The Buckstones

Books by

PAUL I. WELLMAN

NOVELS

Broncho Apache
Jubal Troop
Angel with Spurs
The Bowl of Brass
The Walls of Jericho
The Chain
The Iron Mistress
The Comancheros
The Female
Jericho's Daughters
Ride the Red Earth
The Fiery Flower
Magnificent Destiny
The Buckstones

HISTORIES

Death on the Prairie
Death in the Desert
 (Republished together as
  The Indian Wars of the West)
The Trampling Herd
Glory, God and Gold
A Dynasty of Western Outlaws
Spawn of Evil
The House Divides

BIOGRAPHY

Stuart Symington

REMINISCENCE

Portage Bay

FOR YOUNGER READERS

Gold in California
Indian Wars and Warriors: East
Indian Wars and Warriors: West
Race to the Golden Spike
The Greatest Cattle Drive

The
Buckstones

A *Novel* by

PAUL I. WELLMAN

TRIDENT PRESS   NEW YORK   1967

Copy 1 ✓

Library of Congress Catalog Card Number: 67-15193

Published simultaneously in the United States and Canada by
Trident Press, a division of Simon & Schuster, Inc.,
630 Fifth Avenue, New York, N. Y. 10020

Printed in the United States of America

TO LAURA

How can I ever thank you, my dear, for forty-three years of devotion?

Contents

Contents

I

Turkeytoe

Chapter 1

1.

Colonel Bion B. Buckstone issued from the door of Peebles' Tavern, and halted at the top of the steps leading down from the veranda to the muddy street. The morning had dawned clear and warm after a night of rain, and the Colonel appeared to be in a genial mood. He was perhaps forty years old, with a ruddy, smooth-shaved face, widely opened blue eyes, and a good, though somewhat plump figure. On this day he was dressed impeccably, as was his custom, in a plum-colored coat with a high rolled collar, fancy checkered waistcoat, dove-colored trousers with a strap under the insteps of his varnished shoes, white ruffled shirt with a silk cravat, and a bell-crowned hat of a shade to match the trousers. Altogether he was a sight to please the eye, and most evidently a gentleman in the world's catalog.

The landscape upon which he gazed was worthy of his regard. The month was early in June, and in this year of grace 1833 nature was as yet little spoiled by man in northeastern Tennessee. To the eastward wooded hills climbed toward the moun-

3

tains, which in their turn rose to the blue Cumberlands as their
crest. All about stood the vast solemnity of the forest, which had
hardly been invaded by civilization, save for a few small farming
patches here and there, cleared with infinite labor by frontier
families, and so concealed and shut off from each other that they
made little impression on the mass of feathery verdure that
stretched away on every hand.

From the inspiring natural panorama, Colonel Buckstone's
gaze descended to the village before him. It presented a prospect
far less pleasing than its surroundings: a mere straggle of log
cabins and clapboard houses of mean appearance along a muddy
roadway that passed for the single street. A few of the structures
were whitewashed, but otherwise paint of any kind was notably
lacking, the citizens of the place in general making it their policy
to follow the lines of least industrial resistance.

At the upper end of this street, which sloped down almost
all the way to the river, stood the tavern from which the Colonel
had just come forth, bearing on its front a sign: DREW PEEBLES—
ENTERTAINMENT. Farther down, about the middle of the settlement, was the town "square," an open area of indeterminate shape
and proportions, within its center the courthouse, of two stories
and boasting a "cupola"—built in the general style of a chicken
coop—to house the cracked bell. Behind the courthouse stood the
jail, with its stocks and whipping post.

Peebles' Tavern and the courthouse were the two principal
edifices in the town. There were a few stores and shops, a small
church, three saloons, and a livery stable or two. The general
atmosphere was sleepy, indolent and contented.

The name of the hamlet was Turkeytoe. It was an odd
name, even in early Tennessee, but a name not easy to forget.
Since that day and time it has been changed in favor of another
name, less original, characteristic, and memorable; but then it
bore the title given it by the first settlers, from the circumstance
that three creeks, running together at this point to form a small
river, radiated out in such fashion that men thought they resembled the spreading toes of a wild turkey track.

In spite of the lack of bustle and prosperity in the scene before him, Colonel Buckstone smiled upon it benevolently. He foresaw great things for Turkeytoe, and for the country surrounding it, and more important, for himself.

On this morning he was waiting for his daughter Prudence, who had rooms with him in the tavern; and as is frequently the case when a gentleman waits for a lady, the wait was of some duration. His daughter was engaged in that last-minute consultation with the mirror which is every woman's privilege and pleasure. But presently she left her room, nodded a bright good morning to sour-faced Mrs. Tabitha Peebles, the tavern keeper's wife, and at last joined her father on the veranda.

Colonel Buckstone turned to her with a smile and lifted his hat in a courtly manner. And indeed she was enough to bring a smile of pleasure to his face, for she was slender and young, on the miraculous threshold of womanhood, and already fulfilling a spring promise of great beauty. Beneath her demure little bonnet, her eyes were magnificent, wide and violet colored, and seemingly weighted by wonderful dark lashes. Her lips were pink and sweet, her chin round and firm, and her hair a honey-colored cloud. She was, in short, lovely.

"Prudence, my dear," said the Colonel, "you look fresh and pretty as a daisy this morning."

She rewarded his lifted hat with a smile. "Thank you, Daddy," she said. "Did I keep you waiting?"

"Not long, and I was enjoying the sunshine."

She opened a trivial little parasol and raised it over her head. Colonel Buckstone took her arm.

"The street appears slippery this morning," he said.

Together they descended the steps and he assisted her across the roadway, which was wretchedly muddy after the night's rain. This was a feat somewhat difficult and worthy of remark, showing no little skill and agility on the part of both, for they stepped —almost hopped at times—from one fairly firm hummock to another.

They were, however, accustomed to this, and when they were

safely across, the Colonel took from his pocket a large handkerchief and with it wiped the slight muddy stains from her slippers.
In every regard he treated her with the kind of gallantry he would
have extended to a lady of consequence, rather than to the mere
seventeen-year-old girl she was.

2.

The street crossed, the two advanced down a board sidewalk that
ran before the few business establishments that lined the street
in this block. The walk sloped toward the river, where the street
encountered the stage road from Knoxville, which lay to the
south and east, the chief vehicular egress to the outside world.

By no means was the walk level or even. At some places it
was high, forming a platform to permit the loading or unloading
of wagons; and one mounted two or three wooden steps to reach
such a level. At other places it descended to an uneven stretch
lying close to the ground, before later mounting another loading
platform in this series of acclivities and declivities.

With his daughter on his arm, the Colonel swung a gold-
headed cane, which he carried less as a support than as an acces-
sory to give him a dashing air. And to all who passed, he spoke
with impressive, stately courtesy.

"Good morning, Mr. Tidmiller," he said to Henry Tidmiller,
the little bow-legged harness maker, who was standing in front of
his shop.

"Fine mornin', Colonel—Miss Prudence," said Tidmiller.

"I shall, one of these days soon," said the Colonel in his
imposing manner, "stop in to discuss with you a matter of business. I contemplate the purchase of a horse—none of your livery
stable crocks, mind you, but a horse fit for a gentleman to ride.
I shall need saddle and furnishings worthy of the animal."

"Glad to serve you any time," said Tidmiller.

The Colonel bowed and passed on with his daughter. Looking
after them, the harness maker reflected that the Buckstones were
certainly high-toned people, the Colonel most impressive, and his

daughter a sweet thing in that blue dress that followed her lines to her hips and then billowed out, indicating a nice swell of bosom and an almost frail-looking stem of a waist.

An elderly Negro was sweeping the walk in front of a dram-shop. This was slaveholding territory, though few in Turkeytoe were prosperous enough to own a slave. The manner in which this one dawdled at his light chore added little to any impression of industry or activity the street might have presented.

To him the Colonel said, "Good morning, Joe."

"Mawnin', Colonel. Mawnin', Miss Prudence," said Joe with a pleased grin. Colonel Buckstone occasionally patronized the bar where he was employed, though he usually took his brandy at the tavern.

A little farther along the two encountered a slatternly middle-aged woman, with a basket on her arm. Though he did not know her, the Colonel lifted his hat to her with a bow. Her surprised smile revealed that several of her teeth were missing, and that those remaining were discolored from chewing snuff.

What with the man's dignified courtesy, and the girl's adoring way of looking up at him, few could help smiling at the sight of them. But at one place, near the second saloon they passed, a group of slovenly loafers lounged, leaning with their backs against the wall and spitting tobacco juice on the walk, so that Prudence daintily gathered her skirts as she avoided the ugly brown slime.

Two of the men Colonel Buckstone knew. They were the Blevins brothers, rowdies and ne'er-do-wells. The elder of the two was perhaps thirty years old, huge and burly, with a week's growth of whiskers and an appearance generally shiftless and dirty. His face never had been handsome, but it was further disfigured by an empty eye socket, wet and red beneath the drooping lid, which advertised the result of a rough-and-tumble fight some years previous, in which the optic was gouged out by his adversary. This man's given name was Elias, but because of his quarrelsome nature, especially when drunk, he was usually called Bad 'Lias.

His brother, two or three years younger, was smaller—almost

undersized—yet sly-looking and vicious, and equally unkempt. He had a lascivious grin and was given to telling foul stories. His first name was Elijah, and he was generally known as Little 'Lige. Though both had bad reputations, Colonel Buckstone spoke to them with his invariable courtesy.

The men nodded, and boldly eyed Prudence, especially when she lifted her skirts to avoid the tobacco spittle. As she passed them she kept her eyes lowered, but she heard Little 'Lige behind her say something that brought a snigger from his companions; and she had the unpleasant feeling that whatever he said must have concerned her.

At seventeen she had already become accustomed to having men look after her, and male admiration was not unpleasant. But the mere attention of a creature like Little 'Lige made her shrink inwardly and brought the color of embarrassment to her cheeks.

The Colonel, however, was unruffled. Perhaps he did not attribute the laugh behind them to anything concerning his daughter. At any rate, as he walked along bowing here and there, he exuded an air of satisfaction with himself, his fellow beings, and the world in general.

3.

In his short residence in Turkeytoe, Colonel Buckstone had made a considerable impression. From remarks he let fall, people gathered that he had lived a varied and at times adventurous life, as an educator, a physician ("though not in present practice"), a merchant, a member of the legal profession, a soldier, even a poet; and also that he was a landowner of some importance.

To his military career in particular he referred not infrequently; and at times, especially after a glass or two of brandy, he could be brought to mention his services in the great New Orleans campaign during the War of 1812, when the American army under Andrew Jackson smashed the invading British. If pressed, he might even admit that he and Jackson were on terms of some intimacy, that the general "set a great deal of store" by him, frequently conferred with him "on the deeper questions of strategy," and had, in fact, "expressed unbounded admiration and obligation" to him, for his invaluable assistance in winning the most important victory of American arms during the war.

Perhaps nobody would have been more astonished at these statements than General Jackson himself, who at this very time was President of the United States. In actuality, though Buckstone had fought in the Battle of New Orleans, it was as a humble private in a militia company, and he never so much as exchanged words with his commander.

For, painful as it is to record, the imposing Colonel Bion B. Buckstone was a fraud. He was a likeable fraud, however, and well-meaning; and in his favor it should be said that though he made a practice of somewhat exaggerating his own importance, his motives were not sinister or dishonest, but sprang rather from a sort of innocent vanity. Thus, though he allowed it to be known that he would not be offended if he were addressed as Colonel—and Turkeytoe cheerfully and immediately accorded him the title—he would not have dreamed of using it to defraud or otherwise take advantage of anyone.

His satisfaction this morning was understandable. In his life he had been put to sundry shifts to maintain an often precarious existence, but now he could think back on those shifts with the relieved pleasure one feels in contemplating hardships past and done with. For example, though he spoke largely of being an "educator," he had no more than taught in country schools for a few terms. His claim to being a "physician" was based on a period when he peddled patent medicines from house to house. As a "merchant" he had only clerked in two or three stores owned by more important men of business. His "law" experience consisted of having for a time copied briefs for a legal firm in Philadelphia. Even his reference to himself as a "poet" was somewhat broad, for though he had indeed written occasional verses, none of them had ever enjoyed publication.

In none of these pursuits had he achieved any marked suc-

cess, nor for that matter in many other occupations he attempted
—any in fact that were honorable and did not require that he
soil his hands. For he always maintained that he was a gentleman
and above crude labor.

These failures, however, he admitted to nobody, certainly
not to his daughter for whom his affection was deep and genuine.
After her mother died eleven years before, he had somehow
managed—at times by going shabby and even hungry—to keep
her in a small convent school in North Carolina, because he
believed, although he was not a Catholic, that a girl could gain
the best education under that tutelage.

Only within the last three months had he been able through
a sudden new affluence to have her with him. And his joy in her,
though he did not understand her, and her adoring belief in him,
though she understood him no more than he did her, made all
his sacrifices seem worthwhile. So now they lived in love based
on their complete misunderstanding of each other.

One thing Buckstone indubitably had been: a soldier, though
not a colonel. And as a veteran he had succeeded in obtaining a
tract of three hundred and twenty acres of government bounty
land. Having discovered an unclaimed area in the foothills of the
Clinch Mountains, he located his tract there. He went further
by taking advantage of the Land Act to acquire an additional
one thousand acres, at the minimum government price, to be paid
within a year.

It was this speculation in land that brought him to Turkeytoe
to "administer his estate," which lay not many miles east of the
village. In his somewhat dreamy way, he regarded this land as his
patent to future prosperity and he did not allow his mind to be
troubled by thoughts of how he was to meet his obligation to the
government which would become due in less than nine months
now.

Unfortunately he had already been forced to dispose of fifty
acres of his bounty property, which he sold to Drew Peebles, the
portly and grasping owner of the tavern. Buckstone did not like
Peebles, who had too much of the oily publican about him, and

Peebles had driven a miserly bargain with him, taking advantage of his necessities to pay him only two hundred dollars, less than half the land's worth. Yet Buckstone felt impelled to accept the price, chiefly because he owed Peebles money for accommodations; and also various other tradesmen for clothing and "necessaries" for himself and his daughter.

Upon the land remaining to him, some one thousand two hundred and seventy forested acres, he talked of laying out a townsite—in some pleasantly distant future—and growing wealthy on the lots he would sell. The scheme was entirely visionary. He had made no computation of the costs, nor did he consider how he could induce people to move to his town, or indeed any of the other myriad details of such a project. He cherished his dream and felt secure in the possession of his land, which even in its unimproved state was worth—by his somewhat optimistic estimate—more than ten thousand dollars, a tidy sum for the times.

On this morning, he felt his daughter's hand on his arm, looked the world in the face, and saluted everyone he saw with stately courtesy. Perhaps Bion B. Buckstone was not, in some respects, a man one could admire, but it would be difficult for the average person to find it in his heart to dislike him.

Yet there were those who did. And for reasons he least suspected: his very urbanity of manner, his daughter's beauty, the way in which people accepted the two of them and appeared to value them.

4.

As he neared the end of the block Buckstone saw a tall young man wearing a white planter's hat and high riding boots, which he impatiently flicked with a short whip as he gazed searchingly about him.

He knew the man: Captain Troy Lassiter. With his elder brother, Dr. Tracy Lassiter, he owned Beechwood, the only large

plantation in the county—more than a thousand acres cleared
and in cotton, with at least a hundred slaves, a fine house, quarters
for the servants, barns for the livestock, and a gin and storage
sheds for the cotton. Neither of the Lassiters was married, but
they were quality; nobody would deny that. Troy Lassiter had
attended West Point, been commissioned in the army, and pro-
moted quickly for creditable service during the recent Indian
troubles.

As Buckstone and Prudence approached him, Lassiter turned
toward them. The man was in his twenties, and his features were
striking—dark, lean, restless, even reckless. His eyes were so intensely black that it occurred to Buckstone that they might reflect
light at night, like the eyes of a wild animal. Yet he moved with
a certain alert grace, and his speech and manners were those of
a man of some education and culture.

Buckstone was never fully at ease with the Captain, and
his unease lay in this: Troy Lassiter was a regular army man,
with a legitimate rank. He might conceivably have access to
military records. It would be acutely embarrassing if he discovered
the truth about Buckstone's army service.

"Good morning, Captain," he said, and offered his snuffbox
with a flourish.

"Good morning, sir." Lassiter waved aside the snuffbox, but
his hat came off with a bow, and he gave a smile of very white
teeth. "Miss Prudence, your most humble and obedient."

She colored quite charmingly, murmured a word of greeting,
and passed on. His words were light, but she had snubbed him
because she thought she detected an undertone of irony in them.
Or some amused secret understanding. And neither of these would
she abide from Troy Lassiter.

The Captain's smile faded as he returned his hat to his head,
and his eyes followed her with a curious half-whimsical, half-
puzzled expression as she hurried away and into a store on the
corner. He was thinking that she was very beautiful. A beautiful
woman is never easy for a man to understand. Her very beauty
surrounds her with mystery, so that the simplest thing she does

seems invested with exaltation and miraculousness. And this in spite of the fact that she may not even know that it seems so. Troy Lassiter at that moment would have very much liked to know the thoughts that lay beneath the girl's smooth face and lowered eyes.

But when he turned to her father his look changed.

"You're in town early, sir," said Buckstone, taking snuff himself, and returning the box to his pocket.

"Necessity," replied the other. "Two horses were stolen from our place last night. Prime-blooded stock. My brother is away— affairs in Virginia. So I came in to report the theft. I find the sheriff absent and nobody to report to." He sounded wrathful.

"I regret to hear of this misfortune, Captain."

"You should, sir. And everybody interested in law and order should." Lassiter's face darkened. "I'm not the only one to suffer from thievery lately. Do you know, sir, that only a few days ago a traveler was stopped on the trace east of here and everything taken from him—horse, money, jewelry? He was glad to get off with his life. And a farmhouse in this very vicinity, belonging to old Ashton Moomaw, was robbed during the week. They evidently knew the arrangement of the place, for they entered it while Moomaw and his wife slept, and took five hundred dollars— the old people's life savings—from a drawer in the very room where they slumbered. What do you say to that, sir?"

"Naturally, I deplore all criminal activity."

"Why has the sheriff made no arrest, or even an investigation?"

"That I can't answer."

"I'll say this to you, Mr. Buckstone." The gentleman addressed noted with an inward wince that Lassiter did not say *Colonel* Buckstone. "I believe there's rascality and mystery here. The laws aren't enforced. Our high sheriff, Dode Taney, has performed as the chief feat of his office the arrest of a half-witted boy on a charge of a rather disgusting nature—though hardly dangerous to the peace of this community—described as an 'unspeakable crime.'"

"May I ask the nature of this crime?"

Lassiter gave a little gesture of distaste. "I understand he is accused of having had sexual commerce with a domestic animal on the farm where he was employed. The act, if true, is that of one little better, if any better, than an idiot. Disgraceful and shameful, yes, but a menace to nobody, save perhaps himself." He shrugged the matter aside. "Meantime bandits prey on wayfarers and rob houses and steal valuable horses—almost within sight of this town."

Buckstone uttered a deprecatory murmur.

"I regard you as a gentleman, sir," the Captain went on. "Can I speak to you in confidence?"

"My word on it, sir."

"Then," said Lassiter, "I have a suspicion—nay, more than a suspicion, a belief—that the devil's to pay in this county. Sheriff Taney is an oaf who is under the thumb of a certain individual who is highly influential in terms of mortgages held and people under obligations to him in one way or another; and also under the thumb of a lawyer in this town, who has made a considerable fortune out of juggling land titles—and perhaps in other ways I do not mention just now—and who has succeeded in intimidating all the other lawyers. Our judge, the Honorable Tobias Redding, is a dotard who is the creature of these two—nothing more, nothing more than that, sir. I believe that even if certain lawbreakers were arrested and brought into court, they'd be released at once by the old driveler who occupies the bench, if he got his orders to do so."

"This sounds incredible!" exclaimed Buckstone.

Lassiter looked at him keenly. "Law enforcement, sir, has broken down. And when law enforcement breaks down, upright men sometimes of necessity have to take direct means to combat outlawry. What are your sentiments in regard to that?"

To Buckstone, Troy Lassiter seemed turbulent by nature, and this had the sound of trouble.

"Why—" He hesitated. "I've always followed the policy of respecting the statutes as made and provided——"

"This is all you have to say, Mr. Buckstone?" Again the

omission of the *Colonel*. Buckstone fancied that in the other's manner there was a hint of skepticism, even suspicion.

"Of course," he amended hastily, "under circumstances where the laws are being flouted, I would naturally place at the disposal of the community all the resources at my command."

He did not go into detail as to what those "resources" might be. Lassiter again flicked his boots with the whip.

"I'm glad to hear this from you, sir," he said. "You may be called upon if need arises." His eyes wandered up the street. "Yonder is perhaps an illustration of what I'm talking about—those Blevins brothers. Has anyone ever seen either of them do a day's work? Do they have any visible means of support?"

"I never thought of that, but—" Buckstone's gaze followed that of Lassiter to where the ruffian-looking brothers stood with their crowd of loafers in front of the saloon.

"How is it," asked Lassiter, "that they always seem to have money enough—and more than enough—to go on their sprees and hell-raisings? Is it true that they are not unwelcome guests at Peebles' Tavern?"

"I've seen them there on occasion, yes."

"A well-operated tavern would not tolerate such characters."

"Are you saying——"

"I say nothing. But I intend to keep alert."

There was a moment of silence. Then Buckstone said, "I believe I'd better see what my daughter is doing in the store. Come up to the tavern, Captain. I'd count it a privilege to have you as my guest at dinner. Prudence would enjoy your company, too."

Lassiter hesitated. "Thank you, but not at this time. Later, perhaps." The whip flicked nervously against the boots. "By the way, when will you bring Miss Prudence out to Beechwood again?" He gave Buckstone an oddly inquiring look.

"Why, I hadn't thought——" said the latter.

"The latchstring's always out for you, sir."

"Thank you. In due time we'll be delighted to visit you again."

Buckstone turned away. He was inwardly disturbed. No

telling to what lengths a man like Troy Lassiter might go. A mob movement? That was what the Captain rather broadly hinted. Buckstone hoped he would not be personally involved in anything so violent and lawless.

Other things had been hinted by Lassiter. The "certain individual" who was influential "in terms of mortgages and other obligations" might easily refer to Drew Peebles, the tavern man who was reputed to be the richest man in Turkeytoe. And that lawyer, who among other things "juggled land titles," sounded suspiciously like Ezekiel Rockcastle, the prosecuting attorney, who was, as everyone knew, an intimate of Peebles. This was suggesting suspicion of leading men in the community, a dangerous practice always, and one which Buckstone wished if possible to avoid.

5.

Above the door swung a sign:

JARED HUME, GENERAL MERCHANDISE.

Below the sign, but attached to it, was another:

U.S. POST OFFICE.

The store, as Buckstone entered it, was redolent of the goods it carried: smoked hams and side meat, salt cod, dried apples, onions, bolts of new cloth, and other scents, with an overhanging odor of stale tobacco smoke. Here and there about the floor stood cuspidors for tobacco spitters. On the walls hung pots, pans, axes, hoes, steel traps, guns, and other hardware. Barrels contained dried beans, meal, and such things. Across one end of the room was a waist-high counter and behind the counter a set of pigeonholes hung on the wall, with a cigar box to hold stamps and envelopes. This corner was the post office—all the post office Turkeytoe possessed.

Jared Hume, who combined the offices of postmaster and storekeeper, did so without appreciable difficulty, since the stagecoach from Knoxville came up only twice a week and he was therefore not burdened with any excessive amount of mail. It was, indeed, something of an event when he was able to deliver a letter to an addressee.

At the sight of Buckstone his eyes brightened and he came forward, a smallish man, balding and round bellied, with an apron tied about his middle and paper sleeve-protectors on his arms.

"Mornin', Colonel," he said importantly. "They's a letter come addressed to you."

"Indeed, Mr. Hume?" said Buckstone. He went to the counter as Jared Hume, assuming his official status as postmaster, took from one of the pigeonholes an envelope, well thumbed, and after squinting at the address, handed it to him.

Having performed this official duty, the little storekeeper waited expectantly, as if he hoped for some revelation of its contents. At that moment, however, a woman entered the store, and Buckstone raised his hat to her, meantime placing the envelope in one of his coat pockets.

"Miss Sally," he said in his courtly way, "you look charming this morning."

She flushed, whether with pleasure or embarrassment it was hard to determine. Miss Sally Quintal was twenty-eight and unmarried. By the standards of the time she was an "old maid," and she was what some called "plain," so that compliments came to her so rarely that she was almost flustered by them.

Yet her plainness was perhaps in part due to her humbleness. She was so retiring that she perpetually seemed to try to efface herself; it was as if she avoided doing anything to enhance her appearance for fear that it might call attention to her.

On this morning she was dressed in black, with a gray shawl over her shoulders. She had an abundance of thick, dark hair, but instead of arranging it attractively she wore it drawn straight back and parted severely in the middle with a bun at her crown, a style that did little for her face. There might have been beauty in her fine dark eyes, but her complexion was somewhat sallow, and her cheekbones wide so that they gave an appearance of unnecessary hollowness to her cheeks. Her mouth showed a kind of interminable patience with the lot life had forced upon her; yet when on rare occasions she did smile there was a flash of charm, lips curving up at the corners and perfect white teeth.

It was not often that Miss Sally smiled, for she knew little of happiness. At one time she may have dreamed of a husband and a home of her own, but the dream had long since passed. She was alone in the world and worked hard and long at an exacting toil. She made her small living as a seamstress in her tiny log house at the lower end of the town, not far from the river. Nobody did better or finer needlework than Miss Sally. She had made dresses for Prudence; and in the process she and the girl had become friends. As for Colonel Buckstone, with his stately manners and handsome face, he had made upon her a far greater impression than he had dreamed, or she would have confessed even to herself.

"Miss Sally!" Prudence cried to her with a smile. "Come help me choose a pair of slippers here!"

Less than three months out of convent school, the girl was delighting in the feminine heaven of pretty clothes. At this moment she was hovering over the wonders of Mr. Hume's slipper shelf, for just now dainty footwear had for her a special allurement.

The seamstress joined her, and Buckstone indulgently watched as the two of them examined the display item by item, until at last Prudence selected a pair of slippers, shiny blue satin, with a pretty design embroidered in red silk over the instep and on the sides.

"Oh, but they're two dollars!" she cried in horror.

"Try them on," said her father.

She did so, and when she posed before him, drawing back her skirts to show how well they fitted her slender foot, he laughed and paid for them—noting, as he did so, that he was growing a little low in ready cash.

"Prudy," said Miss Sally, using the girl's pet name, "I have your rose silk almost finished. Can you come for a fitting?"

"Oh, surely!" cried the girl.

The smile was still on Buckstone's face when she departed with the sewing woman, her new slippers in the package hugged to her breast. The smile disappeared, however, as he thought of his brief conversation with Troy Lassiter, and the perhaps dangerous implications that lay behind it.

Chapter 2

1.

When Prudence came out of the store, she half expected to see Troy Lassiter again, but he was gone.

She was relieved and at the same time somewhat disappointed, for her feelings concerning him were a distressing mixture of righteous feminine indignation, a vague feminine wonder, and it must be confessed—a very real feminine interest.

Men were a relatively new and wholly exciting experience in her life. In the convent school almost the only member of the male sex she saw was Father Donahue, the superannuated chaplain, who came to the convent to conduct Mass and hear confessions. Since her arrival in Turkeytoe, however, she had encountered maleness in various manifestations. Most men she met, of course, were older than she, friends or acquaintances of her father. There were a few boors like the detestable Blevins brothers, whom she avoided. But there were also younger men. The gazes of these she had learned to ignore, yet accept as her due, for they usually contained admiration, and admiration she discovered was important to a girl.

Through her father's openhanded bounty, she had pretty clothes; and her tastes ran to softness in fabrics and colors which well became her blonde graces and enhanced those admiring male gazes. Little arts came to her by instinct, such as the sidelong glance, or the half smile, or the gesture with a fan concealing all but her eyes so that her expression was a mystery to the beholder, or even the simple expedient of walking past a young man, small chin in air, eyes taking no notice of him, which sometimes had an effect the reverse of cooling his interest in her.

One young fellow, Will Koble, son of Henry Koble who ran the small Turkeytoe Bank, had even asked permission to call; and her father suggested that she give the permission. But when the youth came and sat awkwardly in the parlor of their apartment, he proved to be a gosling in white duck trousers, pumps on his feet which looked large enough and flat enough to be webbed, and hair scented with a perfect pestilence of cinnamon and bergamot. During this distressing ordeal he could think of nothing to say, nor could she. At last he managed to get to his feet, gave her hand a limp shake, asked if he might see her again sometime, and to her infinite relief, fled.

About Troy Lassiter, however, there was nothing of the gosling; and her experience with him had been brief and so tingling that she still could not think of it with complete serenity.

She had met him first with his brother, the doctor, who was acquainted with her father, at the tavern on the occasion of a visit they made to it. It was then—and this was just two weeks ago—that she and her father were invited to Beechwood, and were next day driven there in the Lassiter coach which was sent for them. The white-painted house, with its four pillars on the portico and its tree-shaded yard, seemed to her quite large and beautiful; and though to a captious eye the interior might have shown too much the defects of being a bachelor abode, to the convent-bred girl it was pleasing.

Dr. Tracy Lassiter, the elder brother, was in his thirties, and unlike the Captain, inclined to comfortable flesh. He had for a time practiced medicine in Nashville, where he met and became a friend of Andrew Jackson, but later he gave up his profession to join his brother in operating the plantation. He flattered Prudence dutifully and chivalrously, but his mind was occupied with weightier matters than conversation with a young girl. So while he discussed the new tariff laws, and cotton prices, and politics, and the English bid for world empire with Buckstone, Troy Lassiter undertook to entertain their feminine guest.

With Troy, Prudence, who was at first shy and a little stiff, soon discovered that unique stimulation which femininity so often discovers in the company of an attractive man. She thought him quite handsome, in a dark, rather saturnine sort of way, and young enough so that she found herself relaxing with him. He had her laughing, and he laughed with her. She seemed to become lighter, perhaps more frivolous, certainly more graceful and charming, without really trying to be.

As for Troy Lassiter, he was delighted with her, and after a few minutes of quite pleasant discourse with her, he suggested that he conduct her on an inspection of the house and grounds.

In the library she saw two portraits on the wall: a somewhat austere gentleman in an old-fashioned stock and blue coat, and an aristocratic lady, dark and thin faced, wearing a wide lace collar and a little lace cap on her black hair.

"My father and mother," Lassiter told her. "They died within a week of each other. Yellow fever. They were in New Orleans when the epidemic broke out."

"Oh, I'm so sorry," she said with ready sympathy. And she added politely, "Your mother must have been beautiful."

"Not exactly," he smiled. "I got this hatchet face from her. You can see that she was quite dark—French by extraction. That was what they were doing in New Orleans when they got the yellow jack—visiting some of her Creole relatives."

"Do you miss them?"

"Now? I hadn't really thought. You see this happened years ago while I was a cadet at West Point. And I've been busy since then, first in the army, and then with this plantation which my brother and I bought and improved with the inheritance they left us."

It sounded somehow cold to her, and she hardly knew what to say.

But after a moment he said, "You must have your own portrait painted, Miss Prudence—and soon."

"Why? I've never really considered it."

He smiled, and she liked his smile, the white gleam of his teeth in his dark face. "A lady should be caught by the artist's brush at the height of her beauty. Life has a way of adding lines and making contours a little less perfect as she grows older. Or don't you believe this?"

"But I'm only seventeen——"

"By which I'm to understand that you expect to be more beautiful still?"

She colored at that, and he laughed, but not derisively.

"I mustn't tease you, Miss Prudence, for really you are distracting when your cheeks grow pink like that."

It was hard to resist him and she fell in with his gay spirits. They were chatting quite intimately as they went outdoors and he showed her the paddocks with their beautiful Thoroughbred horses, the barns, the cotton gin house farther beyond by itself, the slave quarters with little half-clad black children tumbling in the dust and their mothers quaking with laughter. A cottage near the main house, quite pretty, with rambler roses growing over it, attracted her attention.

"Our overseer's house," he said. "Oh, here he comes now."

The man approached and was introduced to Prudence. His name was Melton, and she sensed in him a coldness, even a sullenness. Perhaps he envied his employers and resented them.

Then they came to the orchard where the apple trees were in full bloom, and she exclaimed with joy at the sight.

"Would you like some?" asked Troy. "I'll help you pick them."

In a few minutes she stood with her arms full of blossoms, smiling at him with a sidelong upward look from her eyes and a

curving of her lips that was pure coquetry, except that it was
entirely natural with her and not studied.

"Oh, you lovely creature!" he exclaimed in a kind of ecstasy.
"You *yourself* are the most beautiful of all these blossoms!"

And to her entire surprise and confusion he kissed her.

It was unpremeditated, and he was almost as thunderstruck
as she. At his momentary embrace she dropped her blossoms, and
he covered his own abashment by stooping to gather them for
her. When he stood erect she had gone some distance toward the
house, almost running. He hurried after her.

"Here—your flowers," he said.

"I don't want them!"

"Please stop," he pleaded. He took her by the arm and she
faced him, cheeks vivid, eyes stormy.

"I must apologize," he said contritely. "It was an impulse.
You must try to understand——"

"I understand *perfectly* that you are not a gentleman!"

It restored his equanimity. He smiled at her ironically. "There
are a few other things perhaps that you will understand better,
when you're a little older and wiser," he said. "One is that the
charm of beauty is sometimes irresistible. Another is that men
are weak about resisting temptation. A third is that a kiss never
left a scar."

She broke away from him and hurried on to the house. And
he, seeing that she was much offended, tossed the apple blossoms
to the ground, lit a cheroot, and followed her.

They managed, without words, to enter the house in apparent serenity. The rest of the evening, including the fine dinner
when the men toasted her with their wine, passed without event,
although she once or twice caught Troy Lassiter's eyes on her,
with inward speculation in them. Of all this she mentioned
nothing to her father when they were driven back to the town,
or later.

She did not know it, but the questioning look Lassiter
had given her father that very morning, when inviting him to
bring her once more to Beechwood, was to discover if she had

revealed the episode to Buckstone and perhaps aroused his
resentment, for a kiss was not a light matter for any girl in those
times. But Buckstone's face was serene, and it was clear that he
knew nothing of the occurrence.

Two weeks had passed since the visit and Prudence found
herself looking back to that moment in the apple orchard with
less indignation. Perhaps Troy Lassiter had spoken the truth about
the weakness of men—and he meant himself—in resisting temptation. In a way this was a high compliment, for it seemed a
tribute to her feminine power of attraction.

True enough, a kiss did not leave a scar, at least one that was
visible. But a kiss taken by surprise, almost by force, left confusion and resentment behind it. That was why she had behaved
so coldly to him when she met him this morning. She was
determined to give him no opportunity for further familiarities.

And yet . . . he was cynical and baffling, and at times he
seemed amused at her; but he had undoubtedly shown admiration
for her. And it came over her that the admiration of most people
was somehow tepid in comparison with the admiration of Troy
Lassiter.

She ought to hate him, and she knew it. But surprisingly she
found herself measuring herself against him. She was seventeen
years old and inexperienced; he was twenty-four and, in her eyes,
worldly wise. Was there too much disparity in this? Did she seem
immature to him?

But why, she suddenly asked herself, should these things
matter? It was not as if he meant anything to her. She took
herself in hand and tried to stop thinking along this silly and
fruitless line. And she found herself not entirely successful in
doing so.

2.

"You're so silent," said Miss Sally, walking beside her. "What's
on your mind, Prudy?"

"Nothing," answered Prudence. "I was thinking about my school."

And in a manner of speaking she was. Her life in these days—even with a slight disturbance of emotions by someone like Troy Lassiter—was secure and happy in the sheltering affection of her father. It contained the spice of change and variety. And even of adventure—of a sort—although adventure, she assured herself, was not what her nature really sought. None of this was true of her life in the convent school.

A long recollection of loneliness hung over her. She remembered how she and her mother lived in a boardinghouse in Chapel Hill, North Carolina, where the great university was. She hardly knew her father then. He visited them at infrequent intervals, but almost always he was gone on a mysterious errand called "business," and her mother pined, and grew thin with a cough. He was not at home when her mother simply gave up the struggle to live, and neighbors did what they could. He arrived in time for the funeral.

She was six then, and bewildered and frightened by the solemnity of the occasion, a feeling of great loss, and the grief of her father, although she hardly knew him as yet. Childishly, she did not question when he took her away to the school where she was to live and learn her lessons until he could send for her. She was at that time a thin little thing with great eyes seeming too large for her face.

The convent was poor, and the girls in the school were from the poorer classes. Their families could pay only the smallest of tuitions, so the girls, as they grew old enough, were expected to do much of the work of the convent, to defray part of their own expenses.

Prudence's desolation and her longing for her mother, the gentle creature now in her grave, at first made her almost indifferent to the routine she underwent. But with time, as she grew sensible to it, that routine became dreary. The nuns, though not unkind, were stern and discipline was inflexible. Punishments could be severe when that discipline was violated.

All girls, from children to virtual young ladies, dressed alike in uniforms of cheap blue cotton—except that when they grew old enough so that the sight of their legs was considered sinful, they were put into long dresses. All girls wore their hair in braids down their backs. It was an ugly uniformity which she at first accepted, but as she grew older she hated it.

Everything went by the bell: a bell at five in the morning to awake and dress for Mass; bell at six to go to Mass; bell at a quarter past seven for breakfast; bell at nine for morning classes or work details; bell at noon for dinner; bell at one for afternoon classes; bell at four to begin the hour and a half allowed for leisure time; bell at five-thirty to get ready for evening prayer; bell at six for evening prayer; bell at seven for supper; bell at nine for bed and lights out.

Except for herself, all the girls were Catholic. They went to confession, which Father Donahue, the portly old chaplain, heard every Saturday night; but she did not. Her father was not religious, but her mother had been brought up in the Episcopal faith, and one of her last requests to him was that her daughter likewise be brought up in that church. So Buckstone would not permit her to become Catholic, and had a strict understanding in that regard with the heads of the school. Prudence, therefore, in a measure, felt left out of things.

All this she accepted with patience. Humility and patience were in fact drilled into her constantly, and so were the sins of pride and self-indulgence. Even though she was not a Catholic, she received a full measure of instruction about mortal sins, deadly sins, venial sins, and original sin, much of which she never fully understood.

The workings of conscience likewise were powerfully impressed upon her, and she learned that there were at least five different kinds of conscience. Doubtful conscience was bad, lax conscience was worse, but false conscience was worst of all. Correct conscience was acceptable, and scrupulous conscience was to be prayed for and achieved if possible.

Prudence was quite sure that she did not possess a scrupulous conscience, for a scrupulous conscience, as described by her preceptors, interpreted almost every act of life as sinful. Perhaps she did not even have a correct conscience, for that kind of a conscience should have caused her to tell her father about the episode with Troy Lassiter in the apple orchard. She had not told him, not because she felt any guilt in being kissed without her consent, but because she did not want to cause trouble between her father and the Lassiters. And that in turn was because—well, she did not want, for some reason, to erect an impassable barrier between Troy Lassiter and herself which such a difficulty might create. Why this reluctance on her part? She could not have defined it to herself, and she perhaps would have shrunk from the thought of it; but it is just possible that the brief tingling moment of his embrace and his stolen kiss, which had so disturbed her, had also awakened something she had not known before—the woman in her.

At any rate life was different with her now. She compared it with the regimentation of the school where routine was so wearying that even attending Mass and evening prayer were welcome diversions. Her plain uniform was cut severely and fit her ill; her knit stockings were of wool; her shoes were cheap and clumsy. Comparing this garb with the pretty dresses she now wore brought almost a shudder at the recollection.

She hugged the new slippers to her. Until recently she had not fully realized how essential becoming clothes were to a girl. They gave her a whole new sensation of preciousness, of being pleasing to others. That soft blue gown she wore out to the Lassiters assuredly had a most surprising effect on Troy. There, she was thinking about him again. Were men the only things that mattered?

Men. Except for the priest, men were rarely seen about the convent when she was there, and then only on matters of business or when repairs were to be done by workmen. She lived in a world exclusively female, and at that time she did not know the difference. At rare intervals her father paid a visit and she sat with him in the formal reception room, hardly knowing what to say.

Once, toward the last, she begged him to take her away, and she could not forget the tears in his eyes as he comforted her and told her it was impossible, at least for that time. It was then that he gave her a ring, a cheap enough one of silver with a simple design hammered into it. The ring she was allowed to wear, but otherwise the nuns forbade ornaments.

Unhappy but resolved, she went back to the convent school. By a rigid system of rotation she did various work tasks—in the laundry, the kitchen, the sewing room, the garden. She did the dishwashing, the mopping of floors, and other necessary chores. To this she made no objection, since all the girls were called upon to work and she took it for granted.

Her classwork was spotty. She learned to read early, for she had a quick mind in some directions; and she did well in French and even in Latin. But she felt herself a hopeless dunce in mathematics.

Music was her greatest love. Though she had a fresh, clear voice, singing was not her chief joy. Sister Mary Felicia, who taught music, instructed in choral and even solo vocalizing, and also gave the girls lessons on the spinet and the violin. Most of her pupils lacked talent, or interest, or both. But Prudence took to the violin as if she were born to it. As soon as she learned to run the scales, she knew that she had found an instrument she could love.

Practice was essential and the girl spent much of her free time in the music room where the nun, a fine violinist herself, lent her own prized violin to this pupil who showed such promise. Prudence had an exceptional ear, a fine touch, and an instinct for emotion. In her last year she played the beautiful "Ave Maria" by Franz Schubert with such feeling that she brought tears to the eyes of the gentle nun. The song was a favorite of hers, and when she learned its history she thought how remarkable it was that music written by a Jew, for a Catholic prayer, could be so dear to a Protestant girl.

After she left school one of the things her father bought her was a violin. It was not an expensive instrument, but at least

with it she could keep up her practice. There had been, in connection with this, an annoyance. For some reason, which Prudence
did not understand, she was not liked by Mrs. Tabitha Peebles,
the tavern man's wife. And Mrs. Tabitha put a stop to her playing in the tavern, although Prudence could not see how she disturbed anyone, since she never played by night. The episode
created an unpleasant situation, for her father protested to Drew
Peebles. If there had been another tavern available, he would
have moved away, he told his daughter.

Miss Sally offered the solution to this. Prudence was welcome
to practice in the little log house at the lower end of the street,
so she kept her touch, and solaced her yearning for music.

3.

Somehow, as she grew older in the convent school, Prudence
escaped the awkward stage through which most girls pass, and
she knew she was as pretty as anyone in her classes, prettier than
most. This was a matter of intimate personal knowledge and it
did not necessarily mean vanity in her, especially since she had
instructors who did not quite approve of feminine beauty and
saw to it that she was kept humble.

Her heart was naturally open and eager for friendship and
when she was twelve she found a friend for a time, a girl named
Carrie Callan, a year older than she, who had entered the school
only recently.

For a thirteen-year-old, Carrie exhibited surprising sophistica-
tion, and she kept little Prudence agog with recitals of the ways
of people in the world outside the convent. She described the
clothing worn by women of fashion, and the balls and parties
where there was dancing—even waltzing, in which men danced
with their arms about their feminine partners.

Prudence was shocked. "Why would women let men put
their arms around them?"

"Pooh, that's nothing," she said airily. "They let men do a lot more than that."

"What?"

"Don't you know anything?"

"I—I guess not," said Prudence humbly.

"You *are* a booby, aren't you?"

"Maybe. But tell me—please."

Carrie became superior. "If you don't know, I don't think I ought to tell you," she said importantly.

But Prudence, of course, was wild with curiosity. She pleaded so eagerly that at last Carrie looked cautiously around the playground to see if anybody was in hearing. Nobody was near.

"Promise never to tell?" said Carrie. "Not anyone?"

"Yes, yes! I promise."

"All right. Remember you promised. If you have to know, I'll whisper it."

Mystified and eager, Prudence inclined her ear. Carrie put her lips close and whispered. In this unwholesome manner Prudence learned something of the purport of sex. To be sure, Carrie's version was garbled, because she did not know nearly as much as she pretended. But garbled or not, it horrified Prudence, whose naïve little mind could understand no reason or meaning in it.

She recoiled. "What do men want to do *that* for?" she asked.

"Because they're that way, that's why."

"All men?"

"All men. Every one. They *like* to do it."

"Even Father Donahue?"

Carrie was a little taken back. "No. I guess priests are different. So are nuns."

"But other women let men——"

"Yes, they do."

"Why do they?"

"Because they have to. They get married and it's the law. You have to obey the law. You *have* to let them do it."

Poor Prudence was left bewildered. She kept her promise not to tell, but of course Carrie Callan did not. When she went to confession she revealed the conversation, although she put it in such light that the blame for the "nasty talk" was all on Prudence.

Very soon Prudence was summoned before the mother superior. But the mother superior was wise and not unkindly. After a little questioning she saw that the frightened girl had no knowledge of the forbidden subject beyond what she had heard in this one conversation. So Prudence was not expelled from school.

In a later day the mother superior might have helped her by explaining the power and mystery of the process of generation and its beauty and necessity. But the nuns were all extremely prudish, and the mother superior only gave Prudence some homilies about purity of thought and the excellence of hard work for keeping the mind off unheavenly speculations. The girl was also forbidden further intimacy with Carrie Callan, who soon after left the school.

In time Prudence came to accept Carrie's revelations, though she still did not fully comprehend them. She supposed that marriage and what it evidently entailed happened to a girl by a sort of fatal continuity, and was one of the crosses female creatures were ordained to bear. As her body underwent changes and her mind became more mature she found that she even became interested in the thought of men, strange and terrible as they must be, and the outside world in which they lived and moved.

One reason why she loved her father so sincerely was her gratitude to him for at last taking her out of the convent, which seemed by then almost a prison to her.

She was seventeen and would be eighteen in October. She was fully formed and perhaps lacking only depth of understanding for womanhood. The months since she left the school had given her feminine instincts a chance to play and develop. With

the frivolities of clothes and ornaments that went with her
nature, and a gay, apparently light-minded manner, she was in-
nocently charming in a way that sometimes caused her to be
surprised at the interest and attention men displayed toward her.
This was at times confusing, but it was not entirely displeasing,
in the main. Of course the incident in the apple orchard ... but
that was an experience apart. She would not allow herself to
think any more about Troy Lassiter.

To banish such thoughts from her mind, she broke her
silence and began chatting with such vivacity that Miss Sally
glanced at her in surprise. Prudence had not told the seamstress
about the apple orchard. They were friends and even confidantes,
but the virginal Miss Sally was hardly wiser in matters of emotion than the girl.

Perhaps her chatter was occasioned in part by the sound of
a horse coming up behind them and an intuitive feeling as to
the rider of that horse. They were near Miss Sally's cabin, and
she glanced around. So did Miss Sally.

The horse was a splendid one, but the girl saw only the
man on its back. He was Troy Lassiter.

A fine rider on a fine horse is always a spirited sight, and
Lassiter rode with the style and dash of a hussar. At the sight
of him Prudence experienced a maidenly fear that he might stop
and try to talk with her, and a maidenly wish that he would
do just that. She was sorry already for having snubbed him in
front of Hume's store, but her mind was in a state of confusion
concerning him.

Lassiter did slow his horse as he came abreast of them and
lifted his hat. His eyes were on Prudence, and his face was
expressionless as if he was not entirely sure of his reception.

Had she read the look in his eyes, she might have behaved
differently. He was thinking of how delicately lovely she was,
and how much she had been in his thoughts lately, and that
he had offended her perhaps beyond forgiveness, and how he
hoped she would relent.

But she did not read the look. When he bowed and said, "Ladies, a very good morning to you," she looked downward and let Miss Sally return the greeting.

Lassiter replaced his hat on his head and cantered away.

Now Prudence lifted her eyes and gazed after him with a mixture of relief and disappointment. If he had stopped, she told herself, and been properly penitent, she would gradually have allowed herself to be very nice to him. But now he was gone.

She had little to say the rest of the way to Miss Sally's cabin.

4.

After his daughter was gone Buckstone also left the store. He expected to see Lassiter, but the young man had departed, so he turned up the street toward the tavern. Ahead he noticed a knot of loiterers, among them the Blevins brothers, listening to a gaunt farmer.

Buckstone knew the farmer—Reedy Halcutt, who raised a little corn and a few hogs on a small cleared place not far from Turkeytoe. He paused on the sidewalk at the edge of the crowd.

"Homer's his name," Halcutt was saying. "Homer Phipps. He's big enough to make a hand, but he ain't quite right in the haid. I tuck him in, an' I give him his vittles an' a place to sleep in the barn, fo' what leetle he could do about the place. Seems like he's too dumb to do anythin' right. Set him to hoe, he's as liable to chop the corn as the weed. He's big an' lubberly an' good-natured enough, but clumsy an' unhandy as all git out. Try to talk to him, like as not he'll be lookin' off somewhere not follerin' anythin' you say. My ole woman, Sairy, she didn't like him from the fust. Said it give her the creeps to have him around, he's so consarned looney."

Halcutt paused to fill his pipe with tobacco from a leaf he crumbled in his hand. He lit it and took a few puffs to get it going before he continued.

"Wall, then this happened. Sairy was the one seed it fust. She heerd somep'n goin' on in the barn, an' peeked through a crack atween the logs. Then she come hustlin' an' got me. I looked through the crack too."

He paused, as if for dramatic effect.

"What was it you seen?" It was Bad 'Lias who spoke, and Buckstone saw his ugly face, avid for sensation.

"Wall, thar he was," said Halcutt. "He'd tied my leetle .jenny mule in her stall. You know, she's a runt. Not hardly big enough to work any good. I got her from Hap Miller for ten dollars an' a sack of shelled corn two year ago——"

"Go on," interrupted Bad 'Lias. "Whut was Homer a-doin'?"

"Wall, fust he give her a bait of corn. Good corn, like we gits milled for our own pones. That jenny mule ain't entitled to corn like that, an' it made me b'il at the sinful waste——"

"Yeah?" cut in Bad 'Lias impatiently.

Halcutt's voice lowered to a confidential tone. "Then Homer, he got aroun' behind her, an' by God, he up and mounted that leetle jenny, jest like as if he was a stud jack!"

"Did she object?"

"Naw. That's the thing that struck me. He must of done it before, becuz the jenny didn't make no objection. She could of kicked him clean out of the barn, but she never. Fact is, she seemed to favor it, an' when he was ruttin' away she never even laid her ears back. Why, that Homer acted as if he'd of kissed her if he could."

A roar of laughter. Men slapped their thighs and guffawed, and some of them repeated to each other the last sentence as if it was the choicest of witticisms.

"Wall, that's whut we saw," went on Halcutt, obviously pleased by his success. "Me? I thought it was funny as hell, jest like you boys. I busted right out laughin'. At that Homer, he quit whut he was doin' an' come out of the barn lookin' queerer than ever. Then I did give him the big hooraw. I called him everythin' I could think of, an' made fun of him somep'n fierce."

"Whut did he do?"

"He jest had that fool look on his face, an' kind of slunk off. I reckon I'd of let it go at that, but the ole woman, she was plumb scandalized an' red-faced. Nothin' would do but she would have Homer in jail. He's in thar now."

Another guffaw from the crowd and the farmer swelled with importance at the attention he was receiving. Buckstone felt a sensation of acute disgust. This, evidently, was the half-wit to whom Troy Lassiter had referred earlier as being charged with an "unspeakable crime."

"Whut'll they do to him?" someone in the crowd asked.

"He'll be cowhided at the whippin' post, shore," said another.

"That ain't enough," suddenly broke in Bad 'Lias. "Feller like that oughtn't git off that easy."

"Whut's your idea, 'Lias?"

The unsavory ruffian looked about him with a mean grin. "Wall, I reckon we could have some fun with him."

"Like what?"

Bad 'Lias, in look and voice, became conspiratorial. "Why, I say we'd ought to ketch him some night, an' jest simply cut out his balls. A man would do sech a thing as that ought to be gelded, jest like a boar pig. I bet he'd squeal, but it might make him lose interest in jenny mules——"

"Good God, 'Lias, you wouldn't do a thing like *that?*" Halcutt was horrified. He knew Homer Phipps as harmless and not unamiable in spite of this disgraceful episode.

Bad 'Lias pushed through the crowd and confronted the farmer, their faces not more than a few inches apart.

"You want to try an' stop us?" he asked.

"Why—why—" stammered Halcutt, backing away from the baleful glare in the bully's single eye.

"You approve of whut he done?" demanded Bad 'Lias. "You think we oughter give him a vote of thanks, mebbe, for doin' what no man that calls hisself a man would do?"

"No—no—it ain't that. But whut you're sayin' is turrible——"

"He's got it comin' to him! I say sech a feller ought to be made a example of. Whut do you say, fellers?" Bad 'Lias swung his gaze around the crowd.

They were his kind—shiftless, disreputable, half-drunk. They nodded and some of them vocally assented.

At this point Buckstone intervened. "I'd go mighty slow, gentlemen, in endorsing a scheme like that," he said.

"Whut's this?" Bad 'Lias turned on him with a scowl.

"What you're suggesting would be a worse crime than what that poor idiot did."

"Jest whut you gittin' at?" The ruffian's scowl deepened.

"No man has any right to go beyond the law's penalties," said Buckstone. "What you're proposing is a felony, and a serious one. The law has a name for it—*mayhem*."

"Anybody invite you in on this?" In the unshaved visage, with the red wetness of the empty eye socket and the vicious lines of the face, Buckstone recognized the unreachable criminality of the man, his sadistic eagerness to maim and hurt, his utter selfishness, his brutal lawlessness. And beneath all this there was a hatred of Buckstone himself, because he represented a class considered above the bully in the social scheme. A stench of bad liquor expelled itself in a belch—Bad 'Lias was drinking and therefore doubly dangerous.

Nevertheless, Buckstone answered him steadily. "Nobody asked me. I simply gave you some sound advice."

"Jest keep out of it, hear? We ain't needin' no soft-handed jack-lawyer to tell us our business."

Buckstone looked him in the eye. "I'm going to say one thing to you, Blevins. And it's a warning. If any harm comes to Homer Phipps, on my honor I shall denounce the guilty parties before a court of law."

In the silence that followed he turned and walked away.

Behind him he heard a fist smack angrily into an open palm.

"*By God!*" said Bad 'Lias explosively.

Chapter 3

1.

Drew Peebles sat in a wide slat-bottomed chair on the veranda of his tavern. It was a habit of his to sit there when the day was fine—and this day was superb.

Mr. Peebles was past his prime, but still vigorous; a big, potbelly-fat man, with an appearance remarkable yet hardly pleasing. His face was broad and double-chinned, and his eyes were heavily bagged and of a peculiar, indiscriminate color called "cat-eye" locally. In those eyes lurked a continual gleam of cunning or speculation.

In one fat hand he held what was commonly called a "fly flicker." This was an instrument in common use, sometimes no more than a leafy branch, but frequently a more permanent article like a dried horse's tail with the hairs shaved off the shank to form a handle and a tuft at the end with which flies were whisked away from a dining table during meals, usually by a servant appointed for that office.

The fly flicker in Mr. Peebles' hand, however, was more

elaborate. It consisted of a wooden stick perhaps two feet long
with horsehairs at the end, to be sure, but not loose. Instead
they were woven into a sort of screen or flap that made the
device excellent for killing flies instead of merely shooing them
away.

Flies were always numerous, particularly where there were
stables or garbage dumps near at hand; and the tavern, like all
public houses in its day, was plagued by them. Mr. Peebles on
this morning, as on others, devoted himself to killing flies. He
even seemed to take a kind of pride in his skill at this occupation.

When one of the insects lit within reach, Mr. Peebles
would cautiously lift the fly flicker, poise it above the intended
victim, and then with a quick flip of his wrist bring it down
smartly, crushing the fly with the horsehair flap at the end. If
he killed the fly—and he rarely missed—he would contemplate
it for a moment with satisfaction, then use the fly flicker to
sweep the small quarry into a little pile of other victims of his
fly-killing prowess. After he had been sitting there for as much
as an hour, he always managed to amass quite a heap of dead
insects; and in this nasty little hoard he seemed to take a gloating
sort of gratification.

Fly killing would appear to be a childish occupation for a
man of affairs, and Mr. Peebles unquestionably was a man of
affairs. But it amused him and was in fact a mask for a lurking
line of thought so furtive and concealed that it would have been
hard to follow it to its conclusion. The crushing of insects indeed
might have been something of an index to his inner personality.

It was believed that Peebles was the richest man in Turkeytoe. He owned his tavern, but beyond that he had many other
interests. Looking down the street, he could see a livery stable,
a store, the town's one bank, a harness shop, a saloon, and several
dwellings that were his property outright or were controlled by
him. Acquisition not only satisfied his innate greed, but also
his lust for power. Mortgages were a source of power over other
men. So many mortgages were owned by Peebles, not only in the
town but in the country around, that he wielded heavy influence

in political and other affairs. Men found it expedient to follow
his wishes and "vote their bread and butter" as the saying was.
Besides real estate he dealt also in slaves, horses, liquor, and
goods; and he had other transactions of a nature so secret that
he never spoke of them.

One friend he had. At least they tolerated each other, perhaps because their interests chimed together so closely. This
was Ezekiel Rockcastle, the county prosecutor, whom nobody
ever dared call by the usual shortening of Zeke, or trifle with in
any other way. For he was as deadly as a rattlesnake when
angered or thwarted. Between them, Peebles and Rockcastle
ruled in many ways not only Turkeytoe but the entire county,
and even beyond.

In the intervals of his fly killing, the tavern man saw Colonel
Buckstone approaching up the street. At the foot of the veranda
steps that gentleman paused and looked up at him with a smile.

"A fine morning, Mr. Peebles," he said.

Mr. Peebles' attention at the moment was directed toward a
fly that had the temerity to light upon his knee. Little knowing
its peril, the small creature was busy polishing its wings with its
hinder legs. Without replying to Buckstone's greeting the tavern
man slowly lifted his fly flicker to a killing position. Buckstone
waited for him to achieve his triumph. The fat man did not so
much as stir his knee while he poised his weapon. An instant
later the fly flicker descended and the fly lay dead on the
veranda floor.

With his fly flicker Peebles swept it into the heap of other
proofs of his singular prowess. Only when this was done did he
answer Buckstone's civil greeting.

"Yeah, nice mornin', Colonel," he said.

"You seem to be in excellent form today," said Buckstone,
his eye on the heap of dead flies.

Peebles only grunted. He felt that he detected amusement
in the voice of the other.

"Well, good hunting." Buckstone mounted the steps and
entered the tavern.

Peebles suspended his fly killing to turn his head and look

after him. His broad jowled face showed for an instant that
Buckstone's light gibe had created in him the kind of resentment
that is always felt by men who regard themselves as too important to be laughed at.

He disliked Buckstone. The Colonel made him feel his own
provincialism and his inferiority of demeanor and address. Mr.
Peebles disliked feeling inferior to anybody. There was his wife,
too, Mrs. Tabitha Peebles. Mrs. Tabitha centered her particular
aversion on Buckstone's daughter. In her was that peculiar an-
tagonism, based on jealousy, that an unattractive woman past her
prime sometimes feels toward a girl of superior charm and evident good fortune. More than once Mrs. Tabitha had expressed
to her husband the opinion that Prudence Buckstone was "high
and mighty," as well as "trifling and giving herself airs," and
darkly predicted that she would "get her comeuppance one of
these days, and a good thing, too."

When the door closed behind Buckstone, Peebles turned
his attention again to his fly killing. But the savor had departed
from it. He sat glaring off into the distance and a fly settled
upon his arm, then flew away, never dreaming how close it
had come to extinction, or how the man's abstraction had saved it.

2.

Buckstone went directly to his room, which was one of a suite
of three. The room farthest from his was his daughter's and
the room between them had been converted into a sitting room
sometimes used as an office. He had intended to do some corre-
spondence, but as he put his hand into his pocket he felt the
letter he had received that morning, and which he had not as
yet read.

With no particular interest, for there was nothing about
the envelope to suggest anything unusual in the contents, he took
the letter to a window and slowly read its message. As he did
so the color seemed to drain from his ruddy face.

Slowly he turned from the window and sat down rather

heavily in a chair. After that he gazed for a long time at the
wall, like one in a trance.

From this he aroused himself and read the letter once more,
as if to assure himself that he had correctly interpreted the message it contained. Then he replaced the letter in his pocket, rose,
and left the room. All his recent blithe mood was gone. Bion B.
Buckstone had experienced a stunning blow: one of the severest
reverses of his life, which had been filled with reverses. So serious
was it that he hardly knew what to do.

He had honesty. Having received news of a most unhappy
sort, his first instinct was to impart this news to someone else
who also was affected by it, even though he dreaded the task.

Drew Peebles still sat on the veranda when Buckstone opened
the door. With him now were two other men, patrons of the
tavern, who stood in idle conversation, gazing out at the vista.
Buckstone hesitated a moment, as if embarrassed or at a loss.

Then he said, "Mr. Peebles——"

The fly killer turned toward him his curiously expressionless
countenance.

Buckstone tried again. "Mr. Peebles, might I have a word
with you?"

"Go ahaid," said Peebles, without stirring from his chair.

"I'd like to see you in private, please."

"What for?"

"A matter of confidential nature, sir."

Peebles sat still, as if making up his mind whether to accede
to this request. Then he rose heavily from the chair.

"Come to my office," he said.

Buckstone stood aside for him, then followed him down the
hall. Past the bar they went and the smell of stale liquor was
in the air. Beyond the barroom Peebles opened a door and motioned Buckstone into a small room, which contained a book-
keeper's desk, a set of ledgers, and two or three chairs. It was
illuminated only by one small and very dirty window, but the
light had gone out of Buckstone's day long before this.

Peebles closed the door. "Now what is it?" he asked.

His voice was suspicious, as if he suspected that Buckstone was about to ask a favor. Peebles had a prejudice against doing anyone a favor.

For a moment Buckstone did not speak, as if he were trying to think of some way to open a difficult subject. Finally he said, "Mr. Peebles, I have received some bad news."

Suspicion appeared to grow in Peebles. "What kind of bad news?"

"I came to you directly, because I'm more concerned about you than about myself——"

"Concerned about *me?* Now what d'you mean by that?"

"I feel a certain responsibility——"

"Listen here, Buckstone, if you've got me into trouble somehow, you're going to be goddamned sorry."

In Drew Peebles' life there were matters that he was anxious to keep secret. If one of them was being brought to light, he wanted to be the accuser right away and make the other man shoulder whatever blame there was. So his voice rose, as it always rose, when he wanted to cow down somebody.

"I haven't got you into any trouble, sir," said Buckstone. "Not exactly——"

"All right, out with it! What's this that's happened?"

With the air of a man about to plunge into icy water, Buckstone drew the letter from his pocket and tendered it.

"I just a little while ago received this," he said.

Peebles hesitated about accepting it. No telling what that letter contained. It might be embarrassing to himself.

Buckstone continued, "There's been an error—a ghastly error——"

At that Peebles accepted the letter.

"Notice of ejectment," he said, reading aloud, though to himself.

He went on reading, skipping parts and coming out with certain salient snatches of the document: "Heirs of the late Horace Waterman of Philadelphia . . . notice hereby given of prior title . . . ten thousand acres herein described . . . all and sundry now

occupying . . . full penalties of the law for trespass and such claims
for damages caused by such persons as rightfully due the legal
owners . . . entries, surveys, patents on file . . . dating to 1814. . . ."

Peebles' voice died. He looked questioningly at the other
man.

"Don't you see?" asked Buckstone. "It looks as if that land
I thought was legally mine isn't mine after all."

"Is this the land you sold me?" demanded Peebles.

"I sold you part of it."

Peebles' eyes narrowed. "You're telling me that you filed
on land without looking to see if there were original patents
on it?"

"How could I possibly know there were previous patents?"
Buckstone spoke almost pleadingly. "The land was represented
to me positively as public land."

"You goddamned fool! Any child ought to know that a
title should be searched!" Peebles' face now was flushed with
evident anger. "Jest what do you propose to do, Buckstone, about
that two hundred dollars you took from me for fifty acres of
that lousy land that wasn't yourn—an' never was yourn?"

"I paid you thirty-four dollars——"

"For room an' board! It was a legitimate debt to the tavern
an' had nothin' to do with this here!"

"Mr. Peebles, that's what I want to talk to you about."

"I'm listenin'." The voice was uncompromising.

"I intend to pay that two hundred dollars back to you——"

"Two hundred an' thirty-four is what it amounts to—you
cain't pay me out of my own money." The tavern man thought
a moment, his jowled head on one side. "Yeah, an' since then
there's additional bills. Twenty-seven dollars an' mebbe more.
Say two hundred an' sixty-five all told. I'll know as soon as I
check the ledgers. An' besides that, I'm entitled to interest."

"Just whatever's right, Mr. Peebles." Buckstone was anxious
and his face showed it. "I want to tell you what I propose to do.
I've thought it all out. I'm going to organize a school here—
a grammar school and perhaps an academy. I've had experience—

the need for education in Turkeytoe, even in the bare rudiments of reading and writing, is obviously great——"

"How much cash you got?"

"I—well—a few dollars at most——"

"You've spent the whole two hundred?"

"My daughter and I needed clothing. There were necessary fees to pay in connection with that land. And I've been living here in the tavern right along—your rates aren't low——"

"Complainin' about my rates?"

Peebles' manner was bullying, and Buckstone flushed at having to answer diplomatically; but he was thinking of his daughter.

"Well—no—not exactly—" he said. "I'm sure that the high standards of the house support the tariff."

But efforts to mollify him seemed only to further anger Peebles.

"Jest how much you think you'd make teachin' school in this town?" he sneered. "I'll give you an idee. Most people don't give a damn for education. They think it's weakenin'. You couldn't git twenty scholars. Even if you could git 'em to pay eight dollars a head per term—in *cash*, which they'd never do, becuz most of 'em would insist on you takin' corn or hog meat or cordwood for part of it—that wouldn't come to more'n a hundred an' sixty dollars a year. An' out of that you'd have to fend for yourself an' that gal of yourn. Why it'd take three, mebbe four years, to pay me back. Think I'd give you four years? You got another think comin'! I want my money an' I want it quick!"

"I haven't got it, I tell you. Maybe I could borrow——"

"Hell, you couldn't borrow a thin dime. Now you jest move out'n my place, Buckstone—you an' that snooty leetle gal of yourn—an' don't you be a-takin' nothin' from your rooms, either. I know my rights. An' I got a right to levy on anythin' salable for what it's worth. Git out of here an' stay out!"

Not knowing what else to do, Buckstone retreated from the office and hurried out of the tavern. He felt that he had been foolish in not taking every precaution about those lands. And certainly Peebles must be conceded cause for being disturbed.

But his manner had been unnecessarily furious and insulting. Why? Considering his own case, Buckstone knew that he had acted with honesty, and that he still would pay back everything if Peebles would only give him time.

But Peebles was not going to give him time. The way the tavern man blew up indicated that he intended to make matters as difficult as he could. What the fellow intended to do Buckstone could not think. But he knew that he was in some serious trouble and that Prudence might be in trouble with him. Having an important man like Drew Peebles out after you was decidedly unpleasant. He was filled with anger, self-blame, and apprehension—for himself, but most of all for his daughter.

Buckstone quickened his pace, hurrying down the street to find Prudence and prepare her for whatever portended for her and for himself.

3.

When he approached the small cabin where Miss Sally Quintal lived, he heard feminine laughter. For all her somewhat joyless bearing, Miss Sally upon acquaintance had proved a pleasing companion for Prudence. They found matters for amusement, which was good for the spinster. And the girl, who had learned some needlework in the convent school, liked helping the seamstress, even on dresses intended for herself, although she could not do the fine work Miss Sally did so beautifully.

Sometimes Prudence played on her violin, and sometimes they sang together over their handwork. Miss Sally taught her songs of the country, such as had not been allowed in the convent—innocent enough, but folk music, which was considered frivolous by the nuns. She even learned to transfer some of these songs to the violin, for example "The Hunters of Kentucky" and "Show Your Pretty Foot" and "Wait for the Wagon" and "The Jolly Miller." In return Prudence taught her preceptress some airs more classical. They had their little private feminine jokes and mutual interests; and they got along with each other famously.

Before knocking on the door of the cabin, Buckstone paused a moment. He could think of no way to break this news to his daughter, and he hated to chill her happy spirits. Presently, however, he squared his shoulders and rapped with his knuckles.

A brief wait, and the door was opened by Miss Sally. Her eyes widened at the sight of him.

"Why, Colonel Buckstone," she said. "Please come in."

Beyond her, in the single room, Prudence rose at his appearance and put some needlework on the table. Then she came to greet him.

Buckstone stepped in and closed the door. Shaken as he was he could not help appreciating the fact that the place was quite pretty for a log cabin. There was a bed in one corner, a plain deal table, and two or three chairs. At one end was a fireplace, for warmth and cookery, with the usual utensils.

All this was standard. What was not standard was the way little decorative touches had been added here and there. Upon the table was a crocheted cover with a pink rose design about the edges. White lace curtains hung at the two windows. The bed was covered by a handworked spread, and each of the chairs had a needlepoint seat pad. In a corner cupboard opposite from the bed were china cups and saucers. Two or three pictures hung on the whitewashed walls, not well painted, but giving color. The puncheon floor had the look of being scrubbed every day, and upon it was a round braided rug of soft colors. It was evident that she who lived here took interest and pride in her surroundings, however humble they were.

Buckstone made no full inventory of these things. His daughter, intuitively seeing that something was wrong, came to his side.

"Daddy," she said, "what is it?"

"Prudy," he began, "I—I don't know how to say it——"

Her eyes, very wide and searching, were on his face. Miss Sally stood to one side with a look of concern. He glanced at her and then at his daughter, whose slim hands were on his arm.

"I suppose," he said, "there's no reason for secrecy." He hesitated, then half stumbled on. "The fact is, Prudence, that I'm afraid I'm in trouble—no fault of mine, please believe me—a legal difficulty arising unexpectedly——"

Again he broke off, looking at the two faces so distressed in sympathy with his distress and trying to decide whether he should go on and explain the whole wretched business now or later. While he hesitated there was a knock on the door.

Miss Sally opened it. Outside stood Dode Taney, the sheriff, a big, club-jointed man, with a wen on the side of his face and an expression of dull wistfulness arising from his stupidity.

"Miss Sally," he began, "sorry to bother you, ma'am." Then he looked past her and saw Buckstone. "I figgered I'd find you here, Colonel," he said apologetically. "Not meanin' no offense, but I got a warrant fo' you, Colonel. You're s'posed to come with me."

"A warrant?" exclaimed Buckstone. "What on earth for?"

"Fraud," said Taney woodenly. "The jedge'll have to explain it to you, becuz I cain't. Now you shorely ain't a-goin' to give me no trouble, are you, Colonel?"

"Why, no, Dode," said Buckstone. "I'll accompany you of course. Prudence, please stay here with Miss Sally. I assure you, Miss Sally, that there's been some mistake. I'll be right back."

"I want to go with you," said Prudence anxiously.

"No," he answered. "Why, this thing is preposterous! I'm certain it will be explained and everything settled satisfactorily at once. On my honor, I'm not conscious of having defrauded anyone—ever."

Obediently the girl remained in the cabin with the seamstress. Through the open door the two watched anxiously as Buckstone walked away with the sheriff.

4.

In his oxlike way Dode Taney was considerably awed, for he had never had in custody before a person of such consequence

as Colonel Buckstone. He said nothing, but walked along in
respectful silence because the entire situation was a little complicated for him.

The courthouse was two blocks away and Buckstone's mind
was seething with speculations. So he opened the conversation
which the sheriff was too bashful to begin.

"How long ago was this warrant issued, Sheriff?" he asked.

"Why, jest now, I reckon, Colonel."

"You must have hurried to serve it."

"Mr. Rockcastle said for me not to waste no time."

"Who swore to it?"

"I dunno, Colonel."

With annoyance Buckstone observed that several loafers,
who saw him apparently in the custody of the sheriff, were falling
in behind and following them.

The courthouse was of stone, the only building in town so
constructed, except for the small jail which stood directly behind
it. Taney conducted his prisoner up the stairs to the second
floor, where the doors of the courtroom stood open.

As they entered, Buckstone saw with surprised apprehension
that Drew Peebles was there with Ezekiel Rockcastle, the prosecutor.

Rockcastle was a formidable looking man, about Peebles'
age, somewhat less than six feet tall, and gaunt in contrast to
the tavern man's obesity. He had a wide mouth turned down
at the corners, grizzled gray hair balding on top, and cold gray
eyes. The old-fashioned suit of gray he wore seemed to match
the hair and the eyes, and his ruffled shirt always showed the few
scattered grains of snuff that fell between his lengthy nose and
his gold snuffbox.

Noting this combination of Peebles and Peebles' legal artil-
lery, Buckstone reflected that they had moved with remarkable
celerity in bringing him to court. The lawyer was known to be
fierce in conducting a legal case, tough on witnesses and a terror
to opposing counsel.

"Set down at that there desk," said Taney, and Buckstone
took a seat at one of two tables before the judge's platform.

Peebles and Rockcastle already were sitting at ease at the other table. Spectators who had followed the sheriff into the courtroom took seats back of the bar separating them from the arena of legal conflict.

In no more than a few minutes Judge Tobias Redding entered the courtroom with a feeble, shuffling walk. He was old, being in his eighties, much decayed, almost entirely bald; and his jaw sagged so that at times it shook and he had to support it with his hand.

Buckstone remembered that Lassiter had spoken of the judge as a "creature" of the others; yet at one time Tobias Redding had been a conspicuous man in the courts of Tennessee. He was senile now, and vague much of the time. But on occasion he was still able to speak out with surprising force. In politics the old judge was a member of that disappearing party known as Federalists, and an admirer of Chief Justice John Marshall. It followed that he believed so fervently in the paramount rights of property, that any attack on this principle aroused his fury. He was much given to platitudes and Latin phrases, uttered in a quavering voice, and he required frequent libations of brandy.

Behind the judge came the clerk of the court, George Rivers, a cadaverous individual, who assisted the ancient up the two steps to his dais and saw that he was safely seated behind his desk.

"Order in the courtroom," proclaimed Rivers, and he took his place at his own small desk below, upon which were the paper, inkwell, and quills for recording the proceedings of this august tribunal.

At once Rockcastle stepped forward.

"May it please the court," he said, with an expression that indicated he had no desire to please the court or anybody else, "the matter to be heard is the case of Bion B. Buckstone, here present, on a warrant issued by your Honor."

His Honor seemed to remember that he had signed a warrant, but he was not quite clear in his mind concerning the charges contained therein. After carefully wiping a pair of steel-rimmed glasses while his jaw sagged in its disconcerting way, he placed them on his bulbous nose and gazed at Buckstone.

"Is this the accused?" he asked in the high, tremulous voice of age.

"Yes, your Honor," said Rockcastle.

"Ahem. Colonel Buckstone, will you stand?" said the judge.

Buckstone obeyed, and any unbiased observer beholding him would have said he was by far the finest-looking man in the room.

The judge blinked at him behind his spectacles. "Are you familiar, sir, with the charges against you?"

"No, your Honor," said Buckstone.

"The clerk will read the warrant," directed the court.

George Rivers rose and read the document in a monotonous voice, stumbling over unfamiliar words, and putting a great deal of emphasis on the "whereases" and "wherefors" that, in the manner of all legal instruments, obscured the text.

Listening, Buckstone made out that, according to the accusation, he had "maliciously and feloniously, with intent to cheat, defraud, and misrepresent," sold to Drew Pebbles "a certain property, to wit, fifty acres of land"—with the legal description set forth—"well knowing at the time when he received for this property from the said Drew Peebles the sum of two hundred dollars, good and legal money of the United States, that he had no right or title to the ownership of the said property."

The judge looked over his spectacles, which was rather easier than looking through them. "What say you to this, Mr. Buckstone? Do you plead guilty or not guilty?"

Buckstone's emotions almost choked him. He was unjustly accused, and he was sure that these people knew it. He fought to control his anger against Peebles, against Rockcastle, against the foolish old judge himself.

"Not guilty, of course, your Honor," he said, speaking calmly with difficulty. "Mr. Peebles is well aware that I had no way of knowing that the title to the land was defective at the time I sold it to him. As soon as I learned of this—this unfortunate situation—I hastened to inform him of it personally——"

"Do you deny," interrupted Rockcastle, "that you did receive two hundred dollars in payment for this property?"

"No, I do not deny it. But I intend to make restitution——"

"Can you present proof that you did not know of the defects in this title?" demanded Rockcastle.

"I—well—I suppose only my word of honor that I had no intimation of it—until I today received a letter from an attorney representing the heirs laying claim to the property——"

"To which the plaintiff says contrary," cut in Rockcastle. And Peebles nodded his fat head.

The old dotard on the bench held his chin in his hand and looked perplexed. "A court of law," he said at last, "cannot accept words of honor as evidence——"

"Defendant has been asked a plain question," interrupted Rockcastle again. "Does he have documentary or other proof?"

Buckstone was now confused as well as angry. His face flushed as he groped for an argument.

"If the court will permit," he said, "I will endeavor to secure a statement from the surveyor who marked out the land for me——"

That he might obtain just such a witness appeared to be one of the things Rockcastle and Peebles wished to forestall. Once more the lawyer intervened.

"May it please the court," he said, "plaintiff has stated on oath that the defendant, Bion B. Buckstone, at this very time owes him the sum of two hundred and sixty-one dollars, including not only the original payment for the worthless land, but bills for lodging and board at his tavern, for defendant and his daughter, incurred by defendant before and after said payment; and plaintiff further states that said defendant has failed and refused to pay this debt or any part of it."

The judge seemed to hesitate. Then, still holding his poor jaw, he began in a weak voice, "As *amicus curiae*," the sonorous Latin seemed to give him confidence, "counsel for plaintiff has offered a *causa sine qua non* in this matter. Are you prepared, Mr. Buckstone, to pay the injured complainant the debts which you justly owe him?"

"At present I cannot, your Honor. But if Mr. Peebles will only grant me a little time——"

"To which we object!" broke in Rockcastle. "Time? Perhaps to make an abscondment? No, your Honor. By his own words defendant convicts himself of obtaining money from the plaintiff which he cannot repay—and has no real intention to repay."

Buckstone was not without intelligence. He saw that the whole proceeding was a vicious farce, carried on before a doddering judge who was predisposed by various influences to favor Peebles and Rockcastle, and who was at the same time sufficiently remote from higher courts so that he had little concern over any interference. But he fought back.

"Your Honor," he said, "it is true that I have no actual witnesses here present able to testify as to the circumstances under which I acquired the property in question. But I can get them. As to the statement that I have no real intention to pay my debts, that is false, preposterous, and ridiculous on the face of it. How can the lawyer for the plaintiff know what is in my mind——?"

But now Judge Redding, senile or not, saw his way clear. "We have no time to listen to lengthy oration," he said. "You have admitted——"

"I demand a trial by jury!"

To Buckstone's surprise the old judge's face flamed red with anger. "Let me inform you," he said in a voice that even gained some strength from his rage at this challenge to his authority, "that this court has taken cognizance of this case and has assumed jurisdiction over it." His face, with its twitching jaw, had a look so hostile that Buckstone could hardly believe he was the same man who appeared to be so futile and groping a moment before.

"And let me warn you," continued the judge, "that this court will hold you in contempt if there are any more such outbursts from you. There is a whipping post for contempt. Ten, well laid on the bare back, might teach you respect for this court!"

Buckstone realized that he was at the mercy of an arbitrary power, in which the judge, the sheriff, Rockcastle, and Peebles all apparently were united. He knew that if it suited the whim of the touchy old fool on the bench, he might well be condemned to a public flogging. The shame of it, more than any fear of the pain, held him silent.

Having uttered his threat the judge sat back, hand under jaw, as if the effort had exhausted him.

It was time for Rockcastle once more to step in and direct the actions of the court.

"Your Honor," he said, "inasmuch as the charges of fraud are denied by the defendant, and since much time and expense would be involved in seeking and obtaining witnesses, and also since the defendant is customarily given the benefit of the doubt, we are inclined to be merciful. With the indulgence of the court, the complainant will hold in abeyance—but without prejudice to future action—the criminal section of this charge."

Judge Redding looked somewhat at a loss, and Buckstone felt an amazed relief. But the relief was momentary only.

"In such cases as this," Rockcastle continued, "I need not remind your Honor that the law in its wisdom provides a remedy. Defendant has admitted the debt, and that he cannot pay it. A portion of this debt is for food and drink consumed by defendant, and for lodgings and other services rendered him, all at the expense of the plaintiff, which makes the offense more serious. Therefore, since the statute provides the penalty, we pray the court that the defendant be held in prison for this debt until he makes full and complete restitution of all moneys which he owes to the plaintiff, Mr. Drew Peebles."

The judge nodded. "It is so ordered," he said. "The prisoner will be conveyed to the county jail and there confined, until he discharges the debts as set forth in the complaint."

"Your Honor—the matter of interest—" said Rockcastle eagerly.

"The interest, certainly," said Judge Redding. "The judgment of the court further stipulates that said debt owed by defendant to Mr. Peebles shall carry, from the date it was incurred until it is paid in full, interest at the rate of eight percent per annum, and that such accrued interest shall be considered part of the debt owed."

"Your Honor—" cried Buckstone desperately.

"What have you to say?"

"How can I pay my debt to Mr. Peebles, if I must lie in jail, unable to earn the money with which to pay him?"

At these words the old judge, who up to now had appeared feeble, almost vague, seemed to rouse himself. He leaned forward on his desk, and even his loose jaw seemed to strengthen as he began a discourse, at first in a stern though reasonable manner, but growing in violence.

"That, sir, is something you should have considered before you got yourself in this situation. The law is designed, sir, to protect honest men from sharpers. From earliest times the justice of imprisoning debtors, particularly debtors who were guilty of fraud, or *suspicion* of fraud, has been recognized. It has been on the statute books since our first ancestors came to this continent. Indeed it has the consent of even greater antiquity, for it is part of the *lex non scripta*, the great English common law, on which our entire legal system is based."

Thus far he had spoken in a moderate tone. But it was as if he suddenly remembered that the man before him had in a manner challenged the very law he was expounding. His voice grew stronger as he resumed, and the speech he directed at Buckstone was in the nature of a denunciation.

"Were it not for such a law, sir, what would prevent sharpers like yourself—yes, I say *sharpers*, sir!—from plunging the whole country into insolvency by obtaining money under false pretenses and then pleading inability to pay? Why, sir, property would become valueless! The honest man would be the victim! There would be no motive for industry or providence, sir, since the industrious and the provident would be without their rewards! The entire legal system would become impotent! A state of anarchy would exist! This nation would go to the dogs, sir, if there were no safeguard against *defaulters like you!*"

All this was uttered in a high railing voice, as if the aged

judge was working himself into a fury. Evidently it was an old
and sore point with him, and the prisoner realized the futility
of argument. Already the court had threatened him with the
whipping post. He stood silent, his head lowered and his face
reddening, until the tirade was over.

As if exhausted, Judge Redding sank back in his chair, the
wavering of his jaw once more apparent.

"Your Honor, if I may suggest—" said Rockcastle solicitously.
He extended a bottle across the judicial desk. "A slight restora-
tive is due to your age and exertions."

The honorable court accepted the brandy bottle eagerly and
from it took several swallows. After that he appeared to feel
better and he straightened himself in his chair.

"Mr. Sheriff," he said, "do your duty."

Buckstone was led away to prison.

5.

As Dode Taney conducted him down the stairs, Buckstone's humiliation was increased by the actions of the crowd of curiosity
seekers and idlers who had watched the "trial." Among these he
recognized the unfragrant Blevins brothers.

These two began a chorus of coarse epithets, hootings, and
catcalls in which the others quickly joined, all of them mani-
festing the unadmirable satisfaction which the mediocre feel in
the downfall of their betters. Clear across the yard to the jail
they followed the sheriff and his prisoner, and Buckstone's face
was burning with indignation at their insults, and with his sense
of the injustice of his treatment, though he gave no other sign
of his feelings.

The Turkeytoe jail was of stone, like the courthouse, and it
contained two compartments or cells, with a small corridor about
six feet in width between the hand-wrought iron bars that fenced
off the cells. Each compartment also had one window, high up,
guarded by iron bars.

Into one of these cells Sheriff Taney thrust his prisoner
and locked the iron door. Then he went out of the jail and also
locked the door leading from the outside into the corridor.

Buckstone looked about him. His place of confinement was
small. Against the wall opposite the window were two wooden
bunks, one above the other, and in a corner was a wooden bucket
for excretory purposes. Otherwise the cell was bare of furniture,
and it stank with the immemorial stink of prisons the world over.

He glanced through the bars into the cell on the other side
of the corridor. Lying on a bunk was a loutish youth, perhaps
eighteen years old, over-fat, with a vacant face, pursed-out lips,
straw-colored hair, and china-blue eyes, the lashes of which were
almost white in color. He was Homer Phipps, the poor oaf
charged with the "unspeakable crime," against whom Buckstone
had heard threats made by the crowd on the street, and in behalf
of whom he had expressed himself concerning those threats,
arousing the evil resentment of Bad 'Lias.

The charge against Homer was disgusting, but Buckstone was
not particularly shocked by it. A man of the world, he had heard
of instances of such unnatural acts before. But it seemed to him
that the depth of his own degradation was measured by his being imprisoned here with a near-idiot accused of sexual degeneracy.

Neither he nor the youth spoke. He turned away and sat
on the edge of the lower bunk, his head in his hands. He believed
that his arrest and sentence were both illegal, but he could see
no way that he could do anything about it. The malignancy of
Drew Peebles was evident; and he was sufficiently acquainted
with the law for imprisonment for debt to know that a malignant
creditor could keep him in confinement as long as he pleased,
unless by some means or through some agency the debt was
paid in full. Without resources and with the whole town jeering
at him, it appeared to Buckstone that he might remain imprisoned in this squalid jail for the rest of his natural life.

His depression was further embittered by the mental picture
of the figure he had cut in this miserable succession of events.
The public humiliation had been sufficiently hard to bear, but

Buckstone faced something far more lacerating to a man of his temperament: a consciousness of failure, a downright loss of self-respect. He had ridden so high on the wings of his unreasonable expectations; and now he realized that those expectations were impractical, even fatuous. He remembered Peebles' scornful, "A child ought to know that a title should be searched." That he had neglected to take this extra precaution was due no more to the surveyors' assurance that everything was all right than to his own instinct to let matters drift rather than go to the trouble of making certain. So for all this time he had been living in a fool's paradise based on an utterly worthless premise. It had been his lifelong fault—a series of hopes based on spurious conclusions, all of which had come to nothing. And this was the worst of all, because it not only showed him to himself for the hapless fool he was, but because it involved with him his daughter. He despised himself and felt the bitterest acids of despair as he sat there on the bunk in his jail cell.

After a time he heard the sheriff's voice. "Hey, Buckstone! Come to your winder. You got visitors!"

He rose and went to the window. Because of the slope on which the jail was built, the window was so high above the ground that he gazed down on those outside. They were, of course, Prudence and Miss Sally. As he looked down at the two below him, his hands grasped the bars of the window in the instinctive pathetic attitude of prisoners since the beginning of time, the attitude of utter helplessness.

Prudence was weeping silently, and it was Miss Sally who uttered the first words.

"We just learned——" she began, and broke off.

He was naturally affected by the sight of his daughter's grief, and he tried to comfort her.

"Don't cry, Prudence," he said. "I want you to know—and you, too, Miss Sally—that I've done nothing in any way dishonorable or dishonest. A set of circumstances nobody could foresee has occurred——"

Miss Sally's eyes, honest and grave, met his. "I know—we

both know—that you could never be guilty of anything dishonorable."

"Thank you for that. I'm disgraced, my misfortunes are terrible, but your belief in me makes things a little easier to bear."

"Daddy—oh, Daddy," sobbed Prudence.

"Keep up your courage, daughter," he said. "Remember I love you—you're all I have left in the world."

The jail window was much too high for her to reach to him, but she looked up, her eyes sparkling with tears. Then, her cheeks still wet, she somehow summoned a proud, tender little smile that was exquisite and very touching.

"I will, Daddy—I'll remember," she said.

His eyes sought Miss Sally's. "I'm nearly bereft of reason. What's happened to me isn't important. But what's going to happen to *her?*"

The sewing woman's arm went about Prudence. "I'll see after her. She shall have a home with me."

He was profoundly moved. "The thanks of a despairing father to you, dear lady, my everlasting thanks!"

When the two left him, Miss Sally's arm still about the girl's waist, Buckstone watched them as long as he could see them. Then he went over and sat once more on the bunk, and thought bitter thoughts. The incomprehensible caprices of fate stunned him. Only a few hours ago he was a man of position, of means, with a beautiful daughter and prospects of great advancement. Now he was a pauper, and worse than a pauper. His daughter was dependent on the charity of a sewing woman; and he was in prison for a debt incurred, he hardly yet understood how.

6.

Homer Phipps had been sentenced to the whipping post, twenty lashes with the cowhide whip—the allotted number. There were those in Turkeytoe who thought the sentence too light. A horse thief customarily received thirty strokes, besides imprisonment,

and the feeling in some quarters was that the unnaturalness of
the poor fool's crime required some especially exemplary punishment.

Homer sat silent, staring dully about his cell. He seemed
hardly to understand the feeling against him, or the nature of
the penalty he must suffer.

Once or twice that day Buckstone, in a kindly spirit, tried
to talk with him. It was a vain effort. The poor stupid creature
hardly responded and behaved almost as if he was without human
perceptions. So Buckstone gave it up and left Homer to stare
into space.

It was next morning that the sheriff came for the youth,
shackled him, and led him out into the courtyard. Buckstone,
going to his window, saw the whipping post and the considerable crowd that had gathered about it. He noticed that both
Peebles and Rockcastle were there, together with Hume the storekeeper, Tidmiller the harness maker, in fact most of the male
population of Turkeytoe, including Bad 'Lias Blevins and his
fox-faced brother. Reedy Halcutt was present, perhaps summoned
to witness the punishment of the one he had accused, but
Mrs. Halcutt was absent, though there were several women in
the crowd. Buckstone was not surprised that neither Miss Sally
nor Prudence was there. They were too fastidious to participate
in such a spectacle, and they could never have borne the cruelty
about to be enacted. Another whom he missed was Troy Lassiter.
He presumed the young Captain also felt disgust at these proceedings.

Homer was led to the whipping post, which was planted in
an open space a few yards from the jail. His shirt was removed,
revealing his white, bare back. Buckstone saw him obediently
lift his arms at the sheriff's order, so that his wrists could be
fastened to short iron pegs, driven into the post on either side
and above his head.

Even yet the poor oaf hardly seemed to comprehend what
was to be done to him. The crowd, however, did. There was a
stir in it as Sheriff Taney took in his hand the cowhide whip,

and it sickened Buckstone to see the massed cruelty, the eagerness to see suffering, in the circle of faces.

The whip was made of braided rawhide, rough and stiff, about five feet long and capable of cutting open the skin with a single lash. Taney measured it in his hand, took a good grip on the handle, looked at the white back before him, and suddenly, with all his might, struck at it.

At first Homer did not utter a sound. It was as if the pain took a long time to penetrate to his dull brain. But his back flinched shudderingly. A weal appeared across his shoulders, already beginning to grow bloody. And at length he gave a cry, a harsh animal howl of startled agony.

A second slash cut his back. Homer's body twisted and squirmed. His arms strained at their fastenings above his head and his feet stumbled about in a pathetic and futile effort to avoid the whip. He screamed, a long-continued, blood-chilling howl of mortal anguish as the whip continued to descend until the twenty strokes were finished.

A pail of water was thrown on his back, which now looked like a piece of flayed and bloody meat. He was hanging by his wrists, in collapse, but the cold water in a measure revived him so that he weakly regained his footing. Taney released him from his fastenings, and though he seemed barely able to stand, he was handed his shirt and ordered to get out of town.

This at least penetrated his mind. Staggering like a drunken man and holding his old shirt in his hand, he stumbled off into the woods, still shuddering from his torment.

Buckstone did not watch it all. The sight was too much for him. He went to his bunk and sat, elbows on knees, his ears covered by his hands, trying to shut out the horrible sounds. And he thought almost despairingly of the cruelties and injustices of the world.

Chapter 4

1.

Miss Sally Quintal's colorless existence had been radically changed.

The spinster, who had lived alone these years with nobody to be responsible for or to take any interest in her comings and goings and the small routine of her life, found herself sharing her home, her very identity almost, with a creature who was not colorless and anything but routine.

At first Prudence, woeful over the fate of her father, wept much. But after the first day or two she rallied and faced her altered circumstances rather bravely. It is hard for a girl of seventeen to remain in a mood of dejection forever, especially a girl who is lively and playful by nature. Sometimes she smiled and even sang quietly while she was doing her tasks.

In those first days Miss Sally sometimes wondered if her charge was too frivolous of mind to understand the gravity of her situation. Her own instinct was to be intensely serious, and what had happened to Colonel Buckstone was assuredly a very serious matter. Yet in spite of herself she found herself smiling now and then at some little prank of Prudence's or some light remark.

Like most women of settled life, Miss Sally had her ways of doing things, amounting almost to a ritual. She woke at dawn, made her light breakfast, and did her housekeeping before sitting down to begin her work. Prudence had a tendency to disrupt this routine by perhaps scurrying around and making the bed before doing the dishes, which was not Miss Sally's custom, and then perhaps sweeping and dusting in a perfect flurry of activity. These were small things, but they sometimes bothered Miss Sally because they were not according to her usual ways.

Yet she could not really complain of the girl's behavior. Prudence was naturally willing and helpful. She had been taught simple sewing in the convent school, and although she could not hope to equal Miss Sally's exquisite needlework, she could baste, do plain sewing, put in hems, and do other tasks that saved time in the creation of a garment. By thus pooling their efforts they finished work more quickly, and this partly solved the problem of their livelihood, because by making more dresses they earned more.

They even speculated together about the possibility—through strict frugality and long working hours—of eventually putting aside enough money to pay the debts that imprisoned Buckstone. But they decided not to tell him of this plan, for even by the most optimistic reckoning it would take years.

There had been times in the past, before the disaster, when Miss Sally was almost jealous of Prudence. In those days when the girl tried on a new gown and looked at herself in the mirror, tilting her graceful head this way and that, very critical and yet often pleased, she was unconsciously beautiful as Miss Sally was not and never had been.

But any such feeling was ended now. Prudence was hers, and sometimes when the girl did not know it, the sewing woman would look at her with tender yearning, a mothering instinct from a heart which all its life had known only barrenness and frustration.

To have someone to plan for and work for gave a new meaning to Miss Sally's existence. Where she had first assumed the care of Prudence for her father's sake, she now thought and planned for the girl's sake alone.

Colonel Buckstone . . . always she prefixed his name with the military title, because to her it became him and belonged to him. Even in his adversity she thought him noble in his bearing and in his mind; and in the days of his prosperity he had never failed to bow to her and speak to her in his stately and polished way, as if she were not an ordinary little plain-faced sewing woman, living in a one-room log house.

Yet she felt he was so much her superior in wisdom, in personality, in experience of life, and in masculine good looks that her own lack of feminine charm seemed pathetic by comparison. She did not dream that she might ever win his regard, and the mere memory of his gratitude to her for believing in him, while it was precious to her, brought a certain sadness, for she knew that her own feeling for him must always remain humble, self-denying, and unspoken. She could not even permit him to become aware of her hopeless devotion, for that would be a humiliation she could hardly bear.

She had given much thought to his imprisonment and wondered how it could ever end. And she would gladly have paid his debts herself, but her resources were far too small, even if she sold her little cabin and all its belongings. And now she must keep her home for the sake of Prudence.

The girl and she slept together in the same bed, worked together, and went together on such errands as were necessary. One daily errand was a visit to the jail to try to cheer the prisoner.

2.

As the days passed Prudence was shocked and Miss Sally was pained to see the change in Buckstone's appearance, and neither of them knew that their visits to the jail sometimes embarrassed him.

To Buckstone himself the worst feature of his imprisonment was the filth in which he was forced to live. Naturally cleanly, he was forced to sleep in his clothes, on a bunk with dirty blankets and not even a mattress. His garments grew rumpled and stained. He could not bathe. He had asked for a razor, but this was denied him, and he was ashamed to show his daughter and Miss Sally his unshaved face. Yet this he must do or refuse to see them, and he was shamefully conscious that the growing beard made him appear more unkempt than he could remember having been in his entire previous lifetime. More than once he apologized for this to them, but they pretended it was nothing and sought to make him smile.

Then one day the seamstress and the girl went on an errand that brought a disaster for which they were not prepared. It was Miss Sally who suggested it.

"You must be tired of that dress you've been wearing," she said, for Prudence had no other garment.

"I wish I had some of the clothes I left at the tavern," sighed the girl.

"Maybe if we asked they'd let us have them," said Miss Sally.

"I'm frightened to ask."

"We can at least try. They can't do worse than refuse."

In that last sentence Miss Sally did not know how badly she guessed.

Together they walked up the hill to the tavern which stood at the top of the town. Drew Peebles, as usual, sat on the veranda killing flies. He scowled at them as they stopped at the foot of the steps.

"What you want?" he asked.

"We thought—" began Miss Sally, and stopped because he looked so threatening.

"Well?" Peebles did not rise, or invite them up on the porch, or display any other courtesy.

Prudence took up the gauge. "Please, Mr. Peebles—I'd like to get my belongings that are here——"

At the words Mrs. Tabitha, Peebles' wife, stepped out on

the veranda, as if she had been listening from behind the half-open door. She was a black-haired woman, but there were streaks of gray in her hair. Her chin was long, her voice harsh, and she looked as if she was quarrelsome by nature.

"There ain't nothin' of yourn here," she said before her husband could find his tongue.

"But my dresses and things——"

" 'Dresses an' things'," mimicked Mrs. Tabitha in a mincing voice. Then her anger flared up. "We ain't got one solitary thing here that belongs to you!" She snapped her mouth shut as if she were biting off the words.

"But—they're mine——"

"Yourn? They ain't yourn! Now git this through your haid. Your no-good pappy owes us money. A whole lot of money. An' you're his minor child, ain't you? What you had was in his name, not yourn. Well, the law done give everythin' he had to us, for what little they're worth—an' that includes them frilleries of yourn. Now git along!"

She had a habit of hackling up and yelling when her rage mounted.

Peebles had not relaxed his scowl. "The law give us all your property to apply ag'in your debts," he said.

As if to emphasize this statement he destroyed another fly with his fly flicker.

There was nothing more to say. Miss Sally and Prudence turned away to go back to their cabin.

The tavern man stared after them appraisingly, and his face relaxed somewhat. Miss Sally wasn't so much, but Prudence Buckstone had a way of walking and carrying her head that had a tendency to make a man glance at her more than once.

He gave a half chuckle. "That gal of Buckstone's is a likely lookin' little wench," he said.

"Likely!" Mrs. Tabitha was scornful. "Sometimes I think you talk jest for the pleasure of hearin' your head roar. Little snip! Always was high-nosed an' snotty. Common folks wasn't good enough for her, with them fancy dresses, an' them hoity-toity airs of hers. Well, now she's sewin' for a livin', along with that dressmaker—I jest hope she likes it!"

Peebles slaughtered another fly. "You've give me an idee," he said, slowly sweeping the insect across the floor to the little collection of its conmpanions in death.

"How's that?"

"You mentionin' about her bein' her father's minor child."

"Well, that's what she is."

He rose laboriously from his chair. "I'm goin' to pay a visit to Rockcastle. Have that no-'count yaller maid of yourn sweep them flies off."

He walked down the steps and toward the village.

3.

Once each day Buckstone was permitted to step out of jail. This was from no humanitarian motive. It was only to enable him to carry his own pail of slops across the jail yard and dump the contents into a hole at the back. On his return from this errand he was allowed to wash his hands and face at the jail well before returning to his cell. And in every move he was followed by Dode Taney, armed with a rifle.

To Buckstone the whole process was annoying, and in time it became almost ridiculous. One day he said:

"Look here, Sheriff, I'm not going to try to run away from here. I'm unjustly imprisoned, having committed no crime. But to escape from prison would be a crime, and of this I won't be guilty. So you needn't carry that gun for me. As a matter of fact you're perfectly safe in letting me exercise a little every day outside my cell. Those quarters are pretty confining."

Dode Taney was not overburdened with brains, but he had his orders.

"Hit ain't my say-so, Colonel," he said. "*You* may know you ain't a-goin' to scoot off, an' *I* may know it. But I was told to keep you locked up, an' locked up you'll stay."

The sheriff's quarters consisted of two or three rooms at the rear of the lower floor of the courthouse, next to the jail. There he lived with his wife, a youngish woman with frowsy blonde hair who preferred to paddle around in her broad, flat bare feet. Mrs. Taney cooked the prisoner's meals, which monotonously consisted of boiled beans and sowbelly. Water was furnished him in a jug formerly containing liquor, and the taste, though faint, still lingered in it.

Sometimes Mrs. Taney would bring the prisoner's food and water, but Taney usually reserved this duty for himself, for he admired Buckstone's powers of conversation. On such occasions he would lounge in the corridor between the cells and listen to his "guest's" discourse with pleasure. His particular interest was the Battle of New Orleans, and concerning that conflict Buckstone, glad even for this company, gave him many, and colorful, and not always entirely fictitious details.

"I admire your mind, Colonel," the sheriff said once. "Too bad you're in here. But naturally, you're too smart to be honest."

Buckstone was too amused by the naïve remark to feel irritated.

It was while they were thus conversing one day that the news came which rocked the whole town of Turkeytoe.

Homer Phipps, the half-witted youth who had suffered whipping for his "unspeakable crime," did not return to the Halcutts' after he was released by the sheriff. Nobody was surprised, since it was quite generally agreed that even an idiot was entitled to feelings of resentment against those who turned him over to the law.

His whereabouts were unknown; but though there was some idle speculation concerning this, the subject was soon forgotten. On this day, however, while he was visiting Buckstone in the jail, Taney heard his name shouted.

He went to the jail door and Buckstone to his cell window.

A bearded man on a gaunt horse was galloping toward the jail.

"That's Tod Redfern," said the sheriff.

"Homer Phipps! They done found Homer Phipps!" yelled the man as soon as he saw Taney at the door. He was lanky, ill-clad, and shoeless.

"Wall, supposin' they did," said the sheriff.

Redfern was obviously in great excitement. "Homer Phipps—" he gasped, sliding off his horse. "The feller they caught doin'——"

"Never mind," said Taney. His wife had come to the door of their quarters, and he had a backwoodsman's regard for the niceties as he understood them. Besides, he already knew what Homer Phipps was "caught doin'."

"Wall—shore—'scuse me, ma'am," said Redfern politely, bobbing his head at Mrs. Taney. "Dode," he said solemnly to the sheriff, "he's daid."

"Daid? Whar'd they find him?"

"He was washed up on a gravel bar in the river below town, two-three mile. Drowned I reckon. But that's not all——" Redfern looked uneasily at Mrs. Taney.

"Git back into the house, Lily," said the sheriff. The woman gave him a look of disgusted disappointment, but took herself inside and closed the door.

In a lowered voice Redfern said, "He'd been damaged bad." He hesitated, then almost in a whisper added, "Somebody done butchered out the pore devil's testicles—both of 'em."

The sheriff and Buckstone gazed at him with similar expressions of horror.

"Looked like," elaborated Redfern, "when they got through cuttin' him they let him go an' left him. He managed to crawl to the river an' roll into it. To end his sufferin's likely. We found the trail of blood he left."

Taney was shocked. "Who'd do a thing like that?"

"I know exactly who did it!" exploded Buckstone from his window. "Days ago, when Homer was first arrested, I heard a gang of men, right on the street of Turkeytoe, talking about this very thing."

"Know any of 'em?" asked Redfern.

"Yes. The two Blevins brothers were there. I ventured

to remonstrate and Bad 'Lias grew threatening. I told them that
if anything happened to Homer, I would personally denounce
them."

"Now, wait a minute," said Taney. "I don't think them
boys would do no sech thing as that——"

"I *know* they did it! I want to see the prosecuting attorney
—I'll swear out a warrant!"

"Mr. Rockcastle is awful busy," said the sheriff uneasily.

"Take me to him at once," said Buckstone. "Poor Homer
Phipps will never be able to name those who committed this
dreadful atrocity upon his person. But the authorities must begin
immediately to make a proper and thorough investigation."

"Hold on," said Taney. "I ain't a-goin' to bother Mr. Rockcastle. He'll be talkin' to me soon enough—when he gits around
to it. Then I'll tell him whut you said. But right now I reckon
I'll mosey uptown with Tod Redfern, here, an' see what else is
knowed about it."

4.

At three o'clock that afternoon Ezekiel Rockcastle arrived at
the courthouse. He briefly conferred with Taney, then ordered
him to bring the prisoner to the prosecutor's office. This was a
plain room, off the judge's chambers, with a long table, some
law books on shelves, a few chairs, and many cluttered papers
beside an inkwell with a quill pen and sander.

"Mr. Buckstone," began the prosecutor, "it comes to my
ears that you've been making accusations with reference to the
death of Homer Phipps."

"I have, sir," said Buckstone. "I personally heard the plot
concocted against him."

"You may have heard some loose talk, but I suspect that is
all there was to the 'plot,' so-called."

It was difficult for Buckstone, with his soiled and wrinkled
clothes and his unshaved face, to appear dignified. But he managed to draw himself up and spoke out stoutly.

"I heard Elias Blevins, in the presence of witnesses including Reedy Halcutt, say that he intended to have some 'fun' with the murdered boy. And further, that some night he and his gang would catch Homer and 'geld him just like a boar pig.' Isn't that exactly what's happened? They ruthlessly and cruelly emasculated him and left the poor bleeding imbecile to drown himself in the river. I say that's murder, sir! Conscienceless, inhuman murder!"

"Did you witness this act?"

"No. How could I? I was in the prison when it was done. But I am so morally certain that Bad 'Lias and his crowd did it that I stand ready to swear out a warrant against him and his brother."

Rockcastle deliberately took the quill pen from the inkwell, drew a penknife from his pocket, and proceeded to cut a new point, splitting the nib carefully. At last he said:

"You're too impetuous, Buckstone, and you evidently know little of the law. On such a statement as yours I could never feel justified, as prosecuting attorney, in issuing a warrant—even if you were a respectable citizen. And a respectable citizen, sir, you are *not*. Whatever motives you may ascribe to Elias Blevins, he at least *pays his debts*."

With that bitter sneer he thrust the pen back into the inkwell and turned to the sheriff. "I call your attention, Taney, to the judge's sentence. He ordered you to take this man to the jail and there *confine* him until he makes full and complete restitution to the man he defrauded. 'Confining' him does not mean spending your time conversing with him, or carrying his wild stories about and relating them to others. There's such a thing as misfeasance in office, Mr. Sheriff. See to it that the charge is not made against you. Now take this man back and *confine* him!"

Later, in his cell, Buckstone pondered the unreasonable injustice of Rockcastle. Imprisonment for debt, in his case at least, was unjust. The whole debtor's law was unjust and one of the blots on the nation's legal system. It led to countless oppressions, for the creditors counted on the sympathies of other persons to relieve friends or relatives from confinement. Wives, fathers, brothers, friends, were laid under contribution by heartless creditors, using prison as a means of extortion. Thousands of men, and even women, lay in jails over the country at that very time under this cruel law. How long would it take for the nation to awake to its injustice and abolish it? Buckstone groaned inwardly in his feeling of being miserably victimized and abused.

But injustice went farther than his own case. He was sure in his own mind that not only had Rockcastle made no investigation of the torture-murder of Homer Phipps, but that he would make none. It seemed that the prosecutor did not *want* any proof that might incriminate Bad 'Lias and Little 'Lige. He would not turn a finger to inquire who were the fiends who committed the dreadful outrage.

Why? Turkeytoe, Buckstone reflected, was like a little self-contained despotism, here in the forest country on the frontier remote from civilization. Was there, as Troy Lassiter had suggested, some shadowy connection between men supposedly upright and worthy, like Rockcastle and Peebles and Judge Redding, on the one hand, and criminal ruffians like the Blevins brothers on the other? If so, what was the connection, and why did it exist?

That night he slept fitfully, tossing on his hard bunk and filled with bitterness at the malignity of the men who hated him for some reason he could not understand. Yet he did not dream how much farther that malignity could go.

5.

In the middle of the next morning he heard his name called from outside and went to his window.

It was Miss Sally. She was alone and in tears.

"Oh—Colonel Buckstone—" she sobbed. "There was nothing I could do—truly there wasn't——"

He did not understand what she was trying to convey, and he spoke to her almost sharply to halt her increased weeping.

"Miss Sally! Stop crying! Tell me what's wrong!"

"They've taken her—Oh, Colonel—they've taken *Prudy!*"

An incomprehensibility. "What? Who's taken her?" Buckstone cried.

"The court. This morning the sheriff came and told Prudy and me that we must go see the judge. They wouldn't even let us speak to you. We went—and that terrible old man, Judge Redding—he told me I couldn't keep her." She began to cry again.

"But why? Why couldn't you keep her?" he insisted.

"Because I couldn't post a five-hundred-dollar bond to guarantee that she—she wouldn't become a charge on the county. Oh, I promised to keep her and take care of her! I begged. I prayed. It was no use. The judge bound her out and made her go with them."

"*Bound her out?* To whom?"

"To Drew Peebles and his wife."

In the stunned silence that followed, Miss Sally even stifled her tears. The knuckles of Buckstone's hands, holding the bars of his window, whitened with the desperation of his grip. She longed for him to speak, but he did not.

"Don't hold it against me—please—" she faltered at last.

She saw his face twist, and knew he was wounded almost past bearing by the thought that his daughter was in the power of his enemy. But with an effort he controlled himself, and after a few moments he was able to look down on her almost with pity.

"Don't cry any more, Miss Sally," he said. "You can't blame yourself for this, Prudence doesn't blame you, nor do I. I could never thank you enough for taking her in, even if—it—could be only—for so short a time——"

Despair shook his voice, but he mastered it.

"Prudence—how did she take it?" he asked.

"She cried bitterly—and clung to me. But she had to go. The sheriff took her."

"And so she is Peebles' bound girl—his white slave! Miss Sally, it comes over me that it is I who did this thing to her. She might have been left with you—if I——"

He stopped. Her eyes, still tear-starred, searched his face.

"If you had—what?"

Drearily he said, "I have the unfortunate habit of speaking my mind. I did so after the—mutilation—of that poor boy, Homer Phipps, which caused his death. This new cruelty to Prudence is a further blow at me for accusing certain persons of complicity——"

Again he broke off. In reality his charges against the Blevins brothers were not directly responsible for the action taken against his daughter. It was the visit of Prudence and Miss Sally to the tavern and the hate of Mrs. Tabitha that immediately triggered Peebles' legal steps. Not knowing this, he blamed himself. Presently he went on:

"I spoke from a sense of public responsibility. Should I have kept silent? But Prudence, my poor child, suffers for it."

They were both silent for a time. Then he looked down at the woman and saw that the tears again were slowly running down her face.

"You must go," he said. "Will you try to see Prudence? Tell her I think of her continually. And I'm trying to reason some way out of this dreadful situation."

"Yes. I will."

She turned away, her handkerchief at her eyes. But he called after her.

"Miss Sally—" She halted. "Do you know Captain Troy Lassiter?"

"Yes, slightly."

"If you should happen to see him, in such a way that you can speak with him, would you ask him if he could find time to come and see me?"

She nodded and was gone.

He turned back into his cell and his mood had changed from grief and bewilderment to dull, red rage against the men who had so abused his daughter and himself. He had told Sheriff Taney that he would not attempt to escape. But now, if he saw a way, he was in a frame of mind to attempt it. Unhappily, there was no way that he could see.

6.

When the sheriff took Prudence to the tavern, Peebles was sitting on the veranda. He rose at sight of them.

"Here she is," was all Taney said.

"Bring her into the office," said Peebles.

They followed him and entered the small room. Mrs. Tabitha was awaiting them there, and she had lit a candle the better to illumine the dark place. The tavern man's wife was a heavy woman, in a dark red dress belted too tightly about the middle so that her huge bosom and large hips were made more prominent by contrast. Her black, gray-streaked hair was fluffed about her temples, then drawn back over her ears from a central parting, and her eyes were deep-set, dark, and unfriendly. Prudence could only look down helplessly, before the stare in those eyes, wondering what was to be done with her.

"So here we are!" said Mrs. Tabitha, in a voice at once mocking and triumphant. "The high-toned *Miss* Buckstone, ain't we? In silks an' fancy slippers an' perfumed up like quality. Wall, things is goin' to be difficult for you, gal. It ain't goin' to be Miss Buckstone no more. Niggers don't have no last names, an' you're jest the same as a nigger here. You'll be plain Prue. An' when I say Prue, you jump! Understand?"

"Y-yes," said the frightened girl.

"Yes, *ma'am*. Whenever you speak to me it's *ma'am*, or Mrs. Peebles, from now on. An' when you speak to Mr. Peebles, it's sir."

"Yes, ma'am," said Prudence obediently.

The sheriff cleared his throat. Even he found this bullying of a helpless girl hard to watch. "I reckon I'll be gettin' back to the courthouse," he said.

"Go ahaid, Dode," said Peebles. "This gal understands she's under our authority by law. You do, don't you?" he snapped at Prudence.

"Yes, sir," she replied, although in reality she still could hardly comprehend what had happened to her, or why.

"Lissen to me," said Peebles grimly. "You're a pauper. An' your old man's a jailbird. You're legally bound to work for us, an' you're goin' to learn what work *is*. You cain't work in that fancy dress you got on. Mrs. Peebles will show you to your quarters an' give you somethin' to wear that's more in keepin' with a servant."

At this Mrs. Tabitha led the way out of the office and ordered Prudence to precede her up a narrow stair. The tavern was built ramblingly on a single floor, the guest rooms at the rear, the bar and dining room at the front. The kitchen was in a separate structure connected with the dining room by an open-sided porch. There were several lean-tos about the place, for storage, and there was a low attic or garret above. In this there were two or three small cubicles, with wretched cots in them, the servants' quarters. Mrs. Tabitha indicated one of these.

"You'll sleep there," she said. "Take off that dress an' them slippers, an' put these on."

Prudence obeyed, although she was embarrassed at being seen in her underthings by this coarse woman, for she did not know what else to do. She was handed a rough homespun dress, dyed brown with butternut, which did not fit her, and a pair of heavy, ugly shoes, made of half-dressed leather, which assuredly bore little relation to the feet that went into them.

"Another thing," said Mrs. Tabitha. "No fancy hair fixin's for servants. Put your hair in braids, an' come down to the kitchen."

She gathered up Prudence's silk dress in her arms and flounced her red skirts out of the room.

For a few minutes tears were in the girl's eyes in her unhappiness and bewilderment. But she realized that she was expected downstairs, so she braided her thick hair in the style commanded, and dried her eyes. Mrs. Tabitha had overlooked her slippers. They lay on the floor, and Prudence picked them up. These were the very slippers, blue satin with hand embroidery, that her father had bought for her just before the great calamity befell them. She hid them beneath her cot and went down the narrow dark stairs.

Two Negro women were in the kitchen. One was huge, fat, and very black, with a somewhat ugly, pockmarked face.

"Dilsey," said Mrs. Tabitha to her, "this is Prue, who's goin' to help you."

"Dis white gal goin' to help *me?*" inquired Dilsey, as if hardly believing.

"She's a bound girl now."

"Oh," said Dilsey. "Wall, Prue, yo' might as well start peelin' on dem taters."

The second Negro servant was a light mulatto woman, about thirty, with protruding chocolate-brown eyes.

"Daisy," said Mrs. Tabitha to her, "Mr. Peebles sold you to Mr. Koble, the banker, this morning. You go right over there, hear?"

"Yass'm," said Daisy, and she followed Mrs. Tabitha out of the kitchen to take her few belongings and go to the house of her new owner.

II

The Waif in the Wilderness

Chapter 5

1.

The worst of the drudgery was the dishes at night. Prudence stood with one tired foot on top of the other, and the greasy water in the dishpan almost turned her stomach. Yet she continued, because it was ordained, to scrub the tavern's coarse tableware, piling the dishes one by one on the worktable; and after that she dried them with an old flour sack. When this was done there still remained the forks and knives and spoons, as well as the pots and pans to scour and wash. And the worktable and sink must be cleaned, the dishrags and towels hung up to dry, and all of the dishes and utensils placed on their shelves or in their drawers before she was finished.

It was late and there was nobody to help her. Dilsey, the cook, had gone to her quarters in the garret, next to Prudence's cubicle, as soon as her own tasks were done. Formerly the mulatto slave-woman, Daisy, had done this scullery work, but as soon as Peebles was sure of his bound girl, he sold Daisy and pocketed her price. One slave was enough to do the cleaning up in the kitchen, even if this one was white and young and frail looking.

By the time the girl finished her labors and crept up to her bed in the attic, it was near midnight. She heard Dilsey snoring. The fat slave who did the cooking had proved to be a friendly soul —when Mrs. Tabitha was not around—and sometimes she sang as if her heart was carefree while she made corn-batter cakes and fried sausage in the morning, or prepared more elaborate dishes later. Occasionally—again when Mrs. Tabitha was not around— she addressed Prudence as "honey," and even obligingly turned a hand now and then to help her. But when the tavern man's wife was present, Dilsey's conduct toward the white girl was severe, almost haughty; and since she understood the reason for this, Prudence did not resent it.

How Dilsey could sing and sometimes relax to laugh her great quaking laugh of surplus flesh, Prudence found it hard to understand. Slavery was too dreadful. She did not think she could ever become reconciled to being a bound girl.

At times she remembered the canting lecture old Judge Redding gave her when he announced to her that she was in-dentured to Drew Peebles. The judge had been well braced with brandy, and he held forth at some length on how she owed gratitude to the tavern man. Peebles was so "good and kind" as to agree to keep her, feed her, clothe her, and see that she was brought up "under Christian precepts," so that when her term of bondage was finished she could go into the world with a good character and habits of industry.

"Habits of industry" she was learning in earnest. She had done the work required of her in the convent school, but it was nothing compared to this. From early morning to late at night Mrs. Tabitha kept her running, at times helping the cook woman in the kitchen, at times making beds in the guest rooms, at times waiting table in the dining room, at times sweeping the floors, at times scrubbing them on her knees, at times serving as barmaid in the bar.

Always she was bone-tired when she went to bed, and she was still tired when she was awakened to begin a new day of drudgery. And all day long her work was done to the maddening clack of a scolding tongue; for Peebles' sour-faced wife never allowed her a minute's rest, or spoke to her except in strident criticism.

Prudence knew that Mrs. Tabitha had personal malice against her; but she did not know that it was for the very same reason that Miss Sally loved her—because she was pretty and winning even in her dingy clothes, while Mrs. Tabitha could never be anything but a broad-hipped, hard-faced shrew. Peebles bullied his wife, and Mrs. Tabitha in turn bullied everyone over whom she had authority. To bully Prudence seemed an especial pleasure to her; and more than once she brought the girl to tears, and gloated when her venomous words caused her victim to wipe her eyes and hurry on with her work, sometimes hardly able to see what she was doing because the tears still flowed.

Prudence, who once delighted in pretty things, had now nothing pretty. The shapeless dress of homespun and the clumsy shoes were her uniform of servitude, except when she acted as barmaid. Then she tied on the apron that must be washed every night to get the spots out of it; if she failed to get it clean, she ran the risk of hearing Mrs. Tabitha's vindictive tongue.

She was barmaid in the evenings, when she was not waiting on tables in the dining room. And serving the men in the barroom was something she disliked even more than the drudgery of dishwashing.

There were reasons for this. For one thing, it was humiliating. Among the patrons of the bar, of course, were men who were considered gentlemen. She dreaded the night when the Lassiters might come in, for she cringed at the thought of being seen in this servile condition by Troy Lassiter in particular. But the Lassiters did not come, at least for the time being.

There were others with manners and good clothes. One she noticed came in late in an evening with Mr. Rockcastle, the lawyer, and sat with him at a small table at the rear of the room, where they engaged in some discussion, probably legal. She had not seen this gentleman before, but he was well dressed in dark

clothes, and had well-cut features and a head of curly hair. He
did not look up at her when she brought the drinks Rockcastle
ordered, and after a time he and the lawyer left together. She
remembered this gentleman later, though she did not know his
name.

For the rest, she took orders from customers, and carried trays
to them with glasses of brandy, or whiskey, or flip, or rum, or
beer, or negus, or whatever their fancies dictated. And her pretty
face and her figure, graceful even in the ugly dress she wore,
attracted the attention of men too often, and sometimes the
patrons of the bar, growing tipsy, would try to become familiar
with her.

The worst were the Blevins brothers, who occasionally came
to the bar and who, strangely, not only were tolerated by
Peebles but seemed welcome there in spite of their rough appearance and uncouth manners. Frequently, indeed, the tavern
man stopped at their table with a jovial remark or two, and
even sat down and chatted with them, or bought them drinks,
which Prudence hurried to bring them, enduring with a flush in
her cheeks their knowing grins.

Both ruffians were heavy drinkers; and when Bad 'Lias, the
larger of the two—the horrible one-eyed one—became drunk,
he was mean-tempered and hard to please. But Prudence preferred
even his surliness to the furtive lasciviousness of Little 'Lige,
which she could never quite escape. 'Lige had an insinuating
way of putting his hands on her, feeling her soft feminine body.
Sometimes he patted her posterior with a lecherous grin, sometimes he tried to put an arm around her, occasionally he pinched
her arms or legs. When he could do so, he would even catch hold
of her and whisper in her ear indecencies which she hardly
understood.

She loathed the Blevins brothers, but when after a particularly insulting familiarity by Little 'Lige she complained to Mrs.
Tabitha, that worthy matron scolded her angrily, threatened to
"take a stick" to her, and sent her back for further humiliation.
Peebles himself seldom spoke to her. Prudence did not know
that he might have attempted a seduction of her, for he had an

eye for a pretty woman, but in this regard Mrs. Tabitha saved
her, though not from friendship. She kept an eye on the girl
so constant and jealous, and spoke her mind to her spouse with
such force when they were in private, that Peebles, for the
present at least, left the bound girl alone.

Not so his guests. Only the fact that the bartender frequently needed her enabled her to cut short her unpleasant visits
to the Blevins' table. She was thankful and relieved when the two
did not come to the tavern for some days, and people said they
were out of town.

2.

At times Prudence grew almost dizzy from the heat of the kitchen
and her own weariness. She would dream of being out where the
air was fresh, trees offered comforting shade, streams rippled
in meadows, birds sang, and the sky was a blue and benign
mystery with perhaps little fluffy clouds floating coolly across
it. She even had inward visions of herself all alone, bathing in
a pool, her body white and slim, natural and at ease and unafraid.

But dreams quickly faded when she heard Mrs. Tabitha's
harsh voice, and she was brought back rudely to the realities of
her drudgery, the carrying of glasses of liquor to gross, pawing
men, and the endless, unpleasant toil of life as a scullery slave
to which she had been condemned through no fault of her own.

Often she wept at night, but even then she tried to keep
her tears from staining her pillow, fearing the anger of her mistress. Yet, though Mrs. Tabitha frequently threatened to "take a
stick" to her, she refrained from carrying out the threat for a
time.

One evening Miss Sally appeared at the kitchen entrance and
asked to see Prudence. The request was legitimate and polite,
but she was at once ordered off the place by Mrs. Tabitha in a
manner so arrogant and insulting that she went with her head
lowered in angry shame.

"But she only wanted to speak to me," Prudence protested.

"I won't have that *thing* around here," said the beldame. "Everybody knows what she is."

"And what is she?" asked the girl, indignation overcoming her usual fear.

"Since you ask," said Mrs. Tabitha spitefully, "I'll tell you. She's nothin' but a whore. A common whore. That's what she is. Everybody knows it."

"She is not! That's not true!"

"Oh, ain't it?" sneered Mrs. Tabitha. "I hear different. If you want to know the truth, she was layin' up with that smooth-faced old goat you call your father——"

"You can't talk that way about my father!"

"An' jest why cain't I?"

"Because it's a lie! A lie!"

Mrs. Tabitha's face turned purple. She reached for a stick that stood in the corner of the kitchen.

"Call me a liar, you little bitch?" she shrieked. "I'll show you who you're talkin' to!"

She struck the girl across the back.

She did not strike a second time.

Right at the heavier, bulkier woman Prudence flew, and tore the stick out of her hand. The insults to her father and Miss Sally had for the moment changed the humble little bound girl into a creature fierce with anger.

It was Mrs. Tabitha's turn to cower. Frightened by the blazing fury in the girl's face, she shrank back, expecting to feel the stick wielded on her own fat body.

Prudence did not strike her.

"Don't you ever lift your hand against me again!" she said in a low, intense voice. She took a step forward, the stick clutched in her hand. "And don't you ever again dare to say anything against my father or Miss Sally!"

Quaking, Mrs. Tabitha retreated. "Now don't do nothin' rash——"

She scuttled out of the kitchen.

Dilsey, the cooking woman, had seen the whole thing from

the back of the kitchen. Prudence gave her one look, snapped
the stick across her knee, and tossed both ends into the fireplace. The Negress stared as if she could not believe what had
happened.

"Whut yo' goin' to do?" she asked.

Prudence did not answer, but turned to the dishpan.

" 'Pears lak yo' made ole Missus mighty mad," said Dilsey.

In her own mind Prudence agreed that this was true. Now
that her first anger had cooled, she began to dread the outcome
of her defiance. But she continued silently with her work.

Mrs. Tabitha did not come again into the kitchen that
evening. She had sought her husband, and finding him away from
the tavern on some business, went to her room, shaken by rage,
and took to her bed.

The episode, however, was not ended, and Prudence knew it.

3.

The tavern was silent. Voices and laughter in the barroom had
ceased, and Prudence at last crept up to her room in the loft. It
was deep night.

The girl could not sleep. Weary as she was, she lay wide
eyed in her narrow cot, staring at the dimness of the rafters
above. Something scurried across the floor. A mouse. But she
was used to mice. At first they terrified her in this attic with
their squirmy little tails and their scratchy little feet. But now
she paid hardly any attention to them. In the next room Dilsey
was snoring as usual.

Prudence was thinking of the she-devil down below and what
might happen next. Not for one instant did she regret snatching
the stick from Mrs. Tabitha, or what she said to her, but she
knew the woman would never forgive or forget.

Wistfully the girl's mind went to her imprisoned father,
whose name she had defended. Not once since she was brought
to this tavern as an indentured servant had she been permitted

to see him, and she wondered how he was faring and how he felt.

Often and often she had heard him tell of his friendship with that great man, Andrew Jackson, and the manner in which he helped the general win the Battle of New Orleans. A sense of supreme injustice flooded over her when she thought of how, after a career so glorious, he was reduced to the shame of imprisonment for debt.

If President Jackson in far-off Washington only knew of what was happening to his old friend and comrade in arms! Prudence believed he might do something to help the prisoner. Once, in the past, she had thought of writing a letter to the President. But she did not know how to address a person so lofty, nor did she feel well able to put her thoughts into writing of a nature that might stir the heart of one so far away, and so famous, and probably so burdened with his duties to the nation. Furthermore, though she knew very little about the world, an instinct told her that a letter is a cold and impersonal thing at best, and that a missive was little likely to achieve the object for which it was designed, even if such a letter arrived safely at its destination. So she gave up the idea of trying to write.

It was too late now, in any case. She must face tomorrow. That she would be whipped, perhaps by Peebles himself, she did not doubt. And she felt that she could not bear the shame of being punished in this manner like a slave. Although in all actuality she was a slave—a white slave.

The thought of being whipped and being forced to cry out and weep and beg for mercy with Mrs. Tabitha looking on in gloating triumph brought Prudence out of her bed in a quiver. She crept to the small dormer window of her room and looked out of it. A moonless sky, studded with the countless sparks of stars, seemed to brood over the dark earth. Below her window the roof of a shed lean-to sloped downward. She knew that Peebles used this shed to store firewood.

All at once the girl came to a sudden resolution, based partly on fear, partly on a half-formulated impulse, but chiefly on desperation. Another look down at the lean-to's sloping roof and she began feverishly to dress. The thin drawers went on first, and then the cambric camisole which seemed to cling to her soft, warm breasts. These undergarments at least they had not taken from her. They needed laundering and she could smell her own body, the really not unpleasant scent of a healthy young girl. Then the muslin petticoat went on. And after that the hot unpleasant homespun dress.

She did not dare light a candle for fear of waking Dilsey, but by feeling about she pulled on the coarse shoes in which she worked and made up a small bundle containing the few little things she still possessed, her comb, some hairpins, a few small articles of intimate wear, a spool of thread with a needle thrust under the threads. Another thought. From beneath her cot she brought the little slippers her father gave her, and wrapped them with the other articles.

Dark, oh so dark. With the bundle in her hands she stole toward the window and stopped again to listen. Dilsey snored on in uninterrupted, discordant slumber. Complete silence seemed to reign outside, except for a tireless chorus of frogs down by the river, and the distant whimpering of a whippoorwill.

With infinite caution she put one leg out over the window sill. Her dress hampered her, but no one could see her and the shed roof began at the inn wall, so that she could just reach it with her foot.

In a moment she was out on the roof, cautiously working herself on her hunkers down the boarded slope to the eaves. How far down to the ground it was from there she could not tell. In the darkness it seemed frighteningly far.

Nevertheless she dropped her bundle over the edge. Then, with a deep breath, she turned face down and began to squirm her legs out into space. Her body slid downward until she could no longer keep her balance. A last-minute gasp of fear, but now it was too late. Her hands slipped off the eaves and she had barely the presence of mind to give herself a little push so that she would fall clear of the building.

The drop was no more than a few feet, but it sent her prostrate in a thicket of weeds. For a few minutes she lay still, recovering her breath and her self-possession. No sound from the tavern. Presently she moved. The fall had not hurt her.

When she got to her feet she spent a few seemingly endless minutes groping in the darkness before at last she found her bundle where it had fallen among the weeds. With it she stole away.

The village was asleep. Down the street one or two windows were lighted, but the tavern stood at the higher end of the town and she hurried on up the hill from it, as quietly as she could, to leave behind her every habitation.

4.

She really did not comprehend the incredible impossibility on which she was embarking. Alone, without food, with no knowledge of the wilderness, lacking even any specific knowledge of the direction of her goal or the ways leading to it, she, Prudence Buckstone, seventeen years old and far from strong, was setting out to journey all the long distances across the country to Washington, where the President lived. Vaguely she knew that the nation's capital lay somewhere towards the east; but where it was or how far, she had not the slightest idea.

Ignorance may sometimes be protective. Had the girl understood how many hundreds of miles she must travel, what forests and mountains she must cross, what wild beasts and wilder men she might encounter, she might have despaired even before she started.

But she did not know these things. She was fearful, but she walked on into the night; and her very terror gave her a desperate kind of courage. It came to her that she could not go back now even if she wanted, for it was impossible to imagine what penalties might be exacted if it were discovered that she had tried to escape and failed. Because she did not dare retrace her steps, she went forward.

Almost at once she was out of the limits of Turkeytoe and the night forest closed about her. As she proceeded into it, it seemed to grow blacker and more menacing with each step she took. She stumbled forward over the dark, uneven ground until she came almost straight up against a huge, rough tree trunk. The collision bruised her arm, but she worked around and felt her way onward.

Beneath her feet dead leaves rustled, and there were intervals of silence when she crossed slippery moss and mold that had never been disturbed. Continually bushes and brambles and low branches caught at her clothes. So intense was the gloom that to move at all seemed almost impossible, but the girl with dogged determination pushed her way forward through the tangle.

She walked now with one arm held before her face; and more than once that arm, as she groped her way in the almost palpable blackness of the forest night, encountered tree limbs that might have gouged out an eye, or huge trunks against which she might have blundered. All about her were the trees, some great, some smaller, thickly though irregularly set, their boughs so interlaced overhead that looking upward she could not see a single star through the leafy entanglement.

Once she was trapped where the trees grew so closely together that she could not pass through them; and at another time she encountered a small jungle of underbrush she could not penetrate. In both instances she groped her way around until she found a different place where she could continue forward.

In her nostrils was the bitter-sweet scent of the forest at night. Her cheeks were scratched and her clothes were torn. Yet when she halted to try to reckon how far she had come she heard a distant dog barking. That dog was in Turkeytoe, and by the sound she knew that she had gone only a little way.

So she fought her way on, hour after hour it seemed, until at length she could no longer continue, and sobbing with weariness, she collapsed among the leaves in the darkness of the forest floor. After a time the sobs ceased. The poor little waif was asleep.

But it was hard to sleep in the forest. She had no covering and felt chilled. Sometimes there were scurryings in the bushes and each of these brought her awake with a start. She did not know what animal had passed so close. Once she caught a faint musky odor, but the beast from which it came did not approach near to her. She could not see in the darkness and she had no fire; but even had she been able to kindle a fire she would not have dared do so, for fear that someone might see it and investigate.

Toward morning she sat up gasping, her hands clutching at her breast. A bitter, uncannily lonesome wail lifted to the sky. She knew it was the howl of a wolf, because she had heard the sound before. Wolves came close to the town in winter.

To her mind a wolf was perilous. She remembered one she had seen, held captive by a collar and chained to a post about which it continually ran, long and gaunt, with a drooping tail. She read hunger and murder in the veiled eyes of the wolf, and it would snarl and snap at anyone who came close to it. Disliking it and half-fearing it even though it was chained, she drew away and did not go near it again. Later the wolf pulled the collar off over its head and escaped into the forest. Perhaps this was the same wolf!

Eyes wide with fear, she stared about in the utter dark, half-expecting at any time to see the green glint that people said came from the eyes of the beast at night. But no glint appeared and she then remembered that there must be a fire before the green gleam, which was really a reflection from the fire, could be seen.

This thought was the reverse of comforting. She could not be sure that the wolf was not creeping up on her at that very moment. The howl was not repeated, but she sat awake for the rest of the dark hours, her back rigid against a tree.

An overpowering sensation of dreariness took possession of

her. She was tired and lonely and fearful. And she was friendless and chilled with cold. It seemed to her that she had never seen or felt anything that was not cheerless.

5.

Dawn came palely at last, and with the first half-light a mockingbird in the top of a dead sycamore began to warble its improvisation of songs, borrowed from the whole world of other birds. Soon after, a cardinal not far away whistled its clear call, and one by one other birds awoke and took up the chorus until the forest seemed full of their twitterings and warblings.

As soon as the sun began to tinge the tops of the trees with gold, and she could see, Prudence rose, cramped and stiff. By daylight she found that her dress was stained and damp where she had lain on the leaves and moss. The poor, cheap garment was also torn in places from her struggle with the night forest. With the invincible instinct of femininity she got her needle and thread from the little bundle and hurriedly mended the worst of the rents.

In her mood of discouragement she wondered if she had not made a terrible mistake. The question occurred to her again and again. Perhaps she should have remained at the tavern and accepted whatever punishment was to be meted out to her ... but at once she knew that she ran away simply because it was the only solution for her. Pride could not have borne any further abuse and humiliation.

She wondered what her father would think when he learned that she was gone, and Miss Sally, also. And she found herself asking where Troy Lassiter had been during this time. In the days while she toiled at the tavern she dreaded having him find her in her degradation, fearing he might despise her. Yet she was the same girl whom he had called beautiful ... and kissed. The memory of the kiss and the way it set her emotions into a whirl of confusion lingered with her. Why had he not come? Womanlike she blamed him. It was almost as if he had deserted her, even though her good sense told her he could not have known of her condition at that time.

Now she heard, somewhere, not far away, the gurgle of water. She traced the sound and found a spring running down into a hollow below it. This morning she was hungry and she reflected that even water might help ease her hunger. So she stretched herself on the ground by the spring and drank her fill.

After that she washed her face and hands, combed her soft hair back from her eyes, gathered it behind, and tied it at her nape with a bit of ribbon she had brought. It is a natural feminine style and has become women since mankind's earliest days. Ragged as she was, with her cheeks pink from the cold water and her eyes bright in the early light, if anyone had seen her then he might have thought her very lovely.

But of this she did not think. The comb went into the bundle again and having tied the wrapping she picked it up and once more set out on her journey. She knew the sun rose in the east and Turkeytoe was behind her, so she worked her way eastward.

There was beauty in the forest. Flowers peeped out at her from their hiding places: purple trillium, pink columbine, delicate springbeauty, stonecrop, and other blooms, together with ferns which made the forest seem not so terrible by day. But it still was enormous and frighteningly wild.

In general the land sloped upward toward where the mountains lifted skyward in the east. There were places where the heavy woods gave way to small areas of open grassy ground, sometimes marshy, but offering easier walking, and there she saw red lilies and white hepaticas and pink maypops. Always, however, after she traversed such a place, the shadows of the great trees fell upon her again, and she made her way with difficulty through the undergrowth beneath what seemed a vast green roof of treetops, cavernous and lonely.

Once she heard a rustle in a thicket ahead and stood, limbs all a-quiver. From the opposite side a large animal broke, with a flash of white against a reddish body: a deer, its white tail flaunting as it leaped away, beautiful and harmless.

The sight of the creature caused her to think of the wolf that howled the night before. Perhaps, she told herself, it might not have harmed her even if it found her, for someone once told her that wolves were only dangerous in winter when snow was on the ground and they were hungry. Yet she remembered with a shiver the captive wolf with its eyes of hate and murder and was not sure.

From time to time she came upon small streams. Unless she found precarious steppingstones, she waded these, removing her brogans and lifting her skirts high about her dainty legs as she splashed through the little rivulets. But after crossing she always put the old ugly shoes on again, for her feet were too tender to walk barefoot for any distance.

In a small glen something leaped before her, moving with the incredible speed of a black whiplash—a snake. It frightened a gasping squeal out of her, but the black racer was only anxious to escape, and she watched it traveling away, as fast as she could have run, to lose itself in a mask of underbrush.

Snakes of any kind turned her stomach cold. She shuddered and made a wide detour to avoid encountering that black menace again. It was some time before she recovered from the start it gave her.

Late morning came, and the forest was thicker. In addition to the tangle of trees and undergrowth, climbing vines—wild grape, wisteria, Virginia creeper, poison ivy—laced the trunks together. She knew the treacherous three-fingered leaves of the poison ivy that seemed to reach out as if to cast their venom against her sensitive skin, and she took care to avoid them.

By this time she was savagely hungry. In a stream that formed a little marsh in an opening she recognized watercress growing. She pulled some of the plants and ate the tender, though pungent, leaves and stems. For a time the cress allayed the worst pangs of her hunger, but it caused a burning sensation in her stomach. This was the only food she had that day.

Up ahead, trees upon trees rose ever more darkly, losing themselves in what seemed an almost impenetrable wall of trunks and verdure, knitted togther by vines, their shadows growing dense. So heavy did this forest appear that she changed her course, following the slope downward until after a time she came upon a road in the hollow below.

It was not much of a road, no more than a seldom-used wagon trail through the trees, but she knew it must lead somewhere. For a time she made her way along the trail; but she was oppressed by fear that someone might see her, so presently she took to the woods again, staying close to the road and slinking along like a small shy animal. A limp bothered her now, for there was a blister on one heel. Her legs were scratched and bleeding. With her growing hunger came weakness, and at times she felt faint. Yet she kept doggedly on.

Once, sitting down to rest, she tried to compute the distance she had come from Turkeytoe; and she was forced to admit that it could be no more than a few miles. And how many miles was it to Washington? Hundreds at least.

She wondered how she possibly could reach that distant goal, starving, afoot, sleeping wherever night found her in the woods, with nobody to help or protect her, and a new enormous discouragement overwhelmed her. She could have wept, but it would not help anything. So with her bundle she rose from the log and limped on.

6.

Toward evening she heard a sound that caused her to forget her hunger and weariness. From far away it came, a long bell-like note. The bay of a hound—and it came from the direction of Turkeytoe. Another joined it. Others. A whole pack was coming, their voices vying with each other.

It flashed into her mind that they must have discovered her flight and were pursuing her. Terror crowded everything else from her mind. Bloodhounds, she had been told, once they took a trail, followed it inevitably until they tracked down whatever they pursued. The fierce beasts were sure to discover her. Perhaps they would leap upon her and mangle her, even before men came up and captured her.

With the instinct of a hunted thing she hid off from the trail in a thick clump of rhododendrons. And the pink masses of flowers made a canopy above her, too beautiful to be in harmony with her spirit. There she lay, her heart pounding so that she was sure it could be heard, in an access of dread as the heavy baying came nearer with each minute.

Now, on the trail, she saw the hounds and the men that were with them. There were six of the brutes, tugging at their leashes, two men on foot holding three dogs each by the leather thongs attached to their collars. Raising an incessant clamor, the hounds strained forward so eagerly on the scent that the leash holders were pulled along behind them, almost at a half trot.

Behind the men with the dogs came three other men, all mounted, and leading the horses of the hunters with the hounds. As she recognized the leader, the world seemed for Prudence to swim; it almost dimmed. He was Troy Lassiter, his face grim, riding and gazing ahead at the hounds. So even *he* was interesting himself in running her down and dragging her back to her masters.

Her heart went sick at this faithlessness.

But the hounds, bawling their fierce hunting chorus, reached the road at a place just opposite from where she lay cowering. One of the animals, with a half bellow, started over toward her rhododendrons, as if he scented her. She had a moment of terrible panic. But the leash holder jerked the hound back into the pack, and then to her relief they went on by her, baying in their bloodcurdling eagerness.

Her relief was tempered by fear. She believed that those dogs had missed her because she had not followed the trail itself, but kept to one side of it in the woods. Once they discovered that they had passed her, they might return, and this time they would surely hunt her down.

Trembling in the rhododendrons, she saw the procession go

by, not one hundred feet away. Each of the men was armed, and the sight of the rifles and pistols seemed to her the last excess of cruelty. Why should big men—and Troy Lassiter among them—bring guns and bloodhounds to trail and capture a defenseless girl?

The dogs did not come back. In a few minutes the whole troop, hounds still bellowing, men grim and silent, disappeared where the trace made a bend in the forest.

For a long time Prudence did not stir from her covert. The baying of the hounds receded, gradually growing indistinct. By the time she felt able to go on, the sun was setting behind the trees in the west and night was approaching.

She rose, and her terror and hunger together had so weakened her that she found it difficult to walk. Would she die of starvation out here in the wilderness, with nobody ever to know of her death? Once more tears trickled down from under her eyelids, but she forced herself forward.

The growing darkness made it necessary for her to follow the trail again, even though it was the trail which the hounds had followed. On either side of the dim path the forest pressed down upon her, and it seemed to talk endlessly to itself. Trees rustled and whispered. She heard the hunting call of a great owl, so uncanny and somehow so menacing that it brought gooseflesh to her arms.

In the strange and mighty gloom that descended, her despair grew greater. There was only the faintest sliver of a moon. The few stars glimpsed now and then through the tree tops seemed remote and unfriendly. As if driven by blind instinct to go forward until she died, the suffering girl plodded ahead.

Chapter 6

1.

In the darkness a large beast rushed suddenly out at her. She shrank back with a little shivering scream of terror.

It began a hideous barking. A dog. What was it doing out here in the forest?

Not knowing what else to do, she stood perfectly still, trembling. The dog, undecided, remained at a little distance, barking and growling, but for the moment not coming nearer to attack her. Now her sharpened senses made out dimly that she was on the edge of a small clearing. There must be a house and people here.

She could not advance, for when she attempted to do so the big cur redoubled its furious barking and seemed on the point of charging at her with bared teeth. She did not dare to flee, for that would encourage the beast to pursue and snap at her.

While she stood in this pathetic quandary a light suddenly gleamed in the darkness ahead. It was a small window, evidently,

and someone had lit a candle inside. Desperately she wondered
what story she would tell if people came out and found her.
How could she explain her presence, her bundle, her torn clothes?
She was sure that they would immediately suspect what she was,
a runaway girl; and they would probably take her back to her
masters.

Yet she stood rooted, unable to move because of the menacing cur which still snarled and barked fiercely close in front of her.

Now she was able to see against the darkness of the woods
a darker blob of shadow. A cabin. A very small, very wretched,
very humble log cabin, with its single spot of candlelight.

A voice called out, an old man's voice.

"Who dah?"

Negro voice, she realized. She was almost glad it was not a
white man.

"C-call off your dog," she answered with a half sob.

A dark figure approached, half hesitating, neck craned forward
trying to see.

"Hi-yah, Clitto! Shet yo' noise!" said the old man.

With a half snarl, half whine, the cur ceased its barking.

Cautiously the old man came near and peered into her face.

"Why—hit's a white gal!" he exclaimed. "Lady—whut yo'
doin' heah at night?"

"I—I'm lost," she said. Now she was crying freely.

"Wall, now, Miss—don't take on." His voice was concerned,
even sympathetic.

"I—I'm so—hungry—" she wailed.

"Hongree? Po' chile. Will yo' come into de cabin? We git
somep'n to eat." He turned and spoke severely to the dog that
raised another bark. "Now, yo' Clitto! Yo' shet yo' trap, or Ah
lay, Ah'll lam yo' good!"

Stifling her sobs, Prudence in sheer weakness followed him.
The door of the cabin stood open. By the light from within she
could see an old woman who had pulled on some kind of a wrap
and was hastily binding up her head in a red kerchief.

On the threshhold Prudence hesitated. She had never been in a Negro house before. Indeed, she had had little contact with colored people. The half-friendly black cook at Peebles' Tavern was the only member of the race she had known. She had grown up in the belief that Negroes were creatures apart, born to servitude, hardly to be regarded as human, indolent, uncleanly, with curious superstitions, practices, and mental processes.

The old man said, "Jessie, dis yere li'l lady done got los', an' she's hongree. Git her some food."

Prudence entered. By the light of the single tallow candle she saw them clearly for the first time. Both were old, in their seventies at a guess. Jessie—if that was her name—was large of bosom and haunch. Where her husband's skin was light brown, she was very black. Both had grizzled hair and the man a thin grizzled beard, also. In the faces of both, wrinkles were deeply graved. They gazed at the girl kindly, but as if awed or embarrassed by her presence.

"We got col' fish," said the old woman. "Kin yo' eat col' fish? Ah got some cawn bread." She hesitated. "Ah kin light a fire an' warm de fish."

Prudence was famished. "No," she said, "I can eat it cold."

"Ain't no trouble in de world to start a fire——"

"It's all right as it is," said Prudence, and added, "thank you."

Old Jessie moved about, placing the food on a cracked china plate, which she set on a rude board table.

The interior of the cabin was very mean. Rough log walls, a dirt floor, and a blackened fireplace were its chief features. It was old and run down, and its simple furnishings were in the same category. In one corner was a one-poster bed—a primitive affair, using two walls for the support of three corners, with the fourth corner held up by a single post planted in the earthen floor. Two or three rough stools, a packing box, and a broken rocking chair provided the only seats.

"Heah 'tis, Miss," said Jessie.

Prudence sat on a stool at the table. The provender was coarse, but she was starving and she ate eagerly until she was filled.

Neither of the old people sat while she ate. They stood watching her; and she sensed a humble, apologetic air about them, as if they felt they were not doing sufficiently well by their guest.

"Thank you very much," she said when she finished, to relieve their minds of this worry. "I feel much better now."

"Mah name's Weaver, Miss," the old man said. "Ah b'longs to Waite Corbell, who owns dis land an' lives in de big house up de road. Master say me an' Jessie too ole to work, so he give us dis cabin, an' dis li'l patch ground to raise garden stuff."

"That was kind of him," she said, hardly knowing what else to say.

Weaver looked at his wife. "Jessie was nuss to Master when he was a chile. Ah was in cha'ge of de stable an' hosses an' drove de kerridge. Dat's why he's so good to us. De chillen— we has four—all b'longs to Master, an' lives in de quarters up yondah. Sometime dey brings us a bit of smoke meat, or mebbe somep'n else to spry up our eatin'. Sometimes Ah ketch fish an' othah times Ah snares rabbits. We makes out." He hesitated. "If yo' likes, Ah'll show yo' de way up to Corbell's house—it ain't no mo' dan a mile——"

"No! I don't want to go there!" cried Prudence in alarm.

Silence fell in the room. After a few minutes old Weaver said gently, "If yo' in trouble, chile, Jessie an' me won't tell a soul."

So obviously and genuinely friendly were they, having fed her and having offered to help her with such simple, sincere kindness, that Prudence, in her inexperience and fear, felt an impulse to tell these two of her predicament.

"I'm—well, I'm running away," she said.

"Yo' is?" They spoke at the same time, with astonishment.

"I was bound out," she told them. "The people used me bad. I don't want anybody to see me—anybody *white*—for fear they'll take me back there. Oh, please don't tell anybody that I was here!"

Weaver moistened his lips, looked at the floor, and shuffled his feet uneasily. She understood that he was fearful of being involved in trouble because of her.

"I'm going on now," she said, rising. "Thank you for the food. Goodbye."

But now they protested. "Yo' cain't go in dis dark, chile. Weah would yo' sleep?"

"I slept in the woods last night."

"Ain't fitten fo' a white gal to sleep in de woods. Yo' jes' take dat bed. Hit got a good straw mattress, no cawn shucks."

They were offering her their own bed.

"Where would you sleep?" she asked.

"Oh, flo's good enough fo' us. We sleeps on flo' lots o' times in hot weathah. Cooler theah."

Prudence shook her head. "No. I'll not take your bed."

She was firm. At last, however, she allowed old Jessie to make her a shakedown of quilts in the corner of the cabin opposite from the bed. The old woman did this only after many protests that it was not "fittin" for a white girl.

Prudence crept under the dingy quilts. The candle was snuffed. She was asleep almost instantly from utter exhaustion.

2.

Much later that night she was awakened by the dog, which again was barking outside.

She heard, rather than saw, old Weaver rouse himself and sit on the side of the bed to draw on his breeches, and after that he lit the candle. A knock came at the door and Prudence, morbidly afraid of everything, wondered if somehow she had been traced to this place. Weaver opened the door and stepped out.

There was a whispered colloquy and she covered her head

with the quilt as someone was admitted to the cabin. More whispering. She felt that they were looking at where she lay. Then the candle was blown out and the newcomer lay down on the bare floor, near the fireplace, she judged by the sounds.

Another Negro, she thought. New alarm came over her. Was it a son of the couple in the cabin? If so, he would return to the slave quarters at the Corbell place in the morning. Inevitably word would circulate among the slaves that a white girl was at old Weaver's cabin. That word very speedily would reach the master, who assuredly would look into the matter.

The bitterness of her situation swept over her anew. Only a short time ago she was happy; the world was opening like a rosebud before her. Now, in dizzying sequence, everything had changed. Her father was in prison, she herself a fugitive, sleeping in a slave's cabin, accepting the charity of food and shelter from slaves. She wondered what new peril awaited her with a strange Negro in the cabin.

Yet so weary was she that even with these tormenting thoughts she fell off again into slumber—a troubled sleep, but at least sleep.

When she woke it was early morning, dim in the cabin. The others were up. In the fireplace a fire was going and old Jessie was stooping her bulky form before it, preparing breakfast. Bent old Weaver was talking in an undertone to the strange Negro who had come in during the night.

Prudence sat up. Near the door she heard the old man say, "She ain't goin' to make yo' no trouble."

"But if she went up to de big house——"

"Ah tol' yo' she ain't goin' to Corbell's." In a lower voice Weaver added, "She's a runaway."

They heard her stir and turned toward her as she got up. She saw that the man talking to Weaver was a strapping fellow, and that the expression on his square, dark face, as he looked at her, was like that of a criminal bracing himself for inevitable detection. Yet this man seemed no criminal. She wondered if he, too, was running away.

"I heard you talking," she said. "You needn't be afraid. I won't do anything bad against you."

"Miss," said the man, "Ah shore hopes yo' don't."

His rough clothing was smeared with half-dried mud.

She said, "Weaver told you that I'm running away. It's true. Are you running away, too?"

For a moment he was silent, his eyes on the floor; then, as if putting his fate in her hands, he lifted his eyes to hers and said, "Yes, Miss."

She thought for a moment. "Yesterday afternoon I saw men with bloodhounds and guns on the trace. I thought they were after me, but the dogs went by and didn't stop."

"Dey wasn't afteh yo', Miss. If dem dogs been on yo' trail, dey'd of found yo', shore." He looked at her, a question in his eyes. "Did yo' know any of de white gen'lmen?"

"Yes. I saw Captain Troy Lassiter."

"Dat's him! Dat's de man owns me. Dey was afteh me, Miss."

"Perhaps they were hunting someone else."

"Couldn't be. Ah spent 'most all night wadin' in de swamps to throw dem dogs off'n mah trail."

"I counted five men, all armed. Would they take five men to catch one slave?"

"Ah dunno, Miss. White folks is mighty partic'lar 'bout black folks gettin' away from dem."

"What will they do now? Where are they?"

"Mebbe dey stop some place. Mebbe dey go back wheah dey come from. Mebbe dey go on up de trail."

Jessie called. "Yo'-all come git breckfuss."

Prudence combed her hair and tied it at her nape. The Negroes stood politely aside as she washed her face and hands in a wide brown crock filled with water. Then they followed her example.

The meal was the same as the night before, except that the catfish and corn pone were hot and there was blackstrap molasses for the bread.

They ate in silence, but like a refrain one thought ran
through Prudence's mind. The men with the dogs were not
pursuing her after all. Then Troy Lassiter was not helping hunt
her down. Perhaps he did not even know she had run away.
A small flicker of hope grew in her breast. Troy . . . he had seemed
interested in her, more than interested, once. Perhaps, if he knew,
he would befriend her.

But this speculation was idle . . . in all probability she would
never see him again. The hope faded.

The runaway slave said, "Ah gotta be movin'. If dey fin' me
in dis house, go mighty hard fo' yo' folks."

Prudence suddenly realized that her own presence might be
an equal source of trouble for Weaver and Jessie.

"I'm going, too," she said.

"Yo' welcome to stay," said old Weaver, but she thought
she detected in his voice a note half reluctant, as if though he
would offer his poor hospitality as long as it was desired, he
hoped he might be rid of these dangerous guests as soon as
possible.

"No, I'm going," she said.

"Wheah-at yo' goin'?" asked Weaver.

"To Washington," she said.

From the looks on their faces she knew that as far as they
were concerned she might as well be trying to reach another
planet.

"Hit's mighty long ways," said Weaver doubtfully.

"I'm going to see the President," she informed him.

Oddly, they appeared to accept this statement as far less
miraculous than that she would ever reach Washington.

"Ah 'spect dat Pres'dent, he be pow'ful glad to see yo',"
ventured Weaver. She realized that he had no conception of
what the President was or what he did, or that he might not be
as accessible and hospitable to a stranger as was Weaver himself.

"I hope so," was all she could say.

"Which way yo' goin'?" asked Jessie.

"Well—Washington's east somewhere."

"In Virginny?"

"I don't know. I'll have to ask people."

"If yo' goin' east," said Weaver, "yo' got to cross de mountains. Cumberland Pass best way. As been theah oncet. Dey brung me heah from Virginny. Dem's mighty big mountains fo' a li'l gal to git acrost."

"I'm going to try," she said resolutely.

After a moment of thought, he said, "Young lady like yo' might find it dangersome on dat road."

"Why?"

"Bad men sometimes on dat road. Law cain't ketch 'em. Yo' might come to harm."

"I won't walk on the road," said Prudence. "I'll cling to the woods where nobody will see me."

Weaver still was doubtful, but she was determined. She had a streak of real courage, but this was not merely a matter of courage to her. In truth she had hardly an inkling of the true nature of the perils she thus confidently undertook to face.

Old Jessie put up for each of the fugitives a package of johnnycake wrapped in paper. They said their goodbyes and set out together, the slim white girl and the burly black man. The last thing Prudence saw of old Weaver was his eyes, fearfully gazing out of the shadow behind his half-closed door.

3.

She did not want the Negro's company, and he perhaps wanted hers no more. He did not look vicious, but she reflected that he was a runaway slave, and a runaway slave was always an outlaw. When they started out, he did not walk beside her. Instead, he followed her two or three paces behind. Perhaps this was out of deference, but it made her nervous.

After a time she stopped and turned. He halted also.

"What's your name?" she asked.

"Jeff, ma'am," he said.

"Well, Jeff, my name is Prudence, and I want you to walk in front of me instead of behind me. How will we get around the Corbell place?"

"Out through dem woods, Miss Prudence."

He spoke respectfully and obediently took the lead, going out into the forest. Fortunately the growth of trees was fairly open here and they had little difficulty in making the circuit. They crossed a small stream by stepping stones, and returned to the trail at a place considerably beyond the Corbell farm buildings. After that they, for a time, followed the trail. But in two or three miles she sensed that she was walking too slowly for him.

"Jeff," she said.

He stopped and turned inquiringly.

"You go on," she said. "I can't walk any faster."

He gazed at her with bright spaniel eyes. His face was square, his skin chocolate colored, his expression attentive and diffident.

"Miss Prudence," he said, "it would jes' be wuss fo' either of us to git kotched togetheh. Yo' say yo' wants to go east. Ah got to go nawth. Up nawth is freedom kentry."

She nodded.

"Up ahaid a li'l ways," he went on, "'pears lak dey's a fo'k in de road. Straight trail mus' go to de Cumberland Gap. Lef' hand fo'k should lead up nawth into Kaintucky. Ah aims to take dat."

To this she assented.

When they reached the forks, Jeff took the one that branched left, although it was little more than a footpath. With hardly a farewell to her he followed its windings among the trees until he disappeared from her sight. Prudence went on, her little feet winking in the dust, until she remembered her danger and once more took to the woods. As the slave had pointed out, for a runaway white girl to be found alone with him might be embarrassing in more ways than one.

On this day, having slept and eaten, she felt much stronger, but the blister on her heel had broken and the place was sore. So when she reached a small pool formed by a stream at some distance from the trail in the deep woods, she stopped beside it to form a sort of padding inside her shoe with some soft leaves.

The sun was warm in the little opening around the pool and the cool water tempted her. She was far from the trail and hidden from it, so presently she began to undress. Now nude, and indeed charming in her nudity had any been there to see her, she stepped into the pool. The water was cold, but she sank into it, finding the bottom sandy and clean. As thoroughly as she could, lacking soap, she washed her body and her hair. When she came out of the pool her body was rosy from the coldness of the water, and she dried herself as well as she could, then hurried half-shivering into her clothes. After that there was the problem of her hair. It was lovely and honey-colored and long, reaching down to her waist; and she spent nearly two hours drying it in the sun and combing it before at last she tied it again at the nape of her neck.

When she resumed her journey she felt better, the leaf poultice in her shoe easing the soreness on her heel, and she almost returned to the trail again for easier walking. But there came a sound of horses' hooves and men's voices, and she hid herself, her heart thumping from the danger into which she had almost blundered. She could not see the men, nor they her, and they passed on riding in the direction of Turkeytoe. She wondered if they were Troy Lassiter's party, but if there were hounds with them, she did not hear them.

Evening found her farther along her way. As the daylight began to fade, the forest seemed peopled by strange shadows. Again she wondered how far she had come, but when she computed the time she had used up in bathing and washing her hair, and the time in making the detour around the Corbell place, and the time she was in hiding when she heard the mounted men, she felt discouraged. Yet she limped on.

4.

Dusk was descending fast when she came to a deadening—a place where the trees had been killed by girdling, the first step in clearing forest land. The bark was cut away all around each trunk so that the sap could not rise and the trees died. When sunlight was able to come to the ground through the leafless branches, some cultivation was possible. To be sure, the trees eventually must be cut down and the stumps removed to make the land more productive. But a family could scratch out a living in a deadening, until the real clearing began. It was a process endlessly repeated through the great forest country by the frontier families.

To Prudence a deadening meant people, so she began a wide detour. Presently, however, she noticed in the half-light that there were no this year's crops in the soil, and that where there had been corn rows the small field was choked with weeds. Then she saw the cabin—a wreck, the roof fallen in. Nobody lived there.

She thought that she might at least find shelter for the night under its sagging roof—it would be better than sleeping in the open. So she stole across to investigate.

From the cabin erupted a flight of bats and she shrank away from the rustle of their papery wings. But the presence of bats made it more certain that the place was deserted and had been for a considerable time.

Logs from the roof had fallen in, partly filling the interior of the cabin. Cautiously she peered inside as she drew open the door, which swung out on rotten leather hinges. In the dimness and through the debris she made out a mud-and-stick fireplace at the end, with a rusted iron kettle before it. A rough plank table had been overturned and she saw a stoneware cup that had rolled from it almost to the door. Evidently the cup belonged to nobody, and it might be handy for drinking. She reached out to pick it up.

As she did so, her head came within the door far enough so that she saw a bunk at one side, on which was a roll of rotten blankets. To her a blanket, rotten or otherwise, would be a precious acquisition. So, though the interior was filmed and laced with old spider webs, she entered the tottering structure at some risk, brushing the cobwebs aside as well as she could, and put her hand on the corner of the topmost blanket to draw it off the bunk.

All at once she jumped back with a cry of horror. It was no roll of blankets. The top blanket as it came away revealed an indescribable dreadfulness.

She saw a skeleton head, with pieces of dried scalp still adhering to it, but the face was gone and only the grinning skull was left. An odor of ancient corruption rose from the disturbed blankets.

One glance was enough. Out of that abode of death she turned and fled. As she did so she dropped the cup from her hand, for she could not bear even to think of taking anything from the ghastly place.

So revolted was her system that she was retching with the nausea of sickness and terror as she fled out of the deadening and away from the sight of the ruined cabin and its horrid occupant.

After a time she was forced to stop running to gasp for breath, holding her aching sides and leaning against a tree for support. Now she could ask herself what had happened to that person and why he or she had been abandoned in the cabin. She knew the probable answer. Smallpox. The dreaded scourge of the frontier. Men would not venture into a cabin where smallpox had stricken down a victim.

Was she herself perhaps infected? The thought was frightening, but then she reasoned that the cabin had been deserted with its dead a long time before—perhaps years before, to judge by its tumbledown condition. The elements and time must have swept away all the plague infection.

Yet even though she comforted herself with this reasoning, when she heard ahead of her a running stream she went to it, lay down beside it, and washed her hands over and over, bathing her arms and face, trying to remove any possible trace of the pestilence which might be clinging to her. After that she rose, splashed across the creek and plunged forward into the dark woods, anxious only to put as much distance as possible between herself and that charnel house.

Presently, however, progress became so difficult with the deepening darkness that she felt she must stop. A cold night wind swept down from the mountains, and when she discovered another brook she halted beside it.

Once again she laved herself with desperate thoroughness, using sand which she groped up from the bottom of the stream to scrub her hands until they were sore. Hunger was insistent; so at last, when she felt that she was cleansed as thoroughly as was possible, she ate a few bites of her precious corn pone. It had diminished from previous nibbles, so that she knew it would not last nearly as long as she needed it. After it was gone, how could she live?

5.

A very old tulip tree stood near her stopping place and at its roots the trunk contained a huge hollow. In the chill of the mountain wind any shelter was welcome, so with her bundle she crept into the cavity. The place had an unpleasant, fetid odor, as if it was the abode of a beast or beasts of some kind. But she tried to accustom herself to it, and curled up into a little ball for warmth.

Warmth did not come and that night she slept little. There were scurryings and squeakings around her hollow; and once she was frightened by a shadow, appearing huge in the darkness, that floated just past the opening. It was a great owl. A moment later it pounced on some small creature not far away. A squeal and a scuffle, and the owl dispatched its prey, to fly away with it in its talons.

In the distance wolves began to howl; not one this time, but several. Prudence thought of the offensive fetid odor in her refuge. The smell of wolves? Perhaps she had invaded the den of those very creatures she heard far off.

New panic came over her, and she moved as if to leave even this partial shelter. But then she remained.

She was thankful when it began to grow light and no harm had come to her. As she crept out of the hollow in the tulip tree she felt that she was more weary than she had been the night before. This morning, also, she was stiff and sore, and her foot was painful.

The early sunlight revealed some small bones in the hollow where she had lain, and there was dried dung with hair in it, purged by some carnivorous animal. But perhaps it was not that of a wolf. More probably it was a fox or coon. She wondered if, during the night, the rightful possessor of the hollow had come, found its den tenanted by her, and watched her at close hand while she slept. The thought sent a shiver through her and once more she went to the little stream to scrub herself thoroughly. Then she brushed every vestige of wood punk and other dirt from her dress, and combed her hair. After all of this she still almost felt that some of the smell of the place continued to cling to her clothing.

By this time birds were singing in the treetops, a red squirrel chattered from a nearby tree and peered at her from around the trunk, and the wind had died down. She found a sunlit spot to warm herself while she ate a cheerless breakfast of cold corn bread washed down with cold water.

Wretchedly her mind continued to return to the ruined cabin of the evening before and the skeleton she had uncovered. Was it that of a man or a woman? She hated to dwell upon it, but she decided it must have been a man, because the few shreds of dried scalp on the skull had had hair that seemed too short for a woman.

Were there other dead in that rotted cabin? She had not taken the time to investigate. Again she worried about the pestilence that must have caused the death; and she hoped she had washed away every taint of it from her hands and face.

Prudence was never to learn who the unfortunate was, or the cause of the death; but for all future time she could hardly bear to think of what she had seen in that ruined shack.

But now she must go on. With her meager breakfast fin-

ished she started wearily to parallel the road once more. The
way led more steeply uphill, for she was approaching the mountains, and she continually had to descend into little gullies, then
climb out again, struggling through the underbrush which made
her progress painfully slow and tiring.

Once she was forced down on the trail itself. This was when
she came to a rushing little river, too wide and deep and swift
to ford. So she worked down to the road, thinking there might
be a bridge there. She was right. There was a crude bridge of logs.

After looking fearfully in both directions, she came out on
the trail and went over the bridge in a limping, scurrying rush,
diving at once into the brush after she had crossed. There she
lay for some time, listening hard to learn if anyone had observed
her.

Travel like this was exhausting. Again and again she changed
the leaf padding in her shoe. Each time she stopped to rest she
thought, with a sinking heart, how short was the distance she
had come and how far it must be to Washington; and she now
began to wonder if she could ever possibly reach the city beyond
the mountains.

Thus far she had traveled in the quite childish hope that
she would find her way and even the means of subsistence, but
without really planning. It was true she had found food and
shelter—once. In the cabin of the slaves. But would she encounter
anyone else so kind? Discouragement began to take possession
of her.

The day warmed somewhat and near noon she reached a
small open glade in the woods where grass grew and the sun
came in. There she stopped, ate the few crumbs remaining of
her johnnycake, and sat on the soft earth in the sun. In the
trees about, robins, thrushes, vireos, and others of their musical
kind made a sprightly chorus. A riot of gorgeous azaleas bordered
the little glen, and above her grew a perfect maze of blossoming
rhododendron, shell-pink and radiant. Bees droned drowsily from
bloom to bloom, and a brilliant yellow butterfly made a flare
of bright color.

There was beauty here, but Prudence, who was usually entranced by beauty, on this day hardly noticed it. Instead she looked at her dress and saw that the coarse homespun was so tattered that, if only for decency's sake, she must mend the worst tears in it. With her needle and thread she again made some shift at repairing the garment, but presently she put away the small sewing implements and in sheer weariness lay down on the grass and slept. In sleep the childlike purity of her face, with the long lashes of her closed eyes against her cheeks, was touchingly beautiful, but of this she was unaware.

When she woke she felt somewhat better, but as before she regretted the time she had lost. By the position of the sun she guessed that she must have been there two hours or more. Once again she examined her foot. The heel was inflamed where the blister had broken, and it was sore. She found fresh leaves to replace the old, and this poultice eased the pain.

A new concern worried her. Her shoes, poorly and cheaply made, were beginning to go to pieces. Repeatedly they had been soaked in the morning dew and had gotten wet in places where she crossed. The leather of one shoe was pulling away from the worn sole, while the other gave signs of equal disintegration. Where they had dried after being soaked they were stiff; and broken places appeared where the half-tanned leather creased.

She opened up her bundle and took out the blue satin slippers. They were the last thing her father had given her, and though she might now put them on, she had hoped to save them, perhaps to don as at least one decent article of wear when occasion warranted it.

In the end she returned the slippers to the parcel, and put on the broken shoes, once more to resume her painful progress.

Chapter 7

1.

The country had now lifted into the lower mountains and the girl, weary and lame, found that climbing through the trees and undergrowth was almost beyond her fading strength. Only a few miles away, it seemed, loomed the high peaks and ridges, and the trace below her now wound its way between stony cliffs, which sometimes were tree covered but sometimes showed bare rocky sides. Pines and other conifers appeared on the heights, darker and gloomier, it seemed to her, than the prevailing deciduous trees of the lower lands.

Toward evening she found herself above a gorge, between the rough sides of which the trail seemed to twist in a tortured manner. Before her, on the rise she was climbing, appeared broken rock ledges.

These must be surmounted. She put a foot on one of the broken rocks. Suddenly she halted, stock-still.

Never in her life had she seen anything so menacingly ugly as what lay quietly on the flat rock before her. Its flattened

length cupped into every hollow and depression and curved about
a slight projection, the sinuous back marked with sinister geo-
metrical blackish rhombs. It was a huge, seven-foot, diamondback
rattlesnake.

Perfectly still, she stood looking at the death at her feet.

The big rattler was old and experienced. There was no fear
in his cold heart. His ugly, wedge-shaped head, nearly three inches
broad, contained the fangs and poison sacs, which gave him the
confidence that made him contemptuous of all other living creatures. One lightning strike from him, his venom-dripping fangs
injecting their deadly spurt into the flesh, and the strongest of
his enemies died.

His tongue licked out and a dry whirr came warningly from
the rattles on his tail. As if spellbound by the great serpent, the
girl stood like a terror-stricken little statue.

A puff of breeze fluttered an edge of her skirt. The movement brought a sharp, menacing action from the supple, gleaming thing before her. All in a single whipping motion, the rattlesnake shifted his body from an extended prone position to that
of a coiled spring.

She saw the loops of his body arched back, his flat ugly head
poised on his slightly crooked neck, and heard the long dry warning rattle. And then she leaped. Backward, not looking where.
With a blind instinct to escape the certain death that lay coiled
before her.

Downward she fell for several feet, among broken rocks and
rough vegetation, and rolled yet farther. The instinctive celerity
of her backward movement saved her from the fatal strike of the
snake which still remained coiled above her on the rock.

She was bruised and cut by her fall; but in spite of her
hurts she caught up her bundle and began a leaping, panic-
stricken flight down the face of the gorge. If she were seen it
made no difference to her now. She only wanted to get as far
away as she could from that horror on the height.

Only when, after another tumble and a slide, she reached
the bottom did her presence of mind return. The trace here

seemed little traveled, but she once more began cautiously to limp along it, close to the bushes at one side, ready to hide in them at the slightest alarm. Her thigh and elbow were painfully bruised, and a new scratch was bleeding on her cheek, but she was shudderingly grateful that she had escaped with as little hurt as this from the loathsome reptile that for a moment seemed to hold her in his power.

2.

Just at dusk the alarm came. Up the road ahead she heard men's voices and scurried into a thick clump of hazel shrubs.

A shout, harsh with menace: *"Stand!"*

It was followed by two shots, echoing up and down the canyon.

Peering tremblingly through the bushes Prudence saw a fearful sight. A short distance up the road, at a place where the rocky walls narrowed almost together, two rough men stood, each with a lifted rifle. A third man, well dressed, was clinging to the saddle of a rearing horse, trying to control the frightened animal, though he was handicapped by a smoking pistol in each hand. He had fired both weapons and missed.

As she watched, the shorter of the two men on the road tried to seize the horse by the bridle. But the snorting, rearing beast prevented it.

Pale, cursing helplessly, the man in the saddle looked at the two who had halted him. The taller of the two coldly raised his rifle and shot the rider through the body.

Instantly the horse bolted down the road toward Prudence. Just as it passed the hazel bushes where she was hiding, the rider pitched out of the saddle, rolled over on the ground, and came to rest face down, with a last twist of his legs, almost beside her.

The horse galloped on, and the murderers came running to make certain their victim was dead, and to go through his pockets.

As they turned him over, Prudence felt a sickening horror. The violence and danger in themselves were enough to make her feel faint, but here was something more. She knew the man who had just been brutally shot down. He was Dr. Tracy Lassiter, brother of Troy Lassiter.

And she knew the men who killed him. One of them, tall and burly, with an empty eye socket, was Bad 'Lias Blevins. The other was his brother, Little 'Lige, who had made himself so detestable to her at the tavern.

Even as the bandits hung over the murdered man, robbing him, like a wild animal's eyes, the shifty, ferret eyes of Little 'Lige glanced here and there, ceaselessly alert. She prayed that she was fully concealed, but she could not be sure, they were so close to her. The outlaw's glance passed over her, and she shivered. The glance returned, fixed itself.

"Hell's fire! Somebody's in thar!" yelled Little 'Lige, bringing his gun to his shoulder.

With a fearful oath Bad 'Lias bounded over. The cowering girl was revealed and dragged roughly from her place of concealment.

"Hit's that gal from the tavern!" cried Little 'Lige.

"An' she seen the hull damn thing!" exclaimed Bad 'Lias. He whipped a long knife from its sheath at his belt.

"Hold on!" said his brother. And to Prudence, "Who's with you?"

"N-nobody," quavered the girl.

"Cain't let her go. Got to finish her," growled Bad 'Lias. Again he lifted the dreadful knife.

"Not here!" said Little 'Lige quickly. He pointed at the prostrate figure beside the road. "Bad enough when they find *him!*"

"Wall, then, git her away from the trace," said Bad 'Lias. "Somebody might come any minute. I'll put him out'n the way an' make a cast up an' down the trail."

He turned to complete the robbery of the corpse.

"You come with me," said Little 'Lige. He seized Prudence

by one of her slender wrists and began to drag her away, into the woods beyond the place where the cliffs came almost together.

"Don't—please don't—" she begged. "Let me go—I'd never tell——"

"Shet up!" he snarled.

She was too terrified to disobey him and too weak to resist as he pulled her along, though she clung, as if by instinct, to the little bundle under her arm. She was afraid to think what was going to happen to her, but her beating heart told her that it would be terrible.

Once she glanced fearfully up at the man's brutal, unshaved face, and for the first time the enormity of the double jeopardy of woman was fully realized by her. This man, she was sure, meant to rape her: an unspeakable violation which her mind scarcely understood, but which her female instinct understood all too well. And beyond that she was to die, another conception that her youth could hardly accept as a thought, but from which her body shrank in abject fear.

"What're you doin' out here all by yourself?" he asked her once.

"I—I got lost—" she managed to say.

He gave her a look. "Runnin' away, ain't you?"

She was silent. He gave her wrist a painful twist.

"Answer me!" he said.

She gave a little cry at the pain and nodded her head.

"Thought so," he said, releasing the twist on her wrist, though he still held her. And he added, with a half grin, "That's mighty interestin'!"

At this place the valley widened, choked with trees and undergrowth and walled all around by a steep scrap of living rock above. Perhaps a mile farther along the trail it narrowed again into a second tight pass like that in which the murder was done. But Prudence hardly observed this as she was hauled along; and they had progressed quite a distance into the woods when they reached the foot of a stony cliff.

Around this buttress he dragged her, and all at once they were at an opening in the rock, six feet high and perhaps as wide, the mouth of one of the caves which were quite common in that country.

"In thar," the man said.

She hung back. "I—don't want to——"

For answer he gave her a brutal push, the force of which sent her flying into the cave and almost caused her to fall prostrate. When she turned, frantic to escape, he was there in the cave mouth to seize her and drag her in more deeply.

At the end of the cave, which widened into a fairly large chamber in the rock, were the glowing embers of a fire, indicating a crevice that allowed the smoke to escape upward. Still holding the girl, about the waist now, Little 'Lige kicked some dry twigs and small branches on the embers from a pile lying near. Flames quickly licked up, illuminating the interior with a flickering light.

He turned her about, holding her by both arms, and looked into her face with a grin on his wet red lips.

"Now, gal," he said, "you seen somethin', didn't you? We ought to cut your throat for that, but we ain't goin' to do it. No, you an' me's goin' to be friends. Good friends. *Real* good friends, ain't we? You come along jest right. I been a-hungerin' for a woman, an' here you are. I allus did like your style, an' that li'l shape of yourn. You jest be nice to 'Lige, an' 'Lige will be nice to you. Understand?" One of his hands made a sleeking motion down her back and along her soft hips.

"No—I don't—" she said desperately. But she understood all too well. She knew what he wanted of her. *Hungerin' for a woman.* His coarse way of putting it. It wrought her to a higher pitch of terror and horror. Everything in her loathed him. His dirtiness. His bad, rancid smell. His breath, sour with liquor. His insufferable clutching hands. Above all his lascivious mouth, grinning gloatingly in his unshaved face.

"I reckon you understand," he said banteringly. "You done a little screwin' now an' then, ain't you?"

"I—I don't know what you mean——"

"Oh, yes you do. I bet you've been screwed plenty of times. Purty gal like you is bound to git screwed. But 'Lige'll teach you some screwin' tricks you never knowed before."

"Oh—please—please—" she pleaded.

For answer he pulled her to him, one of his hands grasping at her breasts, and she felt his sickening kiss on her cheek, his liquor-sodden lips reaching for her mouth. In an access of desperate revulsion she twisted her body and somehow managed to break away from him, looking at him with eyes of hate and disgust through the tangle of hair that had fallen over her face.

"Leave me alone—you dirty, filthy pig!" she cried.

"Oho!" He surveyed her with that grin of his. "High an' mighty, eh? An' this is Drew Peebles' white slave! Wall, you want to be treated like a slave? Mebbe a taste of the snake whip will change your notions."

From a niche in the rocky wall he took a whip, coiled and dark, and shook out its length.

"I'm a-goin' to learn you, gal," he said, his face gone suddenly cruel. "Afore I git through with you, you'll be a-beggin' an' prayin' for me to screw you, an' thankin' me while I do it."

She turned away from him into a corner, covering her face with her arms to protect her eyes from the lash.

Near her ear she heard the whip whistle and snap like a pistol shot, as the ruffian amused himself by trying to break her nerve.

Then suddenly she felt the lash. It seemed to lap itself like a red-hot wire about her body.

She screamed.

Again the whip wrapped about her body, leaving a weal of pain and a terror of the next blow that was coming. She gave another cry, screaming at the top of her voice in sheer uncontrolled agony.

Someone said roughly, "What in hell you tryin' to do?"

Little 'Lige was seized by a shoulder and jerked around.

3.

"I was jest explainin' a few things to her," said the lesser bandit.

Bad 'Lias said, "You kin hear her yellin' all the way to the trail. Want to bring somebody to look in on us?"

"I wasn't goin' to lick her much."

"She wouldn't lay for you, I reckon."

"Jest needs a little more of the snake whip. She'll lay for both of us. She'll be a real good little gal, ready an' glad to do anythin' we want with her. Won't you, gal?" He grinned at the sobbing prisoner.

But Bad 'Lias was in an ugly humor. "You're so woman-crazy it's sickenin', 'Lige. Whilst I do the work, you only think about amusin' yourself."

"Now that ain't so," protested the other. "Ain't I allus figgerin'? What about them Lassiter hosses, an' the Moomaw job? An' didn't I find whar that Phipps kid was hidin', so we could ketch him an' do the what-for to him?"

In their wrangling they hardly looked at the girl, who stood cowering in a corner of the cave, like a small field mouse before two venomous serpents.

But now the single eye of Bad 'Lias glowered at her. "I told you to git rid of her."

"Shore. But why not have a leetle fun with her fust? Lissen, I've found out somethin'. She's run away from Peebles' Tavern. She's by herself—nobody knows she's here, or whar she is. We kin keep her awhile, an' nobody any wiser. She kin cook for us. An' when we want a li'l frolic with her—say, I wasn't gittin' her ready for me only. You kin have the fust turn with her if you want."

"Huh!" Bad 'Lias gave her another, more appraising look. "Wall, she kin wait," he growled. "Business before pleasure, as the feller says. Let's see what kind of a haul we got. After that—" he broke off.

It was evident that Little 'Lige stood in some fear of his brutal brother. Also, that both men were more than a little drunk. The girl, listening to the dispute that so intimately concerned her, had no illusions that either outlaw felt any mercy toward her. She expected every moment that the ravishment would begin, and she would gladly have died before submitting to that ultimate disgrace and shame.

But Bad 'Lias had other ideas at the moment. "Gal!" he said. "Make yourself useful. Thar's meat in that piggin. Cook some supper."

They were between her and the cave entrance and escape was impossible. Weakly, hoping to placate them, she obeyed. From the small wooden tub she took some strips of smoked pork, put them in a large frying pan, and placed the pan on the fire. The meat began to sizzle.

The bandits turned from her, and Bad 'Lias took from a rocky shelf a crockery jug, corked with a piece of corncob.

"You know that was Dr. Lassiter we killed?" he asked, uncorking the jug.

Little 'Lige nodded. "Too bad we didn't ketch the hoss. Hit's worth three hundred dollars if it's worth a dime. Besides, it might show up somewheres down the road, an' start people askin' questions. What did you do with the body?"

"Lugged it off'n the trail a ways an' piled some ol' logs an' trash over it." Bad 'Lias lifted the jug to his mouth and began to swallow noisily, his Adam's apple going up and down with each gulp in the forest of coarse hair that covered his throat.

"Buzzards will find him thar," said Little 'Lige.

"We'll be long gone afore anybody notices buzzards." Bad 'Lias wiped his mouth with the hairy back of his hand and gave the jug to his brother who in turn drank deeply.

Prudence, crouching beside her cooking fire, could hear their talk and see them handing the jug of liquor back and forth. It came over her that these were not merely criminals. These men were something infinitely worse: they were *mad*, as rabid dogs are mad, insanely intent on murder and destruction and cruelty. They talked over their evildoings in her hearing as though she were incapable of understanding what they were saying. She knew well why. She would never leave that cave alive. The thought of it shook her, but there was nothing she could do but await her fate.

Coins clinked on the stone floor at the entrance of the cave as the murderers emptied the money belt taken from Dr. Lassiter.

"We done all right," grunted Bad 'Lias.

They began greedily to count the gold coins, arranging them in little piles, and continually passing the jug back and forth.

"Five hundred an' forty in gold," said Bad 'Lias at last. He took still another drink. "What was in his pockets?"

"Jest a li'l change in silver an' some Kaintucky bank bills. Not wuth much," replied Little 'Lige.

Both men were talking thickly. Evidently they had been half drunk when they murdered Dr. Lassiter. They were becoming swinishly drunk now.

Prudence, penned in the cave by the cooking fire, dreaded what was coming. As soon as these beasts finished counting their loot and filling their bellies with the meat that now sputtered in the frying pan, they would turn to her . . .

She wished she was not a woman. She wished she was already dead.

Bad 'Lias was not quite through with his inventory. "Thar was his watch," he said, and belched disgustingly.

"Here 'tis." Little 'Lige took it from his pocket. Both men examined it.

"Gold," pronounced Bad 'Lias. "An' a gold chain. Of the best."

Little 'Lige nodded. "It'll bring a hundred at least."

"Thar was a ring," said the bigger ruffian. "You took it off'n him."

"I did take it off," said Little 'Lige. "It wasn't wuth nothin'."

"Hit's gold, ain't it? An' it's got a big ruby. I seen it."

"Ruby?" Little 'Lige gave a sarcastic laugh. "Hell—it was nothin' but glass. I throwed it away."

There was a sudden, startling roar from Bad 'Lias.

"*Throwed it away?*"

He came to his feet, swearing horribly. The other rose also.

"Whar'd you throw it?" demanded Bad 'Lias. "You know goddamn well that Dr. Tracy Lassiter wouldn't be caught wearin' no glass! That ruby ring's wuth a thousand at the lowest!"

"I didn't reckon——"

"'Lige Blevins, you're lyin' to me! You got that ring on you, an' you're figgerin' on keepin' it for yourself——"

"No, honest, 'Lias!"

"You're a liar!"

"I ain't no liar—now, 'Lias—cool off—ain't no reason to git all het up—I'll give you the damn ring——"

Bad 'Lias had been drinking heavily and he was always dangerous when drunk.

"I hate liars!" he shouted. "An' I'm tired havin' you lie to me!"

In his rage he struck out, a blow that hit his brother on the side of his face. It staggered Little 'Lige but he recovered.

"'Lias, lissen to me!" he begged. "Now wait—let's talk this thing over——" Real fear was in his voice now.

The big man seemed to gather himself and leaped forward. As he did so Little 'Lige seized a heavy stick of wood from a pile on the floor and lashed out desperately.

The club brought a tearing grunt from Bad 'Lias. For a moment the two flung apart, glaring at each other. Then they closed again in drunken fury, the club swinging against the flailing fists.

For the moment the girl was forgotten. She had risen and stood with her back against the cave wall, both hands braced back against it to support herself. This was violence and terror beyond her experience. Never had she seen men fight hand to hand, nor had she ever pictured in her mind a combat of such animal brutality as that now taking place in the cave entrance.

It was no clean-cut, fist-to-fist encounter. The human brutes grunted, swayed, swore, battered, with no rules and nobody to stop them. Down they went, together. Then they were up again.

As they scrambled to their feet Little 'Lige saw his chance and brought down his club upon his brother's head with such furious force that the wood was splintered. Bad 'Lias fell.

At once Little 'Lige made a break for the cave mouth to escape. But his murderous brother was not too badly stunned or too drunk to see this flight.

He hoisted himself upright. Prudence saw his knife come out of its sheath, flash through the air as he threw it, and bury itself hilt-deep in the fleeing back. A dreadful, choking scream came from Little 'Lige as he collapsed on the floor, throwing himself about and coughing up blood. Over him stood his snarling slayer.

A few paroxysms and the prone figure lay still. Cursing drunkenly to himself, Bad 'Lias began going through his brother's pockets.

"Here 'tis," he growled. "I thought so."

He held up a gold ring with a red stone that sent out crimson sparks reflected from the fire.

But as he looked at it his fingers, clumsy with drink, lost their hold on it. The ring fell to the stone cave floor and rolled away a few feet to one side.

Instantly Bad 'Lias lurched after it.

In that brief flash of time, while he was groping to pick up the treasure, Prudence, who had been crowding against the opposite wall, slipped toward the entrance, stepped over the dead man, and ran like a deer into the night-darkened forest.

4.

She heard a great oath from the murderer and he came plunging out of the cave after her. Had it been day he surely must soon have caught her. But night had fallen. Even so, had he been less tipsy, he might have searched for her until he found her.

The darkness and the man's condition, however, favored her. She lay in the undergrowth, her heart beating so that it seemed almost ready to burst from her ribs, while she listened to Bad 'Lias threshing about through the bushes, hunting for her. He was very drunk and consequently very savage, cursing continually.

After a time, however, he abandoned the search at least for the present, and staggered back to the cave. There the girl had a chilling sight of him, sitting in the opening beside his murdered brother, outlined by the fire within, while he seized the jug again and continued to drink until he nodded in hoggish slumber.

A long time later she rose from her hiding place. Very carefully she stole away, trying to make no noise that would rouse the bloody-minded criminal. But when she had put a considerable distance between herself and the cave, she made more speed.

If Bad 'Lias overtook her he would murder her immediately and without pity, for she had now witnessed the two slayings he had committed. Very prayerfully she hoped that his drunken slumber was so deep that he would not pursue her. But every sound in the forest caused her to start, fearful that he was upon her.

She had not the faintest idea in what direction she was going. In the darkness her only thought was to escape as far into the forest as possible. She was lost. No doubt of that. And the trail might be in almost any direction. But even had she known where the trace was, she would hardly have dared return to it for fear that the fiend with one eye might be lurking on it.

After a while she sank down. She was conscious of thirst, and she was hungry, also. Her extreme excitement, the heights and depths of fear, despair and even fleeting hope she had experienced, now combined to increase her bodily needs.

For a time she lay very still, listening, hoping to discover the sound of running water that would show her the way to some nearby spring or stream. But only the ceaseless murmur of rustling leaves and the occasional call of some night bird came to her ears.

In her shrouding of bushes, her face in the direction from which she had come, she lay weary to death.

Chapter 8

1.

A mountain wind, colder than that of the night before, had sprung up, causing the branches of the trees above her to thresh and sough so that other sounds were made dim.

It was instinct, therefore, rather than any warning to her eye or ear, that made her suddenly aware of the dark figure stealing up on her. Even in the night gloom beneath the trees she could make him out, approaching slowly, as if not quite certain where she lay hidden, yet in a manner that made her somehow sure that he had traced her to this last refuge.

She had hoped that Bad 'Lias would be too drunk to continue his search for her; but he must have followed her almost at once. She now remembered that in her hurry, after her first stealthy movements when he failed to find her and returned to the cave, she became careless. Working her way through the underbrush she must have made sufficient noise so that even his alcohol-sodden senses detected it.

When first she saw him her wild impulse was to run. But

she knew at once it would be useless to do so. He was already too close to her. By fleeing she would only reveal her presence and her course. Her sole hope was to lie perfectly still like a fawn huddled under a bush, on the chance that the darkness and her concealment might baffle him again, as it had done before, until he gave up the hunt and returned to the cave.

But no such good fortune seemed possible now. He appeared to *know* that she was in the near vicinity; and though he was no more than a menacing shadow in the gloom, he seemed to be quartering the area like a hound on the scent. She could visualize that fearful death knife in his hand, and she knew his abysmal ferocity. He was a madman, a subhuman beast, without conscience, pity, or normal feelings of any kind. Already she had seen him heartlessly commit two murders, one of his victims being his own brother. She had heard how he and Little 'Lias had hunted down, trapped, and maimed poor young Homer Phipps so that he drowned himself. How many other outrages against decency and humanity the outlaw had committed, she could not even imagine; nor could she imagine any deed, however bloody or vile, at which he would hesitate.

Closer she hugged the earth, trying not to breathe, fearful that her beating heart might reveal her presence. The brooding dark figure came near, then passed her by. He halted, and she held her breath.

Now he began again his quartering movements, moving away a short distance, then returning, all in complete silence—the more menacing in its indication that he was straining his ears to catch any slight movement of hers, ready to pounce on her.

Once he seemed about to stumble on her very covert, but he missed it, passed by. She could make out his shoulders, his stealthy walk, the intent attitude of his head, although in the darkness she could not see his features. It was not necessary that she see them. Her mind pictured them vividly, too vividly: the coarse visage with its stubble of unshaved beard, the wet eyeless socket, the expression of blank, animal ferocity.

Now he stopped again and listened. Then he took a different angle which led him behind her, on the other side of her bushes. She prayed that he would not come back, that he would go away.

For a long time he seemed to stand perfectly still, as if listening for her breathing. Then she heard him moving again.

She was unable to tell what he was doing, until a movement of the very bushes among which she crouched told her that he was almost upon her.

She looked upward, and gave a little quavering cry of despair.

Looming right over her, where he had parted the bushes above her, she saw the black shadow of his head and shoulders. He was looking directly down at her, at her very face.

No use to struggle now. No chance to escape. With a kind of hopeless resignation she awaited her certain fate.

He spoke.

"Miss Prudence?"

It was Jeff!

2.

With a sob of relief and joy she recognized him now. The darkness of the night and her belief that he was Bad 'Lias had prevented her from knowing him before.

"Oh, thank God, it's you!" she cried.

He made a hushing sound. Then he took her by the arm and helped her to her feet.

"Ah seen yo' run from de cave," he said in a whisper. "Ah was shore it was yo'. Afteh dat man went back in, Ah could heah yo' comin' dis-a-way. So Ah follered."

Not for one instant did she ask herself if he intended her harm. Instead, she clung to his arm, grateful to her soul that in her most dreadful adversity she had at least this support.

"We got to git further away," he whispered.

Without a question, she went with him, and it seemed to

her that they were climbing steeply with the woods all about
them. At last he halted.

"Set down heah, Miss Prudence," he said, still in a whisper.
"Yo' need to res' awhile."

She sank upon the ground and he squatted beside her. For
a time they were silent, both breathing heavily from the rapid
climb.

"Jeff—what are you doing here?" she whispered at last. "I
thought you took the other trail."

"Wasn't no trail," he answered in the same hushed tone.
"Jes' went to a farmhouse. Ah come back to de road yo' was on.
All 'long dat trace Ah was keepin' a eye out fo' yo', Miss Pru-
dence. But Ah nevah seen yo'."

"I was high above the road," she said. "I stopped once to
rest first day. Later I found a cabin—with a dead man in it. At
least I think it was a man—it was so——"

She shuddered.

"Yes, Miss." The Negro's voice was understanding.

"I slept in the woods, that night, in a hollow tree," she
went on. "Last evening, just at dusk, I saw those men kill someone and rob him." Hesitating, she looked at him in the darkness. "It was Dr. Tracy Lassiter," she finished.

"Him?" Jeff seemed shocked. After a moment he said, "Ah
heerd de shots. Ah was up de trail only half a mile away."

"They took me to their cave," she told him. "Then they
got into a quarrel over their—loot." She did not enlighten him
on the fact that she herself was part of the "loot" over which
they quarreled. Instead she added, "They had a bad fight and
the big one killed the other. I saw a chance and ran."

"Yo' know who dey was?"

"Yes. The Blevins brothers. The one called Bad 'Lias killed
the one called Little 'Lige. He murdered Dr. Lassiter, too."

"What dey do with him?"

"I don't know, except Bad 'Lias said he covered up the body
with some logs and things."

He said, "Dey'll find him. Dis place be swarmin' with people when dey finds Dr. Lassiter's daid. We got to move."

"Can we get back to the trail?"

"Wouldn't do us no good, dat trail."

"Why?"

"Ah went up it a ways. Theah's people up theah. A li'l settlement, two, three cabins. An' dawgs. Too many dawgs. Ah come back. Dey'd spot us sure dat-a-way."

"We can't go back the way we came," she said. "He—Bad 'Lias—would see us. What can we do?"

He looked upward. "Onlies' thing Ah kin think of, is if we goes ovah dat mountain," he said.

She followed his glance. Through the tops of the trees she saw the beetling cliffs that surrounded the valley, black against the night sky. In unbelieving astonishment she looked back at him.

"Over the mountain?" she asked. "How can we?"

"Ah don't know. But Ah'd ruther try anythin' dan git caught."

In the tone of his voice, dull but set, she caught a glimpse of what it must be to be a slave. Others—even a bound girl like herself—might have hopes or dreams. But Jeff knew that while he was a slave nothing better than mere physical existence, extreme degradation, a life of unremitting toil under tyranny and indignities, would ever be permitted him. He would rather perish than return to it.

But they were trapped in the widened valley. Jeff's fervent "ruther" and the thought of her own dreadful experiences made up her mind.

"When will we start?" she asked.

"Might as well do de fustest part right now," said Jeff. He looked at her. "Miss Prudence, Ah'll he'p yo' all possible."

She said, "I'll need help, Jeff."

He did not speak again but led the way up the ever-steepening climb among the trees toward the mountain scarp.

3.

To climb in the mountains even by daylight is taxing to the strength of a powerful man, and far more so for a delicate girl. Jeff, however, had no intention of making the really difficult part of the ascent by night.

"Hardes' climb is right at de top," he said. "We stops befo' dat."

They were ascending a mountain spur, rounded on top, but falling abruptly at the sides. It was covered with a growth of pines, the acrid needles of which kept down the undergrowth so that their progress was relatively unimpeded. Though there was only a sliver of a moon, the conifers did not grow so closely together as the oaks, elms, and beeches of the forest below, so they could see their way better.

Once they came to a stand of hickory shoots in an opening, and Jeff took from his pocket a jackknife and cut a long slender pole. From this he trimmed off all the branches, leaving a short, thick stub sticking out like a hook at the lower end.

"Better to hol' on by," he explained the stub. "Ah kin use dis heah pole to he'p yo', if yo' git wheah yo' need it. Ah'll pull yo' along by it."

The spur they were on ascended toward the cliff steeply and from a rounded hogback it became sharper and narrower, with each side pitching off more precipitously and severely into deep gorges as they climbed higher.

To the girl, the ascent was exhausting and her thirst grew worse. More than once she was forced to ask the Negro to stop while she caught her breath, and each time he halted without question. His powerful legs made less difficulty of the steep they were climbing, and though he breathed deeply he did not seem nearly as tired as she was. Frequently she was glad to grasp the end of the hickory pole when he offered it to her, and be helped up some especially difficult place.

After a time they came out on a narrow open space and saw above them the cliffs, grim and forbidding. At the base of the escarpment lay heaps of detritus fallen from the rocky walls, at places swept down into the gorges by storms of the past. Here Jeff halted.

"Wouldn't want to try an' git acrost dat big pile of rocks in de dark," he said. "Bettah wait daylight time."

She looked back down into the valley they had left and was surprised at the elevation they had already reached. Though the wind blew colder, the sky was clear, and even in the night dimness she thought she could make out the narrow passes that trapped this valley.

Jeff said, "Ah don't think we kin be seen heah from dat cave. Hit's below de ridge. Might see a fire, but we ain't got no fire, an' we couldn't light one if we wanted. Ah ain't got no flint an' steel—jest mah jackknife."

They looked about for shelter and she found a rough sort of nest down among the boulders where the wind was cut off from her. The slave discovered a similar hollow. In silence they took to these refuges, not ten feet from each other, to await the dawn.

Though she was not so cold, Prudence was uncomfortable among the rocks, and she could not sleep because of her almost unbearable thirst. For the first time she now remembered that she had left her bundle with all her little belongings, including the new slippers, in the cave when she fled from it. It made her feel mournful because those slippers seemed almost her last connection with her imprisoned father.

After a long time she asked, "Are you asleep, Jeff?"

"No, Miss," he replied.

So for nothing better to do they conversed, and Prudence told him about the events at Turkeytoe that put her father in jail and herself into flight. In return, he told her that he had been a field hand on the Lassiter plantation, but he could not stand the treatment given him by the overseer.

"De Lassiters was all right," he said. "Mastah Doctah an' Mastah Cap'n, dey didn't do nothin' mean. But dey wasn't 'round de place much, an' dat overseer, Will Melton, he's mean."

She remembered Melton. Troy Lassiter had introduced him to her during her visit to Beechwood. At that time she had had the impression that he was cold and sullen and perhaps resented his employers.

"Overseer, he tuck a dislike to me," Jeff continued. "Ah was a house se'vant befo' de Lassiters bought me, an' didn't want field work. So anytime any nigger steal a chicken, he whup me. Nigger not finish his row, he whup me. Somebody see a nigger out at night, he whup me. Dat man whup me ten times fo' things Ah nevah done."

"Why didn't you complain to your masters?" she inquired.

"Slave bettah not evah complain. Mastah, he stan' up fo' overseer every time. Makes matters only wusser fo' de one dat done complained."

"I told you that Dr. Lassiter is dead."

"Oh, Lawd!"

"They robbed him and piled logs on him."

"Oh, Lawd!"

"The man who murdered him is going to kill me if he can."

"Oh, Lawd!"

"So I'm just like you—I've got to get over this mountain."

He fell silent, but after a few minutes he said, "Miss Prudence, Ah'm skeered to death. But Ah'd almos' ruther be in my shoes than yourn. Come mornin' we tries. We more'n tries. We *does* it!"

Weariness at last overcame her so that in spite of her thirst and discomfort she slept in the rough hollow among the boulders.

Jeff's voice woke her. "Miss Prudence? Sun, he 'bout to come up. Time we gits started."

Uncomplaining, she climbed stiffly out of her hollow.

It was dawn and the sky was bright, though the sun had not yet risen. When she looked at the towering cliffs above them, they seemed awesome.

"Hongree, Miss?" he asked.

She smiled wanly. "I'm so thirsty that I couldn't eat even if there was some food to be had."

A smile crinkled the sides of his nose. "Ah'm thirsty, too, but Ah'm hongree beside. Come on, let's go try dat clift."

They began to climb over the rocks and boulders, a difficult task especially for her. All at once they heard the sound of running water.

"'Pears lak a li'l crick runnin' down under de rocks," he said. "Mebbe when we gits up to de clift we finds wheah it come from."

She nodded, not speaking, saving her breath.

The scramble over the heaped detritus at the base of the escarpment proved to be not only hard but even dangerous at times. Again and again the Negro reached back to her his ten-foot sapling pole as an aid in surmounting steep or treacherous parts. Fifteen minutes brought them to the cliff wall itself, and Jeff gave an exclamation.

"Ah guessed wrong," he said. "Thought we could fin' a way along dis steep part, to wheah it would be easier to git ovah."

He gazed at her with a look as guilty and apologetic as if he had deliberately planned this impasse.

Above them the precipice, chipped in places and with rocky projections here and there like all limestone cliffs, appeared to be so perpendicular that it almost overhung them. Prudence looked up at it with a sinking heart. Then she looked down. On either side of the narrow ridge where they stood, the sides fell steeply away to gorges that seemed hundreds of feet below.

"But there's water!" she cried.

Out from a horizontal crack in the cliff flowed a spring, and they hastened with gratitude to quench their thirsts.

Then she sat on a boulder to rest. "What will we do now, go back down and try another place?" she asked.

He was gazing back down into the valley.

"Ah 'spect...Ah 'spect..." He swallowed. "Miss Prudence, we ain't got time."

She turned and looked in the direction he was staring. The half circle of the forested valley was clearly visible, and she could see in places through the trees the trail that transected its arc.

But what brought a gasp from her was a running figure, small at this distance, yet recognizable to her as it crossed an opening in the woods.

Bad 'Lias.

He had seen them and was running toward them. In one hand he carried a rifle.

4.

To descend into the gorge and up to the next spur was impossible. To scale the cliff before them seemed equally impossible.

The girl had a horror of heights and she was not strong. But she preferred to die rather than fall into the hands of that vile beast, running toward them in the distance, but now momentarily hidden by the trees.

"We've got to try to go up!" she cried.

Jeff nodded. She saw him take off his cotton shirt, and with a ripping sound he tore it in two. From the pieces, including especially the sleeves, he made a rough sling.

"Put dat 'round yo', under yo' arms," he said.

Wordlessly she obeyed. To the end of the sling he lashed, with a piece of cord from his pocket—firmly, she hoped—the hickory pole just above the short thick stub at its base, which served to keep the fastening from sliding off.

Then he turned to the cliff and his dark torso gleamed in the sun which had just risen above the high mountains to the east. On his back, crisscrossed, she saw the gray scars of whip marks, the floggings that had driven him to flight.

"Ah thinks Ah sees a way," he said.

"Wait," she said. "I'll take off my shoes. I can do better with my bare feet."

The shoes were almost worthless anyway. She left them under

a rock and followed Jeff, who had started up a sloping shelf no more than a foot wide, along the cliff face.

Only extremity could have caused them to make this attempt. The precipice seemed absolutely vertical, and to the girl it was terrifying.

But she saw Jeff's foot on a jutting spur of rock, and when that foot left its resting place she put her own foot there. She did not dare look down as they slowly inched across the cliff face, because the ghastly gorge three hundred feet below them yawned dizzily and at its bottom were broken rocks as sharp as teeth.

Nor did she dare look up, because the distance she must go to reach the top of the cliff might frighten her as much as the horrible drop below. Clinging like a little lizard to the rocky wall, hampered by her loose dress at which the wind caught and tugged, she followed almost blindly.

She was weak with hunger, sharp edges of rock cut her bare feet, her breath came in gasps, but she struggled on. Once she half lost her footing and almost swung out from her precarious stance, but she grasped a pine tuft growing out of a crevice, and the toughness of the rooted seedling saved her.

She regained her balance and for a few moments stood with every limb trembling, almost robbed of volition to move. Then above her she heard Jeff's voice encouraging her. "Jes' a li'l fartheh. Ain't got to go much fartheh. Ah got yo' safe by dis pole."

She gathered courage and helped by his steady pull on the sapling fastened to the sling under her arms, she managed to scramble up until she found herself standing beside him on a vertical shelf of stone.

But there vast disappointment overwhelmed her. They had not reached the top. This shelf was only a resting place, and it was no more than two feet wide. The top of the cliff was still ten feet or more above, and at this point it was abruptly, grimly, straight up and down.

Something knocked chips of rock off the precipice a few

feet away from them and went screaming off across the valley. It took her a moment to comprehend. That was a bullet . . . Bad 'Lias was shooting at them!

She ventured a glance backward. The outlaw was again running toward them. He would try to get closer before he reloaded his gun and tried a second shot, for he was at extreme range from them. They had . . . no more than three or four minutes to reach safety . . . if it was possible to reach safety . . .

Jeff looked at her, his face strangely expressionless. "Hold dis pole," he said, handing it to her.

She took it, and felt even more bereft now that he was no longer grasping it to support her. He glanced upward.

"Ah got to risk it," he said, as if to himself.

There was an angling crevice in the rock just above the very end of the ledge on which they stood. He tried to reach for it, standing tiptoe. It was almost two feet beyond his hands.

"Miss Prudence," he said, "heah goes."

And then he did an act of real, profound courage.

Gathering himself he made a bold spring upward.

If he missed, he could not help plunging downward, to his death on the shattered rocks far below.

But his fingers just reached the crack, hooked into it.

For a moment he dangled there, hundreds of feet above the bottom, held only by his crooking fingers in the crevice. Then she saw him seem to summon his strength. He began to work slowly, hand over hand, along the crevice which angled toward the top.

It seemed to her hours, though it was moments only, before at last he managed with an effort, to get one hand over the brink, followed by the other. Then he had his arms over. And now, by what could only be described as a magnificent feat of slow gymnastics, he drew his body up—and over. Out of her sight.

Alone on that shelf, trying to cling to the cold inhospitable rock of the precipice, Prudence heard nothing from him. Had he fallen over on the other side? Was she to die here, like a fly on the wall?

She could not retire the way she had come even if she

wished, for to climb downward is far more difficult and dangerous than to climb up. And she had no help.

Then she heard his voice. "Han' up de en' of dat pole to me."

Now she saw his head and arms over the brink.

"Don't yo' git skeered now, Miss Prudence." He spoke in an easy, confident tone, to reassure her. "Yo' been mighty spunky so far. Jes' he'p yo'self as much as yo' kin, but don't kick or push yo'self away from de clift. If yo' fin' any li'l knob, put yo' foot on it, an' yo' kin see a crack at de top fo' yo' han's. Now come on. Ah'm goin' to raise yo' up, jes' like an angel goin' to glory!"

It was her only hope. She took a deep breath.

"All right," she said.

She felt the sling tighten about her body, and then she was lifted off her feet. For a horrifying moment she knew she was dangling out over space. But she remembered not to struggle. One hand instinctively caught a crevice. A foot rested its bare toes on a small projection, taking a little of her weight off the sling.

Spang. Another bullet struck close by, followed an instant later by the report of the outlaw's rifle.

Jeff's hold on the hickory pole seemed to slip. For a long moment she thought she was about to plunge down into the depths below.

But then the grip above tightened. She felt him raising her up and wondered desperately if the sling and its fastening were strong enough to hold all her weight.

Jeff said, "Ah got yo'!"

He had grasped the sling itself.

Helpless, she felt herself drawn up. The Negro's face was strained, as if because of some superhuman effort, and the muscles of his powerful arms seemed to crack with his exertions.

Then her hands grasped the rim. He gave a prodigious heave, her body was over the top. Another pull and she was safe.

A third bullet whined over the rim of the cliff. But now they were out of the shooter's view and the searching leaden slugs could not reach them.

Side by side they lay gasping for breath. She looked over

at Jeff. His body was streaming with sweat, and blood ran down the side of his face.

"You're wounded!" she cried.

"Jes' a li'l splinter of rock knocked off by dat bullet," he answered. "Ah'm all right."

That must have been when he almost slipped his hold on the stick that bore her up. But he did not let go. She owed her life to him.

It was sweet just to lie there on the rough cliff top, where the man with the gun could not get at them. She found that she was perspiring, partly from her exertions and partly from her recent fears. She closed her eyes and inhaled deeply.

Jeff moved and she opened her eyes. He had drawn himself to where he could peer over the cliff edge.

"He's goin' back," he said to her. " 'Pears lak he's in a hurry. When dey fin' Doctah Lassiter's body, dey'll be lookin' fo' him." He looked straight downward. "Ah cain't hardly believe we come up dat wall—look lak a squirrel couldn't do it."

He relaxed again on his back and gave her a tired grin.

"Hit's mighty lucky yo's jes' a li'l bit of a gal," he said.

"It's mighty lucky you're about the bravest man I ever knew," she answered.

Chapter 9

1.

The sun, just rising above the heights to the east, still threw into shadow the west side of the ridge, the top of which they had reached by their incredible effort. But they could see that the mountain on the west side sloped down more gradually, and it was covered with pines to the top. Prudence glanced eastward. Clouds were forming about the higher mountain peaks in that direction.

"Might be makin' a li'l weathah," said Jeff.

They had caught their breath and now they began a descent. There were some scrambles but nothing to daunt them, except that Prudence was hurting her tender bare feet. On the inside of the left foot was a cut that bled, leaving a mark on the jagged rocks whenever she set that foot down.

Limping more slowly with every step, she descended with him until they reached a mountain brook. There they drank deeply and she bathed her feet. Jeff tore the remnants of his shirt into rags which he helped her wrap about her feet.

They were still in the heights. Looking about her, it seemed to Prudence that one tree-clad ridge succeeded the next, like huge waves following each other in endless succession. She saw no sign of anything resembling a human habitation in this wilderness.

"Mighty wild kentry," commented Jeff.

She nodded.

"'Pears lak dey ain't no trails heah. Might take lots of scramblin' 'round to fin' a road amongst dese mountains."

She assented.

"How yo' feel, Miss Prudence?" he asked at length.

"Used up," she said. Hunger and weariness, combined with reaction from their recent perils, had told on her.

"Dem rags ain't goin' to do much fo' yo' feet," he said. "But we cain't stay heah. Why don't yo' rest awhile? Ah'll go down an' see if Ah cain't fin' some way to git out of dese mountains. Ah oughta be back in a hour or so."

She was too tired to question.

Having drunk again from the stream, Jeff started down the slope between the two ridges. She watched as he went, a powerful black torso above a pair of ragged cotton pants. He receded, appeared smaller with distance. Down below he disappeared among the trees, reappeared momentarily much farther down, and then she saw him no more.

For two hours or so she lay half dozing by the brook. Then she sat up. She noticed that the sky was clouding over, as if the promise of the cold winds from the high peaks was about to be fulfilled. Jeff had been gone far longer than he had promised. She wondered if something had happened to him; and as the hours lengthened, she became increasingly concerned about her own situation.

By mid-afternoon heavy swollen clouds were sweeping over the mountain tops and the sun was completely shut away. She came to a decision.

Jeff had not returned. She could not remain much longer where she was. So she rose and began a slow, limping progress down into the valley in the direction he had gone, hoping to find him if some accident had befallen him, or meet him if he was returning.

All about her the wild confusion of ridges and ravines, growing more heavily wooded as she descended, formed a labyrinth which so confused her that presently, looking back, she could not decide from what place she had come. She was suffering more and more from her lacerated feet as she made a zigzag descent, now along a rocky slope, now down some torrent bed. It came over her that Jeff might have become lost just as she now was.

At last she sat down on a stone, unable to travel farther.

And now the wind began rising to gale force. She saw two crows above the trees fighting against it, only to cease the struggle and quickly seek shelter in a lofty, blowing pine. The day darkened ominously. Thunder boomed and echoed from mountain to mountain, and with almost night blackness the storm came howling over the forest.

She huddled with her back toward it. The sound of the wind became a mighty, open note. Drops of rain, at first each large and separate, came spattering down on the leaves and ground.

Within a hundred paces from her, a vivid lightning flash struck a tall tree, and this was followed instantly by a terrific clap of thunder ending in an earth-shaking roll.

Then, with a gasping roar, the full tempest struck.

So hard did the rain lash down that she could not face it or breathe in it. She took refuge behind the trunk of a huge old oak; and the mighty fury of the storm shook the great tree so that it gritted and ground within itself as its tough fibers strained to their utmost to withstand the wild hurricane that strove to tear it down. Thunderclap followed thunderclap almost incessantly, until it seemed they must deafen her. She was soaked to the skin and trembling with cold.

Now and again tall trees crashed to the ground. But the oak held.

The rain turned to a biting sleet which added an icy touch to the atmosphere and she found it almost impossible to shelter herself from it. When the sleet ceased the ground was covered as by a strange, harsh snow, infinitely discomforting and numbing to her poor feet.

After half an hour the fury of the wind abated somewhat and the sleet, turning to rain again, settled to a steady, cold downpour.

At last, toward evening, her clothing soaked, her body faint with hunger—it seemed that forever she was hungry—the shivering girl tried to find a better shelter for the night. A flat leaf of stone had fallen across a boulder in such fashion that it provided protection from the direct lash of the storm. But water from the ground surfaces came into it and about it. When she crept into this inhospitable place she found that the soil beneath the rock was a mire, her clothes were clinging to her in their wetness, and she could not sleep because of the cold of the unseasonable storm.

Dawn came at last, gloomy and wet, with a slight drizzle still falling. She crept out from under her rock, and stood up, trying to wipe the mud from her dress. Even more severely than before she felt the cold and wetness, and this morning she had a cough.

She was starving. Her pangs of hunger were so severe that they almost made her forgetful of her wounded feet. As she made her way miserably through a thicket at the bottom of a gorge, she stopped at the sight of a reddish gleam and beneath it a bright yellow eye that seemed to glare at her. A moment later a large bird, bronze-brown, leaped out of the covert and took to wing.

A wild turkey—a hen. In the midst of the thicket, Prudence instinctively looked for and found the nest. There were in it four yellowish eggs, quite warm.

She seized upon them. They must be fresh, for she knew that turkey hens sometimes laid as many as a dozen eggs before they began to set. There was no fire, but she resolved to try to eat the eggs raw. A week ago her stomach would have turned squeamish at the mere thought, but now she felt that she could eat anything to ease the dreadful gnawing within her.

After a moment of consideration, she sat on the wet ground, put three of the eggs in her lap, held the fourth in her hand, and with a sharp stone cracked its tip. From the hole thus made she drained the whole egg into her mouth and swallowed it.

It was glutenous, saltless, disgusting, and in spite of herself, she almost gagged. But it was warm and there was nourishment in it.

As she swallowed she discovered that she had a very sore throat. Nevertheless, her body needed food. Sitting there, she swallowed the contents of all four eggs.

From where she sat she could see around her, but she had no idea of which direction to take. She had given up hope that Jeff might reappear. So great had been the confusion of the storm that she could not even think what way he had gone.

One thing was certain, however. She could not stay where she was. So presently she rose and began again to limp painfully down toward the valley, coughing frequently, her lungs growing sore. All that wet day she wandered, feeling weaker and sicker with each hour. The drizzling rain ceased at last, and the sun shone feebly through the clouds. But now she shook with a chill.

Somehow she staggered along, coughing in fits, driven blindly on by an instinct to get somewhere, anywhere, to find help. If she found nobody to help her, she must just die when she could not force herself any longer to move.

2.

Late in the afternoon she at last found herself on the road again. Or perhaps it was another road. At least it was a way where people traveled.

By this time she had a high fever, and she was so ill with her cough and sore throat that when she heard the rattle of an old wagon behind her, she did not have the strength or the will to hide as she had always done before. Instead, she sat down and huddled by the side of the road.

The wagon stopped. She heard a gruff man's voice.

"Say, thar. Whut ye doin' thar?"

At this she managed to look up. The wagon was small and old, with a very weather-beaten canvas tilt, and it was drawn by two scrawny horses. In the driver's seat a man was bending toward her, looking at her.

"I—nothing—" she gasped, with another fit of coughing.

"Say—you're sick——"

The man got down from the wagon and the horses slacked off in their harness, as if they were accustomed to standing until called upon to move. Prudence sat in her pathetic huddle, her arms on her knees, her head on her arms. The man approached her and put a hand on her arm.

"Why, it's jest a young-un," he said. "Say—gal—ye live here-abouts?" He answered his own question. "No, nobody lives here-abouts." He seemed to ponder a moment. "Gal, ye got folks near here? Campin', mebbe?"

She did not answer.

He pulled her arm aside from her face. Then he saw that she was crying.

"Say, gal—" he began.

She looked up at him through tear-filled eyes. He was a thin dark old man, with a bent back and a battered wool hat pulled low on his forehead. In his lean face the cheek bones stood out and his eyes were deep-sunk in their sockets. A huge iron-gray moustache drooped over his mouth, giving him the grim expression of a brigand. She was afraid of him.

"Say—ye cain't stay here, gal," he said. "Lissen. I'm Corbie Wilson. Corbie Wilson, the peddler. Everybody knows me—knives, dry goods, buttons, needles, thread, kitchenware, sech articles. I sharpen knives an' scissors, too. Carry a few axes an' tools like that, an' I got a line of proprietary medicines. Say—why don't ye come, git in my wagon? I'll take ye whar there's folks."

"No—leave me alone—" she whimpered, shrinking from him.

But the cough came again, and when the paroxysm was over he took her by both arms and lifted her to her feet. Her knees trembled with weakness when she stood, and she turned upon him a face so woebegone that he was struck silent with pity.

When he began to lead her toward the wagon, she did not have the resolution to resist. What happened to her now did not seem much to matter.

The canvas tilt of the wagon was fastened shut at the rear, to keep out the weather. He spent some time untying the canvas strips with one hand to open the back, while he supported her with the other. At the rear of the wagon, below the endgate, was a step to aid in getting into the vehicle or for fetching goods out of it.

"Say now, gal," said old Corbie, "kin ye git in thar? Ye'll find a bed of sorts. Ye may say it's a hard bed. Wall, it is. But I like a firm bed to sleep on. None of them there soft, sickly feather mattresses for me. Ye kin lay down in thar, an' cover yourself up, an' rest."

The thought of a bed—however "firm"—and a chance to lie down and rest, seemed to answer a hidden want that Prudence had not even expressed to herself. She allowed him to help her mount the step, then crawled into the wagon.

Under the canvas cover the interior contained boxes and bundles of varying sizes and shapes, bolts of cloth, cheap garments hanging from the wagon bows above, and sundry other articles arranged on the floor, or in sacks and bales. She was far too ill to pay attention to the contents, but she saw a wretched little pallet at one side of the wagon bed, just behind the seat, and to this she crept, almost collapsing in it.

Old Corbie followed her into the wagon. "Pull them quilts up over ye," he said, and helped her do so. "Now ye jest lay thar an' git warm."

She had another spell of coughing.

"Say—we got to do somethin' for that," he said.

At the front, directly beneath the seat, was a box the width of the wagon bed, with a hanging lid. He unfastened and lifted the lid, revealing under it two shelves on which were arrayed numerous bottles, labeled in startling hues of red, black, yellow, or green, and sometimes with crude wood-cut pictures of faces on them, supposed to be the portraits of whoever concocted the particular nostrums contained in the various bottles.

"Now lemme see," he said. He began lifting bottles one by one and reading their labels, including the claims as set forth for their curative powers. "This here's 'Seneca Chief Rock Oil, good for heart diseases, dyspepsia, dysentery, cholera, causitiveness, an' elderly people.' Ye ain't got none of them ailments. 'Dr. Ludlum's Specific, for the cure of gonorrhea, gleets, whites, strictures an' complaints of the organs of generation.' No, not for ye. How about 'Sands' Sarsaparilla, cures cutaneous eruptions an' has an admirable effect on the general system.' No, I reckon not. An' ye don't need 'Dr. Fitch's Specific for Restoring the Powers of Manhood.' I do a good business in that article some places, though the men who buy it usually has to sneak up to git it, so's the wimmin won't ketch 'em. 'Burnett's Cocaine, efficacious for stoppin' baldness an' restorin' the hair.' Ye shore ain't in no need of a hair restorer. 'Jonas Whitcomb's Remedy for Asthma.' No. 'Gardner's Compound, a sure cure for rheumatism, neuralgia, an' salt rheum.' No, again. 'Hegeman's Camphorica with Glycerin, will keep the hands soft in coldest weather.' No. Here's whut I been lookin' for—'Dr. Wister's Balsam of Wild Cherry, for coughs, colds, sore throat, bronchitis, asthma, croup, whoopin' cough, an' incipient consumption.' Sounds like that fits your case perfect."

He looked down at Prudence. "I'm a-goin' to open this bottle. Costs a dollar, an' I'll have to knock off some of the price if it's opened, but I won't charge *ye* nothin'.'"

With this magnanimous statement he drew the cork by means of a corkscrew and poured a thick pink liquid into a pewter spoon. "Here," he said.

With the pathetic obedience of the sick, the girl swallowed the dose. It was sweet and not unpleasant to the taste, and indeed seemed to assuage some of the soreness of her throat. Still holding the bottle and spoon, old Corbie looked down at her.

"Say, gal—whut's your name?" he asked.

She did not want to tell him her real name. "Alice," she said weakly.

"Alice whut? Ye got a last name, shorely?"

"Alice—Hankins." She gave him the first name that came into her mind.

"Wall, Alice, whar ye headed for?"

On the spur of the moment she concocted a feeble piece of fiction.

"My aunt's."

"Whar's she live?"

She could think of no plausible location, for she did not know where she was or even in what direction he was heading. So she went into another spell of coughing to avoid a direct reply.

"Here—take some more of the Balsam." He gave her another spoonful.

"Your aunt live anywhere near here?" he persisted.

She shook her head.

"I got to find out *somethin'* about ye. She live in Kaintucky? I'm headed north to the Ohio River. She live that way—north?"

Dimly she realized that in some manner she had crossed the line from Tennessee and was now in the state north of it. Just where she crossed she did not know. Perhaps it was after she escaped from Bad 'Lias, and that frightful climb over the cliff. When Jeff, the slave, left her on the mountain, she remembered that she had wandered aimlessly, sick most of the time and half dizzy, until she stumbled on this wagon trail. Of one thing she was sure: this was not the road that led across the Cumberland Pass. It went north, not east.

Again she began coughing.

"Don't sound good," he muttered. "It's early, but I'm goin' to camp." He put the bottle, lightly corked, within reach of her, together with the spoon. "If ye git to coughin' bad, take a leetle more of the Balsam."

Before he left her he inquired solicitously, "Ye comf'able?"

She nodded feebly.

"Them fur bales in the back ain't exactly perfume," he said.

"Wisht I could take 'em out, but I cain't. Ye'll say fox stinks.
Wall, fox does. An' so does mink. Hides gener'ly stinks, but none
of 'ems a patchin' to skunk. I jest won't take skunk. Lots of folks
in these mountains don't have much cash, an' wants to trade.
Wall, I trade—up to a p'int. Them furs will jest about be my
profit for this trip."

"They're all right," she said weakly, and indeed with her
heavy cold she did not so much notice the smell of the baled pelts.

He got out of the wagon, fastened the back flaps carefully,
climbed into the driver's seat up front, clucked to his horses, and
a slow progress began.

3.

The girl was too grateful for the warmth of the quilts in old
Corbie's bed to think about the roughness of the road. Sometimes
the wagon jolted over rocks, and sometimes she heard the splash
of the horses' hooves and a sucking of the wheels as they crossed
miry stretches caused by the recent storm. Above her the canvas
top jerked and swayed, and the garments, tools, and other articles
fastened to the wagon bows, jerked and swayed with it. After a
time she heard a prolonged rough rumble, as they crossed a considerable river on a long bridge made of logs. Then they came
to a stop.

The peddler leaned back in his seat. "Say, gal—" he said.
"We're a-goin' to camp here. Kin ye git down?"

She made an effort, but succumbed back into the pallet.
A great lassitude seemed to possess her. The Balsam of Wild
Cherry which she had taken, like most cough syrups of the day,
no doubt contained an opiate, but she did not know it. She
attributed her weakness to her illness alone.

Old Corbie studied her a moment. "Wall, jest lay thar,"
he said.

She heard him get out of the wagon, unhitch the horses,
move about to water them, and probably tether them where

they could graze. After a few minutes he returned to the wagon and took from it a box and an ax. The sound of chopping came to her and afterward she smelled wood smoke and heard the crackle of fire. Then she dozed off.

His voice aroused her. He had opened the tilt at the rear of the wagon and was standing there with a tin plate containing some greasy meat and a piece of the inevitable corn pone of this country. In his other hand he bore a cup of steaming coffee.

"Kin ye set up?" he asked.

She managed to struggle to a half-sitting posture. Her throat was very sore, and she had no appetite, but at his urging she tried to get some of the corn bread down. The meat she could not abide. When he put the coffee cup on the floor beside her she tasted it. Too hot. She let it cool for a little time, then tried again. The coffee was black and very bitter, and in the past she had been accustomed to cream and sugar with it. But she swallowed some of it.

"That's all I want," she said, and thanked him.

Old Corbie took away the dishes to make his own meal outside by his fire. Again the wagon flaps were fastened. The girl lay down on the pallet and pulled the old quilts up about her. Warmed somewhat by the coffee, and with the Balsam now taking its effect, she fell into an uneasy sleep, broken again and again during the night by her racking cough.

Daylight shining through the canvas tilt awoke her. Birds were chirping and singing in the trees and she heard old Corbie moving about outside. Only then did it occur to her to wonder where he had spent the night. Assuredly it was not in the wagon, for she had possession of his bed.

She felt sorry about that, but the lassitude still remained upon her, depriving her of any volition to move. Presently she heard him unfastening the wagon flaps, and then his gaunt face with its wide cheekbones, grim moustache, and deep-sunk eyes was thrust in at her.

"Awake?" he asked. "Say, now—I got somethin' here ye kin eat. Soup. Will ye try it?"

She struggled up and took the crockery bowl he offered her. It contained some kind of broth, and he gave her a piece of corn bread with it.

"Break it in the soup," he said. "Makes it go better."

With the pewter spoon she made an effort to eat and found that she seemed able to swallow more easily than the night before. The soup was salty and somewhat greasy—boiled from smoked side meat—but old Corbie stood outside the wagon and encouraged her with every sip she took.

"That's it—a leetle more—it'll do ye good—jest another taste ——"

She could not, however, finish the soup, and he took away the bowl and spoon. Weary, she lay back.

He returned to fasten the flaps and all at once her eyes filled with tears. The kindness of this old man with the brigand's face touched her heart. He had taken her word about herself, cared for her gently as a mother, and all out of his own goodness, for he owed her nothing, could hope for no recompense from her, and she had not even asked for his help.

He saw the tears. "Now, now there—" he said in some alarm. "No use takin' on. We'll git ye to your aunt——"

"Oh, Corbie!" she wailed. "I haven't got an aunt!"

"Ye ain't?" He stood blinking with surprise.

"I—I told you a lie," she sobbed. "I haven't got an aunt—and my name isn't Alice Hankins—it's P-P-Prudence. And you're so good to me—I—I—just can't bear it!"

"Say, now—wait a minute," he said. "A gal like ye ain't jest out in these woods, sick an' hungry, for no reason at all." He puzzled over that for a moment, then added, "If ye ain't got no aunt, ye must be goin' *somewhar*. So don't let it bother ye—jest tell ole Corbie whar ye want to go, an' we'll git ye thar."

"You don't understand," she wept, "I'm a *runaway*. I'm a bound girl, and I'm running away from the people I was bound out to."

"Hum," he said, and appeared to be considering all aspects of the case as it now presented itself.

"Ye know," he said at last, "I don't hear very good, an' I didn't make out that last thing ye told me. No—don't repeat it. Sometimes I cain't hardly hear at all. About all I kin remember is ye said ye had an aunt somewheres. In Ohio State, mebbe? We'll say in Ohio State."

She was quick enough to see that he did not want to admit openly that he knew she was a bound girl running away, for this might in some manner involve him with the law for helping her. Also, that he was determined to give her that help. Her heart went out to him in gratitude.

But because of this she never told him how she came to be bound out, or of her father, or Miss Sally . . . or Troy Lassiter. Nor of the slave that helped her, or those terrible men, the Blevins brothers.

"Oh, Corbie—th-thank you—" was what she said.

For a moment he studied her, his brows knitting in a frown as he considered the various complications that might arise.

"It's goin' to take a few days to reach the Ohio River," he said. "I got to stop here an' thar to do business. Folks in these hills expects me, an' the wimmin is usually all ready with their leetle lists of things they want—an' a bigger list of things they'd like to have but mebbe cain't afford. They want to look at 'em jest the same. Wimmin always looks, even if they don't have no real idea of buyin'. It's part of bein' wimmin, I reckon. If I'd of sold everythin' wimmin jest looked at, I'd be richer than any banker in Louisville."

Having conferred upon her this piece of mercantile wisdom, he thought again for a moment.

"Now I'll tell ye, Prudence—ye say that's your name? Wall, Prudence, when people come I'll have to git things out'n the wagon, but ye jest lay thar. I'll tell 'em you're a sick gal, belongin' to some friends of mine, an' I'm takin' ye to your aunt. See? Don't ye even speak. Kin ye do that?"

She nodded.

"Wall, we might as well be movin' on," he said.

He shut the back of the canvas tilt, hitched up his horses,

climbed up on the driver's seat, and they were traveling once more.

She took another swallow of the Balsam.

4.

Two or three days passed in a sort of slow dimness to her. She was feverish, and in spite of the Balsam—of which she consumed nearly an entire bottle—her lungs were sore from her coughing. Vaguely she was conscious that the wagon stopped at intervals and that people gathered about it. Old Corbie rummaged in the wagon for goods to sell, and when his business was concluded, drove on without bothering her. When they stopped to camp at night by some stream, he cooked for her.

"Look whut I got for ye," he said the second night, "a chicken. Missis Nippert, back thar the last place we stopped, give it to me when I told her I had a sick gal. Awful nice people, the Nipperts. Her husband's in jail right now. Hog stealin'. But he'll be out next month. You'd like 'em."

The chicken, when he boiled it, was tender, and she ate of it, the best meal she had taken in days. Afterward she began to feel stronger. By the third day she was able to eat even the smoked meat he offered her, with a helping of cooked greens on the side.

Her bare feet with their lacerations aroused his concern. He insisted on putting lard on the cuts. "It'll keep 'em soft an' make 'em heal up better," he told her. It required days, however, for the worst of her cuts to heal entirely.

She was beginning to be alert as to what was going on about her; she knew that old Corbie slept outside by his fire. Fortunately the nights since the big storm had been fine; and each evening she saw him take from the wagon a plaid woolen cloak, in which she supposed he wrapped himself as he lay on the bare ground. But when she tried to protest he waved it aside.

"Does a man good to sleep on the ground," he said. "Ye git strength from the soil."

The frail elasticity of youth was hers, and sheltered and warmed and given food, she fought off what in those days might have become a serious case of pneumonia. By the fourth day she was strong enough to insist on getting up when they camped. In spite of his misgivings, though with his help, she tottered out into the evening sunshine and sat for a while to enjoy it. Next day she progressed even further. When they stopped for nooning she made her way up a gentle stream, where she was hidden by undergrowth, and there bathed herself.

What with her adventures and her sickness it was her first real bath in days, and although old Corbie was alarmed about it and feared she would "bring on that cough again," she told him that she felt almost well.

The following day, although he insisted that she must continue to lie on the pallet in the wagon while they traveled, she quite disobediently climbed up to the front seat and sat beside him. She so beguiled him with smiles and talk that thereafter he no longer treated her as an invalid.

All this time wooded mountains loomed high about them, but here and there rail fences appeared and occasional cattle were encountered. Every few miles, also, there were, on hillsides or near the road, cabins built of logs chinked with mud, the roofs usually of hand-riven shakes all weather-beaten to a neutral gray. Where the ground sloped, the downhill side of a cabin would be raised on posts or blocks of stone to make the puncheon floor level. Hogs liked to lie in the shade of these open spaces beneath, and so did dogs and even children. Sometimes there was a shack-barn behind the cabin, with perhaps a solitary mule in it. Chickens pecked and scratched under the very feet of old Corbie's horses when he drew up near one of these primitive abodes.

Unkempt people came out of the cabins to the wagon. In most instances the men were gaunt and whiskered; they had flapping wool hats crammed shapelessly on their heads and rough clothes of homespun or cotton. Almost all of them chewed tobacco or smoked charred corncob pipes. The women, however, usually chewed snuff, plying the slimy snuff paddle while they talked. They were slatternly and lantern-jawed as a rule, wearing slat bonnets, which they hastily donned before issuing from their homes. Their figures were stoop-shouldered and shapeless, if they were matrons, and they were clad in ill-fitting dresses of calico or homespun.

Children were plentiful—shock-headed little tykes whose hair appeared to know neither comb nor shampoo—for procreation seemed to be a universally popular occupation with these people. A woman at fifty might be a grandmother and a great-grandmother, for the girls married young and had babies early and frequently.

Some of the older girls were not unattractive in an uncombed slab-sided way, and the youths were awkward and long-legged. Prudence saw one couple—married, according to Corbie—the wife, very pregnant, could not have been more than twelve or thirteen years old, and the husband, without a beard as yet, was only a year or two older.

All these people, young and old, knew old Corbie and appeared to like him. As he had said, the women would be first with their lists.

"I need a dozen buttons, six needles, three spools plain thread—now, good strong thread, mind—an' a butcher knife. The ole one's ground down to whar it's almost no knife at all, jest a sliver of steel," a matron might say.

Corbie would gather the articles and name the prices.

"Hain't that awful high fo' a knife—twenty-five cents?" would come a protest.

"Missis Hungate," Corbie would begin, as if patiently instructing, "when ye figger what I had to pay for that knife in Louisville, an' the time I had to carry it in stock, an' the investment I got in it, thar ain't hardly no profit at all in that knife."

"Wall, mebbe," the woman would concede. "Whut kind of goods yo' got?"

"I got beautiful selections," Corbie would say. "Look at this gen-u-ine imported calico—ain't them flowers in the design natural?"

Thereafter Corbie would display, one by one, every bolt of cloth he had, to be inspected and fingered. At the end would come the question:

"How much fo' that calico with them flowers?"

"Thirty-five cents, Missis Hungate—but *thirty* to ye."

"*Thirty* cents?"

"It's a sacerfice, Missis Hungate. Import taxes, ye see." (The calico was really made in Providence, Rhode Island, but "import taxes" provided a favorite excuse for peddlers to charge high prices.)

After long haggling perhaps five yards of the material would be purchased—at twenty cents a yard, or a dollar all told—because Corbie followed the principle of pricing goods high, and in the end magnanimously coming down to a figure that represented only about one hundred percent profit to him, thus pleasing both the customer and himself.

The men might want a new ax, or some hand-wrought nails, a new bullet mold, or pig lead to make bullets.

Younger women would ask to see the few cheap dresses he had brought; although they would yearn for them they rarely would buy any because the price was beyond their means and making their own clothing was cheaper.

Continually in these trading sessions, old Corbie extolled his wares. "Now that ye've bought that calico, how 'bout lookin' at this pink gingham? Make a mighty fetchin' dress for your young daughter thar—an' she does git purtier every time I see her. An' how are ye for pins? Pins is dear now—ten cents a paper. Them big fact'ries in the East holds up prices on them. But how kin ye git along without pins? I got some ribbon here, too, that'll make your mouth water. An' look at that lace! Would ye like a hand mirror? Ye kin have that one with the purty lady on the back for only a quarter—it's like stealin' it at that price. What about tea an' coffee? Spices? Now here's somethin' new in graniteware—

a coffee pot with a handle an' bail both—won't burn your hands."

Lengthy periods would be devoted to talk in which no business at all was discussed, for the cabin folk were as eager for gossip and news as they were for the necessities he brought them. And for this they exchanged their own gossip, so that his stock of talk was constantly being renewed. Nobody was in a hurry. The peddler's visit was an event and the mountain people wanted to enjoy it fully.

Usually old Corbie managed to bring the conversation around to the subject of epidemic or sicknesses, and then he would shine:

"I hear they's smallpox spreadin' in the South. Better lay in a couple bottles of Seneca Chief Rock Oil, an' the same of Sands' Sarsaparilla. Gardner's Compound is mighty good, too. If I was a mother—an' with children inclined to be croupy like most young-uns is—I wouldn't be without Dr. Wister's Balsam of Wild Cherry. Look at that gal"—he would indicate Prudence, sitting on the wagon seat—"four days ago she was dyin'—absolutely dyin'—with black pneumonia. The Balsam saved her. Didn't it, Prudence?"

Prudence would confirm this, for she indeed attributed her recovery in large measure to the treatment.

"She b'longs to some friends of mine down south of here, an' I'm takin' her up to her aunt on the Ohio," he would explain.

The mountain people saw nothing strange in the girl's riding with the peddler, especially since her tattered garb and appearance indicated that she was very much of their own kind.

But Corbie, launched again, would look around roguishly.

" 'Pears like a lot of ladies in this neighborhood is lookin' forward to blessed events. Mother Eaton's Elixir for Expectant Mothers is the best thing I ever run onto for helpin' childbirth an' bringin' strong, healthy babies."

There would be a cackle of self-conscious laughter among the women and Prudence noticed that he usually sold some of his bottles by these tactics.

Or a lanky man might sidle up to the wagon opposite from where the women and children were gathered. Old Corbie knew at once what he desired.

"Hi, Jason," he might say with a confidential leer, "I understand ye been sparkin' that good-lookin' Widder Simpson. Wall now, I don't blame ye. If ye want a woman, an' a widder is avail'ble, take the widder every time. A young gal's too skeary an' walleyed. An' a old maid's too over-powerin' anxious to please without really knowin' how. But a widder—now thar's a woman that knows what it's all about. She knows what a man's like, an' by an' large, she likes what she knows. She kin lead him on an' yet hold him off jest enough so that what's comin' is twict as grateful to him. She knows that a pie ain't worth nothin' without sweetenin' an' she's always ready to sweeten up a feller if required. But some kind of tartness is needed in a pie, too, an' she kin spry things up with a leetle tartness if she needs to. A widder knows how to dress to please a man an' how to act to please a man. Ye don't need a lot of false-startin' an' sashayin' to git her to come your way. Of course some will an' some won't, but I've observed that most all of them will if ye go at 'em jest right. An' a widder ain't dumb, neither. She knows that givin' a man a sample of whut she's got makes him want the whole stock in trade; an' she gener'ly winds up marryin' the one she likes best."

At this exhortation Jason would get red, and grin in a bashful manner, and usually wind up buying a bottle of Dr. Fitch's Specific for Restoring the Powers of Manhood which, by inference, was considered an aphrodisiac.

After all the wares had been examined there would be a further period of haggling. Sometimes the peddler accepted trade since cash was scarce. This trade ordinarily was in furs, which he added to the bale in the rear of the wagon, or in ginseng roots. which had a market in China. He did this was apparent reluctance, always proclaiming that the merchants "in the East" were not much interested in pelts or "sang roots" this year—this enabled him to get the products at a very reasonable rate, so that he made a double profit when later he sold them to wholesalers at a higher price.

Finally, when he made a good sale, he would often top it off with a present—a ten-cent jackknife, or a pewter mug, or sometimes a yard or so of ribbon.

To Prudence those hours of trading and haggling and gossiping were tiresome, but she was patient. And once the wagon was again on the road she came to life.

Her cough abated and the sore throat disappeared. Though she still was very thin and had distressing hollows under her eyes, her strength was returning. Old Corbie gave her a cheap comb, and she was able to make some improvement in her appearance by arranging her hair. No physician examined her and perhaps this was fortunate, for it was a day when doctors were more notable for their ignorance rather than for their skill in the medical arts.

One day, in a blithe mood, she sang a song for old Corbie. He was surprised and delighted, and thereafter she sang often. Sometimes it was a hymn, and the peddler might lend a discordant bass rumble to it if it was one he knew. But he took especial pleasure in some of the old songs, as when her clear voice took up "Drink to Me Only with Thine Eyes," or "Hark, Hark the Lark."

She knew a few country songs, too, taught her by Miss Sally, and old Corbie would nod time to them and smile under his huge moustache. So the days passed, and she was well enough now to help with the camp cooking, and to spend time with good effect in repairing the rents in her poor dress. Her feet healed also, and she felt so much better that at times she was almost merry.

But there were other times, particularly at night when she lay beneath the canvas on her pallet, that she thought of her situation with a catch in her throat, almost a sob. She was only a girl; and she had not foreseen the dangers and hardships through which she had passed, nor had she by any plan of her own gotten through them. She recognized her unparalleled good fortune that enabled her—with the courageous help of the runaway slave—

to escape from that horrible creature, Bad 'Lias. And she knew also that had not kind old Corbie come along just when he did, to take her under his care, she might have died back on the trail. For these things she was inexpressibly grateful.

But in her there was a hard little core of determination, and she still was intent on her original plan—to help her father, if by some means she could reach Washington, and obtain an audience with the President of the United States. After the experiences she had already been through, it sometimes seemed to her that it would be impossible for her to achieve that goal. But each time discouragement came over her, she remembered the poor prisoner in the jail at Turkeytoe and her resolution stiffened.

She knew that she had missed the direct route across the famous Cumberland Pass, and she was wandering northward with the old peddler in his leisurely progress. At least with each mile she was farther away from Bad 'Lias Blevins and so, for the present, she was content just to ride with Corbie, and hope, womanlike, for some turn of fortune that might somehow further her journey.

And with that sort of resignation she would be able at last to go to sleep and dream shadowy dreams of perhaps happier times in the past when her future had seemed bright with many promises.

Chapter 10

1.

It was big country, mountainous and broken and beautiful to look upon. Sometimes, after they toiled up a long and crooked trail to the top of a ridge, Prudence would exclaim in enchantment at the vista below, wooded green slopes flooded with sunlit crystal brightness, and at the higher mountains above with opalescent clouds trailing their skirts across the pine-clad peaks.

Old Corbie, the realist, did not share her enthusiasm. To him the high country only wore out the horses. Besides, cabins were fewer there and, consequently, opportunities for trade were fewer.

"Them laurel slicks may look purty," he would grumble, "but thar ain't no plow land thar."

On the seventh day of their leisurely journey, as old Corbie drove slowly along and both of them for the time being were silent, two tall bearded men armed with rifles stepped out from behind a thicket beside the road.

Prudence felt her heart leap with alarm. But Corbie, his face expressionless, drew his team to a halt.

The two men came toward them. They were lanky and wore the usual garb of the hills. At a distance, because of their long brown beards, they appeared to be of middle age, but as they came nearer, the girl saw that they were relatively young, in their middle twenties perhaps. Moreover, they were twins, slouching in the same way, their clothes equally slovenly; they fell unconsciously into similar attitudes, the very hairs of their whiskers seeming to be identical.

"Hi, boys," said old Corbie.

"Hi, Corbie," they replied, both speaking at once, resting their rifle butts on the ground.

"Huntin'?" asked the peddler.

"Nope," said one of them. "Notifyin'."

Old Corbie looked at the two solemn countenances with an expression of slight embarrassment. "Long as I've knowed you boys," he said, "I still cain't tell which one is Rufe an' which is Lafe."

The twins grinned as if they considered this a tribute.

"Few kin," said one of them, and added, "I'm Lafe."

"I'm Rufe," said his brother.

"What's the notifyin'?" asked the peddler.

"Hit's on account of Nelly," said Rufe. "She done got married yest'day—to Jud Tooley."

Old Corbie looked surprised. "Jud *Tooley?*"

Both twins became serious.

"They run off," said Lafe, "an' got hitched by the Freewill Baptis' preacher down in Hickory Holler."

"Then—the feudin's patched up?"

The twins exchanged solemn glances as if debating this question in their minds. Then the one called Rufe said, "As to that, we ain't in no position to say. But the Big Hoss says thar's to be a infare tonight fo' them new married people."

"The Tooleys is invited," said Lafe. "We-uns is heah to notify all comin' by the road."

The peddler gave Prudence an odd look.

"We'll be proud to come," he said to the twins.

"See yo' thar," they replied.

Old Corbie slapped the reins on the backs of his horses and the wagon creaked forward. When they were well out of earshot, he said to Prudence, "Them's the Hostetter twins. We've got to go up to the Hostetter place. When ye git 'notified' in this country, it ain't polite to refuse." He paused. "Sometimes it ain't very healthy, neither. Folks is mighty touchy about sech things."

"You mentioned something about feuding," said the girl.

"Yeah. This here's feudin' country. Thar's been hard feelin's betwixt the Hostetters an' the Tooleys for a long time—mebbe twenty years. Now an' then both sides has done some shootin'. What started it, I dunno. Wall, whoever does know what starts a feud? Might be over a woman, or a argyment over who owns a cow or a hog, or a gamblin' dispute, or even a election. Everybody in these hills totes a shootin' iron, an' in the quarrel somebody kills somebody else. So purty soon a relative or friend of the party that was killed downs the killer. Next, the relatives an' friends on both sides begins goin' after each other. Sometimes it lasts a long time—a generation or more, or until one side or t'other is all killed out. I reckon ten or twelve men has been killed in this here partic'lar feud, divided 'bout even betwixt Hostetters an' Tooleys. Now a Hostetter gal marries a Tooley man. This might be interestin'."

"Will there be trouble?" she asked.

"Mebbe not. Not at an infare. But this here weddin' they'll be celebratin' may not be easy to swaller for either clan. I jest hope shootin' irons will stay out of it."

Prudence had seen enough of violence and she hoped so too.

"See that ridge yonder?" asked old Corbie, pointing with his whip. "That's the dividin' line betwixt Hostetter country an' Tooley country. We take the road that branches off here."

As they turned into the "road"—mere wagon-wheel tracks up a small valley—he elucidated further.

"Ye take them boys, Rufe an' Lafe. They got married, five-six years ago. Double weddin' it was. In the shivaree afterwards, some were feelin' mighty jovial on account of the licker they'd been drinkin' and arranged so's the couples got mixed up in their rooms some way. Lafe with Rufe's wife, an' vicy-versy. In the dark, an' feelin' irresponsible that-a-way—the wimmin natcherly took their drinks right along with the men—neither couple found they was wrong matched until too late. Nine months later—give or take a leetle—both them brides had a baby. To this day neither they, nor the twins, nor nobody else knows whether it was Rufe or Lafe that sired their partic'lar infant."

Prudence was shocked. "It sounds awful," she said. "Those poor women!"

Old Corbie spat tobacco juice over the wheel. "Not so awful when ye knows the people. They jest got their own ways. Each of them wimmin had a baby to fuss over. As for them twins, they're so clost to each other that either of 'em's welcome to what the other's got, if it's wimmin, kids, or drinkin' whiskey. Mebbe they still trade wives oncet in awhile."

Prudence did not reply. Old Corbie's devastating frankness sometimes brought a gasp from her. He went on.

"Fact is, thar was talk that later on, when Betsey—that's Rufe's wife—was pregnant with her second, Lafe an' Rufe took turns sleepin' with Keziah—that Lafe's wife—until Betsey was usable again. Well, Keziah comes with child, an' now thar's more confusion than ever."

"Don't they have any *morals?*" the girl asked.

"The Hostetters? Shore. They're fine people. So's the Tooleys, as far as that goes. Not like the Skaggs, over on Porcupine Crick. Old Man Skaggs has four daughters—kind of purty, too. Everybody knows, 'cause he told it hisself, that he broke in them gals, every one of 'em, as soon as she was old enough. Them Skaggs is a low outfit. They ain't worth an intelligent man's bother. I never stop over on Porcupine myself."

2.

On the crown of a tree-covered hill lay the Hostetter place. It consisted of a good-sized clearing in which stood a big old log structure and several smaller ones. The main building, called the "Big House" by members of the clan, had originally been built two stories high, then it was added to with lean-tos and ells until it stuck out on both sides and behind. It had no less than three stone chimneys, a matter of boasting for all the Hostetters.

In the clearing were three lesser cabins of ordinary size, evidently the homes of married sons and daughters, although others of the family lived in clearings all up and down the valley. Behind the Big House stood a barn of unusual dimensions for this country, with a hayloft. And there were several other outhouses of varying sizes—granaries, a cook house, privies, and the like.

As Corbie and Prudence, in their wagon, turned into the clearing, a hoarse, half-whispering roar greeted them.

"That's Joel Hostetter, him they calls Big Hoss," the peddler whispered.

Awaiting them beside a stone-well curb, which had an old-fashioned sweep to raise the water bucket, Prudence saw a tremendous old man. He was more than six feet tall, with a great hooked nose above his vast gray beard, prodigious eyebrows, and a deeply lined forehead. It was evident that at one time he had been a man of exceptional strength and power, but age had sapped his muscles and turned his hair and whiskers gray. His voice, once a booming bass, had become a husky growl, as if—it was whispered—the ardent whiskey he had drunk all his life had eaten his vocal cords.

"Well, Corbie!" he said in his curious half rumble. "Glad to have yo'. Notified, was yo'?"

"Yep. The twins," said the peddler.

The old giant came up beside the wagon and put his hand on Corbie's knee.

"I reckon yo' know my feelin's about this," he said earnestly. "They say that in these mountains if a man's got a leetle dog hair in him, the mountains'll bring it out. It shore done so with the Tooley breed. Nelly, she's the youngest darter of Larkin, my second son. Leetle fool, she ain't no more'n fourteen, but her an' Jud Tooley—he's Ole Tom Tooley's grandson by Rachel, that married Clem Tooley, Tom's son by his second wife that was the Widder Caleb—'pears like them two young-uns snuck out a few times in the bushes together, an' nobody the wiser. Nacherly, she got in a family way. I'd ruther she'd marry a rattlesnake, but the harm's done. At least that young devil Jud was honor'ble enough to marry her. So when she come home an' told about it las' night—Jud, he hid out in the woods ontil he found out how the wind was goin' to blow—I was madder'n a big-bollixed bull in a briar patch. But after I got done cussin', I concluded that since nobody was invited to their weddin', it'd be only right an' proper to give 'em an infare. Nacherly the Tooleys is all bid, with the rest of the folks in the country 'round."

While he was giving these particulars to old Corbie, Big Hoss surveyed Prudence, taking in every detail of her face, clothing and general appearance.

"Who's the young-un?" he asked.

"Her name's Prudence," said old Corbie. "She's ridin' with me to her aunt's up on the big river."

Big Hoss nodded and gave her a sociable glare. Then he lifted his voice in a half-whispering roar.

"Z'reldy! We got comp'ny!"

In a moment or two a tall, homely woman appeared. She was gray haired and sun faded, but there were lines of character in her face. Almost at once four others were behind her on the porch—younger women ranging from their teens to their middle twenties.

"This yere young lady's named Prudence," bawled Big Hoss. "Take keer of her while I help Corbie with his team an' offer him a gourd of licker."

Prudence descended from the wagon and went rather timidly toward the waiting group on the porch while the old man and Corbie drove the wagon around to the rear of the house.

For a moment old Zarelda stared suspiciously at Prudence. Then she wiped her hands on her apron and shook hands limply.

"Come in," she said. "Gals, git back to your work! Plenty of time to see what ole Corbie's got to sell tomorrow. Folks'll be landin' here 'fore we know it."

The younger women hastened inside and Zarelda conducted her guest into the house.

"Whar yo' from?" she asked. And before Prudence could answer, she followed with a barrage of other questions. "Corbie a relation of yourn? How'd yo' git that dress tore up so? Whar does yo' aunt live? Hain't yo' got no shoes?"

Prudence replied as well as she was able, and fortunately the inquisition did not last long.

"Yo' go in thar—the settin' room," said the matriarch. " 'Scuse me. I got to get to the cook house. Them Tooleys will be showin' any time now, an' supper's to git."

3.

She was gone and Prudence entered the "settin' room," a chamber embellished with a split-bottom settee, two or three homemade chairs, a melodeon that looked as if it had been brought over in the ark—it had become so rusted over the years that it could not be played—and a center table made of the crate the melodeon originally came in. Upon this table rested a huge old family Bible in which, presumably, were registered the Hostetter vital statistics for generations.

To her surprise, a young girl was sitting alone in the room. She rose with a look of embarrassment when Prudence entered. Her age appeared to be two or three years less than Prudence's, and she was halfway pretty, although her youth was overwhelmed by some inner emotion.

"I'm Nelly," said the girl.

Prudence realized that this was the little bride of "no more than fourteen" who was expecting a baby and had been married only the day before.

"My name is Prudence," she said. "I'm here for the—the infare."

"Thank yo' kindly," said Nelly. "Won't yo' set down?"

Rather stiffly they seated themselves, and for a few moments silence reigned.

"I'm married, yo' know," said Nelly after a time.

"Yes, I heard."

"The folks—my granddad—decided I should stay hyar las' night," Nelly went on. "My husban'—that's Jud Tooley—is to claim me tonight."

She spoke primly, yet with a kind of pathos that went to Prudence's heart. Fourteen years old—so soon she faced the harsh realities of life. This little child-woman across from her should still be playing with other children and learning her book.

"I've never seen your—husband," said Prudence.

Nelly's face colored and for a moment her eyes were starlike.

"Wait till yo' meet him. He's a wonderful boy, even if—" She paused an almost imperceptible second. "Tooley or not, he's a wonderful boy, an' good to me. Yo'll see," she finished.

With that, emotion overcame her and the poor child, criticized by her family, feeling as if she had committed some act of dreadful guilt—not in becoming pregnant, but in becoming pregnant by a Tooley—began to cry.

Prudence went over to her and put her arms about her.

"It will be all right," she said. "You're safely married, and your husband's coming for you, and you'll be happy. Everything will be all right."

The little bride clung to her, weeping hysterically. It took Prudence's kindest words and softest ways to restore the poor thing's composure.

4.

There was a shout outside.

"Oh, they've come!" said Nelly, jumping up and dabbing her eyes. "I got to fix myself up——"

She was gone. Prudence went out into the hall where the Hostetter women were already gathered. Coming up the road, she saw a procession that, in its way, appeared as wild as a band of Indians.

First came a buckboard driven by a lean, stooped man with

a dangling black beard in which not a few white hairs gleamed; he wore a black slouch hat and a gun rested between his knees.

"That's Ole Tom," said one of the women, and Prudence knew he was the leader of the hostile clan, and that the "Ole" was part of his recognized title.

In the buckboard, crowded together, were half a dozen women and children. Just behind the vehicle, on a mule and with a rifle held across his saddle bow, rode a man identified to her as Clem Tooley, father of the groom. Behind him was a wagon containing more women and children. A cavalcade of men and boys mounted on horses or mules, and without exception armed, brought up the rear of the strange procession.

Big Hoss, that magnificent ruin of a man, stepped forward to do the honors as required by mountain protocol.

"Come on in! 'Light down!" he bawled. "Put yo' rigs an' animals in back. Thar's a bar'l an' a gourd dipper onder this hyar tree, fo' one an' fo' all!"

The Hostetter twins, Rufe and Lafe, came swinging across a pasture on foot; from the cabins at the rear appeared other men and youths. Prudence counted ten of them and they were all Hostetters by the look of them. She observed that the Hostetters were inclined to be tall, with brown or sandy hair and beards. The mark of the breed was equally evident in the Tooleys—dark skin, black hair and beards, wiry rather than muscular bodies. The males of the two clans were about equal in number. And this she noticed with misgivings: every one of them, in both clans, carried a firearm of some kind.

In spite of the Hostetter patriarch's hospitable invitation, she could feel the tension in the air. As the Tooley men dismounted and they and the Hostetters approached each other, they all seemed to walk on the balls of their feet, bristling like hostile dogs on their first meeting, eyeing each other for potential combat. They did not shake hands. The two groups stood apart from each other and the air seemed to crackle, as if with electric warnings of danger.

Then old Corbie's cheerful voice broke the silence.

"Come on!" he said. "Say—thar's drinkin' whiskey as good
as I ever tasted—clear as spring water an' beady as a weasel's eye!"

His laugh broke the tension. Distantly polite, still eyeing
each other, the men of both clans headed toward the barrel.
Meantime the women and the younger children foregathered
in the house with their own kind.

Evening was approaching and Big Hoss led the men around
the house to the barn, which had been cleared for the festivities.
Another barrel of "refreshments" stood on a small board platform
in the barn at the rear, with cups and dippers at hand, so that
everyone could help himself. The mountain women also came to
the barn, and Prudence noticed that they were not averse to a
swallow or so of the Hostetter home-distilled liquor, which was in
fact quite famous in the area for its potency and quality.

Within the barn the wide earth floor had been swept clean
and men began, at Zarelda's directions, to set up trestle tables of
planks laid across sawhorses. The women, all of them, regardless
of name, appeared to be on good speaking terms; soon they began
to bring out the "supper."

It was a banquet, a sumptuous feast by any standards, and
in keeping with the Hostetter notions of hospitality. There were
roast wild turkeys, two magnificent hams baked brown and well
spiced, fried chickens heaped on great platters, haunches of
venison roasted to perfection, and wild ducks swimming in their
own gravy. And with these, an almost bewildering array of side
dishes—mashed potatoes, candied yams, garden greens, two kinds
of bread, butter, jellies, preserves, molasses, pies, cakes, and other
sweets beyond counting. There was coffee for those who desired
the beverage, but most of the men preferred a tot of whiskey
beside their plates.

For this occasion the guns were set aside; but it was sig-
nificant, as showing mutual suspicion and scarcely concealed
hostility, that the Hostetter weapons were placed against one
wall of the barn while those of the Tooleys were arranged against
the wall opposite.

This being an infare, however, both factions were on their

best behavior, and drinking warmed them so that they spoke
almost cordially, with a few mountain witticisms. The men sat
along the benches beside the tables; the women served the meats,
for it was considered proper that men be served first, after this
their wives and mothers could see to their own plates and feed
the children. Prudence helped with the serving.

Now the male mountaineers put their elbows on the tables,
leaned over their food, and began to eat to surfeit. The women
ate a little more delicately perhaps, plied Prudence with questions, and gossiped. Stomachs began to fill, adding new geniality
to the atmosphere.

Suddenly, as if it had been noticed for the first time, somebody said, "Say—whar's Jud an' Nelly?"

Neither bride nor groom was present, but this in reality
was no surprise to the mountaineers, for it was a quaint custom
to "bring the couple to the table." Nevertheless, all affected
astonishment.

"Why, they orter be hyar," said someone else.

At this "searching parties" were formed—three or four young
men to look for Jud and an equal number of young women to
seek Nelly. The bride, of course, was found in the house; and
Jud was discovered sitting alone in Ole Tom's buckboard.

Triumphantly they were seized and brought together to the
banquet, Nelly blushing very red, and Jud, looking foolish, a
dark lad too young yet to have more than a little fuzz on his
cheeks. Side by side they were seated; and they ate, or made a
pretense of eating while a shower of "jokes," more notable for
broad earthiness than for humor, was rained upon them.

Prudence, only recently out of convent school and unaccustomed to such primitive badinage, more than once felt embarrassed at hearing some of the quips. But to the mountain
people, living as they did so close to the raw verities of life, there
was nothing exceptionable in the crude "witticisms." If they
made the young couple squirm and flush red, so much the better.
All of their elders had, at some time or other, been through much
the same sort of ordeal before them.

When all had eaten their fill the trestle tables were cleared out of the lantern-lighted barn, and the benches arranged about the sides of the hard dirt floor. On the platform beside the whiskey barrel a plump, red-faced little man stationed himself with a fiddle and began scraping and tuning his instrument. This was Abel Beeson, who had some local reputation for calling numbers and playing for dances.

Obviously the worse for drink already, Beeson suddenly struck up a mountain tune. Surprising, how quickly the couples were on the floor to begin the dance. But a call came from Zarelda, the Hostetter matriarch:

"Newly married folks fust!"

A roar of laughter and applause at this. Nelly and Jud, protesting, were pushed out on the floor; they had to go through a dance together, shuffling and hopping to the squeaking fiddle's tune while the crowd about clapped and joked at their expense.

After that preliminary the dancing began in earnest.

Prudence had never before seen a mountain square dance, and she quickly learned that while such a dance might not be the most esthetic of all things, it did not lack in liveliness. The young men stamped their feet and swung their partners almost violently; and the strange rhythm of the sets, the "sashaying" and "do-ci-doing," all to the wild notes of the fiddle and the caller's voice, made a scene of almost barbaric gaiety.

First one young man, then another, came to Prudence where she sat on a bench by the wall and asked her to dance. She had no shoes and at first demurred on this account, but some of the other girls were barefoot and so were some of the youths for that matter; at last she accepted an invitation from a tall young hunter.

Though she was unaccustomed to the dances, she was naturally quick of foot and reacted well, so that she did creditably and she found herself swung, and led, and turned, and passed from hand to hand until she was breathless, and flushed, and laughing. After that other youths besought her, for in spite of her ruined dress, she was by far the prettiest girl present. For some of the numbers she consented, but she was still not entirely strong after her long period of hunger and sickness, and so she excused herself from the figures that seemed too complicated. She managed to do it with such smiles and appearance of sincere regret that she ruffled no feelings.

"She's purty, an' she's got sperit, an' she lets a feller down easy," said one disappointed swain.

"An' yo' kin bet she's all lady," said another. "She'd shore illuminate this yere commun'ty, if she tuck a notion to stay in these parts."

Old Corbie, when asked for information, disclosed nothing except that the next morning he intended to head north and Prudence was due at her aunt's. This to the general disappointment of all the young bloods.

In the midst of the gaiety there came a sudden stop. Abel Beeson, who stood on the low platform beside the open whiskey barrel to play, had improved the occasion between each number to take a dram for his comfort. Now, all at once, the music ceased. He set his fiddle down on a chair and lurched out of the barn to be sick under the trees in the back, after this he drunkenly slept; he was unable to fiddle any more that night.

The merry spirit of the occasion seemed to dim. Young men and women of the Hostetter and Tooley clans had been dancing freely with each other, but with the spell of the music broken they now insensibly drew apart, each clan together. The Tooleys stood near where their guns were stacked against the wall, and the Hostetters grouped where they were handy to their own weapons opposite.

Prudence looked across at old Corbie by the fiddler's platform; his face had grown suddenly anxious. Hardly understanding what was in the air, but nevertheless feeling the sudden chill, she went over to him. Voices in the barn had lowered and glances were being shot across the space between the factions that suddenly were far from friendly.

When she reached old Corbie her eye fell on Beeson's fiddle, where he had laid it on the chair when he went outside. Hardly thinking, she picked the instrument up.

How familiar was the shape in her hands! The fiddle was old, perhaps brought across the mountains a generation before, and at one time it might have been a fine violin. But now it was scratched and discolored, and when she softly tried it, her sure ear told her it was badly out of tune.

She forgot everything else and became absorbed in the violin, softly tightening strings where needed, working to get it back to the harmony it deserved until she was better satisfied with it. Then she turned to lay it back where it had been abandoned.

5.

At that instant she became aware that a deadly tension had come over the room. Every voice was silent. Every face was taut. Every eye was fixed on something going on at the front of the barn.

She saw what it was. Big Hoss Hostetter and Old Tom Tooley, those ancient enemies, confronted each other beard to beard almost, bristling with some mighty anger.

In the deathly silence she heard the Hostetter patriarch say in his husky voice, "You've et my vittles, an' you've drunk my licker——"

The head of the Tooleys reached into a pocket and what he drew forth was a silver coin—a fifty-cent piece. He held it out in his open palm.

"Here—" he said.

The look on Hostetter's face was terrible. To have pay offered for his hospitality, under such circumstances, was a shooting insult.

From the walls where they leaned, rifles were plucked by the men of each clan. Prudence saw the Hostetter twins, Rufe and Lafe, their faces tense with ferocity, each drop on a knee, their rifles cocked, ready to fire. Opposite them Clem Tooley, father of Jud, had lifted a shotgun to his shoulder. All the others of the two factions, weapons ready, glared at each other with murderous hostility.

Life and death hung on that moment. Any sudden act could fill that barn with the flaming thunder of guns, and a score of lives might be snuffed out in one furious outburst of bloody slaughter.

Behind her, Prudence heard old Corbie whisper, "Kin ye play that thing? Oh, for God's sake, play somethin'!"

Struck motionless by the deadly drama before her, for a moment she did not respond to him.

"Anythin'! Play *anythin'*—" His voice was desperately urgent. The violin was still in her hand. She tucked it under her chin.

She must play, but what kind of music to offer? In that moment she thought back wildly and raised her bow.

What disaster might next have occurred nobody can ever know. But from the rear of the barn came the voice of the violin, in an opening phrase none in that room had ever heard before.

The two old men, hate still in their faces, turned their eyes toward it. Every face in the barn turned likewise.

They all saw the girl, her eyes on the instrument, her face rapt, her fingers sure on the strings, her slim arm moving the bow in timing far different from any songs they knew, as it brought forth the rich and sonorous chords.

It was music strange to the listeners, slow in tempo, floating forth upon the stillness of that room with an undertone of such peace, of such immortal gentleness, that it caught at their hearts.

In the breathless silence the music swelled up, a concurrence of tones unbelievably harmonious, indescribably magnificent, heartbreakingly beautiful. It was as if the very beams of the far-off moon in its serenity had been caught and changed in their softness and in their celestial purity into a prayer uttered in the form of music by a supreme genius.

It lifted to its climax and then came slowly to its perfect ending. It ceased.

What Prudence had played, and played with all her soul, was the song she loved best, the "Ave Maria" that once brought tears to the eyes of old Sister Mary Felicia in the convent days.

A sigh seemed to come from the listeners. For a moment they paid the most perfect of tributes, complete silence.

Then there were words. But these people did not applaud in the ordinary way. They gathered around the girl and their voices were soft, with almost unknown emotion, as they praised her.

The two patriarchs still stood together but the harshness had faded from their seamed countenances. Beside them now stood old Corbie.

"Wall!" said Big Hoss, and the expulsion of his breath seemed to blow his whiskers forward.

Old Tom cleared his throat. Then he slowly began to return the silver piece to his pocket.

"What I was going to say, Tom," said Hostetter, "was that you've et an' drank with me—an' you're allus welcome at this house—yo' an' yourn."

"An' what I was about to remark, Hoss," said Tooley, "was that we ought to start a leetle nestaig fo' the young-un that's to come—an' this half-dollar is a starter an' more back of it."

"The young-un," came old Corbie's voice, "it'll be both a Hostetter an' a Tooley."

"Why, that's right," said Big Hoss. "Tooley an' Hostetter."

Old Tom said, as if digesting this idea for the first time, "Tooley an' Hostetter blood blended together——"

"Say—ye ain't two different families no longer," said old Corbie.

The patriarchs stared at each other.

"The feudin' stops?" said Big Hoss.

"It stops," said Old Tom.

They extended gnarled hands in a strong shake and looked deep into each other's eyes.

"Now that makes me feel fine," said Corbie.

"Makes us all feel fine," said Big Hoss. "That so, Tom?"

"Shore do," said Old Tom. "Let's go find out what that gal was a-playin'."

The title "Ave Maria" meant nothing to them or to anyone else present. Prudence did not try to explain it. Politely they suggested that since she could play the violin—"fiddle" they still called it—she might perhaps know some dance tunes.

She remembered "The Hunters of Kentucky," "Show Your Pretty Foot," and one or two other country tunes from playing and singing them with Miss Sally. Now she tried them on the fiddle, and her perfect ear and sense of timing enabled her to play them well enough for her uncritical audience.

The dancers formed again, old Corbie called the figures, and the jollity went on until midnight, although the girl was nearly ready to drop from weariness before it ended.

At midnight the young couple was "bedded" according to ancient custom. Giggling young women led the bride to the bridal chamber—on this occasion the loft of the Big House. Stalwart youths grasped the groom and hustled him to the same place. Side by side they were placed in bed, the covers pulled up under their chins, and much advice, some of it coarse in nature, was given to them. Then everybody had a drink and the couple was left alone at last to its nuptial privileges.

Long after midnight the guests slowly departed.

In Old Tom Tooley's parting words to Big Hoss Hostetter there was cordial good will.

"Bring over the hull kit an' b'ilin' of yo' family a week today," he said. "By that time we-uns will have the logs got up an' thar'll be a house raisin' an' jollification fo' Jud an' Nelly."

Chapter 11

1.

Next morning, as old Corbie and Prudence prepared to depart, twenty Hostetters of all ages and both sexes, after having gone through the peddler's stock to their hearts' content, said farewell to them. Big Hoss shook hands with the peddler and then with the girl, his immense paw almost swallowing her small hand.

"Yo' done us good, Prudence," he said in his whispering bass. "That's the fust time Ole Tom Tooley an' me has shook hands fo' twenty years. An' we oncet was chums. Many a time me an' Tom has hunted deer an' b'ar an' coon together in these very woods."

"Mebbe ye will again now," said old Corbie.

"Cain't tell. A lot of water's run downhill, an' neither of us is as spry as when we was younger. But give a leetle time visitin' back an' forth, an' a grandchild we kin take turns dandlin', an' I reckon we kin at least swap stories about them ole times."

Of Prudence he asked, "Whut was the name again of that thar tune—the one yo' played fust?"

" 'Ave Maria,' " she said.

"Sounds furrin," said the patriarch. "But it's shore the nearest to angel music I ever heerd. I couldn't believe it was comin' out'n that ole fiddle Abel Beeson's been abusin' all these years."

From Nelly, the bride, Prudence got a hug and a whisper, "Oh, *thank* you—everythin's all right now." Jud, the groom, was not in evidence.

Hearty cries of "Come back ag'in!" and "Goodbye, an' a welcome to the both of yo' if you're ever this way!" followed them as they drove away.

A mile or so down the road two horsemen were waiting for them.

"It's Ole Tom Tooley—an' Jud," said the peddler.

He pulled his team to a halt as the riders trotted up.

"Howdy," said Old Tom. "Thought yo'd be along, an' jest wanted to say goodbye an' wish yo' the best. Jud, hyar's, brung yo'-uns a leetle goin' away present."

The youth untied a heavy gunnysack parcel from his saddle.

"Hit's jest a ham," he said. "But it's a prime one. An' with it goes my thanks—an' Nelly's—fo' last night."

"Thankee kindly," said old Corbie. "Big Hoss give us a demijohn of his corn. Have a goodbye nip?"

The ham was transferred to the back of the wagon and Old Tom and Jud dismounted to take a pull at the demijohn, holding it by the wicker handle and expertly swinging it by one hand to the shoulder to drink.

When Old Tom returned the container he sighed with pleasure and wiped his black beard. "Big Hoss allus could make licker so damn good a feller cain't hardly bite it off," he said.

As they drove on the patriarch of the Tooleys raised his arm in farewell and his teeth gleamed in a grin through his black whiskers.

"Wall," said old Corbie after a mile of silence, "looks like mebbe we seen the end of the meanest feud in Kaintucky."

"They won't fight any more?" asked the girl.

"Nope. Orders is out. Them two ole he-coons has shook

hands an' vowed peace. Ain't nobody goin' ag'in their dictates."
He gave the girl a look of sincere respect. "An' ye done it. I
thought I could already smell powder burnin' when ye begun to
play."

"You were the brave one," she said. "You walked up to
those two old men and they listened to you."

He grinned under his vast moustache. "If shootin' had
started, I'd a-been out'n that barn so fast lightnin' couldn't of
singed my coattails. Ye had 'em quieted before I ever said a
word. I never seen a lady tuck a fiddle under her chin before—
mostly it's men does that. But ye kin make it talk like nothin'
I ever heerd."

Prudence knew she had not played the "Ave Maria" perfectly. But the majesty and the beauty of the music and the
passionate prayer it sent upward carried an appeal that was
universal. Her listeners did not notice minor mistakes, and she
only thanked heaven that the hand of death had been stayed.

2.

Toward the afternoon of the second day after leaving the Hostetters, old Corbie said, "It's all downhill now. We're startin'
into the big valley. Should see the Ohio River 'fore supper."

After a silence he went on, "I been thinkin'. I know some
folks on the river—ole friends of mine. Finest folks ye ever seen.
Name of Glover an' run a wood yard. They'll take keer of ye
until ye git ready to go on. I'll tell 'em ye got a aunt in Ohio.
Ye don't need to tell 'em nothin'."

"Are you going to leave me?" Prudence asked with a feeling
of panic. She had grown accustomed to old Corbie, and in the
days she had traveled with him and experienced his unwearied
kindness, she had become very fond of him. She could hardly
bear the thought of parting.

He was speaking. "Why, yes. Ye told me, didn't ye, that ye
was headin' east? I got to go west, down the river to Louisville."

She gulped. "What will I do without you?"

"Ye'll do fine. The Glovers is church-goin' people. The ole man's name is Alex an' the ole lady is Libby. They got four kids, two boys an' two gals."

"But—oh, Corbie—" Tears sprang into her eyes.

Suddenly, and for the first time, his arm was about her shoulders. "I'll miss ye, gal." His voice rasped with unwonted emotion. "But we cain't go on travelin' like this forever." He gave her a little squeeze and took his arm away.

Prudence wept unrestrainedly on his shoulder. He let her have her cry out, but he was practical.

"Ye might want to fix yourself up," he said. "We'll stop down here by a leetle spring I know. Your hair's right purty. Ever wear it any way except down your back?"

"Oh, yes. I used to put it up," she told him. "But I haven't any hairpins."

"I thought of that. A lady's jest nacherly got to have hairpins. So I rummaged around an' dug some out'n the bottom of my chest—no, don't thank me. They was layin' thar, an' I'd clean forgot all about them. Glad to git rid of them." He paused. "Ye kin keep that ole comb I give ye—ain't worth nothin'. An' here's a hand mirror. That mirror only cost me four cents wholesale, an' I sell it for more, so I ain't sacrificin' nothin'—if ye'll take it——"

"Oh, Corbie! I owe you too much already——"

"Hush up!" he said almost crossly. "I was fair starvin' for comp'ny when I was lucky enough to find ye. An' ye've more'n paid me back for any leetle thing I done with your singin', an' helpin' around camp, an' laughin' to make the days shorter, not to mention what ye done the other night at Hostetters. An'—an'—by jest bein' the way ye are. Now here's the spring——"

The wagon stopped and they descended to the ground. In the new mirror she saw how bedraggled she looked. Her face was pinched by illness and hardships, with hollows under the eyes which made them seem unnaturally large, and hair straggling untidily.

No need to urge her further. She began by washing her face in the spring, then she braided her shining hair after she combed it well, and finally wound the heavy braids about her head, fastening them with the hairpins.

Old Corbie, watching the girl at this very simple toilet, thought, as many another man has thought before and after him, that the play of a woman's arms about her head as she arranges her hair is one of the most graceful of all movements. When she finished, and surveyed herself in the small mirror, turning her head this way and that, her cheeks fresh from the cold water and the sun picking out highlights of gold in her hair, the old man smiled.

"Say—ye look like a little princess," he said.

She smiled back at him. But then her eyes fell on her ragged dress and the smile faded.

He understood. "Too bad ye ain't got somep'n fresh to wear."

But she hastened to head him off from some new bene-faction. "This is all right. Just as soon as I have a little time, I'll fix it so it will be plenty good—for a 'runaway girl.' "

The twinkle with which she said this last was so merry that it made them both laugh.

Not long after they resumed their journey he said, "Thar she is—the ole Ohio."

He pointed out the great river, seen here and there through the trees of the valley into which they were descending.

"Thar was a time," he went on, "an' it's been since I've knowed her, too, when that thar river wasn't safe for a single foot of her way. Thar was the Injuns. An' what was wusser than Injuns, thar was river pirates—like the Harpes, an' the Masons, an' all them other outlaws. They'd kill ye for the fun of it. An' then, after they killed ye, they'd do somethin' terrible nasty. They'd gut ye—take out all your insides—an' fill ye full of stones, an' sink ye in the bottom of a river so's ye'd never come up an' nobody'd ever find ye——"

He stopped at the girl's cry of horror.

"But the Injuns is all gone now," he went on after a moment

in a comforting voice. "An' the outlaws, too. The ole Ohio's as safe as a city street."

Prudence was to remember that statement afterward and think how very wrong the old man was.

Down the steepening road they went and presently they reached a considerable clearing right beside the swirling waters of the great river. She saw a boat landing, and wood piled in ranks on the bank, and a log house with some outbuildings, and a thin haze of smoke issuing from a chimney.

A dog began to bark and a thin childish voice cried, "Hey, Ma! It's Corbie!"

As they drove into the clearing the family seemed to erupt from the house. There was a tall man, clean-shaved, with a rugged face, wide shoulders and sinewy arms; a plump, comfortable, motherly woman wearing an apron; two boys, perhaps sixteen and fourteen, both looking as if they had outgrown their clothes; and two girls about ten and eight years old. The girls were flaxen haired and each appeared to be clad in only a single garment, a sort of loose cotton dress which came to their knees. They were both barefoot.

There was also a dog—an old dog, gray with age, with a small tinkling bell on the collar around his neck, who stopped barking as soon as he recognized Corbie.

Cries of hearty greeting indicated that the peddler was a welcome visitor here. He gave Prudence a hand down from the wagon.

"This here's Prudence," he said to them. And to her, "This is Alex Glover, who owns this wood lot. An' this is Libby Glover, who's shorely one of the nicest ladies ye'll ever know. An' them's their kids." He named them in order of age, "Bud, Babe, Sis, and Susie."

The entire family stared at her with the frank, round-eyed curiosity of the frontier.

"I picked up this child on the road," old Corbie explained. "She was too sick to stand on her feet. I brung her along with me, an' kind of took care of her. She's perked up some, but she's still ga'nt lookin', as ye kin see. Now, folks, Prudence has got a aunt somewheres up in Ohio State, who she's tryin' to git to. Ye know I got to go down the river. Kin ye put her up a leetle while, till she gits her bearin's? She's real good to help, an' won't cause no trouble, an' kin sing like a lark, an' play a fiddle like ye never heerd."

A momentary silence was broken by Libby.

"Why, shore, the pore little starved-lookin' thing," she said, and put a motherly arm around Prudence. "You jest come on into the house, honey."

But the eyes of the children were on old Corbie with a silent expectant stare.

"Wall, young-uns, whut's keepin' ye?" he asked. Then he chuckled. "Thought I forgot, didn't ye? Wall, ole Corbie didn't forget."

From the wagon he took a gift for each of them.

"Boys," he said, "here's two jackknives for ye—them's gen-u-ine Barlows. Sis an' Susie, a purty ribbon apiece, for your hair. Alex, I reckon a new double-bitted ax would about suit ye. An' Libby—here." It was a coffee grinder, ornately decorated with impossible painted animals—cows, horses, deer and sheep—and it brought a gasp of pleasure from the plump matron.

Libby interrupted the chorus of thanks by saying, "Supper'll be ready right soon."

Carrying her precious new acquisition and followed by her daughters, she escorted Prudence to the house while Alex and his sons remained to help old Corbie unhitch his horses, water them, and feed them in the log barn.

The Glover cabin was of the style known as "double," built in two divisions, with a roofed breezeway called a "turkey walk" between them. Each division contained two rooms, and the smaller log structure close behind was the kitchen, with a huge stone fireplace complete with cranes and firedogs. It was large enough to serve as a dining room as well.

The two young girls conducted Prudence on a tour of the house.

"You'll sleep in the room with us," Sis told her. "We got two beds an' Susie an' me kin sleep together, so you'll have Susie's bed. This here's the boys' room. Stinks a little, don't it? They're allus trappin' an' some of the skins they bring home is purty rank. This here's where Paw an' Maw sleep. That's a real feather bed, all goose down. Not a chicken feather in it."

Having displayed this magnificence, the girls showed the other glories of the house. The fourth room was a combination sitting room and family room; also, for state occasions, a dining room. It had a fireplace and mantel. On one wall hung a large framed engraving entitled "The Signing of the Declaration of Independence." On the wall opposite was another engraving "Washington Crossing the Delaware." Over the mantel there was a framed woodcut of a man with bushy white hair and a long lean face.

"That's Gen'ral Jackson," said Susie. "He's President. We're Demmycrats but there's a lot of Whigs around here that votes for Henry Clay."

Prudence looked closely at the woodcut. So that was the President, the friend of whom her father had so often spoken! Actually, like all woodcuts, it little resembled the face it represented, but she could not know that. To her, the expression seemed so reserved and stern that she had a new qualm of fear over the success of her intended mission—even if she ever got to see him in the flesh.

Meantime, in the kitchen, Libby moved back and forth with a rolling gait like that of a sailor on land, but not missing a move as she checked the kettles on the cranes and the huge iron spider with long legs to hold it over the blazing logs. At one side a coffee pot, already bubbling, sent forth aromas from the first coffee ground in the new and splendid coffee grinder.

Libby had magic in her cooking. Within not more than thirty minutes she placed on the table a blue china tray heaped with golden-brown pieces of fried chicken, a dish of fried mush, another of greens, a plate of smoking home-cured ham, a bowl of gravy, hot biscuits, butter still cold from the spring house, honey and jelly, a large fruit pie, coffee, sugar, cream, and other delicacies.

They sat at the table and Alex Glover bowed his head and rumbled a long prayer. Then they ate, and Prudence listened with pleasure to the talk, and looked at this new family around her.

Glover and Corbie at first discussed politics. They were both Jackson men, and commented favorably on the President's recent victory over the monopolistic Bank of the United States which, according to their view, was crippling the country financially. Then Glover told Corbie that he hoped he had cleared enough land to be able to put corn on the hill above the house next year.

"I'm lucky," he said. "Most folks has to burn their felled trees. I sell mine to the riverboats."

After that old Corbie, to Prudence's embarrassment, insisted on telling the story of how "that young-un, all by her own self, an' with nobody to help her, put an end to the Hostetter-Tooley feud an' got them ole he-coons to shake hands." He made a better story of it than the facts warranted, she felt. And Alex Glover wished aloud that they had a fiddle so that they could hear her play.

Meantime Libby corrected the manners of her two daughters with words that were sharp, yet manifestly affectionate. And the two boys ate silently, seemingly tongue-tied; but now and then, when Prudence looked up, she sometimes caught their eyes soberly regarding her, and then quickly turning away.

3.

Supper finished, the family was busy attending to various tasks, and Prudence was left alone. She would have sought out old Corbie, but he was engaged in some discussion with Alex down by the wood ranks. The boys were at their outside chores and she was too shy to speak to them anyway. The girls helped their mother in the kitchen.

For the first time since she ran away from the tavern at Turkeytoe, she was by herself, not in immediate peril of some kind, and not in acute discomfort or hunger. She had come this far through all the dangers and hardships that beset her, and she still hardly realized what a miracle it was. Strangely, instead of a feeling of gratitude, a wave of desolation suddenly swept over her.

It was not homesickness in the ordinary sense, for she had no real home. Perhaps it was partly the reaction of her nerves from the tense days of the past. She was lonely for her father and Miss Sally. And she was suddenly woeful over the thought of parting with that kind friend, old Corbie. Whatever the cause —and who is to understand a girl's emotions?—blank misery took possession of her.

Tears were welling in her eyes when Libby Glover entered the room. One glance and the kindly matron sensed at least part of the trouble.

"Come, dear," she said. "You're worn out, an' you need rest." She took the girl by the hand and led her to the bedroom.

"This is your bed," she said. "It's got a good straw mattress." She went to a clothespress. "Here's a nightgown. You won't want to sleep in that dress."

And Prudence had her choice between one of Libby's, which was much too large for her, and one belonging to Sis, which was much too small. Eventually, wrapped in Libby's voluminous garment, she got into bed.

The matron tucked the bedclothes about her and stooped to give her a goodnight kiss. "We're all your friends here, dear," she said. "You're going to be just fine."

Somehow the affection in the words and the kiss lifted the weight of depression, so that almost at once the girl was asleep.

It was a sleep of weariness so deep, that next morning she did not even hear the two younger girls who rose from their bed and stole out of the room so as not to disturb her. When she did wake it was broad daylight. She was conscious that the others were about; she dressed quickly, made her brief toilet, then went to the kitchen house. The family was eating breakfast.

"Where's Corbie?" was her immediate question.

"He left before sunup," Libby answered. "Said he had a long drive to make today. I think he couldn't bear to say good-bye to his little friend he left with us." She paused. "By the way, he left this for you." She held up the half-empty bottle of Balsam of Wild Cherry. "Should your cough come back on you, he said."

"I didn't even get to thank him!" cried Prudence, with a lump in her throat.

"He knows you're grateful. You'll miss him, but you couldn't ride around with Corbie forever. He's a nice man, but he's got his rounds to make. An' he said you wanted to get to your aunt in Ohio."

Prudence was silent. Reference to the fictitious "aunt" reminded her of her real errand, to seek, if possible, the President of the United States in behalf of her father. The thought came to her of the woodcut portrait looking down so sternly from the mantel of this house; and she wondered if the next part of her journey would be as hard and as frightening as the part she had already completed.

"Eat your mush an' milk," said Libby kindly. "After that you kin have some bacon an' hot cakes."

But Prudence had little appetite this morning. Her heart was heavy at parting in this fashion: without even speaking to the old man who had been so wonderfully kind to her.

Libby did not urge her. When the breakfast dishes were done, she said, "Corbie left somethin' else for you."

"What is it?" asked the girl listlessly.

"Let's take a look at it."

The matron displayed a dress of gingham in tiny checks of blue and white—a cheap little dress of the kind the peddler carried to sell to the mountain people, but infinitely superior to the ragged homespun Prudence was wearing.

"That's another reason Corbie left early," Libby told her. "He was afraid you wouldn't take it if he gave it to you himself."

Prudence felt she must accept the dress, but there was an ache in her heart for the old peddler who had gone out of her life with this last gesture of generosity.

4.

The days at the Glovers passed almost dreamily at first.

Libby took personal charge of her guest, fed her, dosed her with a concoction of herbs made palatable by being mixed with wild honey, and expanded on her own skill as an herb doctor. Her opinion of the medical profession was low—of her own abilities, correspondingly high.

"All the doctors know is to bleed you," she said. "I cure people the doctors has given up jest by using the brains the good Lord give me an' the remedies nature pervides all around us."

She paused to shake out the blue gingham dress on which she and Prudence were working at the time.

"Now you take bowel complaint," she continued. "Sassafrass is good for that, unless you want a real quick purge, an' then you use mandrake root. I mind Link Lukins, he was so bound up he was all bloated an' near to die. Looked like they'd have to take blastin' powder to him. But I brewed him some mandrake tea. He hadn't drunk more'n half of it when he had to hurry so fast, he barely made it to the outhouse in time."

She laughed at the remembrance of Link Lukins' haste, and went on, "Spicebush an' witch hazel is prime for chills an' fever. For morbid fever there ain't nothin' to beat boneset. An' goldenseal, boiled an' sweetened with honey, is a wonderful tonic. That's what I been givin' you an' you look better every day."

Indeed Prudence, with regular sleep and meals, was showing marked improvement in her appearance and in the way she felt. She was eager to be helpful, and Libby came to depend on her for many of the household tasks.

The dress old Corbie left her was too large, particularly in the waist, and it had some tawdry decorations on it. Aided by Libby, she set about altering it, using ideas she had gained from Miss Sally. In the end she succeeded in creating out of the rather shapeless garment something that fit her neatly, with a skirt that flounced gracefully from the waist, puffs on the sleeves at the shoulders, smocking at the neck, and a touch of lace—given by Libby—at the wrists. Blue became her well and she was very pretty in it, but she did most of her work about the house in the old worn homespun.

The family was friendly and kind, and she repaid them with light talk and smiles and willing hands and feet at tasks to be done. The elder boy's real name, she learned, was John, and his brother's Jesse. But it was a custom of the country for the oldest son always to be called Bud—for "Brother"—and the youngest to be called Babe. Similarly, the elder of the girls was really Rosanna, but she was called Sis, for "Sister." Susan, the youngest child, having no appropriate nickname fixed by custom, was simply Susie.

Prudence also made friends with the Glover dog, an ancient patriarch of the canine breed rejoicing under the name of Shadrach, or rather Shad for short. When she left the house she always heard the small bell at his neck jingling as he followed her, hoping that she would rub him about the ears, a trick she had discovered that delighted him.

Soon after she came to the Glovers, with her feet bare, Libby found for her a pair of moccasins, old but usable. Alex promised that "when he got a little time" he would "cobble up" a better pair of shoes for her, like the homemade footgear he and his sons and his wife wore. Yet she liked the moccasins well enough.

With unslaked curiosity Sis and Susie plied her with questions. She told them that she had gone to school in North Carolina, and lived with her father in Tennessee until he was "taken away." At this they fell into respectful and sympathetic silence, for they supposed he was dead.

The whereabouts of the fictitious aunt bothered her until one day she heard Alex mention Columbus as the capital of Ohio. When she hinted that her aunt lived in the vicinity of that city he looked doubtful.

"That's more'n a hundred mile north of here," he said. But then he added, to cheer her, "Once in awhile somebody comes along headin' for up that way. Mebbe we kin git you a ride."

The family life was regular. Each morning as soon as the chores were done and breakfast was eaten, Alex and his two sons went up to the forest where they were busy all day felling trees, cutting them to lengths required for steamboat furnaces, splitting them with mauls and wedges, and bringing them down to the landing in a cart drawn by the family's one mule.

At the landing the cut wood was laid in what were called "ranks," each rank having roughly the proportions of an ordinary cord of wood—eight feet long and four feet high—except that it was not necessarily the width of a standard cord, which is four feet. Steamboats varied in the length of wood they required, so that ranks were of different widths. All were placed where they could conveniently be loaded on the riverboats that stopped at Glover's landing. It was slow, toilsome work, and the rewards were small in proportion to the time and labor, for steamboat captains habitually drove the prices down.

Meantime in and around the house Libby directed the manifold domestic activities, and Prudence took her full share in this, and even hoed weeds in the garden patch back of the cabin.

In the evenings when they had leisure the boys sometimes fished on the river bank. Once Prudence went down to watch them. Suddenly Bud, who was sixteen, with a pale fuzz on his cheeks and a developing Adam's apple, hoisted a fish from the water. She did not know what kind it was, and she watched with a sort of fascinated horror—for she had never seen a fish taken alive out of its element—while he strung it, flapping and wriggling, onto a cord. Then he turned to her, his Adam's apple in agitation, and held it out.

"Here—you kin have it," he said.

Prudence screamed and retreated. "No! Take it away! I don't want to touch the nasty thing!"

He was abashed. "I didn't mean nothin'—I thought you'd like it——"

"I don't! I don't!" She hurried to the house as Bud stared in astonishment after her.

But she could not help hearing his younger brother jeer at him, "Hey, Bud, you look at her jest as if she was a piece of apple pie!"

Without doubt Bud was smitten with her. Thereafter he showed his interest by various awkward attentions. He picked flowers for her. He gave her uncouth compliments. When on Sunday the family walked to the small log chapel, which was only half a mile away at a crossroad, he strove to walk with her, and he was over-solicitous, as if he feared she might stumble.

She adopted the expedient of having the two younger girls walk on each side of her. Unhappily, he followed behind. During the service she was embarrassingly conscious of his sidelong looks at her, although she never let him know that she was aware of him. Instead she paid most decorous attention to the sermon. The preacher was white bearded, bald and somewhat cock-eyed, so that she never knew whether he was looking directly at her, or off in some other direction with his other eye. His name was Thomas Timmons and he was "Reverend" only on Sundays. On weekdays he was plain Tom Timmons, a farmer like all his congregation, who tilled his fields and was a minister without pay. A sincere and excellent man he was, without doubt, but he had the defect of preaching too long, giving many platitudes and Bible quotations—some of them incorrect—and was, from "Firstly" to "Lastly," dull and uninspiring.

In the days following, poor Bud continued to be bashfully attentive to her. She did not wish to wound him, for she liked him; but he was so adolescent.

He admired her, and male admiration is hardly unpleasant to any woman, particularly if she is young. But his admiration caused her to think of another who had admired her. At least once. Troy Lassiter was baffling and enigmatic to her. She was surprised and indignant when he kissed her, but in retrospect that somehow did not seem so grave an offense now. There was the episode of the bloodhounds, and when she thought he was hunting her, she hated him. But it turned out that it was someone else he was hunting: perhaps his runaway slave, perhaps...the outlaws? She found that she did not hate Troy any more. She hoped somewhat wistfully that she might some day see him again.

At the Glovers there was always something to watch in the ever-changing life on the river, that great artery of commerce. Huge flatboats floated down the stream with their cargoes of produce and their unkempt, almost barbaric crews. A Kentucky boat, smaller than the flatboats, might pass. On board a woman with a baby on her hip might be hanging out the family wash on a line stretched from upright poles at the two ends of the craft, a man steering the floating domicile with a long sweep at the stern, and children shouting and tumbling on the deck in imminent danger, so it seemed, of falling off into the flood.

Skiffs often plied the river and occasionally a barge went by with six or eight Negro oarsmen and two or three well-dressed gentlemen might be sitting under a canopy at the stern—land speculators or government officials. Or a great raft of logs, as much as six hundred feet in length, would come prowling around the curves of the river, with sweeps at the sides and ends to guide it and little board shelters upon it for the crew. Sometimes these huge rafts took as much as half an hour passing a given point because of their slow-moving length.

The great spectacles, however, were the steamboats on their way up or down the stream, making a mighty splash and racket with sidewheels churning the water into froth, with walking beams in measured cadence, lofty woodwork painted gleaming white, passengers idling on the decks, and twin smokestacks pouring out clouds of smoke.

Vast excitement occurred when, at rare intervals, a steamboat stopped at Glover's landing for wood. Stevedores and third-class passengers would swarm back and forth across the gangplank like ants with their load of wood, while a mate was shouting and swearing, and sometimes even fighting was going on. But presently the gangplank would be drawn in, the paddle wheels would churn, and the splendid craft would go snorting and splashing on its way while quiet returned to Glover's landing.

Alex Glover was the strength of the family. He was uneducated and tight fisted, and he had need to be the latter, for the wood lot provided a bare existence, prices being what they were. His way was masterful, sometimes abrupt. The children, and Prudence with them, obeyed his mandates promptly. He did not drink or allow alcoholic beverages on the place; he was a powerful man who more than once had thrashed with his fists some swaggering bully from a flatboat who tried to cause trouble because he could not get whiskey at the place.

But he was just, and toward his smiling wife he was awkwardly affectionate. It developed during Prudence's acquaintance with him that he was a man of influence and worth in the rural community, a jury foreman, a supervisor of what slight work was done on the roads, and a trustee of the little church he attended.

Those days were restful for Prudence. She did her work about the house, watched the pageant of the river, and regained her strength and serenity as time went by.

III

The Monster

Chapter 12

1.

On the night when Prudence made her escape from Peebles'
Tavern in Turkeytoe, Dilsey, the cook woman, slept as usual—
which is to say so soundly that the crack of doom would hardly
have awakened her. The Negress was an excellent sleeper. She
could in fact fall asleep anywhere and at a moment's notice, if
given opportunity. Only her fear of consequences at the hands
of Mrs. Tabitha kept her from sleeping in the kitchen, and at
times she nodded even there, while sitting on her stool waiting
for a pot to boil, a roast to brown, or a loaf to bake.

That particular night Dilsey's snores, which were vigorous,
continuous, and stertorous, drowned out any slight sound Prudence may have made in her hurried and hardly-considered departure. But when the first light of morning came, Dilsey woke
by lifetime habit.

For a moment she knuckled her eyes with her fat black fists,
gazed at the cobwebbed rafters above her, and yawned prodigiously. Then she rolled her Amazonian form over and got out

of bed. Close beside her was the thin unplastered wall that separated her small attic cubicle from Prudence's. She tapped with her knuckles on that wall.

No sound came in reply. The cook woman honestly hated to wake the girl. But duty was duty. She tapped louder than before.

"Prue," she said. "Time to git up."

Still no answer.

Dilsey's plump black face assumed an expression of annoyance.

"Ah declah," she grumbled. "Dat chile sleep lak a daid pusson."

She donned her loose working garb and waddled around to Prudence's door. Since this had no latch, she pushed it open.

"Prue," she said, "yo' bettah be showin' a foot, or yo'll heah from——"

In mid-sentence she stopped. The room was empty.

Dilsey's eyes dilated until they looked like white saucers in her face. "Prue!" she cried in consternation. "Whah yo'——"

But Prudence was gone.

A frightening dilemma now suggested itself to the cook woman. She must relay this news to the Peebles. But when and how? Should she waken them now and tell them? Persons aroused abruptly from slumber were usually notorious for their bad tempers; this applied to the tavern man and his wife, too. Dilsey could envision consequences most unpleasant if she broke their sleep with information as distasteful as that which she must give them.

Would it not be better, perhaps, to wait until the couple got up and came to the kitchen? But at once this course seemed to her to be fraught with possibilities even worse than the first. She would be blamed for not informing them at once, because such delay might make it more difficult to pursue and recapture the fugitive. She was sure they would at once set about to do that; and for the sake of her own skin, Dilsey decided to undertake the dire task of waking her masters.

All was quiet in the tavern at this early hour. She stole to the room which Peebles shared with his consort. Within, she could hear two snores in different keys. Timidly, she knocked on the door. One of the snores ceased at her tap, but there was no reply.

Again she knocked.

Through the door came Peebles' surly voice. "Who's thar?"

"Hit's me—Dilsey," said the cook woman in a pleading voice. "Didn't want to 'sturb yo'—but de white gal done gone."

Now both snores ceased. "What was that you said?" demanded Peebles.

"Dat gal, Prue—she gone. Went away in de night."

There was what sounded like a violent upheaval in the Peebles' bed. Both the tavern keeper and his spouse were thoroughly awake now.

Dilsey shrank back as the door opened to reveal Drew Peebles in a long white nightgown, which bulged out over his paunch. Peering over his shoulder was Mrs. Tabitha, wearing stiff curlpapers like garnishes around a leg of roast mutton, except that no mutton roast ever looked so unappetizing.

"Did you say Prudence is gone?" asked Peebles. "Whar did she go?"

"Ah dunno," faltered Dilsey. "She done went sometime endurin' de night——"

"Didn't you hear her?"

"No, suh. Ah nevah heerd nothin'."

Peebles glared at her ferociously. "Did you help her?"

"Oh, Lawdy, no!" Dilsey was in real terror. "Ah nevah dreamed of nothin' lak dat!"

So genuine was her distress that even Peebles was convinced. "Go to the kitchen," he said gruffly, "an' git to work."

2.

For both Peebles and his wife the news they had thus received was unpleasant.

Mrs. Tabitha still smarted under what she considered the

humiliation she had suffered at Prudence's hands, when on the previous day the girl snatched the stick from her hand and threatened her with it. Indeed, she had devoted some time to thinking up punishments with which to break the spirit of that rebellious creature. To be deprived of an opportunity for revenge left a most bitter taste in her mouth.

Her husband's thoughts were several. First, the girl belonged to him by law, and he had sold the slave woman who previously had filled her place as general scullery and chore girl. He might have to buy another slave, and to spend money in this way was unpleasant to Drew Peebles. His second thought was anger. He had enjoyed the humiliation Bion Buckstone must feel at the servitude of his daughter. Her father would undoubtedly be glad if she escaped, and Peebles desired that Buckstone should feel no joy. His third thought was that this flight might adversely affect some plans in which the girl was involved, and this was bad.

Yet he comforted himself somewhat in the belief that she could not have gone very far. She was so young and so weak and so feminine that he could not conceive that she would dare go out in the forest. She might have taken the road south toward Knoxville. If so, she could be overtaken rather quickly. But more than likely she would try to hide somewhere in the village. In that case she would soon be back, either coming of her own accord to take whatever punishment awaited, or be brought back by any one of his numerous adherents who might discover her.

For breakfast he drank some coffee and ate a slice of fried ham; and so distracted was his mind that he hardly tasted the food. When he finished he rose from the table and went out on the veranda. On this morning, though the flies hummed thickly, he did not think of fly killing. He had something more important to crush than a mere insect.

After a moment's thought he descended the porch steps, crossed the street, and walked down the irregular wooden sidewalk. It was early, but a few persons were astir. He ignored them. Such was the expression on his face that Henry Tidmiller, the harness man, who spoke to him and received no answer, felt apprehensive. Though the harness shop was supposed to belong to Henry, it was really owned by Peebles through a mortgage, and times were not pleasant for those beholden to the tavern man when his mood was bad.

Peebles walked on rapidly, bulled his way through a group of loafers in front of the grog shop—which also was his property —and continued on, without pausing, past the store and post office run by Jared Hume. He was heading for the courthouse, or more specifically, the jail.

After arriving there, he first knocked on the door of the sheriff's quarters.

"Dode," he said abruptly, when that official appeared in long baggy underwear, knuckling his eyes and with tousled hair, just as he had risen from his bed, "I want to talk to Buckstone."

"Why, go ahaid, Drew," said Taney hospitably. He smothered a yawn. "He's in thar, locked up. He ain't a-goin' to run away from you."

"I want to talk to him inside."

"Wall, then, wait till I git on my pants an' shoes an' shirt."

A few minutes later the sheriff came out more suitably attired; he conducted Peebles to the jail door, unlocked it, and followed the tavern man into the corridor.

"Hey, Buckstone," he said, "somebody to see you."

The prisoner was lying on his bunk. He rose and stood for a moment blinking to banish sleep from his eyes.

Peebles wasted no time.

"Whar's that gal of yourn?" he demanded.

"What do you mean?"

"She skipped out last night, that's what. You must know whar she's hid."

Buckstone's reaction was not joy but consternation.

"You mean Prudence is gone?" he cried. "What's happened to her?"

"Yes, she's gone, I told you," said Peebles. "You goin' to tell me whar?"

"What have you done to her? Has she come to harm? Have you allowed her to be carried away——?"

"Don't play innocent with me! I ain't no fool. You must've

had a hand in it somehow. She wouldn't of gone off on her own. She had help, didn't she? Somebody you sent, ain't that so? Now jest lemme tell you somethin'—that gal's indentured to me, an' I'm goin' to git her back. If you don't tell me whar she is, I'll keep you in this jail till you rot, to show you what happens to a man that tampers with the law!"

"I tell you I know nothing about this! In the interests of humanity, Mr. Peebles, let me out of here so that I can help in the search for my daughter!"

So obviously shocked and filled with concern was Buckstone, that Peebles left him in disgust. Already the tavern man had another thought. He knew of the friendship between Prudence and Miss Sally Quintal, the sewing woman. Straight to the little cabin at the foot of the street he went.

"What've you done with Prudence Buckstone?" was his first question when Miss Sally came to the door.

"Why—" Miss Sally was at a loss. "She's at your tavern."

"No, she ain't. She's left. Whar'd you tell her to go?"

"I told her nothing. I've had no chance to talk with Prudence. That wife of yours saw to that. I can't imagine—" She looked at him. "Does her father know about this?"

"He shore does. An' won't say nothin'. But I'll git it out of him. You got her hid somewheres?"

An angry spark was in Miss Sally's eyes. "I have not. But let me tell you this, Mr. Drew Peebles. If I *could* help that poor child, I would! And I'm glad she's gone. As for Colonel Buckstone, he's twice the man even in prison that you are swaggering around this street! And as for that awful creature you call your wife—Prudence is worth a hundred of her, and you can tell her that for me! And as for the both of you, I wouldn't spit on either of you, and you can take that back and think about it while you spend your time like a fat toad killing flies!"

One glance had shown Peebles that she could hardly have hidden a mouse in that small cabin. He fled from her as fast as he could lumber away, knowing that a man can never match a woman in this sort of tirade.

Besides, by this time he had decided that he must at once

consult his attorney, Ezekiel Rockcastle. Several matters required immediate discussion with that sharp-witted, if something less than scrupulous, lawyer.

3.

Almost never in her life before had Miss Sally engaged in vituperation such as that which she showered on Peebles. But as she tied on her bonnet, her eyes were still stormy, and she was glad that she had spoken her mind to that pompous swine. Perhaps there might be trouble in this for her, but if so, she would bear it. At least she had routed Drew Peebles. In this mood she hurried at once to the jail.

Buckstone, unshaved and unwashed, was sitting on the edge of his bunk, his head in his hands, when he heard his name called at the window of his cell. He recognized the voice. It was Miss Sally and he did not wish at that moment to talk to Miss Sally. The news he had just received concerning his daughter seemed the very peak of his misfortunes. Bitterness and a sense of helplessness alike corroded his feelings. But the habit of courtesy caused him to rise slowly and go over to the barred window.

Seeing him from the ground below, Miss Sally was shocked and alarmed at his appearance. There seemed little resemblance between the handsome and urbane Colonel Buckstone whom she knew, and this disheveled and ravaged creature. But the change in him did not cause her to recoil. Her whole concern was for him.

"You've heard," he said.

"Yes."

"I had hoped she might have taken refuge with you."

"She didn't come near me," she said. "She must have known they would at once seek her at my house—which they did."

"That's true," he agreed somberly. "She had no other friend but you in this God-forsaken place. They won't permit me even to help in the search for her."

"Where could she have gone?"

"Miss Sally, could it be that in her despair she ran off somewhere—to die?"

"Oh—no——" She protested.

"It's possible. There are limits of humiliation which even she, child as she is, would not undergo. Some day—perhaps—they'll find all that's left of her——"

She refused to admit this. Yet the hopelessness in his voice created an answering loss of hope in her.

Their conversation was brief. Her thoughts were chiefly on him; his thoughts wholly on his daughter.

So, unhappily, she said goodbye and returned to her home.

Next day two printed handbills were posted on the wall of Hume's store. The topmost read:

$50 Reward

Ran away from the plantation of
Lassiter Bros. a negro man, Jeff,
about 30 yrs. old, brown skin,
wt. about 170 lbs., ht. 5 ft. 11 in.,
square face, scar on inside of rt.
arm, 2 teeth missing in rt. side
of mouth.

Wilbert Melton, Overseer.

Below it was another, smaller handbill:

Notice

Prudence Buckstone, legalled indentured
servant of Drew Peebles, runaway.
Description, white, female, age 17 years,
blue eyes, light hair, well featured,
last seen in a brown homespun dress.
$25 will be paid for arrest and return
of this party by subscriber.

Drew Peebles.

When Miss Sally read the notices she was glad that Buckstone could not see this demeaning juxtaposition of his daughter
with a runaway slave.

On the following day a heavy rainstorm with a high wind
came sweeping down from the mountains. It was the storm
that had caused Prudence such misery and illness; and it brought
with it to Turkeytoe the cold that had caused Miss Sally, in
her cabin that night, to worry about the man in the wretched
jail cell with so little to keep him warm. She resolved on the
morrow to carry to him a bed quilt.

4.

Buckstone spent a miserable night. By morning the rain had
abated, but water stood in chill pools in every depression; and
the cold was such that he wrapped his single blanket about his
shoulders when he went to his window to look out.

The sheriff, bringing the tin platter of boiled beans that was
his breakfast, unlocked the door of the jail. As he entered the
corridor between the cells Buckstone heard shouting up the
street beyond.

"What's the yelling about?" he asked.

"Likely they've jest heard about Dr. Lassiter bein' killed,"
said the sheriff. "I jest got word of it myself."

"Dr. Lassiter—*killed?* How?"

"Murdered an' robbed, they say. His hoss, saddled an'
bridled, was found near a farm place, a few mile east of hyar.
Cap'n Lassiter, his brother, was sent for an' they made a search.
Somebody noticed a convention of buzzards in the woods an'
investigated. Then they found Dr. Lassiter covered up with bresh.
His face was purty badly eaten by the buzzards, but Cap'n
Lassiter identified him all right by his clothes an' a day book in
his pocket. He'd been shot through the heart. Everythin' of value
was took from him. The body's bein' brung back to be buried on
the plantation."

"This is dreadful!" exclaimed Buckstone. "Dr. Lassiter was a gentleman and fine citizen. I hope they run the murderers down!"

"I reckon they'll try," was the sheriff's comment.

"Are you doing anything officially?"

"How kin I? I got nothin' to work on. You want me to waste the county's money by gittin' up a posse an' bushwhackin' the woods without nothin' to go on? Hit might not even be in my district—the thing happened right on the Tennessee-Kentucky line."

"Take this mess away," said Buckstone. "I'm not hungry."

The sheriff scowled, but he carried the dish back to his quarters. Buckstone, considering the sheriff's apparent lack of interest in the crime, thought that it was oddly similar to his lack of interest at the time of the death of Homer Phipps.

News of such moment quite naturally became the chief subject of talk and speculation in Turkeytoe. Bad 'Lias Blevins had reappeared in town after an absence of some days, though his brother was not with him. The big ruffian was sober, not drinking at all, a condition most unusual for him. He listened with apparent interest to all discussions of the murder, but offered no theories concerning it.

That afternoon Troy Lassiter brought his brother's body back in a rough box carried in a mule-drawn cart. He did not pause in the town but rode directly through.

Miss Sally saw the grim little procession, Lassiter and two other men on horseback, a Negro driving the mule that pulled the cart with the box. She was on her way to the jail to give Buckstone one of her own beautiful patchwork quilts.

She could just reach the folded end of it up to him; and when he thanked her she told him about seeing Lassiter.

"They say burial is to take place as soon as they reach the plantation," she said. "I saw Captain Lassiter's face. Some people commented that it bore a black look of rage. I thought instead it might have been a look of terrible grief."

"He thought a great deal of his brother," said Buckstone. "I don't think he will let this matter rest."

She agreed that Troy Lassiter would leave nothing undone to bring the murderers to justice, and after a few more words she said farewell and departed.

Next morning Buckstone had a different visitor: no less a personage than the prosecuting attorney, Ezekiel Rockcastle. He was admitted to the jail corridor by Sheriff Taney, and when he entered it he looked around with a fastidious wrinkle of his lengthy nose.

"The surroundings are none too pleasant here," he said to no one in particular.

Buckstone, who had risen at the appearance of his caller, did not trouble to answer. The place stank and nobody knew it better than he. His face was covered by a bristle of unshaved whiskers and his attire was wrinkled and foul.

Rockcastle seemed undisturbed by the lack of response.

"Bring me a chair," he said to Taney.

When the article of furniture was brought, he seated himself upon it. To the sheriff he said, "You may be excused now, to go about your no doubt heavy duties."

Taney, who had almost nothing to do, did not resent this sarcasm, but retired as directed.

When he was gone, Rockcastle gazed through the bars at Buckstone. "I've been thinking over your situation," he said, in a manner surprisingly pleasant. "It seems too bad for you to be shut up here—especially with the disappearance of your daughter."

Buckstone came over toward him and seized the bars with his hands. "If I could only get out of here!" he exclaimed.

"It might be arranged."

The prisoner was astonished. "How?"

"In exchange for a small concession from you, Peebles might drop his claims against you."

Buckstone stepped back. "What concession, sir?"

"It's rather ridiculous, when you think of it," said the lawyer smoothly. "He merely wants you to sign a paper making over to him your interest in that land you formerly claimed as your property."

"My interest in it? I have none."

"Of course not." Rockcastle smiled indulgently. "That's what makes the whole thing rather meaningless. The property, as we both know, is worthless without a valid title. I pointed this out to Peebles. But Peebles, between ourselves, is a peculiar man, and a stubborn man. Snuff?"

He offered his snuffbox, but Buckstone waved it aside. The lawyer took a pinch, dusted from his shirt ruffles the particles that had fallen there, and returned the snuffbox to his pocket.

"He owns," said Rockcastle, "fifty acres that he bought from you—or he did own it before this difficulty arose. Now in his bullheaded way he wants to gamble, hoping perhaps to obtain title on it by exchange, or litigation, or otherwise. But fifty acres is hardly worth fighting for."

Rockcastle drew a handkerchief from his coattail pocket and blew his nose vigorously.

"You, obviously, have not the money to attempt such an action," he went on. "It would be costly and might require a considerable space of time, besides being at best unlikely of consummation. I've advised Peebles against it, but he has some resources and is resolved to make the attempt—if he could control enough acreage to make it worth while." He grinned like a lizard. "He feels that the total acreage to which you formerly had claim—in other words, your three hundred and twenty acres of bounty land, plus your thousand acres of government purchase minus the fifty acres he bought from you, making a total of one thousand two hundred and seventy acres—might make it worthy of the gamble. Therefore he has empowered me to offer you a complete discharge of all your debts to him, amounting to two hundred and sixty-one dollars, with interest at eight percent, and also he agrees to assume all court and attorney fees—which come to a fair figure—thus allowing you to go free from prison. This will enable you to search for your daughter, concerning whom, I regret to say, there's still no word. In exchange for this highly generous offer, you are to grant him all your interests in the entire acreage you once claimed—which I need hardly remind you are not worth a plugged nickel."

Slowly, Buckstone assimilated this astonishing proposal. Then another thought came.

"What about Prudence—if she is found?"

"I'm glad you brought that up." Again Rockcastle smiled. "As a further concession, to show you his goodwill, Peebles has agreed to withdraw any and all claims of servitude he may have against your daughter."

Buckstone walked across the cell to the barred window. After the stormy weather the sun was shining and the sky was blue. His lungs fairly ached for the fresh air of outdoors.

But why, he asked himself, should Drew Peebles be willing to make such an extraordinary offer? Did he possess some secret knowledge that made him willing to risk negotiation with the heirs for the entire property?

Buckstone could not believe that Peebles—or Rockcastle, for that matter—had any particular "goodwill" toward him. But in his present mood it made little difference. He wanted to be free, on any terms, to try to find his daughter.

Turning to the lawyer he said, "Draw up the papers. I'll sign them."

"A wise decision," said Rockcastle with his dry grin. He called for the sheriff and left the jail.

5.

Hardly five minutes after the departure of the lawyer Buckstone again heard voices outside the jail.

"I want to see him in his cell and in private." It was Troy Lassiter speaking.

"What for?" came the sheriff's voice.

"Because I have something to discuss with him. Can you read, Taney? If so, you will recognize this as a commission signed by Governor William Carroll giving me authority as a special justice of the peace; my authority is from the State Supreme Court. This authorizes me to enter all jails in Tennessee and talk to prisoners, as you well know. If you refuse this request, which is legitimate, I'll take it as far as Nashville for an order from the Supreme Court."

The sheriff had some inkling of the reluctance in certain quarters to have a review by the state authorities. Furthermore, the rank Lassiter had displayed did empower him as he had stated.

A key grated in the outside door of the jail and the sheriff appeared in the corridor with Lassiter.

"This all right?" he said.

"It will do," said Lassiter.

"I'll have to lock you in."

"Then stay within call, for I'll not be long."

The sheriff left the jail and the outside door clanged shut as he locked Troy Lassiter in the corridor.

Buckstone had been wishing to see the young man; he had in fact asked Miss Sally to convey a message to that effect. But now he found himself strangely diffident, almost hesitant in his presence. In that moment he saw in the younger man the things he himself was not. Lassiter was a man of action; this contrasted with Buckstone's feeling of his own ineffectuality. He wore a black coat and about the right arm was a band of black crepe. Considering him, Buckstone mentally noted that though he was tall and lean, he was square shouldered and square chinned, and he had a way of looking a man in the eye when he spoke to him that suggested a mind direct and forceful. He was a natural leader, perhaps—a man whose friendship was not lightly given, but once given was firm. The older man envied this native force in the other. And after the unpleasant presence of Rockcastle, Lassiter seemed wholesome and refreshing by comparison. But even when he greeted the prisoner the younger man's face did not light up.

He said, "I'm here—perhaps, sir, you think I come late."

"I have no right to question your comings or goings——"

"I've been away for several days; on business of importance—of great importance I assure you. Latterly I have been much occupied because of my brother's death. His murder, I should say."

"A shocking thing. A terrible thing," said Buckstone.

"Terrible, it is true, sir. The last of my blood, save myself." The young man raised his eyes. "What I started to say to you is that because of—of these various matters—I only just a few hours ago learned of your circumstances . . . and those of Miss Prudence."

"Do you know that she's disappeared?" asked Buckstone. "Poor child—she's gone, nobody knows where!"

Lassiter looked him straight in the eye.

"Have you ever seen these?" he asked. From a small bundle he took a pair of blue embroidered lady's slippers, and in his hands they looked small and dainty—and very feminine.

Buckstone took them. "Why—yes," he said. "They belong to my daughter. I bought them for her the very day I was arrested—" He broke off. "Where did you find them, sir?"

"I was hoping," said the other, "that you'd *not* recognize them."

"Why?"

"If these are hers, I fear I may have heavy news for you."

"Give it to me." Buckstone seemed to brace himself.

"When we found my brother—that is, his body—I scouted that vicinity with two other men trying to discover anything that might help identify the murderers. The search brought us to a limestone cave in the side of a cliff in the woods. It had been occupied quite recently—there were ashes of a fire, some scraps of food, and a frying pan such as campers use, with the grease still in it."

"Yes?"

"I also found, sir, in a corner there—well, those slippers. They were contained in this small parcel. Here, look at it."

With trembling fingers Buckstone opened the little bundle that Prudence had carried.

"This is her comb," he said. "I believe these other things are hers also." He looked up in sudden dread. "Prudence must have been in that cave. Was there—anything else?"

In a bleak voice Lassiter answered, "Yes, sir. There was a large pool of blood on the stone floor of the cave near the entrance. It had dried but was still quite fresh."

"Prudence . . . ?"

"I don't know, but—I fear——"

"Did you look for a—a body?"

"Yes, sir. We combed that area thoroughly. But there had been a hard rainstorm the day before and we found nothing. If there's a grave—or any other trace—we didn't discover it."

Buckstone sank down on the edge of his bunk as if his legs were deprived of their strength.

"I'm profoundly sorry," said Lassiter.

Buckstone gave a half sob. "It's hard to—accept the thought —even harder to get accustomed to it——"

"Hard for me, also." Lassiter hesitated. "I admired your daughter, sir."

"Yes . . . everyone admired her," said Buckstone brokenly. "Have you any idea who . . . ?"

"Only this. The cave is within half a mile of the place where my brother was murdered. In my heart I believe the two Blevinses murdered him." He gulped. "And perhaps—Miss Prudence, also." He paused and added savagely, "If I could find the guilty ones, sir!"

A change came over Buckstone. It was as if, deprived of hope for his daughter, he somehow gained in will and courage.

"Do you know that Elias Blevins is in Turkeytoe now?" he asked.

"No!" said Lassiter in genuine surprise.

"I was so informed—by a friend." Buckstone did not say that the friend was Miss Sally, who had seen the hulking ruffian on the street. "If my daughter is dead she must have been murdered by the same devils who murdered your brother. I believe like you that the Blevins brothers are the prime suspects, and I'm the more convinced by another circumstance. You know of the maiming and death of the half-witted boy, Homer Phipps?"

"Yes."

"I heard Elias Blevins propose that brutal crime. Later, after I was thrown into this prison, I learned of Homer's fate and denounced Blevins to the prosecutor."

"What did Rockcastle say?"

"He contemptuously reminded me that Blevins at least paid his debts—a sneer at my condition."

For a moment Lassiter was silent. Then he said, "I'd consider it a privilege, sir, to personally discharge your debt to Peebles ——"

"Thank you, but I don't want that from you."

"A loan only—it's a bitter shame to hold a man like you in prison for such a petty sum——"

Buckstone shook his head. "Not even a loan, sir."

"But it would be an accommodation easy for me to arrange, sir——"

Buckstone folded his arms and walked to the opposite side of the cell. He stood for a moment as if in some sort of inner turmoil and then turned once more to Lassiter.

"You must allow a man his pride, sir. There's a principle involved here. The law allowing imprisonment for debt is nothing less than a blackmailing measure. It is iniquitous and unjust. In effect, Drew Peebles would be dipping into your pocket because of this hold which he has on me."

Lassiter remained silent.

"I will not deny," Buckstone went on, "that before the news you've just brought me—about my child—I might have been tempted. But as things stand please allow me to remain where I am—at least until certain matters become clear."

"May I ask what matters, sir?"

"This morning," said the prisoner, "Rockcastle made me the strangest proposal. In a nutshell: if I'll sign a paper relinquishing to Drew Peebles all my interests—which are worthless—in the land I once held, now claimed by the Philadelphia heirs, Peebles will discharge my debts to him, withdraw any claims of servitude against my daughter, and I will be set free to search for her."

Lassiter glanced at him sharply.

"Are you wondering," went on Buckstone, "as I'm wondering at this moment, if perhaps Peebles—and even Rockcastle—knew that Prudence was dead before they made that offer?"

The younger man's look was intensely speculative. "They could only learn that from the murderers themselves!"

"Which indicates a connection of some kind. You hinted at something of this nature to me the morning that your two horses were stolen—the morning I was arrested."

Lassiter gave him a straight look. "I hope you'll say nothing about that conversation."

Buckstone returned the look with one as level. "You can be certain of that."

"At the risk of offering unwanted advice——"

"Advice from you I'll always listen to," said Buckstone.

"Then, don't sign any documents presented to you by or for Peebles."

"I won't—I've already decided."

Lassiter called for the sheriff and departed.

After he was gone Buckstone strangely had a lift of confidence. The reason was his realization that his land after all must have importance, therefore he was perhaps not such a pathetic fool as he had thought himself in being tricked by Peebles and Rockcastle. The enhanced status of his land enhanced his opinion of himself. It was a small comfort, but it was the only one that Buckstone knew that day.

Chapter 13

1.

When Rockcastle returned to the jail an hour later, Buckstone was restlessly pacing his cell.

"It took you long enough," he said when the lawyer was admitted to the cell.

"I came as speedily as possible. The transfers of title had to be drawn up in triplicate for your signature." Rockcastle offered the papers.

"This is about as long a document as the warrant on which I was arrested," said Buckstone grimly as he examined one of the transfers.

Rockcastle laughed humoringly. "If you wish to make that your standard of comparison, perhaps so. But these instruments, as you see, are quite different in context."

"But why did it take so long?" insisted Buckstone.

"Well, you see, George Rivers, the court clerk, who wrote these up, is an extremely careful penman. Observe the uniformity of his letters, the exactitude of the lines, the whole general

219

artistic effect of the calligraphy. George is a perfectionist. It takes him not less than fifteen minutes to turn out a beautiful page like that."

"*Always*—for a page of this length?"

"Always. He will not be hurried." Rockcastle was impatient. "Let's to business. We're not here to discuss the penmanship of George Rivers or anyone else, are we? I've brought pen and ink. All you need to do is sign these transfers in triplicate. After that I'll deliver to you Mr. Peebles' complete written discharge of all your obligations to him, including any claims he may have on your daughter's services——"

"Mr. Rockcastle, my daughter is dead."

At Buckstone's tone when he delivered this statement, the lawyer seemed startled. "Why—what do you mean, sir?"

"I have here all her earthly possessions," said Buckstone still in that hard voice. "All, that is to say, which the poor unhappy child had left to her after Peebles—*and his attorney*—got through with her. They were found in a cave near the place where the body of Dr. Lassiter was discovered. There was blood on the floor of that cave. My daughter, Mr. Rockcastle, like Dr. Lassiter, has been brutally murdered!"

Buckstone's eyes seemed to bore into the lawyer's. Rockcastle suddenly became nervous.

"Now, wait a minute," he said. "Let's not jump to conclusions. Where did you get these articles?"

"They were delivered to me less than an hour ago by Captain Lassiter."

The lawyer looked at the floor as if debating something in his own mind.

"Lassiter," he said at last. "Perhaps Lassiter found articles in a cave, but is there any other evidence that anything has happened to your daughter?"

"None that Captain Lassiter could furnish." Buckstone's face was stern. "Can you perhaps furnish it—from your own knowledge?"

"My own knowledge? Of course not! You're mad! What knowledge could I possibly have?"

"From Elias Blevins, perhaps?"

"What do you mean by that, sir?"

"That I believe you are in that man's confidence, perhaps advising him legally, and protecting him—as in the Homer Phipps case—for reasons of your own."

"This is insulting and outrageous!" exclaimed Rockcastle. "You're making a libelous accusation against an officer of this county, sir! Enough of it, sir! I'll have you know that there are means of punishing such slanders!"

His voice was unnecessarily loud and threatening. Buckstone, on the other hand, was coldly silent.

"Do you want to sign these papers and be released from jail, or not?" asked Rockcastle angrily.

"I do not."

"You mean that you prefer to remain in this stinking cell?"

"Some questions have been turning over in my mind, Mr. Rockcastle. I prefer to sign nothing."

"Then rot here!"

The lawyer shouted to the sheriff to unlock the door, and flung out of the jail.

2.

Ezekiel Rockcastle had two offices: one in the courthouse, where he conducted his official business for the county, and the other on the main street of Turkeytoe, in a small two-room building, where he carried on his private practice.

Later that same day Troy Lassiter entered the anteroom of Rockcastle's private office. He found the prosecutor already in conference—with Drew Peebles, in the inner office.

"Just a minute, Captain," called the lawyer through the open door. "Please be seated. I'll be only briefly occupied."

But Lassiter did not take a seat. He waited, standing erect, his black eyes and dark face still and strangely watchful.

Shortly Peebles came out of the inner office, gave Lassiter a surly nod, and left.

"Pray come in, Captain Lassiter," said Rockcastle. "Please be seated. Now, what can I do for you?"

Again Lassiter preferred to remain standing. "I want you to issue a warrant against Elias Blevins," he said.

The prosecutor darted a sharp glance at him. "On what charge?"

"Murder."

"You have evidence that Elias Blevins has committed a murder?"

"I can produce evidence that he planned the mutilation of Homer Phipps. And I believe that he murdered my brother. And perhaps Prudence Buckstone as well."

"You have witnesses to any of these crimes?"

"Not exactly. But with your cooperation, as prosecuting attorney, I think the truth can be brought out."

Rockcastle sat back and placed his hands, the fingers of each touching the corresponding fingers of the other, before him.

"This is a serious step you're proposing, Captain Lassiter," he said. "As prosecuting attorney I must have something definite to proceed upon—" He broke off and an odd little flicker came into his eyes. "On the other hand," he resumed smoothly, "I have no right, have I, to deny the issuance of a warrant? Especially when it is requested by a man of standing like yourself. Will you sign the complaint when it is drawn up, Captain?"

"I will, sir."

3.

An hour later the populace of Turkeytoe had a new sensation.

Bad 'Lias Blevins, as usual standing with his cronies in front of the groggery owned by Drew Peebles, was approached by Sheriff Dode Taney.

" 'Lias," said Taney with considerable diffidence, "could I see you jest a minute?"

Blevins shifted his tobacco quid in his jaw and went over to the sheriff.

"Understand this, 'Lias," said Taney with a note of pleading apology, "I got nothin' personal ag'in you. I'm jest follerin' orders."

"Yeah?" said Blevins, expectorating a stream of tobacco juice on the back of a passing dog. "Wall, I hain't got nothin' ag'in you, neither."

"Mr. Rockcastle told me to serve this warrant on you, 'Lias." The sheriff, with marked trepidation, displayed a written document.

To his surprise and relief Blevins showed neither astonishment nor resentment. He asked, "You mean you're arrestin' me?"

"Wall, yes, 'Lias. Now, please let's don't have no fuss——"

Blevins' single eye had almost a twinkle in it. "I ain't makin' no fuss. Come on, let's go."

The knot of loafers, who had expected Bad 'Lias to fly into a fury, perhaps even assault the sheriff, looked on gap-jawed at this tame surrender. Only when Taney and Blevins went off together did they awake from their astonishment sufficiently to follow the officer and his "prisoner."

In the courtroom the huge ruffian stood before old Judge Redding, with that almost quizzical gleam still in his one good eye.

"May it please the court," said Rockcastle, who was present as prosecuting attorney, "the prisoner before the bar is Elias Blevins. Mr. Blevins is a long-time resident of this community, and he appears here willingly, with no effort to resist or escape arrest, to answer certain charges made against him."

The judge steadied his jaw with his hand. "What are the charges?"

"The warrant contains two sections," said the prosecutor. "In the first, Mr. Blevins is accused of conspiracy and participation in a mayhem committed upon the person of one Homer Phipps, who later was found dead in the river. In the second section, Mr. Blevins is accused of the murder of Dr. Tracy Lassiter."

"What say you to these charges, Mr. Blevins?" asked the judge.

"I say I don't know nothin' about them," said Bad 'Lias. "I'm innocent."

"Let the record show that the prisoner pleads not guilty," said the judge to George Rivers, the clerk of the court.

"Your Honor," said Bad 'Lias, "since them charges has been made ag'in me, I demands a 'mediate trial by jury."

The crowd in the courtroom was astonished at this surprising development.

"Mr. Rockcastle?" inquired the judge.

"The State sees no objection to this request," said the prosecutor. "In fact, it is his right under the Constitution, the Sixth Amendment of which specifically states that in all criminal prosecutions the accused shall enjoy the right to a speedy and public trial by an impartial jury. The State therefore accedes to the request of the defendant."

Judge Redding, chin in hand, considered for a moment. "In that case," he said in his old voice, "the prisoner will be held for trial at the earliest possible date."

"Tomorrow, perhaps, your Honor?" asked Rockcastle. "I'm informed by Mr. Blevins that his affairs make demands upon his time. With the court's indulgence, I suggest that he be placed under bail to appear in this court at the hour your Honor may decide."

The judge nodded. "Set the hearing for tomorrow morning. The bail will be five hundred dollars."

A portly figure heaved itself up from one of the courtroom seats and Drew Peebles went forward.

"I have known this gentleman for many years," he said. "I'll be glad to sign his bond. And," he added smugly, "everybody knows I'm good for it."

A spectator in one of the rear seats of the courtroom had a strange feeling that all this went too smoothly to seem natural. Miss Sally Quintal had slipped in late and attracted no attention. She had small understanding of the processes of the law, but to her this seemed arranged, perhaps rehearsed, before it took place. Without previous legal advice, Elias Blevins would hardly

have demanded an immediate trial by jury. He would not have
known enough to do so.

Judge Redding also seemed to have been coached in his
role. The easy acquiescence of the prosecutor to the "demands"
of the accused and the prompt posting of the bail by Drew
Peebles, all had the appearance of being stage-managed. Miss Sally
wished she could talk to someone about it. She thought of going
to see Buckstone, but decided that a conversation conducted
through the jail window was too public for a voicing of her
doubts and queries.

4.

Jurisprudence, never at a high level on the frontier, perhaps
reached a record low in the trial of Elias Blevins.

Early next morning Troy Lassiter, summoned from his home,
appeared in Turkeytoe. He held a brief conference with the
prosecutor, and came from that meeting with a face that seemed
uncertain and puzzled, expressions most unusual for him.

Before court opened he called upon Miss Sally.

"I understand you were in court yesterday," he said as he
stood hat in hand before her door.

She told him what she had seen, and expressed her feelings
about the strangely smooth progress of events. "Mr. Blevins didn't
even have a lawyer," she remarked.

"He didn't need one," said Lassiter bitterly. "The prosecutor
and the court were both on his side. It looks like a mock trial.
I had a notion not to be present, but then I changed my mind.
If they're going to make a farce of justice, I want to be there to
witness it."

Before he left he asked her if she would attend the hearing.

"I intend to," said Miss Sally.

He gave her a nod. "Then there'll be two of us who are on
the side of justice."

Before nine o'clock the seamstress put on her bonnet and

managed to get a seat in the rear of the courtroom. The trial of
Blevins was delayed for a few minutes by the settlement of a
bastardy case—a frequent court matter of the times.

In the front sat a young country girl, thin and pathetic
looking, with her new baby, to which at one time, quite without
any self-consciousness, she gave a breast with the whole courtroom looking on. Beside her was her father, a lanky, whiskered
individual with a hollow chest and a cough. The defendant was
a young man who Miss Sally thought seemed reckless and lazy,
though perhaps not vicious.

"I call Vince Dow to the stand," said the prosecutor.

The defendant complied and seated himself on the chair
indicated.

"Did you," asked Rockcastle, "at any time or place, have
carnal knowledge of this woman, Liddie Cluny?"

"Have whut?" asked the defendant, obviously at a loss.

"I'll put it another way. Did you engage in sexual commerce
with the plaintiff in this case?"

A light seemed to dawn on the young man. "If you mean
did I rooster her, I got to admit I done so. But thar aren't no
commerce in it, becuz as I understand it thar's money exchanged
in commerce. This here was as free as the air."

A giggle went through the courtroom.

"Tell the court when this took place," said Rockcastle.

"I reckon it was at Apply's cornhuskin'. Fellers told me she
was a good lay. She went out inter the bushes with me easy
enough, an' she *was* a good lay. We went back to the barn an'
shucked some more corn, an' purty soon she sidles up to me an'
wants to go out ag'in. We done so. Then later that evenin' we
went out a third time. Towards the end of the shuckin' she begs
me to take her out for a fourth time. I never seen a gal so plumb
eager an' hankerin', jedge. Wall, I went with her that fourth time,
but I was so tuckered out I couldn't do neither of us no good.
I jest couldn't make it."

There was a roar of laughter at this involuntary admission
and the judge rapped for order.

No smile crossed Rockcastle's face. "The plaintiff, Miss

Cluny, says that you caused her to become pregnant and are the father of her child," he said imperturbably.

"She's jest sayin' that," said the defendant. "They was plenty of others had her. All you got to do is drag your wing at that gal, an' she'll ruffle up her feathers an' spread out her tail."

Rockcastle allowed the courtroom to get its laugh out of this quaint reference to the tactics of a rooster and a hen just before copulation. Then, with impassive face, he moved that it be stricken from the record.

Miss Sally, watching the girl's face, could not tell whether she was embarrassed by the accusations of the young man or not. Part of the time she bent her head over the baby, and at other times she simply looked blank. Evidently she was an easy mark, but the baby in her arms was a reality that the court could not ignore.

Old Judge Redding rested his jaw on his hand and said, "Can you name someone else who might have been the father of this child?"

"Wall," said the defendant, "I know some of the other boys that claims to of had her, but—" He hesitated, then he said, "When a gal runs through a brier patch, how kin you tell which thorn stuck the deepest?"

Another delighted laugh from the crowd.

But the court went into the statistics of the case. The date of Apply's cornhusking bee was established, and the date of the birth of the child in question was known. With the nine-month interval thus shown, evidence was all against the defendant.

"In the presence of this testimony," said the judge, "you are the undoubted father of this child. You therefore must contribute to its support. The judgment of this court is that you shall indemnify this mother by the sum of one hundred dollars, plus costs, which will be ten dollars more."

"I cain't pay that, your Honor," protested the defendant. "I ain't got that kind of money."

"The court will issue a lien on your present assets and your future earnings until this indemnity is satisfied."

Now the father, whose name was Hoke Cluny, rose and

asked that he also should receive some money, for the "loss of his daughter's services" during her accouchement. The judge, however, lectured him severely.

"You are censurable for not keeping a closer eye on your daughter," he said. "Any remuneration to you is denied."

The case, having thus been handled according to frontier notions of justice and propriety, was finished. The girl with her baby, her father, and the accused young man all left the courtroom together. Miss Sally noticed that even after what he had said against her the girl gave Vince Dow a coy smile as they departed.

A woman next to Miss Sally whispered, "With that hundred an' ten dollars hangin' over him, I reckon Vince Dow might think it cheaper to marry Liddie."

"Yes," said another woman with a grin. "They've made their crop. Now they'll build a fence around it."

5.

Immediately after the bastardy case, which required no more than thirty minutes, there was a stir in the courtroom as Bad 'Lias entered it in company with Sheriff Taney.

Miss Sally observed that he was sober and clean-shaven for once, and somewhat more decently clad than usual, though he was chewing tobacco. He had again employed no lawyer to uphold his case, for when he took his seat at the defense table, his only companion there was the sheriff in whose custody he was supposed to be.

Bad 'Lias appeared unconcerned. He looked around the courtroom confidently, grinned at friends he saw, and showed rather adept marksmanship in hitting a spittoon some feet away with a brown ejection of tobacco juice.

During the previous afternoon the sheriff had busied himself rounding up jurors: a task of no great difficulty since the town was full of idlers who were quite willing to accept the juror's fee of a dollar a day for doing nothing but sitting and listening to the trial—which they would have sat and listened to anyway, for nothing. In thirty minutes after the case was opened the "twelve good men and true" were seated in the jury box and sworn in; and it made no difference to the judge or to the prosecuting attorney that not one man on the panel could either read or write, or that many of them were known friends of the accused.

Every eye was upon the principal figures in the drama about to be unfolded: particularly on Blevins, huge and tobacco chewing, and on Troy Lassiter, who wore a band of crepe about the arm of his long-tailed black coat and took a seat beside Rockcastle as the chief witness for the prosecution. Miss Sally, sitting with some of the curious women at the back, thought that the young man seemed uneasy and at a loss this morning.

Prosecutor Rockcastle rose. "May it please the court," he said, "inasmuch as there are two separate charges against the defendant in this case, the State moves, for the court's convenience, that the charges be heard separately."

Judge Redding massaged his jaw. "So ordered," he said.

Rockcastle took out his snuffbox, helped himself to a sniff of the stimulating powder, blew his prominent nose in his handkerchief and, as usual, dusted a few crumbs of snuff from his shirt front.

"Captain Lassiter," he said, when these operations were concluded, "I believe you swore to the warrant upon which the accused was arrested?"

"I did," said Lassiter.

"You of course had evidence upon which to base the accusation?"

Troy Lassiter seemed surprised. "Am I supposed to produce the witness?"

"I would say, sir, that if you can, you must."

Lassiter looked at the judge. "Your Honor, I'm not prepared for this. I thought it was the State which produced the witnesses." He hesitated. "However, if you're going to consider first the case involving the late Homer Phipps, there are two witnesses who should be called. I am not one of them."

"Who are they?" asked Rockcastle, without giving the judge time to reply.

"Reedy Halcutt and Bion B. Buckstone, sir."

"I believe that Mr. Halcutt is in the courtroom," said Rockcastle. "Mr. Sheriff, will you go to the jail and bring up Buckstone?"

There was a delay while the officer was gone, and Miss Sally observed that during this time Rockcastle conferred in a low voice with the old judge, who leaned a large ear toward him and caressed his chin with his hand.

When the sheriff appeared with Buckstone, necks were craned and Miss Sally felt acute pity. He was unkempt and seedy, with a grizzled growth of unshaved beard and uncombed hair. Why did they have to humiliate him so in bringing him before all these people without permitting him to make himself presentable? Her heart went out to him; he seemed to feel the shame of such an appearance, for he looked neither to the right nor the left as he went forward.

"Take the witness stand," said the prosecutor.

Buckstone was sworn.

"You are called as a witness in the case of the State of Tennessee versus Elias Blevins," began Rockcastle. "Have you any knowledge of the circumstances surrounding the death of Homer Phipps?"

"Yes, sir, I do," said Buckstone. "I heard Blevins threaten to emasculate that poor boy——"

"Threaten?" interrupted the prosecutor. "In what manner?"

"He said to a crowd of men, 'We ought to ketch him some night an' jest simply cut his balls out.'" Buckstone imitated quite creditably the defendant's peculiarities of speech.

"Do I understand," said Rockcastle, placing his fingertips together before him and rocking back and forth on his toes and heels, "that Mr. Blevins said it *ought* to be done, or that he *would do* it?"

"My recollection," answered Buckstone truthfully, "is that he said it ought to be done. But," he added, "he said it in such a manner that it seemed to me he was stirring up the crowd to some such action——"

"That is a conclusion," interrupted the judge, "and not admissible as testimony. This court is not interested in what *seemed* to be the case, only in what actually *was* the case."

"I beg your Honor's pardon," said Buckstone. "I was only trying to re-create the conversation as it occurred."

"Then proceed, and bear the injunction in mind."

"Yes, your Honor. After these statements I intervened and told Blevins and the others that what they contemplated was against the law, it being the crime of mayhem."

"And to this what did Mr. Blevins reply?" asked the prosecutor.

"He became threatening toward me."

"But he did not state positively that he seriously intended to perform such an act himself?"

"No—not exactly——"

"That's all, Mr. Buckstone." Rockcastle turned toward the bench.

"But I just wanted to say—" began Buckstone.

"The witness will stand down," said the judge.

Buckstone was plainly disconcerted and angry when he left the witness chair. He had been given no opportunity to bring up what he considered to be important points in the case, including the prosecutor's refusal to investigate the crime. At once he was conducted back to the jail by the sheriff. As he went he caught Miss Sally's eye. He made a gesture that to her seemed to be one of apology or disgust, as if he was sorry that she had witnessed the humiliating episode.

Reedy Halcutt, the farmer who had employed Homer Phipps, and upon whose complaint the youth was arrested, was next called. He added nothing to the testimony. The most he appeared able to say was that he had "heerd some talk of one kind or 'nother," but he could not testify that anybody had suggested direct action of any kind. Under Rockcastle's questioning he even appeared unable to remember that Blevins, specifically, had done the talking. To Miss Sally he seemed vague, confused, afraid; she wondered if he had in some manner been threatened and intimidated.

When the farmer was excused from the stand, Rockcastle said in his pompous manner:

"May it please the court, there is no testimony here to identify the defendant as an actual participant in the crime alleged to have been committed on the person of Homer Phipps. We are wasting the court's time with this line of inquiry. The State therefore moves that the defendant be discharged from this aspect of the case, and that charges against him for injuring Homer Phipps be dismissed for lack of sufficient evidence."

"It is so ordered," nodded the judge.

The first section of the warrant against Bad 'Lias was thus dropped by order of the court. There still remained, however, the more important charge that he murdered Dr. Tracy Lassiter.

It was nearing noon and the honorable court adjourned for brandy and lunch.

6.

When the session resumed Miss Sally had difficulty finding a place to sit. For a time she stood by the wall at the back, then she moved down a side wall to hear better. Buckstone, of course, was not present. Troy Lassiter came in early and seated himself before the bench, his black eyes searching the faces of the judge, the prosecutor, and the jurors, as if he sought to gain some inkling of their state of mind.

He was at once called to testify and as soon as he was sworn Rockcastle approached the witness chair.

"Captain Lassiter," he said, "I believe you swore to the complaint upon which the warrant was issued for the arrest of the accused, Elias Blevins, charging him with the murder of Dr. Tracy Lassiter?"

"I did," replied the witness.

"And after I, as prosecuting attorney, had somewhat demurred over taking this action?"

"I believe you did hesitate somewhat at first."

"I was doubtful that there was sufficient evidence to justify that action. Yet you insisted on going ahead, did you not?"

"That is true," nodded Lassiter.

"No doubt you had good and sufficient reasons for swearing to such charges?"

"I considered that I did."

"Will you explain to the court and jury those reasons?"

A liquid *plop* was heard as Bad 'Lias expectorated a mouthful of tobacco juice into the spittoon beside his table, which contained a considerable quantity of that fluid.

"To begin with," said Lassiter, "Blevins held a grudge against my brother."

"What kind of a grudge?"

"My brother had stated openly that he believed Elias and Elijah Blevins had something to do with the theft of two valuable horses that were taken from our plantation."

"He had evidence to this effect?"

"I can only say that there had been a number of crimes committed in this vicinity; and without doing work of any kind or being engaged in any other legitimate business, Blevins and his brother always seemed to have plenty of money. By the way, Mr. Rockcastle, where is Elijah Blevins?"

"That's beside the question," said the prosecutor. "Mr. Blevins' brother is not a party to this case."

"He might very well be," insisted Lassiter. "I'd like to know where Little 'Lige Blevins is!"

There was a visible stir of interest in the courtroom, and Bad 'Lias expectorated again into the long-suffering spittoon.

Even Judge Redding was interested. He sat up and removed his spectacles, the better to see the accused.

"Does the defendant have any objection to telling us his brother's whereabouts?" he asked.

The courtroom became silent, waiting for the answer.

"I reckon whar he is, is his own business," said Bad 'Lias.

"Where *is* he?" demanded Lassiter.

"Now look here, Cap'n," said Blevins with a surly scowl. "'You've tried to make trouble for me. Now you're aimin' to make trouble for my brother. Wall, I ain't a-goin' to let you do it. Mr. Rockcastle already said it didn't have nothin' to do with the case, didn't he? I'll jest say my brother's out of the kentry at present, an' that's all."

Rockcastle interposed. "All this is incompetent, irrelevant, and immaterial," he said to the judge. "Furthermore the witness has no right to question this defendant. The whereabouts of Mr. Blevins' brother certainly has nothing to do with the merits of this case. We move that all this be stricken from the record."

The somewhat angry manner of the prosecutor seemed to bring Judge Redding back to himself. He nodded. "So ordered."

"Now, Captain Lassiter," said Rockcastle, and his manner had become sarcastic, "will you be so kind as to favor this court with such information as you possess dealing with this case?"

To Miss Sally, standing by the wall, it seemed that Lassiter was at a loss.

"Aside from the man's known bad character," he said after a moment, "his reputation as a drunkard and a trouble maker, and his being suspected of more than one crime——"

"That will do!" shouted Rockcastle. "Your opinion of the character of the defendant has nothing to do with the case, even were you an unprejudiced witness, which you are not. Do you mean to tell this court that you have no witness of any kind to the commission of this crime——?"

"Where's 'Lige Blevins?"

"I've told you that's not material——"

"'Lige Blevins might be a very important witness!"

"I refuse to argue with you, Captain Lassiter. Will you answer the question as to the evidence you can adduce concerning the commission of this crime?"

Lassiter hesitated. "The only piece of evidence that might have bearing on this case," he said, "is a frying pan which I discovered in a cave near where my brother was murdered. That utensil belonged to the Blevins brothers, I believe."

"On what grounds?"

"Jared Hume told me that he sold such a frying pan to them some time ago."

"Did he say that he sold this particular frying pan to them?"

"No. He said he sold them a frying pan of the same style and make——"

"But he did not identify this frying pan, without question, as the same one he sold to the Blevins brothers?"

"No, not exactly," the witness admitted.

"Frying pans are very much alike, aren't they? This could have belonged to anybody, couldn't it?"

"Mr. Rockcastle," Lassiter burst out, "are you prosecuting Blevins, or *defending* him?"

"I resent that!" shouted the prosecutor angrily. "Your Honor, I ask that cognizance be taken of this abusive remark!"

"The witness will refrain from such remarks," said the old judge severely.

"But your Honor——"

"I warn you, sir, that you may stand in contempt of court."

The witness lapsed into silence.

"Have you any further testimony?" asked the prosecutor.

Reluctantly Lassiter admitted that he had no direct evidence.

"Then this whole action is preposterous!" exclaimed Rockcastle, with a great show of indignation. "You are saying that you put this court to the trouble and expense of a trial, with nothing but your unfounded suspicions upon which to base your charges?" He turned to the judge. "Your Honor, I humbly apologize. In the absence of other witnesses, the State rests."

"Has the defense anything to say?" inquired Judge Redding.

The only reply of Bad 'Lias was another squirt of tobacco juice into the spittoon.

"Very well." The old judge turned solemnly to the jurors and spoke, as if he had committed to memory his charge to them. "Gentlemen of the jury, in the absence of one single iota of

direct evidence bearing on this recent regrettable murder, this
court has only one recourse. You are directed to return a verdict
of not guilty. Do you so agree?"

The jury so agreed.

Court adjourned and Bad 'Lias Blevins walked forth a free
man.

Chapter 14

1.

When he left the courtroom Troy Lassiter encountered Miss Sally. He lifted his hat to her, but without a smile.

"You were there?" he asked.

"Yes."

"The trial was a farce."

She nodded.

In him she felt a fury of grief and rage, a kind of angry desperation bottled in by the force of self-control. Troy Lassiter had changed in the time she had known him, within the last few days in fact. She had considered him a slightly sardonic, somewhat carelessly elegant young man who took nothing seriously, except perhaps his amusements. Now he seemed imbued with some secret purpose, perhaps terrible. So foreign was it to her spinster's nature, that she felt constraint, even uneasiness, in the face of the volcanic passion she sensed in him. Yet she could not help sympathizing with his sorrow and resentment against injustice.

237

"A victory for . . . outlawry," he said to her.

His eyes were gazing up the street and her own gaze followed his. Peebles and Rockcastle were walking together toward the tavern. As they passed the groggery near Tidwell's harness shop, the figure of Bad 'Lias appeared in the doorway. In one hand he held a glass, evidently containing spirits. With his other hand he made a gesture toward them, while he half nodded.

"I reckon he's thanking them for getting him off," Lassiter said. "Well, he owes them that kind of thanks."

The lawyer and the tavern man passed the groggery as if they had hardly seen Blevins, and the big man returned inside.

"Now that he's in the clear, he's taken to drinking again," observed Lassiter.

"What will happen next, do you think?" she asked.

"Miss Sally, that man is guilty. He ought to hang."

"It's too late now, isn't it?"

"You mean since he's been acquitted? Well, the law expressly forbids that any person shall twice be put in jeopardy for the same offense. But my brother's blood is on his hands! And there's something more." He paused and looked at her. "Miss Sally, have you spoken to—our friend in prison—lately?"

"No. I intended to visit him this morning, but the arrest of Blevins and his preliminary hearing prevented me. I hope to see him now, though. He's grateful for any friendly visit."

"I saw him yesterday afternoon, and carried heavy news to him. Miss Sally, I believe that Blevins murdered not only my brother, but also Prudence Buckstone."

At her incredulous gasp, he took her by the arm, as if to steady her. "Why do you think that?" she asked.

He told her of what he had discovered in the cave—the bundle, the slippers, and the pool of blood.

"Her father has her things now," he ended. "I took them to him. Miss Sally, I don't know why I should tell you this, except that you were her dear friend: but that girl meant very much to me. And if you think I'm vengeful—well, you're right."

He bowed and left her before the courthouse, her face suddenly paled. She watched him as he passed around the stone building, evidently bound for the jail. But she did not follow. At this moment she did not feel that she could face Prudence's father. No words of hers could help him, and she felt such desolation in her own heart that she hurried to her house.

2.

To Dode Taney, at the jail, Lassiter said curtly, "Please admit me."

On this occasion the sheriff made no objection. There was, indeed, a half grin on his face, as if he knew the frustrations in Lassiter's mind and how helpless he was to do anything about them. So he unlocked the outside door and said nothing.

Within the jail corridor Lassiter once more became aware of the offensiveness of the sordid surroundings, the narrow confinement, the unclean smell. Buckstone hurried at once over to the bars separating his cell from the little passageway.

"How did it go?" he asked eagerly.

"Worst possible," replied Lassiter.

"Blevins was acquitted...?"

Lassiter glanced around to be sure the sheriff had left them alone together. "He was," he said. "And he's guilty as hell. But the jury returned a verdict—instructed—of not guilty."

Buckstone knew as well as Lassiter the provision of the law preventing the trial of any person for an offense of which he has been acquitted.

"He now no longer needs fear prosecution," he said gloomily, "and is free to go on his way."

"Completely free. 'A speedy and impartial trial' is the way the law books read. This was speedy enough."

"But how impartial?"

"Totally lacking in impartiality, sir," said Lassiter darkly. "I've been humiliated and made a fool of. That reptile, Rock-

castle, treated me like the dolt I was and led me on to swear
out a warrant and thus bring Blevins prematurely to trial before
evidence was fully gathered—which it was his duty as prosecutor to gather and present. All this to give Blevins immunity."

Buckstone said, hesitantly, "Was anything brought out concerning . . . Prudence?"

"No. They cut me off before I could even state what I found
in that cave."

Silence. Again Lassiter looked around to assure himself that
they were alone together. The jail door was shut; Taney, that
somewhat less than energetic officer, had wandered off to his
quarters.

"You'll remember that I've been gone from this vicinity for
several days," he told Buckstone.

"Yes, it was during your absence that I was imprisoned here."

It was also, reflected Lassiter, during his absence that
Prudence was indentured to Drew Peebles. That outrage, at least,
would not have occurred had he been near. He could at least
have helped Miss Sally post bond for the girl. Too late now, he
thought heavily.

"I was gone," he said, "on what I thought was a most important errand." He looked keenly at Buckstone. "I have friends
in various parts of this state. Judge John Overton of Nashville is
one. Colonel Orville Shelby of Shelby County is another. There
is also General John Coffee. All of them are friends of Andrew
Jackson, as was my brother. We discussed the crime situation in
this part of the state. The same sort of thing has been reported
elsewhere—in Madison County, Shelby County, Blount County,
even in Maury County, just south of Nashville."

"Statewide!"

"More than that. I believe Kentucky, Louisiana, Mississippi,
Arkansas, and perhaps other states are affected in a wide and
dangerous criminal conspiracy."

"How can you know this?"

"There's a man in prison at Vicksburg by the name of Soril
Phelps. He is under sentence to be hanged for a murder-robbery;

and he's done some talking. Boasting, rather. He's told of some sort of a 'Clan,' probably a criminal organization, which will 'pull down the walls of the Vicksburg jail,' and free him. Of course it only served to increase the guard over him, but it furnished a useful clue. Then Colonel Shelby gave a piece of pertinent information. His plantation is on the banks of the Mississippi River, below Memphis. He told how a flatboat, laden with valuable goods, was attacked by a gang of river pirates not far from his place, its crew murdered to a man, and the boat and its cargo carried away somewhere, apparently among the bayous on the Arkansas side for distribution among the thieves. Colonel Shelby says the head of that gang is a man named John A. Murrell, who is a thief, a highwayman, a murderer, and God knows what else."

"It sounds almost incredible," said Buckstone.

"I know it sounds melodramatic," conceded Lassiter, "but my friends, whom I mentioned, and I believe there is some sort of a gigantic criminal network made up of outlaws, cutthroats, robbers, thieves, murderers, and gallows birds operating throughout the South. And, also, that it is supported and aided in some places by men of *high standing and influence* for various reasons, but chiefly for greed. It's my conviction, sir, that a tentacle of that crime monster extends right here into Turkeytoe!"

"Good God, sir!"

"Do you see how everything fits this theory?" Lassiter went on. "Blevins, who must be a member of that gang, was in trouble. It was necessary to get him out of it—for the sake of this 'Clan.' Who got him out of that trouble? Rockcastle for one, with the judge cooperating. Who else? Why, your treacherous acquaintance, Peebles, who put up the bond so expeditiously." He paused. "It's dangerous to mention such names," he went on. "But we're in a frightening situation in this remote part of the country. Talk is dangerous, for you never know when you might be speaking to a member of the criminal network—and I have, so far, not the slightest iota of evidence to prove the suspicions which I've just voiced to you."

Buckstone was impressed. "You can trust me, Troy," he said.

"I'm sure of that, sir. If I could only get the barest inkling to go on—" A hint of discouragement was in the young man's voice.

"If only I could help!"

"Of course you can't. And I don't know why I burden you with this, except that I must have someone to express my feelings to. Well, I'm going to take such steps as one man can, but it looks ill for honest men these black days."

Lassiter called for the sheriff and was let out of the jail. Going to his window Buckstone watched him as he walked away past the courthouse. He had a soldierly way of striding along, a straight, high-shouldered, unsmiling figure, heading for some unknown errand of his own.

Troy Lassiter was hard to fathom. In him the call of blood vengeance was deep, and Buckstone was sure that he might be a very dangerous man in a personal vendetta. But there was more to him: he had also a thought for others, a sense of responsibility to his state and its people.

No telling what he might do; but in that moment Bion Buckstone felt for him the kind of affection that a father might feel toward a son whom he does not very well understand, but upon whom he wishes that fortune would smile.

3.

When Lassiter was gone, Buckstone sat down and did some hard thinking. And presently he had his second visitor of that afternoon.

Outside he heard Miss Sally's voice, calling his name, and he went to the jail window and looked down at her through the bars. He was disheveled and depressed. But she, looking up at him, was a pitying woman who saw him only as the kind, courtly, even handsome gentleman whom she had idolized. He noticed that her eyes were very bright as she tried to smile at him.

"Miss Sally," he said, with more discernment than might have been expected, "you've been crying."

She nodded.

"Then you've heard about Prudence?"

"Yes, Captain Lassiter told me." The smile faded and she gazed up at him, sharing his grief. But where he accepted the obvious certainty, she clung to hope. "I won't believe it!" she said. "Not even a fiend would harm that lovely child!"

"Unless to silence her," he said drearily. "She may have had some knowledge of Dr. Lassiter's murder."

"We mustn't give up!" Miss Sally cried. "What do we actually know? Her slippers were found in a cave and there was a little blood. That's no proof that anything happened to her!"

He smiled sadly. "Do you really believe that?"

A shadow came over her face, and her eyes fell. "Oh, Colonel Buckstone——"

"My dear," he interrupted, and it was the first time he had ever used such an expression to her, "I want to ask you not to call me 'Colonel' any more."

At her look of surprise he added, "I never was a colonel. It was a title I assumed—for business reasons. Will you think less of me for telling you this?"

"No—oh, no!" she cried. "I could never—ever—think less of you—" She stopped and her face was almost pretty in the way she colored at this involuntary admission.

He smiled. "Nor I you. And I don't want to be under false pretenses—not with you, of all people—" He paused and gulped, feeling that he was on dangerous emotional ground. So he finished rather lamely, "I want to thank you for your great and unceasing kindness in this trying time."

"It's nothing," she murmured.

"I think it is a very great thing," he replied.

She looked down and again he felt the tide of emotion, so he made haste to change the direction of the conversation.

"I've been doing some thinking, and I want you to help me," he said.

She lifted her eyes. "What is it?"

"Do you remember the day of my arrest?"

"I can never forget it!"

"I came to your house?"

"Yes."

"I began to explain my predicament?"

"Yes."

"But I didn't finish my explanation, did I?"

"No," she said. "The—sheriff came."

"How long after I arrived at your house did he come?"

"Why—it couldn't have been longer than two or three minutes."

Buckstone nodded. "Two or three minutes. Almost immediately after I myself arrived." He paused. "Now only yesterday Rockcastle brought me some papers to sign—he had only just had them prepared—releasing my interest in that land of mine to Drew Peebles."

"Did you sign it?"

"No. But there is this oddity. I commented to Rockcastle that the release was about the same in lines and wordage as the warrant. He thought I was uttering some sort of a joke at my own expense and agreed that the written substance of the two instruments was about the same in length—the warrant and the release. Then I asked why it took so long to get the papers to me."

"And he?"

"He said that George Rivers, the court clerk, who prepared them—and the warrant also—takes such pride in his penmanship that he requires not less than fifteen minutes to complete one written page to his own satisfaction."

She looked puzzled.

"Don't you see?" he asked. "The warrant was served on me two or three minutes after I came to your house. It must therefore have been written *before* I arrived—before I even showed Peebles the letter setting forth the claims of the Philadelphia heirs, because I walked directly to your house without stopping."

"How could that be?" she exclaimed.

"I don't know," he said. "It's set my head to running in circles. I've got to think."

"If I could only help you——"

He looked down at her, and the thought of her long, un-selfish friendship came over him again. In all the world she alone seemed to cleave to him, to remain loyal whatever the world might think of him. And standing there below him she seemed to him wonderfully womanly in her neatness, with her dark eyes so concerned for him, and in all her ways which were serious but sweet.

"You've already helped me more than you know," he said. "Now goodbye, my dear—my very *dear* friend."

The way he said the last words had the power to uplift her for days after, even though she tried to tell herself that she read too much meaning in it.

4.

On the single street of Turkeytoe several persons were witnesses when Troy Lassiter confronted Bad 'Lias Blevins.

Now that his trial was over and he stood acquitted, Blevins was again drinking heavily, as if to make up for his period of abstinence. He had stepped out of the groggery, with some of his unfragrant cronies—among them some of the very jurors who had acquitted him—and to these he was bragging as usual.

"I shore made fools of 'em," he said. "I made 'em take water." And he spoke sneeringly of Troy Lassiter. "I made him look like the little end of nothin', an' that whittled to a p'int," he said, and went on to state, "If I ever run onto him, with his slick boots an' his high-falutin' ways, I'm liable to make him look like he's been drug through a brier patch."

These interesting sentiments had just been uttered when Lassiter himself appeared. Paying no attention to the others, he walked straight up to Bad 'Lias.

"Blevins," he said, "I still want to know where your brother is."

The hulking ruffian turned to him. His single eye was blood-shot and malevolent and his breath was foul with whiskey. "I told you in court it was his business—an' none of yourn," he said.

Lassiter's black gaze bored into his. "Elias Blevins," he said, "get out of my sight! And I give you warning: never cross my path again!"

There was a moment's electric silence.

Bad 'Lias was half drunk and he was always dangerous in that condition. He was physically bigger and more powerful than the slender planter. Furthermore, the words Lassiter had spoken to him were fighting words. The onlookers expected a violent explosion.

For a moment they stood, face to face. Then Bad 'Lias deliberately hitched up his pants and slouched away.

Those who saw it could hardly believe the way the coiled steel will of Troy Lassiter had cowed the huge ruffian.

"I didn't want to make no ruckus on the street," Bad 'Lias explained later to some of his associates.

But they remembered his threats made just before Lassiter appeared.

"Besides, I figgered he was toting a sleeve pistol," he added.

A sleeve pistol was a small firearm that could be concealed in the sleeve of a man's coat; it was held by a spring catch that released it for firing when seized by the opposite hand. Such weapons were sometimes carried by gamblers on Mississippi River packet boats.

But it was a lame excuse. Those who had seen Bad 'Lias faced down and ordered to leave were quite sure that Lassiter carried no weapon of any kind. The ruffian's prestige fell prodigiously in Turkeytoe.

Next day Bad 'Lias was gone. The question of the whereabouts of his brother, and of Prudence Buckstone, remained unanswered.

5.

Two days had drifted over the high country, and now as the sun sank below the rough ridge of the mountains, making the gorge dark with the early night gloom, Troy Lassiter came to where his horse was tethered, near a certain cave in a limestone cliff— the cave where the relics of Prudence had been found.

His riding boots, usually kept in such gleaming condition, were scratched and mud stained. His black coat with the band of crepe on the sleeve had a tear in it. He was tired and discouragement overwhelmed him.

Lassiter had spent most of the day about that cave, searching its vicinity. He was alone, because his was a personal vendetta, and he was looking for something.

Elias Blevins had been acquitted of the murder of Dr. Lassiter. But there was another murder, or at least a murder in every probability, of which he had not been acquitted. Every bit of evidence pointed to the slaying of Prudence Buckstone. Troy Lassiter was seeking the final, definite proof of that slaying. If he captured Blevins this time, he wanted sufficient confirmation to send the monster to the gallows.

There was the ghastly gout of blood in the cave, which certainly showed that someone had been killed, and to Troy, this could only be Prudence. What he had searched for that day was something he shrank from seeing with all his being, yet believed he must find: the piteous remains of the girl. There must be a grave, or some repository for a body. He felt sure of that, but his search that day had been fruitless; he had discovered nothing. What *could* the murderers have done with her?

Standing beside his horse, before mounting, he felt the weight of deep discouragement upon him. He was never communicative, and he had ridden on this quest without telling anyone of his plans. That his errand was dangerous he well knew: even to spend time in this vicinity, known to have been a rendezvous of outlaws, was perilous. For this reason he carried two well-oiled and newly capped percussion rifled pistols in his saddle holsters and a shorter barreled pistol in his pocket. He would have almost welcomed the appearance of bandits for the sake of killing or being killed, but nobody had appeared in that day.

For a time, bowed beside his saddle, he debated the question of returning to his home. He had not found Prudence's body, but he was sure she was dead; and secret within himself was the fact that his hatred for the murderer was on this day even greater for what he believed had been done to the girl than for the slaying of his brother.

As in a dream, he remembered that evening with her at Beechwood when she had charmed him beyond all imagination. He had been entranced with her bright moods, her lovely face and wealth of honey-hued hair, her trim femininity, her graceful walk, her way of holding her head, and her manner when she looked laughingly up at him with eyes brilliant and smiling.

His very delight in her caused their quarrel. An impulsive kiss: the tête-à-tête was over.

A kiss? Not so very harmful, even though it was stolen. But it offended her and she left him in anger.

In him, however, that kiss worked a strange alchemy. The girl had caught him; she aroused him. He had tried to think reasonably of her in terms of his life and his work, but he found it impossible to be reasonable in his thoughts of her. He had never considered any plans to complicate his life and his freedom by marriage. And certainly none of the women he had previously encountered had caused him even to contemplate such a step. But when Prudence stepped across the threshhold of his heart, all he could think of was how she would queen it in his home, how lovely she would be to look at, to listen to, to be in company with, to have for his own, and how superior she was to any other woman he had ever known.

Her very indignation at his misstep, he recalled, had heightened his admiration for her. She was a thoroughbred, with not only beauty but also spirit to be prized. Given a little time to repair the damage of that brief moment of thoughtless aggression, he had hoped that she might come to look upon him with kindness again, perhaps even respond to him in the way he felt toward her.

But he had gone on his errand into southern Tennessee, and when he returned it was already too late. That day, when he went to her father in the jail with the pathetic little slippers and the evidence of tragedy, he told Buckstone that he admired his daughter. It was something far deeper than that, which he did not express...

His horse nickered softly, perhaps wondering at this long immobility of his master beside him. Lassiter lifted his head. Then he untethered the animal and mounted.

But instead of turning back toward his home, he guided his mount on up the darkening gorge. The last of his race, he would not turn back from the solitary task he had set for himself.

6.

As he rode in the gloom, another name entered his thinking.

Murrell. John A. Murrell. It was branded on his mind.

Murrell, a vague, shadowy figure, but somehow emerging in recent weeks as a diabolist, a criminal genius, evidently possessing a satanic handsomeness of person, graceful manners, and having a way with women, so that he commanded the favors of many, and with men like Elias Blevins and his brother, so that he commanded their loyalty and obedience.

The picture had been pieced together from divers hints and clues picked up here and there. A planter on the banks of the Mississippi had seen him and had given a sketchy description of him. A woman living south of Nashville had appeared against him in a court case a few years before, and her description, being from a woman's viewpoint, was more detailed. A miserable highwayman, lying in jail awaiting his death on the gallows, had bolstered his spirits by boasting of a "Clan," which had as its "Grand Master" this same Murrell, with far-reaching plans that were incredible in their audacity and evil ambition. Murrell—and here the scattered accounts agreed—was tall and well formed, having a fondness for elegant clothes. He also seemed possessed by a monstrous blood-lust—it appeared to be his most salient characteristic.

Men had been found murdered and robbed in widely separated areas; and it was, according to local conjecture, Murrell's work. Yet it was hard to imagine that any one man could strike so lethally and almost simultaneously in so many different parts of the country.

No, the answer could only be that these murders were the operations of a network of criminals, such as had been described by Soril Phelps, the condemned man in the Vicksburg jail—a network organized by a master criminal, trained by him in bloody practices, and operating under his malign direction.

It was difficult to believe that such a gigantic conspiracy could exist, yet Troy Lassiter believed it. The trouble was in getting other people to believe and recognize their danger. General Coffee, Colonel Shelby, and Judge Overton believed. And they had signed, together with Troy himself, a letter to a certain person in Washington, hoping to get some help from that quarter.

But Lassiter knew that reply must be long in coming. And meanwhile Elias Blevins might get clear out of the country and escape. He was sure that Blevins was a member of Murrell's "Clan"—the man's very barbarity stamped him—and he suspected that others in Turkeytoe were in the conspiracy. He could not wait before he took up his personal hunt for the man who, he believed, had killed both his brother and the girl he might have loved.

He was not even sure that Bad 'Lias had come this way; but now, on a hunch, he rode on in the darkened gorge hardly knowing what move he would next make, but hoping for some turn that might help him in the purpose on which his whole being was now concentrated.

7.

Up ahead lights pricked out in the gloom. A little settlement. As he rode up to it a horde of dogs came bounding out at him, making the night hideous with their barking. His horse minced and shied at the noisy curs, but Lassiter curbed him, and drew rein before the first cabin he encountered.

Four shacks, two on each side of the trace and one other a little farther along—that was the extent of the settlement; and a meaner or less hospitable one Lassiter had never seen.

From the nearest shack an old man came out and held up a lantern to scrutinize the newcomer, meantime directing a well-aimed kick at one of the noisy dogs, which sent the cur off howling. The old man wore clothes apparently too big for him, and he had a voluminous beard, snowy white, except for a brown stain in the center from chewing and expectorating tobacco juice. Like a spot of manure in a snowdrift, was Lassiter's thought.

From the cabins came others, men and women disreputably garbed and children with hardly any clothing at all, to stare at the man on the horse.

"What's this place?" asked Lassiter.

"Hit ain't rightly got no name," said the white beard with the lantern, somewhat sheepishly.

But another in the small crowd said, "Some calls it Cherry's Station," and indicated with his thumb the old man. "He's Laban Cherry."

"Can you put me up for the night?" Lassiter asked.

"Wall," said the white beard without enthusiasm, "I reckon so. But yo'll have to sleep on a pallet. The ole woman'll git yo' supper, but we ain't fixed for no hotel business."

Lassiter dismounted, saw that his horse was watered and fed, then ate a plain country supper. He did not like the appearance of the place, so when Cherry's old wife brought him a bearskin and some quilts, he took them outside and lay where he could see his horse, which was tethered to a tree. Beyond the tree, underbrush and more trees marked the course of a small creek meandering down the bottom of the gorge.

He did not sleep well. It seemed to him that there were whisperings and movements about him in the night. His saddle was his pillow, and the two horse pistols were in the saddle holsters. There was also the shorter weapon, which he took from his pocket and placed where his hand could instantly grasp it.

Once the horse snorted softly and lifted its head to look

at something it apparently saw. Lassiter made out a dark shadow stealing toward the animal.

He leaped from his bed, pistol in hand. At the movement the shadow fleeted away, crashing through the bushes.

No pursuit was practicable; and he did not like to leave the horse unwatched, so he lay down again.

After a time the horse resumed its quiet grazing, by which he knew that the intruder, whoever or whatever it was, had not returned. Catnapping, he lived out the rest of the night until the eastern sky brightened with the pre-dawn light. His horse was standing relaxed, nodding half asleep. He saddled the animal, and led him around to the front of Cherry's cabin. The old man came to the door.

"How'd yo' sleep?" he asked.

"Well enough," said Lassiter. "Something startled the horse during the night. A bear, do you reckon?"

"Yeah," said old Laban Cherry. "We're bothered some with b'ars."

But Lassiter was sure no bear had tried to molest his horse. He watered and fed the animal, and while he was eating breakfast he kept an eye on his mount, which was tethered just outside the cabin. After he finished he said:

"What do I owe you—supper and breakfast, feed for the horse, and pallet?"

"Why—" said old Cherry. Cupidity and caution seemed to struggle in his face.

"How about a dollar?" asked Lassiter, holding forth the coin.

The old man's face was lit with avarice. "Wall, now, Mister, that's right kindly," he said.

So pleased was he by what he considered munificent payment for his grudging hospitality, that he even grew informative.

Yes, he said, he had seen a man such as Lassiter had described. Big fellow, with one eye gouged out. Carried a rifle. Wanted whiskey and food, and paid for them, too.

"Which way was he heading?" Lassiter asked.

"Wall—up this trail," said Cherry. "He done asked about roads leadin' toward the Ohio kentry."

"What did you tell him?"

"I tole him to go on up this trail to the foot of the Cumberland Gap, an' then turn west into Kaintuck."

"How was he traveling?"

"Afoot. Said he was lookin' fo' a hoss, but we didn't have none."

"How long ago?"

"Two days."

The sun lifted over the sawtooth edge of the mountains and Lassiter rode on up the gorge for the Cumberland Gap. He knew what to look for now. Bad 'Lias would not stay on foot long.

Where the Wilderness Trail debouched into the Cumberland Gap, he turned north and rode along the valley of the Cumberland River and through the gap in Pine Mountain known as the Narrows. There, at the little town called Pineville, he struck his first hot clue of the man he was hunting.

It was late in the day, and he stopped at an inn where a small group of villagers gathered to stare curiously at him. While he ate supper he talked in his soft polite way with the innkeeper, concerning horse thieves and their increasing boldness in the country. And presently an elderly farmer crowded forward.

"Air ye a thief hunter?" he asked.

"That's one of the things I do," said Lassiter.

"Then mebbe ye kin ketch the one that stole my mare." The farmer gave a description: gray, almost white, old and thin. "The thief must've rode her bareback, an' he couldn't of gone very far with her, the shape she was in."

To Lassiter, this was almost a sure sign of Bad 'Lias. The man was a thief, he was anxious to get somewhere, and a horse, even an old, almost white mare, was a logical thing for him to appropriate to make his travel easier.

But he asked a question: "Have you seen a one-eyed man around here lately?"

Two or three answered that. Yes. Big fellow. One eye gone and carrying a rifle. When? Why, only yesterday.

So he was gaining on Blevins. "I'll look for your horse," he said.

Sure enough, at Manchester, he found the old white mare from Pineville, in the city pound. She had evidently been too slow for Blevins, who had abandoned her and stolen another horse near the town to take her place.

Following a trail of stolen horses seemed simple, but from Manchester the track was exasperatingly hard to work out. He rode north toward Booneville, then remembered that at Cherry's Station they had told him the "fellow with one eye gone" had asked about the roads toward the Ohio River. So he headed northeast through Jackson, spending a night there; and the following day at West Liberty, in Morgan County, his luck returned.

An irascible old gentleman named Colonel Xenophon Carter was in town when he got there. Colonel Carter was proud of his acres and his horses, and he had just, the previous night, so he told the sheriff, lost a Thoroughbred stallion.

Lassiter, after he talked to the sheriff, looked the old man up; he was bracing himself with a toddy in the local tavern.

"Stolen, sir," Colonel Carter told him, his white moustaches bristling. "His name, sir, under which he's registered, is Hamilcar, out of my mare Charity, by General William Thomas Buckner's stallion, Hasdrubal. On both sides he's got the blood of Sir Archie in him, and there's no better blood, sir, than the blood of Sir Archie's line. I wouldn't take a thousand dollars for that horse, sir, and I'll pay a reward of two hundred dollars for his recovery."

He described the animal: bay, with white stockings on the hind feet, and a white star on the forehead, four years old, fourteen hands high, superb conformation. And the Colonel used some highly inflammatory descriptive language concerning whatever scoundrel had stolen him.

"A horse like that should be hard to hide," said Lassiter. "I'm on the trail of a horse thief and murderer right now. He took two horses from my own place in Tennessee."

"Then Godspeed, sir," said the Colonel. "North's the way you want to look. There's a shifty population in the breaks of the Ohio River—always has been. I'd go with you, if it weren't for the confounded sciatica that bothers me when I ride too much. But I'll give you a letter to a friend of mine, John Boyd, at Vanceburg. He's sheriff of Lewis County, and he hates a horse thief worse than any kind of poison."

So Troy Lassiter, on the trail now for days, rode north to the Ohio River.

Chapter 15

1.

Prudence, as the days passed, began to hope that she was beyond the reach of Drew Peebles. She had of course no inkling of the events in Turkeytoe, or of the belief that she was dead.

But she knew that the entire state of Kentucky now lay between her and the beginning of her flight, and she had seen that much of the area was a labyrinth of forests and mountains. She could not think that so unimportant a creature as a bound girl would be pursued so far.

On her second Sunday with the Glovers she went to church. She had by this time learned to tolerate the awkward attentions of Bud, who hung about her too eager to do things for her, and who blushed so miserably when he blundered that she felt sorry for him. Though she considered herself whole ages beyond Bud in maturity and experience, she liked the lad. So now she allowed him the exuberant joy of walking beside her when the pilgrimage to the meetinghouse was made.

On this Sunday there was a surprise—a visiting preacher. He

sat on the platform with "Reverend" Tom Timmons, the farmer-pastor, and members of the congregation craned their necks to take stock of this prodigy. Something about him seemed oddly familiar to Prudence.

She thought he was quite young for his profession—perhaps in his early thirties—quite sleek and good looking in appearance, with curling dark hair, a good brow, and elegant attire. Two things seemed to her feminine eye perhaps a little at variance with his ministerial occupation. His garb was *too* elegant, almost dandyish; he wore a black broadcloth, most carefully brushed, and a gleaming white ruffled shirt and cravat. And she thought his eye wandered over the congregation a little too much, whereas she was accustomed to preachers who looked sternly ahead, as if ready to grapple with the devil and all his works on a moment's notice.

After the opening hymn, bald, cock-eyed, good-hearted old Reverend Timmons rose to make the usual announcements.

"Be a meetin' of the board of trustees tomorrow night," he said. "Sister May Colwood is down with the bold hives an' folks kin visit her. Brother Caddy Sanger has lost his mule—brown critter, star on its forehead, six years old this spring, collar gall on its shoulder. You folks all know the animile. If you see him, let Brother Caddy know. Sewin' bee at the Killions' Thursday. All ladies invited an' bring along a covered dish for a sociable noonin'. Now folks, it's our mighty good luck that one of the ministers headin' for that big revival up at Portsmouth, on the Ohio side, has paused over here. He's a mighty expounder of the gospel, so I understand, though he is young. Hit's an honor to interduce to this here congregation Reverend Clark Catlett."

Reverend Catlett rose, smoothed the lapels of his coat, and took the pulpit. In that moment Prudence recognized him. He was the young man she had seen at the tavern in Turkeytoe with the lawyer, Ezekiel Rockcastle. So he was a preacher!

She was glad he had not paid any attention to her when she waited on his table, and she hoped he would not recognize her as the bound girl of Peebles' Tavern.

When he began to preach, Prudence found his discourse interesting. He seemed to be a man of some culture; he used the English language correctly and he had a pleasant voice. To judge by his quotations, not only from the Bible but from other works such as *Pilgrim's Progress* and Shakespeare, he had some learning and at times he rose to considerable pulpit eloquence. Before he concluded his sermon, she found herself listening with more than her usual attention to the Word, as expounded by Reverend Catlett.

He finished with quite a lengthy prayer, and afterward he stood with Reverend Timmons at the door of the church and shook hands with everyone. At the ladies particularly, he smiled with gleaming white teeth. Prudence felt a little apprehensive when she was introduced to him, but though he clung to her hand, she thought longer than was entirely necessary, he only said how happy he was to meet such a charming young lady, with rather unministerial warmth.

"Living with the Glovers, you say?" he asked with his smile. "I'll hope to see you again soon."

She was quite sure he had not recognized her, and she managed to release her hand, half thrilled, half repelled by his attentions. Poor Bud, however, on his way home, could not conceal his jealousy.

"What did you think of Reverend Catlett?" she asked him.

"Not much," he replied moodily.

"I thought he was very eloquent and sincere," she said, twisting her feminine knife in his wound.

"Eloquent, mebbe, if that means a gift of gab," he said grudgingly. "But sincere? I bet he's got faces all around his head. I noticed how he hung onto your hand."

She chose to ignore this.

"With that curly hair an' them slick clothes, he's a caution with the wimmin, I bet."

"You mustn't say such things," she told him.

"Jest the same, I don't like a horny preacher. An' he shore acts horny to me. Wonder why he didn't hang onto any of them old, ugly wimmin?"

The conversation was getting out of hand and Prudence scolded him a little for it.

"All right," said the boy, "but jest the same, if he got half a chance I bet that Catlett would snuggle up to you like a sick kitten to a hot rock."

She was a little amused, but she did not show her amusement. And secretly she was relieved when next day Alex Glover told her that the Reverend Mr. Catlett had gone on to his revival meeting. As a link with Turkeytoe, he made her feel uneasy.

2.

The girl had a sense of guilt about remaining long with the Glovers. Alex and his family worked very hard, but they could never "put by" much money because prices paid for their single salable commodity, wood for the steamboats, were miserably low. There were too many wood lots along the Ohio, and boat captains haggled for every rank they took, beating down prices by playing one wood-lot man against another.

Prudence felt that another mouth to feed—her own—must be a drain on their resources, though they never showed anything but warm-hearted welcome to her. Beyond this she had not forgotten her stubborn resolve: to reach Washington somehow and to try to get the President to help her father.

How she could accomplish this she did not know. She was beginning to realize how incredible it was that she had come even this far; and she quailed at the thought of trying to make her way again through the forest.

If she had possessed any money she might have bought deck passage on a steamboat going to Pittsburgh; and that would have been a long step in her journey. But she had no money and no prospect of obtaining any, for she could not even think of asking compensation for what she did around the Glover house, even had the family been able to pay her. So she spent much time in fruitless worrying and in the consideration of various impractical plans.

Then, the very day after she had heard Reverend Catlett preach at the little church, decision was forced upon her.

An upriver steamboat, stopping for wood, left with Alex Glover a printed piece of paper. When the steamboat had gone, thrashing its way upstream, he brought the paper to the house.

"Looks like a handbill of some kind," he said.

Since neither he, nor his wife, nor any of their children could read, he handed the paper to Prudence.

The girl glanced at it and her heart almost stopped beating because the first thing she saw was her own name.

Words seemed to run into each other. *Prudence Buckstone . . . indentured servant . . . runaway . . . white, female, age 17 years . . . $25 will be paid . . . Drew Peebles.*

So they were still after her!

She knew that her face had changed, but she heard Alex's voice say, "Go on, read it."

She must do something. So she began, and as she "read" she wildly improvised, changing the description as she went along:

"Notice. Alice Hankins, runaway, white indentured servant, female, age twenty, well featured, black hair and eyes, reward of twenty-five dollars will be paid by subscriber. Matthew Jones."

The name "Alice Hankins," the first that came into her mind, was the same that she gave to Corbie Wilson when he found her.

Alex Glover was watching her face, and like most frontiersmen he was a good judge of people. Yet she might have carried out her pretense, but for one little flaw which he instantly detected.

"Does it say she's twenty?" he asked. "A gal cain't be held as an indentured servant after she comes of age. An' by law a gal comes of age when she's eighteen."

She had not thought of that. Caught in a lie, Prudence looked guilty and frightened.

"You sure it says *black* hair an' eyes?" asked Alex.

"It's about you, ain't it?" asked Libby with quick perception.

The girl had never dreamed of being tracked down in this manner, and she began to cry.

Libby put an arm about her. "Don't worry your head, honey," she comforted. "Ain't nobody goin' to know nothin' about you while you're with us."

The Glover children gazed at Prudence wide eyed. The face of Alex was stern.

3.

In the night Prudence lay restless in bed unable to sleep. Long ago Sis and Susie had fallen into the deep untroubled slumber of childhood, but the turmoil in her mind prevented her from following their example.

She did not distrust the Glovers. Still, she considered, a reward of twenty-five dollars might be a heavy temptation for a family so straitened in means as they. Furthermore, even if the Glovers had no thought of exposing her, she must now be a serious embarrassment to them, since they knew they were going contrary to the law.

Long before dawn she rose quietly and put on her blue gingham gown. Once more she made a little bundle to contain her few oddments, this time out of the old homespun dress.

She wished that she could say farewell and express her thanks to the family that had treated her with such kindness, and the thought came to her that she might leave a note for them. But then she remembered that none of the Glovers could read, and if they went to somebody else to read the note for them, explanations would have to follow. That would be an additional clue to her movements, supposing the reader was not as friendly as the Glovers.

So stealing about to avoid waking anyone, before the pre-dawn chill portended the coming day, she let herself silently out of the house. Nobody stirred and for a moment she stood still, trying to decide which way to turn. The direction must be up-river, of course. She knew that there was a rough road running generally parallel to the river for at least some miles, and that it was a mile or so away from the stream in most places. But she did not know what houses she might encounter upon that road, or how much traffic it carried. If she was seen she might be recognized by persons who had met her at the Glovers' or at the church.

After a brief hesitation she headed directly toward the forest, which seemed very dark and grim beyond the stumpy area where the woodcutters had done their work. A bell jingled behind her, and she halted. It was Shadrach, the Glovers' old dog, panting happily as he followed her. She stooped and patted his rough head.

"Go home, Shadrach," she whispered. "Go home and lie down."

When she straightened and began once more to walk, the dog remained sitting where she had left him, and finally, with a sleepy yawn, went jingling back to the house.

The forest closed around her and once more she learned how difficult it is to travel through a heavily wooded area at night. At last she gave it up and sat down on a log to wait for daylight.

The darkness was full of sounds. Not far away she could hear the swish and roar of the great river. Above her the trees seemed to whisper and talk to each other. Frogs raised a chorus and there were calls of night birds. But all these sounds were now familiar to her.

At the first brightening of the eastern sky she washed and drank at a spring, then took her bundle and started along the river bank. Many travelers before Prudence had learned the lesson she now learned: that following the course of a stream is the worst possible kind of walking. Again and again she lost time going around almost impenetrable thickets that abounded along the banks of the Ohio. Once she came on a creek, or rather a small river, too deep and too wide to ford. On that occasion she was forced to walk up its course for almost a mile until she came to a tree that had fallen across it in some past windstorm. Over this "raccoon bridge" she teetered, clutching her bundle and making her way around impeding branches by clinging to them, afraid every moment that she might slip and fall into the rushing water.

After she got across she worked her way back to the Ohio, where she had a real scare. In a small swampy glade she saw a large black animal with a tan muzzle. A bear. She was frightened, but the bear, at sight of her, gave a snort and ran away through the woods.

Later she encountered a possibly greater danger, though she did not know it. As she made her way along the river bank she heard a familiar-sounding grunt. Presently she beheld a huge old razorback sow stretched luxuriously on her side, a litter of piglets at her teats. Had the sow, which was wild and fierce, thought her young were in danger, she would have charged the girl. But Prudence gave her a wide berth, and the sow only rolled her small red eyes at her, and continued to lie where she was giving nourishment to her squeaking offspring.

As night began to descend the girl found a grassy spot and sat down upon it. She was very hungry, a sensation with which she was familiar enough, but which still was not pleasant. When she left the Glover house she was too scrupulous to take even one crumb of food. Now as she thought back on it, she was sure that the warm-hearted Glovers would not have begrudged her a loaf of bread. Instead of eating, she drank from a small spring and slept lying on her belly to ease the hunger ache.

In the morning she awoke cold, blue, and pinched about the cheekbones and wet with night dew. But that morning she was lucky. She was famished but she shortly discovered a bank where red tufts seemed to splash a green carpet. Wild strawberries. She gathered and ate all that were ripe, and found her hunger stayed.

Around her the forest by daylight was beautiful with flowers —trillium, wild ginger, dogtooth violet, ground pink, lady's slipper, and all their dainty kind—and for a time she sat and rejoiced in their loveliness. But having rested awhile she rose once more to go on, hardly knowing to what kind of destination she was heading.

By good fortune she came upon a deer trail along the river bank which for a time permitted her to travel a little more rapidly than on the previous day. More than once she saw steamboats, some puffing upstream against the current, others with a great racket going down. She was tempted to run out on some point of land, to wave at an oncoming steamboat, hoping it might pick her up. But then she remembered that the handbill concerning her had been given to Alex Glover by a steamboat captain, and in her inexperience she supposed that every river craft carried similar notices. So she shrank back into the bushes.

Evening approached, ending the weary day. As she walked slowly along the river bank she was surprised to see a cord stretched on the ground across the deer path. It hung over the bank and when she looked, she saw something swirling in the water below—a fish.

A fish was food. She had been repelled by one freshly caught that Bud offered to her, though she ate cooked fish with enjoyment. Now, in her hunger, she took the cord and drew upon it. There was renewed splashing and swirling, and a moment later she had the fish out on the land.

It lay flopping and gasping. The girl looked down upon it, shrinking from it in spite of herself. She did not want to touch the squirming thing, and besides she had no way to cook it.

Behind her a man's voice said, "Dat's mah fish!"

4.

He spoke from a thicket directly behind her. With a little cry she dropped the line she held and the fish began to flop back toward the river.

There was a rush, the bushes parted, and the man leaped to retrieve the fish. He was a Negro and she moved away from him.

The fish secured, he turned toward her.

"Miss Prudence," he said, "Ah thought yo' was a long ways from heah."

She knew him then—Jeff, the runaway slave. They stared at each other.

He was changed in appearance since she last saw him. A

kinky black beard covered the lower part of his face, and he wore an old faded shirt, whereas when last she saw him he was naked to the waist.

"Yo' wants dis fish, yo' kin have it," he said, offering it.

She drew away. "I don't want it."

"What was yo' goin' to do with dis fish?"

"I don't know."

"Cook it, mebbe, fo' supper?"

"No, I couldn't. I haven't any fire." She looked at the fish which hung from a finger he had hooked under its gill.

"Is yo' hongree, Miss Prudence?"

"I haven't had anything to eat for two days—except a few strawberries." She sank weakly down on the ground.

"Wall, now, look," said Jeff. "Ah got dis ole fish, an' Ah'm gwine to take dis ole fish, an' I'm gwine to cook dis ole fish fo' yo' to eat—if yo' wants it."

His voice was kind and respectful. She made a decision.

"Where can you cook it?" she asked.

"Ah got a li'l camp back in heah."

Without a word she followed as he led the way into the bushes. There was a small opening perhaps twenty feet in diameter. In the middle of this burned a fire and he put some new sticks on it to make it blaze brighter.

"Yo jes' set down, rest yo'self, Miss Prudence," he said.

Weary and faint she seated herself on the ground and tucked her feet under her skirt. He disappeared. A few minutes later he was back with the fish, which now was cleaned and skinned.

"Dis ole fish mus' weigh three pound or mo'," he said. Then he gave her a look of apology. "Ah ain't got no dishes. We jes' has to make do."

She sat still, saying nothing.

With his jackknife he cut two switches and with them propped up the two halves of the fish to broil over the fire. After a time he said, apologetic once more, "Hit's ready to eat now, iffen we jes' had some salt. Ah hain't got no salt. Salt would go good on dis fish."

She was so hungry that she felt the saliva rise in her mouth at the mere thought of food. "I can eat it without salt," she said.

He laid the two pieces of broiled fish on a clean flat rock and stood back.

"Go ahaid, Miss Prudence. He'p yo'self."

She saw that he was going to remain standing until she had eaten.

"Aren't you going to eat?" she asked.

"Wall, Ah thought—iffen any was left——"

"I won't eat it all—not even half of this fish. Sit down. We'll eat together."

He was horrified at the idea. "Hit—ain't fitten—a white gal an' a black man——"

"White girl and black man, we're both runaways," she said. "Now, Jeff, sit down and eat."

It was like a command. He obeyed her awkwardly, squatting on the opposite side of the flat rock, and eating shyly, his head down, his eyes on the food he carried to his mouth with his fingers.

When she had finished, she said to him, "Where did you go after you left me in the mountains?"

He raised his eyes. "Ah try to git back to yo'. But Ah git los'—seem like every holler look lak every otheh holler. Ah went up fust one, then anothah. Ah nevah did see wheah Ah lef' yo'. Afteh awhile, de storm come up. I knowed it warn't no use, so Ah struck out acrost de kentry."

"I thought you'd be in Canada by now."

"Food hahd to git. Colored folks he'p me—one ole man give me a flint an' steel an' a hook an' line. Ole woman give me dis shirt Ah'm wearin'. But mos' was skeered to do much fo' me. Ah moved by night an' hid by day, dodgin' de patrollers. When at las' Ah reach dis river, dey was no way to git acrost. De bridge ovah to Cincinnati is guarded. Dey keep a watch on all de ferries, an' yo' cain't ride a ferry nohow 'thout money. Ah been workin' up de river, hopin' to fin' a skiff Ah kin borrow, an' git ovah to the othah side. River's too wide fo' me to swim. So far, Ah ain't found nothin'."

"Would you steal a boat, Jeff?"

"Wall, no, not 'zackly, Miss Prudence. Ah wouldn't take an' keep it. Ah'd jes' row ovah to de othah side an' leave it. Folks what owns it bound to fin' it wheah Ah'd tie it up. Ah couldn't steal no boat, even iffen Ah want to. Yo' jes' cain't tote a boat 'round with yo', kin yo'? Ah don't want to steal it—or nothin' else. Wall, mebbe Ah did hook a chicken or two iffen Ah was awful hongree an' Ah saw one wanderin' 'round, lonesome an' lookin' fo' comp'ny. Or some roas'in' ears, goin' to waste. But nothin' else, Miss Prudence."

In the growing darkness the fire made a cheerful light in the little clearing. The fish, even unsalted, had satisfied her hunger. She felt drowsy.

Once she asked if the fire might be seen from a house or a road somewhere.

"No—hain't no house nowheah neah," he assured her. "Only road a mile south. An' it couldn't be seein' us nohow, 'cause we're in a holler, an' 'twixt us an' dat road is a hill."

The weary girl nodded in the warmth of the fire.

"Yo'll want to sleep, Miss Prudence," he said. "Ah'll leave dis place to yo', an' fin' a place to sleep somewheah's else."

She looked up at him and his kindness touched her. And she knew she need not fear him.

"No," she said. "You stay here. There's plenty of room for both of us, with the fire between. I saw a bear down by the river. I'd feel safer if someone was here."

He seemed to turn this over in his mind. Then, after a moment, he settled down on the opposite side of the fire, saying nothing. She felt he was grateful that he was not evicted from his own campfire.

After a time she said, "Jeff?"

"Yes'm," he answered.

"You know that man who killed Dr. Lassiter?"

"Yes, Miss."

"I'm afraid he's still hunting for me. He'd kill me if he found me, because I saw him do it."

"Yes, Miss."

"So I want to get across the river, too."

He raised up on an elbow.

"Onlies' thing Ah kin think of," he said, "is fo' us to stick togethah, ontil we fin' a boat."

With that she went to sleep. Twice during the night she woke when she heard him rise to replenish the fire. Otherwise she slept as the exhausted sleep, lying on the bare ground with only the leafy branches of the trees overhead as a shelter between her and the sky above.

In the morning she woke when Jeff stirred up the fire and went down to the river to see if he had caught another fish on the line he left in the stream overnight. There was none.

"Li'l mite of dat fish we cooked lef'," he said. "Yo' take dat, Miss Prudence. Ah'll chaw some slippery ellum bark. Right good to keep yo' from feelin' hongree, ellum bark."

But this she would not permit. She made him take his equal share of the "li'l mite of fish," and they were both chewing "slippery ellum" bark as they started up the river.

5.

In the afternoon they heard the rattle of a wagon. By that they knew that at this point the road came close down to the river.

Together they stole to the edge of the road and looked up and down it. The road had been cut through the forest and its deep ruts showed that it was well traveled. But the wagon they heard had disappeared and no other traffic at the moment was in view. So for the sake of easier traveling, they began a furtive progress near the road, keeping a sharp watch lest somebody see them.

An hour of this, and ahead they made out a cabin.

"Got to git 'round heah," said Jeff apprehensively. "Yo' mebbe could go by de road. Seein' a white gal mightn't cause nobody no nevah-mind. But seein' a black man alone would set de whole kentry huntin'. Ah got to go down to de river again."

She went with him. Together they made a wide circuit through the woods around the small clearing in which stood a miserable little shanty.

All at once Prudence stopped. "You gave me an idea," she said. "Maybe if I went up to that cabin and said I was traveling somewhere, those folks wouldn't think it very strange. They might give me something to eat if I said I was hungry. I'd bring back some to you."

He looked dubious. "Ah dunno——"

"I'll come right back."

"If yo' goin', Ah'll stay heah by de river at dis place. An' Ah'll try to git anothah fish fo' us. So don't be gone long."

Prudence made her way to the road, walked back to the clearing around which they had circled and approached the shanty from the front. Smoke curled lightly from the stick-and-mud chimney. In the weed-grown yard a few chickens scratched and pecked. Right next to the cabin was a small pen containing a half-grown pig.

As soon as she appeared a feisty little long-haired dirty gray dog came bounding toward her and began barking. She picked up a stick. At this the dog backed off a short distance, but continued to jump about stiff-legged with rage; it redoubled its barking.

Presently the door of the shack opened. Out of it glowered an ugly old woman, with red eyes, a deeply wrinkled face, and straggly gray hair wandering out from under the shawl she held over her head and shoulders. In her hand was a corncob pipe.

"Dinky!" she called in a cracked voice. "Shet up!"

The little dog retreated toward her, its back hair still raised and its legs still stiff in the manner of angry dogs.

"Shet up, I tell ye!" said the old woman, flourishing a willow switch, which she brought forth from behind the door.

At sight of the switch the dog made a wide circuit and disappeared under the shanty, from the safety of which retreat it continued now and then to bark.

"Who be ye?" the old woman asked, glaring at Prudence.

"Just a poor girl, ma'am." Prudence made a little bobbing half curtsy.

"What's yer name?"

"Alice Hankins." The fib came easily now.

"Anybody with ye?"

"No, ma'am."

"What ye doin' out here all by yerself?"

"I'm walking to some relatives upriver."

"What do ye want here?"

"Well—I'm hungry, ma'am. I—I thought maybe——?"

The old woman stared at her, as if to decide whether or not this statement was true. "Well, come on in," she said at last. Prudence entered the house.

"Set down." She obeyed.

The old woman took a burning stick from the fireplace and applied it to the bowl—or rather the hole—of her blackened corn-cob pipe. After a few puffs she said, "How fur be ye goin'?"

"I—I don't know exactly," said Prudence. "They live over toward the state line."

"Big Sandy country, likely." More puffs at the pipe. "Say— are ye any kin to the Binnses?"

"No, ma'am. I never heard of them."

"Good thing. If ye was a Binns ye couldn't git a pinch of chicken poop from me."

"Yes, ma'am."

"Well—ye say yer hungry. I ain't got much but I won't let no starvin' gal go away empty."

She moved around and put some scraps of cold food, having the appearance of gray meat, on a plate with a piece of corn bread.

"There," she said. "Eat. I'll make ye some tea."

"Never mind," said Prudence.

"It's only woods tea, but it won't take a minute."

But Prudence wished to end the visit as soon as possible. So she refused the "woods tea" and contented herself with water.

The meat was unappetizing—cold boiled sowbelly—and the

pone was dry. But she was hungry; and as she ate the old woman talked to her in the manner of women the world over who are eager for someone to converse with.

"Ye told me yer name, I'll tell ye mine," she said. "Folks call me Granny Colfax. I live here by my lone, not havin' no kin."

"Don't you have a pretty hard time?"

"Well, I got a pig. An' some chickens. An' I keep a leetle garden—it's jest gettin' a good start now. An' that reminds me— I got to start shettin' the dog outside of nights, to bark an' scare off the deer that comes to eat off the young plants."

"Doesn't it frighten you to live here alone?"

"An' what should I be afeared of? I ain't got so much as a shilling to tempt a robber. An' I'm too old to be bothered by men. Not that they wasn't plenty interested in me forty year ago—yes, even *thirty* year ago." She cackled over the memories, then became serious again. "But that's neither here nor there. I go out into the woods an' dig ginseng roots, an' trade 'em for mebbe a ham now an' then, or a piece of side meat, or a bit of tobaccer, or a leetle salt, or such like. But money I never see. Besides, if anybody tries to bother me, I'll witch 'em—an' the hull dang country knows it." She darted a glance at the girl. "Ever see a witch before?"

"No, ma'am."

"Once Joe Gow's wife said some bad things about me, an' I give her fits," said the old woman. "Jest ask anybody if I didn't. When I got done witchin' her, she had high-stericks an' fits till they come an' begged me to take off the spell. I done it, after they give me a measure of cloth to make me a dress. An' old Tobe Whatley come gunnin' 'round here for partridge an' killed one of my chickens. So I stopped his cow from givin' milk. I kin do lots of witchin' things. I kin cure warts an' rheumatics an' dropsy. An' I kin make luck charms an' love powders—say, ye look like a gal that needs a leetle luck yourself. I'm goin' to give ye a charm, an' it won't cost ye a cent."

The witch went to an old dresser in the corner of the cabin. When she returned she held in her hand a small leathery sack-

like object with strings attached, no larger than a silver half-dollar.
"There's goofer dust in that, mixed with love oil. Tie it
'round yer left ankle."

Prudence had no wish to do so, but she was almost afraid
to disobey. She tied the strings of the curious little leathery bag
about her ankle as directed, wondering what it was, and feeling
a shrinking sensation at touching it.

When she rose to go, the witch said, "I'll give ye some things
to remember. If a black cat crosses yer trail, make the sign of
the cross with yer left foot on the ground to ward off bad luck.
Don't never cut yer fingernails on Sunday—the Devil will be near
ye all the next week. Never hand a saltshaker to another person
or take it from them. It's bad luck. The only way to do is let
them set it on the table an' then pick it up. Now that's enough
for ye, child. Yer goin' now? Ye might git hungry again. Here,
take the rest of this meat an' bread, an' welcome. I got more
where that come from."

Prudence thanked her strange hostess, and with the food
wrapped in an old newspaper, hurried down the road. A few score
yards eastward of the witch's shanty she entered the woods and
soon found Jeff, where he said he would wait beside the river.

Chapter 16

1.

"Miss Prudence, what yo' got on yo' ankle?" the Negro asked as he finished eating the food she brought him.

"The old woman in the cabin made me put it on for a charm," she replied.

He eyed the strange little sack uneasily.

"She a conjure woman?" he asked.

"Well, she said she was a witch. If it bothers you I'll take it off."

"Oh, no! No, don't yo' do dat!" he exclaimed, the whites of his eyes showing in genuine alarm. "Yo' take off dat charm, de conjure woman likely be mad."

"She wouldn't know it."

"How yo' know she wouldn't know? Yo' cain't nevah tell when a conjure woman is afteh yo'. All dat woman got to do is go out an' pick up yo' tracks, an' yo' is onder her spell."

"How can she pick up my tracks?"

"Dey picks up de dust of yo' footprints—lak on de road—

273

an' puts it in a hankerchiff an' dey keeps dat an' kin use it to witch yo' any time dey wants. Dey makes yo' stumble an' fall. Dey gives yo' shootin' pains. Dey puts yo' in trouble. Dey makes yo' lose yo' mind."

"I don't believe all that, Jeff."

"Yo' gotta believe it, Miss Prudence," he said earnestly. "Dey does some turrible things. Ah knowed a woman oncet had a snake witched inter her laig. She would screech dat de snake was quilin' 'round in her laig. An' if yo' put yo' hand on her laig, yo' could feel dat snake squirmin' in onder de skin. Dat woman, she finally kilt herself with a knife. Stuck it inter her laig, to git dat snake out, an' cut a big blood vessel an' bled to death."

"What happened to the snake?"

"Ah dunno. Reckon she kilt it when she stuck dat knife in her laig. It shore wasn't wigglin' when dey laid her away."

"Did you feel that snake yourself, Jeff?"

"No, but Ah talked to folks dat done so."

"The old witch told me this was a good-luck charm."

"Mebbe so." Jeff shook his head. "But Ah don't like no truck with conjure doctahs or witches. Yo' shore cain't take it off, but Ah don't like it."

"What's that sack made of?"

He gave her a queer look. "Don't yo' know?"

She shook her head.

"Conjure doctahs gen'rally uses a dried up cod," he said.

"Cod?" She was unfamiliar with the term.

"A he-stone bag," he elucidated. "Sometimes dey even use man cods, iffen dey kin git to a man corpse."

She realized suddenly that what she had tied around her ankle was a horrible desiccated scrotum of some kind. Wildly she tore it off.

"Now yo' done it!" cried Jeff in real alarm. "No, don't throw it away! We gotta lay de spell!"

He took the thing, from which Prudence averted her eyes.

"Hit ain't no man cod," he said. She shuddered. "More lak a dog cod, or mebbe a wolf cod."

He built a small fire, put the dreadful object into the flames and burned it to ashes. When it was entirely consumed he turned to Prudence. "Yo' got a coin? It gotta be silver."

"No," she said.

"Ah hain't neither," he said. He looked anxious.

"Does it have to be a coin?" she asked.

"No, jes' as long as it's silver."

She looked at the silver ring on her finger, the one her father gave her when she was in the convent school. It was the only thing left to her that he gave her. But she felt that she must allay if possible this unreasonable superstitious fear that had possession of the Negro. So she took it from her finger and placed it in Jeff's palm.

Carefully he gathered the ashes into the paper in which she had brought him the food, placed the silver ring with it, bundled it up carefully, tied it with a bark string, and going down to the river bank threw it as far as he could into the stream. As soon as it struck the water he recited a charm:

> Burn to ashes,
> Cross with silver,
> River wash bad spell away.

He watched the paper package float down the current, slowly sinking as it became soaked, until it disappeared. But he still was not easy in his mind.

"Ah jes' hopes it works," he said as he returned to her. And he added, "Ah hain't goin' near dat road again. Not with no conjure spell mebbe still in de air. Yo' cain't nevah tell how far it'll trail yo'. Scare me to death. If dey evah ketch me an' carry me back to Lassiter's on 'count of dat bad spell, dat overseer, he'll cut de meat off'n my back with a whip ontil yo' kin see mah liver an' lungs right through mah ribs."

His depression continued all the rest of the day as they worked on up the river. That night they camped as before and he prepared to fish. Muttering some kind of incantation he spit on his bait—some worms on his hook—before he dropped it into the water.

They sat on opposite sides of a small fire as darkness fell.

Prudence said, "The old woman told me the bag had goofer dust and love oil in it."

He nodded, as if unsurprised.

"What's goofer dust?" she asked.

"Why, dat's de dust tooken offen a grave."

"What's love oil?"

He looked at her amazed. "Don't yo' know *nothin'*?"

"Well, I don't know that."

He thought for a moment and looked at her with some embarrassment. "De onliest way Ah kin tell yo' is dat it's de kind of ile people makes when dey makes love together."

She understood his meaning and felt new distaste. But she tried to reason him out of his mood.

"This is all superstition, Jeff," she said. "Witches can't really hurt anybody."

"Dey cain't?" He was scandalized. "Not meanin' to dispute with yo', Miss Prudence, but dey's scads of ways dey kin harm yo'. Dey puts a man's name in a daid bird's mouth an' lets it dry up—an' he dries up along with it. A hoss's hair, with a snake's tooth an' a pinch of gunpowder put onder yo' doorstep will bring death by sickness for yo' or someone in yo' fam'ly. If dey writes a pusson's name on an aig laid by a black hen—only writes it back'ards—an' den throw it ovah his house, he'll go crazy. Dey bury somep'n belongin' to a pusson with de right spell an' his liver will rot. If dey throw goofer dust on his porch, he'll be sick all de time ontil he dies. Dey kin make a figger out'n wax, name it fo' a man, stick pins in it an' melt it in de fire—he'll die in big pain. Dem's jes' a few of de ways conjure doctahs kin hurt yo'."

She saw she could not turn him from his depression, and fell silent. After a time he went to examine his fish line. She heard him give an exclamation, and there was a splash in the water. When he returned he held the fish line, looped, in his hand.

"Nothin' goin' to be no good," he said gloomily. "Know whut Ah caught on dat hook? A muddler. Uglies' fish God evah made, an' p'ison to eat. Cain't ketch no fish tonight. Ever'body knows dat iffen yo' ketch a muddler no othah fish is goin' to bite ontil de nex' day."

He sat down by the fire and maundered about "witch womans" that left their skins lying in bed at night and flew about the country doing evil, returning to their skins and getting into them before morning, and of a woman who was "deviled" and would have fits and screaming spells, so that the only thing that could be done for her was to hold her down until the devils went away, until their next visitation.

"Scary thing, dat," he said. "Ah done it oncet—he'p hol' down dat ole woman. She grabbed 'round an' screeched an' frothed at de mouth, an' Ah didn't know what minute dem devils might go to me instid of her."

Privately Prudence thought the woman probably was subject to epileptic fits, but she knew she could not shake Jeff's belief in the "devils."

He went on to say that witches sometimes took the form of wolves or cats or rabbits, and you could tell them from the real animals only if they disappeared before your eyes, as they sometimes did after they had worked their spells.

Prudence curled up beside the fire, knowing she must sleep hungry, and wondering how this man, who had proved his courage so conclusively, could be sent into abject terror by the superstitions he had been taught. That night she slept restlessly and woke frequently. Each time she saw Jeff sitting, brooding, on the other side of the fire. He must not have slept during all those dark hours.

2.

Next morning Prudence once more was famished. But the Negro poked around in the woods and came back with some whitish, bulbous objects in his hands.

"Mushrooms," he said.

"But are you sure?" she asked.

"Ah's knowed mushrooms sence Ah was a chile," he assured her. "Dey's good ones an' p'ison ones. P'ison toadstools has a li'l cap at de bottom. Dese is good. Ah been pickin' 'em all mah life." He hesitated. "Ain't much of a way to cook 'em," he said. "Reckon jes' roastin' 'em is all we kin do. Won't taste like much, but dey'll take de aidge off'n hunger."

He washed them and broiled them on sticks over the fire. At first she did not want to eat; but he did so, and she had gained such confidence in him that she tried them. They were flat and tasteless, but she chewed one or two and swallowed. As he said, they relieved her hunger and she experienced no bad effects.

Jeff would not go near the road again, but she ventured toward it to see if any houses were in view. A man riding a mule was coming from the east, the upriver way. He was carrying a gun. As he came nearer to her hiding place she recognized him. He was Alex Glover!

She did not hail him. Instead she cowered even lower in her covert until he was gone and headed back toward his own place. Then she hurried to Jeff.

"I saw the man I was staying with!" she told him. "He knows I'm a runaway, and there's twenty-five dollars reward for me. He's after me!"

The Negro looked alarmed. "We jes' gotta fin' a boat an' git ovah inter Ohio," he said. "No tellin' who might be comin' up dat road next."

They began again working eastward up the river. Prudence felt a bitter disappointment that Alex Glover, and presumably the whole Glover family, had forsaken their friendship for her to gain that money reward. But she now was as anxious as Jeff to get to the other side of the river.

Somewhat after noon they saw a clearing at a place where the road ran rather near to the river. There was a house by the road and a barn behind it, and Jeff gave an exclamation.

"A landin'!" he said. "Boat likely heah."

They stopped and considered. "We might git dat boat," he said. "But dey'd see us. Iffen it was dark—but no use."

She said, "Maybe if I went up to that house—to the front —I could ask questions and beg for food, and keep them occupied. It would give you a chance——"

He was still under his dark superstitious fears. "Ah don't see no good in it. Bad folks lives along heah, looks like."

"We've got to get across," she argued. And at last he agreed, though unwillingly.

"Den Ah'll git de boat, an' bring it right heah, wheah we is now," he said. "Good place heah to hide it onder de trees hangin' low ovah de water. But don't be gone long."

So she went up through the woods to the road, and approached the house from the front, as she had done at Granny Colfax' shanty.

It was a two-story house with clapboard sides and a shake roof; it looked run down and lacking paint, but somebody evidently lived in it, for the windows were glassed and had heavy curtains behind them.

As she mounted the steps to the porch Prudence had an uncanny feeling that she was being watched from behind those curtains. Nevertheless, she knocked on the door.

There was no answer. She knocked again. When she was about to turn away the door opened just a crack and through the aperture a woman spoke.

"What do you want?"

"I'm hungry," said Prudence, "and I thought maybe——"

"Who are you?"

"Alice Hankins." The old lie again.

"Well, git along, Alice Hankins. This ain't no boardin' house."

"Yes, ma'am." Prudence turned to depart, embarrassed.

The woman spoke again. "Wait a minute."

Prudence turned toward the narrowly opened door.

"Who you got with you?"

"Nobody."

"You're alone? All alone?"

"Yes, ma'am."

The door opened wider. It revealed a harsh-faced woman with dyed red hair.

"Where you from?" the woman asked suspiciously.

"I'm from downriver. Trying to get to the Big Sandy country," said Prudence, remembering the old witch's guess. She felt that the woman was looking her up and down, appraising her.

"Why you goin' to the Big Sandy?" was the next question.

"I've got relatives living there."

"H'mm. Well, come on in."

Prudence entered as the door was held open by the rather intimidating female who had been speaking with her.

The interior of the room she entered was dim, having only such light as came through the heavy curtains, but it evidently was some sort of a sitting room, with a plush settee, some armchairs, and a fireplace.

"Know who I am?" asked the woman.

"No, ma'am."

"Ever hear of Mag Binns?"

Binns . . . the name the old witch had spoken with such venom. But Prudence shook her head.

"You might as well have somethin' to eat," said Mag. "We're jest fixin' to eat ourselves." She raised her voice. "Florabelle! We got company!"

She ushered Prudence into the next room, where there was a table set with some dishes. A younger woman came in from what evidently was the kitchen. She stopped, leaning against the side of the doorway, and looked at Prudence with contempt.

"Disappointed it ain't some man, Florabelle?" said the older woman with a malicious chuckle. "Well, this is Alice Hankins. Alice is walkin' to relatives in the up country. She's tired, an' she's goin' to have a bite with us, an' maybe stay a little while."

Prudence half opened her mouth to deny this last, then closed it. She had the feeling of some strange undercurrent here, which she hardly knew how to interpret.

If the two women were mother and daughter there was

little about their appearance to suggest it. Mag, the older one, was thin and sharp featured, with dark eyes, a grim mouth, and hair dyed a violent red. She was in her forties, at a guess. The one called Florabelle was in her twenties, plump, slatternly, and half-way pretty in an unkempt sort of way. Her mouth was petulant, her skin fair, and her light brown hair was wrapped about her head and knotted carelessly behind.

Both women were attired in wrappers. Florabelle's was a tawdry pink silk held closely about her body so that it showed off her insinuatingly large breasts and her full posteriors; and Mag's wrapper was a purple velveteen with spots of grease upon it and, if it revealed anything, it was that its wearer was less than voluptuous. Softness almost to flabbiness was the impression Prudence got of the younger woman and hardness almost to bitterness was her impression of the elder one.

"Set down at the table," said Mag.

With vague disquietude Prudence obeyed.

"Ham hock an' black-eyed peas is what we got," said Mag.

She ladled helpings into three plates. There was corn bread and the girl ate, finding the food not unpalatable.

"Travel much?" Mag asked after a time.

"No, ma'am," said Prudence.

"Ever been in New Orleans?"

"No." The girl wondered where this was leading.

"You'd like it there," said Mag. "Somethin' doin' all the time. You'd meet a lot of interestin' people. How'd you like to take a job there?"

"What kind of job?"

Mag surveyed her shrewdly. "Dependin' on what you kin do."

"I don't know how to do much."

"How old are you?"

"Seventeen, going on eighteen."

"You could sure learn. Men would be crazy about you. You could make your fortune."

Prudence stared at her. "I don't want any job——"

She started to rise from her chair.

"*Set down!*"

The ugly sternness of the command caused the girl to sink back in her seat, breathless and alarmed.

"You ain't what you claim to be, gal," said Mag. "You say you've lived in the Big Sandy country, yet you talk like you're well read. I can tell a Big Sandy native soon's she's spoke two words."

"I—I don't know—what you mean," stammered Prudence with sudden fear.

"I'll tell you what I mean," said Meg grimly. "You ain't headed for the Big Sandy. You got somethin' else in mind. Now, jest what is it?"

"Well, I—I want to go to Washington——"

"Now here's a change! Why Washington?"

"I want to see the President——"

"What kind of a story is that? *You* see the President? He wouldn't spit on the likes of you!" A cunning grin suddenly came over Mag's face. "But that's all right, that's all right. What's a little fibbin' amongst friends? Whatever you're really after is none of my business, is it?"

She sat back and looked at Prudence as if estimating her.

"I'll tell you," she went on, still with that grin. "I kin put you in the way of somethin' pretty good. How'd you like to go on the stage? An actress, hey? You got looks. They pay good money for pretty actresses in New Orleans. Now I got a friend there, an' at a word from me she'd take you right into her own boardin'house an' give you the best kind of schoolin' in all them arts. What do you say to that, gal? Wouldn't cost you a cent— you'd be a companion to the owner of a fancy boardin'house, learn how to meet an' please people, especially gentlemen. No work, easy life, lovely clothes. Your future'd be made! Many a gal I've sent to that very place has married into rich families, an' has their own house, an' coach, an' servants, an' jewels, an' everythin' they want. How'd you like that, hey?"

With difficulty Prudence's mind had assimilated the idea that a monstrous proposal was being made to her.

"I don't want it!" she cried, jumping up. "Please let me go on my way. Thank you for the food, but——"

"Not so fast!" Mag's face suddenly hardened. "Think you're goin' to git off as easy as that? Don't like what I'm sayin'? Not good enough for you? Well, Miss Alice, I've been studyin' you, an' I've got you figgered. You're a *spy!*"

"No, I'm not!" Prudence began to see that she was in some serious danger.

Suddenly she tried to dart from the room. With surprising quickness Florabelle was at the door before her and Mag seized her from behind.

"A spy! A goddamned spy! Who sent you here? Answer me that!"

Now completely terrified, Prudence could not speak.

"Goddamn whore, that's what you are! Playin' it innocent an' pryin' into things! I'll show you what whorin's *really* like! Git her into that closet, Florabelle!"

Hauling and pulling at her, the two women hustled her to a closet, pushed her into it, slammed the door shut and locked it.

For a time Prudence lay on the floor where she had fallen, too dazed by this sudden shift to think clearly. She knew now that she was in the clutches of two evil women, and that they somehow proposed a dreadful destiny for her. But how they planned to carry out their schemes she could not imagine. New Orleans—if that was to be her destination—was far away. She would never go there willingly. Could they force her to do so?

After awhile she rose and made a groping investigation of the dark little cubicle she was pent up in. It was perhaps no more than four feet wide and six feet long, and a stairway sloped over it from the back, as she could tell by feeling the bottom of the steps. A few articles of clothing hung on the walls, but otherwise the closet was empty.

She tried the door, found it tightly locked, and finally knocked on it.

"What do you want?" It was Mag's voice.

"Please let me out."

"You'll stay there until we're good an' ready to let you out."

"But—I want to go—there's somebody waiting for me——"

"Someone waiting? Who?"

Even in this extremity Prudence would not reveal anything concerning Jeff. Besides, it would only make matters worse.

"My—my uncle—" she said.

The only reply to this weak lie was mocking laughter from both women. Prudence sank to the floor. At last, in her despair, she wept.

3.

After a time she realized that tears would not help her, so she stopped crying. Bleakly she thought of the evil people she had encountered—Peebles and Mrs. Tabitha, the terrible Blevins brothers, these Binns women, and now, she felt, the Glovers, whom she had believed were her friends.

Then, with her sense of fairness, she reminded herself of those who had befriended her; and against the evil ones she balanced the affection of Miss Sally, the kindness of old Corbie, the loyalty of Jeff the slave, and the tenderness of her father. Most wistfully she wondered what would be the fate of her father, so that for a time she hardly considered what might happen to herself.

Hours passed. She thought it must be nightfall; she hoped that Jeff had found the boat he was going to look for and safely made his escape across the river. She knew he must have gone long before this time, and she did not blame him, for she had promised to return to him quickly.

Much later someone came to the back door of the house and was admitted with evident welcome by Mag and Florabelle. It was a man and as he entered the dining room with the women, he said, "That's a prime hoss I put in the barn."

Prudence's blood almost froze. She recognized that voice. It was Bad 'Lias Blevins.

"I need a drink," she next heard him say.

"We got some good Monongahela," said Mag. "Couple of river men came up from the landin' last week."

"River men?" Bad 'Lias gave a laugh. "Both of 'em take a crack at you, Florabelle?"

"No," said Florabelle with a giggling whinny. "Only one. The other laid up with Mag."

"Why not?" said Mag, as if defending herself from some aspersion. "I ain't lost my attractions. I may not be as young as I was, but I still got the fire, an' there's tricks to this trade that only experience will teach you."

"I kin bet on that," said Bad 'Lias.

"All they had to pay was whiskey," Mag went on. "No money. We took ten gallon of Monongahela from them. Here, try this."

Her ears had grown acute from hard listening, and Prudence could hear the gulping of the man as he drank.

"Ah!" he said. "That's shore good. How's things goin'?"

"Slow lately," said Mag. "Once in awhile some ridge-runner that's pussy-crazy happens along. Or a river man with a stiff rhubarb. We charge what the traffic'll bear for beddin' with 'em an' sometimes we lift a poke. Especial if it's a young-un from around here. He'd be too ashamed to admit he lost it in this house. Of course we help the boys of the Clan when they need to turn somethin' they got on a speculation."

"But nothin' happens often enough," said Florabelle plaintively. "It's too lonesome here. I got a notion to go back to New Orleans. There's always money an' studs lookin' for a gal in the Swamp District."

"Mebbe I kin take care of it for you," said Bad 'Lias with a chuckle. "You ain't had no man for a week, an' I been without a woman longer than that——"

" 'Lias, behave yourself!" she squealed.

He laughed. "I reckon both of us has got the eagers. Ain't we?"

She did not answer but Prudence heard the sound of a kiss. Mag said, "If you two are goin' to mush, I'll start supper."

"We'll go to the bedroom," said the man. "Come on, honey."

Prudence heard them rise. The bedroom evidently was next to the closet in which she was cowering. She could hear everything through the thin plaster wall.

From the bedroom Florabelle said coyly, "You ain't been near us in three months."

"I aim to make up for that now," he replied.

There was a prolonged and tense silence.

"Ooh," gasped the woman as if half smothered. "You near squeeze the breath out of a person——"

There evidently were preliminaries to be gone through. Once she said, "Look out—be careful, honey, you'll tear it——"

"All right, undo it yourself," he said.

"You always want things your own way," she said with a mock whimper. "There—is that enough?"

"No. Take off every stitch."

"I—I—can't when you keep—doin' things like that——"

Another long silence, followed by a smart slap and a squeal.

The man chortled, "Bare bottom like you got is jest beggin' for a spank."

"But it hurts——"

"I'll make it hurt good. Git down on that bed."

Prudence could hear the man's voice, low and hoarse, saying something she did not understand.

No words now, but the silence seemed to Prudence to be charged with some terrible expectancy. For what seemed interminable minutes she listened to a rustling and a shifting of heavy bodies and labored breathing.

At last, as if from under some asphyxiating weight, the woman uttered a wail, low and vibrant with intimate feeling.

A little later the man said, "Damn." Not in profanity, but as if in some solemn wonder.

Then there was quiet, as if they had drawn apart.

After a time the woman said, "Feel better, honey?"

The man grunted.

"Another little trick?" she suggested.

"Lemme alone for a minute. We got all night." A long silence and he said, "I could use another drink."

"Shall I get dressed?"

"Might as well—for now."

Movements in the bedroom, the rustle of garments.

Florabelle gave a little teasing laugh. "I thought you wanted me to get dressed."

"I jest wanted another feel."

"Now, 'Lias——"

Another straining silence. Then he said, "All right. Mag's about got supper ready."

Prudence heard them pass out of the bedroom into the dining room.

4.

The stallion lustings in the next room had added to the terror of the girl locked in the closet. Nature enabled her almost to picture the scene on that bed—the naked woman, the man, some wild ecstasy. To her it seemed crude and disgusting, and also frightening, as she thought of herself in the hands of these unspeakable creatures.

In the dining room Mag was saying, "Drink hearty, 'Lias. Then let's eat. What you been up to needs food."

It was growing dark, because someone lit a lamp or candle. The light showed under the crack below the door of the closet.

Mag said, "Looks like you owe Florabelle a pretty—takin' on a stud like you."

"I ain't through with Florabelle," he said.

No reply from Florabelle.

The clinking of dishes and cutlery indicated that they were eating. After a silence the man spoke, evidently with his mouth full:

"Reason I'm this far north is I run into a leetle trouble. Had to kill a man to rob him. Name of Lassiter. His brother had me arrested." Blevins gave a chuckle. "Fat chance he had prosecutin' me, with Drew Peebles puttin' up the bond an' Ezekiel Rockcastle handlin' the law. They made a monkey out'n young Lassiter, an' the jury acquitted me. So I can't never be tried ag'in on that partic'lar charge."

He paused, perhaps to take another biteful.

"Jest the same," he resumed, "I thought I'd make myself scarce for awhile. Troy Lassiter's a devil. No tellin' what he might stir up." Another momentary silence, then, "I heard that John Murrell's been up this way. I'd like to talk with him."

"He ain't been near this place," said Mag. "More likely he's over in Arkansaw, in what he calls his Garden of Eden. Always schemin', that man. I hear he's been clear over in the Carolinas, lookin' up fellers with the right grit."

"He's a caution," agreed Bad 'Lias. "The boss bandit of the hull damn Clan. I know for sure he kin call up two hundred or more of the toughest outlaws in the kentry, if he's a mind to. Smooth as silk an' sharp as a razor an' when he wants to be, as mean as the Devil red hot from home."

"He's all that. An' when he gits the slave rebellion all ready an' everythin' else set, there'll be the damndest ruckus this country ever seen—they'll think hell's busted loose an' all the fences down."

"I aim to be in on that," said Bad 'Lias. "But right now I'd like to set him on that cock-a-hoop young Lassiter. He could take care of him, an' no mistake. Lookit that feller who had him arrested in New Orleans. 'Course Murrell was too slick for that an' got himself swore out of the complaint by his own men. But that feller—I kin remember Murrell's own words about him: 'He soon had a nurse that attended him day an' night ontil he found his way to the bottom of the Mississippi River.' Stalked, an' killed, an' gutted, an' sunk, *he* was. I'd like to see that happen to Lassiter. Not that I'm skeared of him," he finished.

Prudence, in her closet, listened with horror and fear to what the outlaw planned for Troy Lassiter. She prayed that there

might be some way to warn him. And she knew again the sick
feeling of her own helplessness.

"Mebbe you'll run onto Murrell," said Mag indifferently.

"Well, yeah. Sooner or later," said Bad 'Lias. "But now let's
git down to business. Thar's that hoss in the stable—he'll have
to be moved purty soon. By night, too. An' here's some joolry
that needs turnin'."

Evidently they examined his loot, for Mag said, "That ruby
ring's a good 'un. An' the watch an' chain is solid gold."

"Ought to be," said Blevins. "The man I took 'em off'n was
one of the biggest swells in Tennessee."

Prudence knew he referred to the murdered Dr. Lassiter.

"I been thinkin'," Mag was saying. "We done some pretty
big favors for you, 'Lias——"

"An' always took your cut."

"Yes. But there's risks an' dangers. That Jew feller, Aaron,
that used to handle stuff for us in Cincinnati, he's gone. I hear
they got him in jail at Covington."

"Thar's other fences."

"Sometimes they're hard to reach. Now, 'Lias, I ain't sayin'
we won't handle this for you. But I'm sayin' it's time for you
to do somethin' for us in turn."

"Like what?"

"Carry some merchandise for us to New Orleans."

"What merchandise?"

"A piece of fancy goods. I got a workin' agreement with
Mother Colby in New Orleans——"

"Mother Colby that runs the big parlor house on Girod
Street in the Swamp?"

"The same. I furnish her with a likely gal, an' she gives
me half of what that gal earns in her first year in the house.
Mother Colby knows how to set prices. A pretty gal who's a
sure-nough virgin might get as much as two hundred dollars from
some gentleman who wants the priv'lege of takin' her maiden-
head. There's studs that's queer that way. An' after that, so long
as she's fresh lookin', she'll get ten dollars a trick from them

New Orleans beaus. An' once she's broke in, she'll turn maybe
four or five tricks a night, or even more. A gal like that might
take in five thousand in the first year. Of course Mother Colby
collects it all, an' I get half of it. Twenty-five hundred dollars.
Not bad."

"Holy Kee-rist, no! But what if the gal objects?"

"Mother Colby knows a million ways to break 'em in. Time
she gets through with an unwillin' little hellcat, that gal's willin'
to go to bed with the Devil himself, horns, hooves, tail, an' all.
I've sent more'n one to Mother Colby, an' not one of 'em but
turned into a first-class whore."

"Whar do I come in on this?"

"The gal I got is pretty as you ever seen. She'll make a
notch gal the bloods will be fightin' to get to. You're to take her
downriver by boat——"

"What kind of boat?"

"We got a big pirogue down at the landin'. It's fixed up with
a sail an' has a closed cabin in the stern. You'd keep the gal in
there where nobody'd see her until you deliver her at the Swamp.
There's money in it for you from both Mother Colby an' me;
an' besides, we'll turn that horse and jewelry for you. One
thing you got to remember. You cain't make free with this gal
on the way down. Mother Colby won't pay for no damaged
goods."

"I don't like it. Seems purty risky to me."

"Others has done it an' never a slip. You'll be out of
this part of the country till things cool down. An' you stand to
make a thousand dollars."

Prudence, listening, could hardly believe what she heard
as this heartless fate was planned for her. Yet the voices of
Mag and Bad 'Lias were pitched on the level of calm business
discussion, as if a girl like herself was no more important than
a bolt of cotton cloth or a keg of whiskey.

Bad 'Lias cleared his throat. "Wall, I shore cain't take the
stuff back to Tennessee for old Peebles to handle for me. It
was took off'n a man from that very part of the state."

"Then you'll do it?"

After a moment he said, "Let's take a look at the critter."

Prudence shrank back in the closet as the door was opened and the light from a candle flared in. The bestial one-eyed visage of the outlaw brought a little squeal of terror from her. A moment later she was seized by a wrist and dragged out into the room.

Bad 'Lias gave a great curse. "*She* ain't goin' to New Orleans or no place else! I know this gal!"

"You do?" asked Mag in surprise.

"Yeah, I shore do! She knows enough to send me an' you an' the hull damn Clan to the gallows. I been huntin' for her all the way acrost Kaintuck!"

"Just a minute!" said Mag. "She's worth a heap of money delivered in New Orleans—twenty-five hundred to me, a thousand to you. You goin' to throw away that kind of money?"

"Money's nothin' to a man's neck!"

"I got an interest in this——"

"Stop blabberin'!"

Still holding Prudence by the wrist, Bad 'Lias drew his knife.

"If you're goin' to do any pig-stickin'," said Mag coldly, "do it outside, away from the house."

The girl begged and weakly tried to resist. But she was no match for the man's brute strength, and his clutch on her wrist was painful as he dragged her to the door.

As the door swung open, a rifle cracked like a snapping whip outside, and a bullet splintered the doorjamb right beside the outlaw's head.

Chapter 17

1.

The sun had set and the gloom of twilight was in the woods.

At the shot Bad 'Lias sprang back into the house and slammed the door shut.

"Douse that light!" he commanded, indicating a candle on the table. Then he leaped for his gun, which stood in a corner.

The outlaw was conscious only of his own peril. Mag blew out the light and she and Florabelle once more threw Prudence into the closet and locked her in.

The terrified girl heard guns thud outside and somewhere a glass windowpane broke with a shattering crash. Blevins cursed as he fired at one of his enemies among the dark trees about the house.

Firearms continued to blast and Prudence heard men shouting directions, or information to one another. In the house more windows broke; bullets seemed to search their way into the interior, for she could hear their whine and thud against the walls. Mag and Florabelle shrieked continually with fear. They were crouching low on the floor, to judge by the direction of the sound.

A smell of gunpowder smoke penetrated into the closet as Bad 'Lias, in the dining room and fighting for his life, fired his rifle again and again.

"Before they take me, thar'll be some new faces in hell!" Prudence heard him say once.

Then the shooting outside ceased for a moment and a voice was lifted.

"Elias Blevins, you are surrounded. Come out of that house unarmed and with your hands above your head, or the house will be set afire!"

It brought a new scream from Mag and Florabelle. "For God's sake do what he says!" they implored.

"Shet up!" snarled the outlaw.

Prudence heard his gun crash in the dining room. Its report was answered by a spiteful spatter of shots outside.

"Give up!" begged Mag. "Oh, Lord, give up!"

"Like hell I will! Them bastards is after *me*, not you!"

"Oh—they'll set the house on fire—we'll all burn——"

"Burn then! You'll frizzle in hell anyhow!"

After a time he said, "It's gotten right dark. I'm goin' to make a break for it!"

It was the back door from which he tried to make his escape. He was too late. Right beside the door where one of the besiegers had crept, a rifle blasted.

Prudence heard a heavy body crash to the floor.

"I'm shot, by God, I'm shot," the outlaw said as if unbelieving. "They shot me, them goddamn fellers——"

The door was flung open and there was a confusion of men's voices and a tramping of boots as many entered the house.

"Oh, God—don't be so rough," came Bad 'Lias' voice, pleading now. "I'm shot I tell you—right here in the side—"

Another voice said, "Tie him up." Then, "All right, you two, who are you?"

The two women of the house who had been struck silent by the rush of men into it began whimpering.

At that Prudence came to herself and began pounding on the closet door with her little fists.

"See who's in there," somebody ordered.

The door was unlocked and opened and Prudence came out, blinking in the light of candles the men had lit in the dining room.

The first face she saw was that of Troy Lassiter. She saw disbelief, then joy in his face.

"Miss Prudence!" he exclaimed incredulously. And, "Prudence—my dear——"

"Oh, Troy!" She went into his arms, her face against his shoulder. "I've been so afraid . . ."

He looked down at the blonde head. "Prudence, what are you doing here?"

She turned her face up toward his, and it was stained with dried tears. "Those women locked me up," she said. "They were going to ship me down the river to some horrible place in New Orleans. Then Bad 'Lias came. He was going to kill me——"

"Why?"

"Because I saw him murder Dr. Lassiter—and—and his own brother——"

"His *brother*?"

"Yes. Little 'Lige."

"You saw that? You'd swear to it?"

"Yes."

"Prudence, come with me."

By the hand he led her into the parlor and seated her on the plush settee. Then he sat beside her, still holding her hand, and the look in his eyes told its own story. Several of the men stood about, all intent on her.

"Prudence, tell me—just what did you see?" he asked.

As briefly as she could she related to him the circumstances under which, right before her eyes, Dr. Lassiter was killed. Then she went on to tell of how she was captured and taken to the cave. And how Bad 'Lias slew Little 'Lige Blevins in the door of that cavern when he was trying to escape.

"So that was *his* blood in the cave," said Lassiter. "We found some things of yours—and with that blood—we thought you were —gone from us forever——"

"Cap'n," said a voice from the dining room, "you're needed in here."

She looked up and saw Alex Glover as he came into the sitting room.

"What's *he* doing here?" she cried, springing to her feet. "He's trying to get me, to send me back to Peebles——"

"Me?" said Glover. "Not me."

"But I saw you hunting me yesterday along the road."

He grinned at her. "I was bird doggin' these here outlaws for the posse."

"I thought you'd turned against me."

"No, gal. We didn't even know whar you'd gone. Why, we'd of helped you if we'd known. You kin come back an' have a home with us as long as you want—an' Libby'd say the same."

"No, Alex, I'm going to take her back home," said Lassiter. "Tell them to wait a minute. I've got a few more questions here."

He turned to the girl, but she forestalled him. "What about my father?" she demanded. "Is he still in——?"

"Prison?" he finished for her. "I'm afraid so. I tried to help him, but he wouldn't let me."

She sat down listlessly.

"Did you hear these people mention anybody else?" he asked her.

"Yes, they mentioned Mr. Peebles and Mr. Rockcastle."

"What did they say?"

"Bad 'Lias said they got him out of jail or something. He said they made—well, a monkey—out of you."

"They did." He nodded gravely. "Was there anything else?"

"They spoke of somebody named Merrill, or something like that——"

"Murrell," he said. "What about him?"

"Something about a slave rebellion."

"You heard that?"

"Yes, and they said he was sharp as a razor and mean as the Devil, and Bad 'Lias was hoping he'd do something bad to you."

"I'll warrant," said Lassiter grimly. "What else?"

"Bad 'Lias thought he was up in this country, but the women said no."

Lassiter turned to the men in the room. "You've heard all this?"

"Aye," somebody said. "His own brother."

He looked at Prudence again. "Thank you," he said. "I can't possibly tell you how glad I am—to see you—to know you're safe. I want to hear everything about you, and I have worlds of things to tell you—when we can be alone together." His voice sounded almost pleadingly tender.

Then he broke off and the sternness returned to his face. "But first I must attend to this business here."

2.

The men left her, all of them, and went back into the dining room where the prisoners were being held. She went to the half-open door from which she could see all that went on there. Her mind was chaotic. She had been *so* glad to see Troy. And he had called her "my dear" . . .

But one thing remained as a question in her state of alarm, which had been almost continuous for so many days. Troy said he was going to take her "home." She had not had time to ask if that meant to Turkeytoe and to Peebles' Tavern. She would rather die than go back to servitude.

Then her whole attention became fixed on the "business" of which Lassiter had spoken.

There were more than a dozen men in the room, roughly dressed and armed with guns and knives, and it seemed to her that all of them looked to Troy for leadership. He stood, tall, booted, grim, and his gleaming eyes went over the prisoners.

"How bad is Blevins hurt?" he asked.

"Shoulder shot but not gut shot," said one of the men guarding the outlaw. "He'll live."

"That remains to be seen," said Lassiter. He chopped off his words.

"Now—these women," he went on. "Know anything about them, Sheriff?"

The man to whom he spoke was stocky and middle-aged; he had a coarse brown beard and deep crow's-feet about his eyes. "They're a bad lot, Cap'n," he said. "Low-down whores, an' workin' with all the criminals of the valley. Fools that visited them has sometimes been got drunk an' robbed of what they had in their pockets, accordin' to our reports."

"Thar's a hoss down in the barn that's been stole, from the looks of him," said Alex Glover. "Bay stallion. Thoroughbred. Somebody's painted over the white star on his forehead an' the white stockin's on his hind fetlocks, to fault identification——"

"The Morgan County horse," said Lassiter. "You can put him in the pound, Sheriff, and send for Colonel Carter at West Liberty who owns him. There's a reward in this."

The sheriff said, "The boys jest found these."

He held up a gold watch and chain and a ruby ring.

"Where did they find them?" asked Lassiter sharply.

"In the older woman's reticule."

Lassiter turned on Mag. "Did you get these from Blevins?"

She was pale and shaking and she sat down on a chair as if she was unable to stand. Florabelle leaned against a wall for support. Bad 'Lias, sitting on another chair, his arms bound, glared with his one eye in rage and pain.

"This is a posse of regulators, representing two states," said Lassiter. "I am from Tennessee. This gentleman is Sheriff John Boyd of Lewis County, Kentucky. You'd better answer my questions."

"I—" Mag stopped and gulped.

"Yes, she did!" cried Florabelle wildly. "'Lias made us take them!"

"You lousy, lying bitch!" snarled Blevins.

"Shut up!" someone said to him.

Lassiter said in an oddly shaking voice, "These articles belonged to my murdered brother. I can personally identify them. That watch was given to him by our father. The ring he bought in Nashville, and it was worn by him for years. Others will vouch for this."

He paused and his voice hardened. "Together, the ring and watch complete the evidence against you, Blevins."

"I'm a-sufferin'," groaned Bad 'Lias. "You-all ain't got no call to abuse me this way. I wouldn't treat a yaller dog like what you're a-treatin' me."

If he hoped to win pity for himself he failed.

"Blevins," said Lassiter, his tone as cold as his face, "Prudence Buckstone has just stated that she personally saw you shoot to death and rob my brother, Dr. Tracy Lassiter."

"She does, does she?" The outlaw forgot his pain for a moment in his contempt. "Even if you could believe a lyin', no-'count leetle bitch like that, thar's nothin' you could do to me."

"And why not?" Lassiter's voice was almost silky.

"Becuz I been tried for that already, before a jury. An' found not guilty. I know the law. You can't try a man twicet for the same offense, once a jury's acquitted him."

"Are you sure?" The same cold smoothness in Lassiter's voice. "Do you want to make a statement?"

"I got nothin' to make a statement about. I demand a lawyer——"

"Where is your brother, Blevins?"

The outlaw's face changed. "What about him?"

"Miss Buckstone saw you kill him, too."

Bad 'Lias turned in his chair. "You found his——"

He stopped, but it was half a question that Lassiter finished for him.

"His corpse you mean?"

"I didn't mean no such thing. If you did, I didn't have nothin' to do with it!"

He looked from one to another in the room.

"You ain't found it!" he exclaimed with sudden conviction. "You cain't convict a man without the evidence of his daid body, an' you damn well know it!"

"You're admitting there is a corpse," said Lassiter.

"I ain't! You're twistin' my words! The hull thing's a goddamn lie! 'Lige Blevins is gone down somewhar in the New Orleans kentry!"

Lassiter's face was icy. "Elias Blevins, you're not facing an ordinary court, with a slick lawyer to twist the evidence in your favor. You're facing a posse of Tennessee and Kentucky men. Your crimes have been committed in both states, and God knows how many other places besides. This posse has sworn to do its duty."

Bad 'Lias looked stunned, as if for the first time he realized that he was not to be taken back to Turkeytoe for trial before friendly Judge Redding and have friendly Ezekiel Rockcastle to defend him.

Prudence saw the sweat break out on his face. She felt his fear and in spite of all his crimes she felt his horror with him.

Lassiter glanced about the roomful of men. "Gentlemen, you've heard what Miss Buckstone said. You've seen the stolen jewelry, and the stolen horse is down in the stable. What's your judgment?"

They were silent for a moment, shifting uneasily from one foot to the other. Then one gathered courage. "Hangin'," he said.

All of the others in the room nodded assent.

Gazing through the half-open door at this scene, Prudence suddenly realized that Bad 'Lias was being condemned and sent to his death *on her word alone.* She wanted to cry out, to avert the awful thing that was about to happen. To send a man to eternity—it was too terrible a matter for a girl to take on her shoulders.

But she kept silent because at that moment Bad 'Lias stood up.

"Goddamn you, lemme alone!" he yelled. "Goddamn you all to hell!"

"Shut your mouth," ordered Sheriff Boyd.

"I won't shut up!" the outlaw shouted. "You cain't do nothin' to me, an' you know it! You ain't got no proof! You ain't worth killin', none of you! I kin whip any man in this crowd, till his eyes roll back in his haid! Turn me loose an' I'll fight anybody amongst you, one-handed like I am, an' lick him, an' use his guts for galluses! What about the law, you sons of bitches? You gotta obey the law! I hope every last one of you goes to the hottest pit holes of hell——"

"Take him out," said Lassiter.

"Ow, don't! You're hurtin' me!" howled the prisoner.

"Take him out behind, gentlemen," repeated Lassiter, still in that chill voice, and the girl knew that nothing she could say would stop them.

"Don't do this, fellers!" Bad 'Lias was pleading now. "Lemme go—I might tell you what you want to know—it's a sinkhole—no don't do this to me—I ain't done nothin' to deserve this——"

The last was shrieked out over his shoulder as he was half-carried, struggling, through the door at the rear of the house. The door slammed shut, but he could still be heard, begging, praying, cursing.

Something suddenly shut off his voice. . . .

3.

Prudence had watched shaking with horror at this violence and feeling somewhat responsible for it. She stood looking through the door into the dining room, and nobody paid any attention to her. A sort of dreadful fascination held her while Lassiter and the sheriff eyed the two women beside the table.

She looked at Troy's face and she felt she hardly knew it. His eyes, always black, seemed to have grown more intense. A white line extending from his nostrils to the corners of his mouth was caused by the clenching of his teeth. In that moment he seemed to her unfeeling, remorseless, cruel.

Mag had become defiant and angry, but Florabelle was weakly sobbing when, after a few minutes, there was trampling on the back porch and the men who had taken Bad 'Lias outside returned.

"Hit's all took care of," said Alex Glover.

Lassiter gave a curt nod, but his expression did not change. "What do you know about John A. Murrell?" he asked Mag.

The woman did not answer.

He turned to Florabelle. "Has he been here lately? Is he around here now?"

The younger woman looked at Mag, then back at him. There was terror in her eyes.

"Afraid to talk?" suggested Lassiter.

"No—we don't know nothin' about any Murrell," said Mag suddenly.

"It might be easier for you if you'd speak up."

"We don't know nothin'!" repeated Mag defiantly.

"Not a thing?"

"No!"

Lassiter looked around at the men in the room. "As to these women, gentlemen, what do you say?" he asked.

There was deliberation, the men conversing together in low tones. Finally Sheriff Boyd said, "Thar ain't no question about 'em. They're whores, an' thieves, an' fences for robbers, an' from what the young lady says, kidnapers who send young gals down to the New Orleans bawdy houses ag'in their will, or wish."

The "young lady"! Was this going to be on Prudence's word, also? She stood in the next room in silence, her nerves seeming to twist and knot within her.

"I vote that we whip 'em both, an' run 'em out of the kentry," said Alex Glover.

"Aye," said another member of the posse. There was a rumbled chorus of assent in the room.

Prudence looked on aghast as the two women struggled in the rough hands of the men who were tying their wrists together. Mag shrieked out foul curses, but Florabelle only squalled in a despairing terrified way.

For the first time Lassiter seemed doubtful. "Whipping women?" he asked. "Isn't that a little drastic?"

"By your leave, Cap'n," said Sheriff Boyd, "them two sluts has done all their meanness in Kaintuck. An' Kaintuck claims jurisdiction over them."

Lassiter, after a moment, nodded and stood back. "I reckon that's proper."

"I got a snake whip outside," said one of the men.

Sheriff Boyd shook his head. "Snake whip would cut 'em to pieces." To Lassiter he said, "Up here we got our own way of dealin' with no-good females."

"How?"

"We bare-ass 'em."

Lassiter stepped back and folded his arms, as if to disassociate himself from what would follow.

"Thar's a buggy whip down in the barn," suggested one of the men.

"That's better," said Sheriff Boyd. "Go git it."

While someone ran for the required lighter lash Prudence only watched Lassiter. He stood silent, his face expressionless, the white lines more definite about his mouth, his arms folded. The others in the room said little. Even the women had ceased their outcries for the moment, waiting fearfully.

"Thar was two buggy whips," said the man returning from the barn.

Boyd nodded. "That'll let us git things over quicker."

"That thar roof beam's about right," said someone pointing.

A rope was quickly tossed over the beam, and one end of it fastened to the bound hands of Mag. At the same time a second rope was cast over the beam, some distance from the first, and this was tied to Florabelle's wrists.

By means of the ropes, when men hauled on the free ends, the arms of the women were drawn to full length above their heads, where they were held as the ropes were fastened.

"What you goin' to do?" whimpered Florabelle.

"You'll soon see," said one of the men. To Prudence the men seemed eager, coarsely avid for the sport to come.

"Bare-ass 'em," directed the sheriff.

"Oh, my God, don't do that!" squealed Mag.

What happened next was to Prudence unbelievably obscene. The wrappers of the women were pulled up over their heads and lashed to their wrists above. Neither of them appeared to wear undergarments, so that thus strangely enveloped, with their skirts shrouding their faces and the upper parts of their bodies, they were naked from their waists down, except for their stock-ings and shoes. In this state their sex was exposed and evident, but there were striking differences in their forms. Florabelle's thighs were plump, her posteriors swelled out almost pendulously. Mag's buttocks were more meager, her hips narrower, her legs lean.

Unable to see what was happening to them because of the garments wrapped about their heads, and held helpless with arms aloft, both women began to beg piteously.

Sheriff Boyd said ponderously, "Do you reckon ten apiece will be enough, gentlemen?"

There were nods. "Yep. If they git out of the kentry in twenty-four hours," someone said.

"We'll see that they do." The sheriff selected two of the posse. "Joe, you take the young one. Denny, you work on the other."

The two whips cracked almost simultaneously. A welt leaped out on the soft buttocks of each woman, and each gave an answer-ing shriek of pain. Thereafter, as the lashes followed one after another, there were continual screams of anguish. The cries, and the vain caperings of the women in their efforts to avoid the cruel whips, and their indecent exposure, sickened Prudence.

She glanced again at Lassiter. He stood with arms folded, watching with a face, it seemed to her, as expressionless as cast iron.

When this dreadful thing was finished, she supposed he would be returning to her, with soft words and looks!

With an overwhelming impulse of horror and revulsion she

slipped out of the front door of the house, into the darkness. The men were all intent on the proceedings in the dining room. . . .

4.

In the night gloom the trees about the house were black. As she hurried around to the rear she almost collided with a pair of booted legs dangling from above.

She shrank back to avoid them and looked up.

Even in the dimness she saw that it was Bad 'Lias, come to his end at last. His arms and legs were bound, and he turned round and round in mid-air, suspended from a noose that twisted his head in a ghastly unnatural angle. He was quite dead. On his breast a crude placard had been pinned: KILT HIS OWN BROTHER.

She felt like retching, but she did not have time to be sick. Within the house the outcries of the women under the lash continued. By the time they ceased she was well down toward the river.

Someone in the house shouted, "Whar did that gal go?"

She hid in the underbrush like a small rabbit. Men came out of the house and began questing here and there. Some ran out to the road to look.

Troy Lassiter called, "Prudence! Prudence, where have you gone? If you hear me, Prudence, come back!"

After a while he ceased calling.

The men began to go back into the house. "We kin put trail dogs on her in the mornin'," one said.

"She shall not be hounded!" exclaimed Lassiter almost explosively. Then he too returned to the house.

She was ready to weep, but she did not. She remembered that moment of joy, when he held her in his arms, and called her "my dear."

But after that came the whole dreadful episode in the

kitchen. Troy Lassiter's face like chilled iron as he pronounced sentence on Bad 'Lias: *Take him out.* And then: *"Take him out behind, gentlemen."*

Out behind to do him to death, with that placard on his chest. He was evil, Bad 'Lias. A monster. But the coldbloodedness of his execution appalled and sickened her. And Troy Lassiter ordered it. She herself, by her words, had brought it about. A terrible self-accusation overwhelmed her at this thought.

Then the aftermath. Those wretched, pathetic women. Guilty as she knew them to be, Prudence recoiled from the manner of their punishment. And she remembered Lassiter's face, the intense blackness of his eyes, the white line from his nostrils to the sides of his mouth, his teeth locked like a wolf's.

She felt she had seen him as he really was beneath his genteel polish: unsparing and cruel. She believed she now knew the bitterness in him, the remorselessness. And yet, with all this, she had to fight back the tears. She had thought so highly of him—how highly she was just beginning to understand; and now she must not allow herself to think of him forever more.

5.

After a long time she rose from where she had been lying and stole down to the river, making as little noise as possible.

A whisper said, "Sh-h-h-h——"

She stopped staring about in the gloom.

The whisper said, "Miss Prudence——"

It was Jeff.

She had thought that long before he must have sought his own safety beyond the river. But perhaps he had not been able to find a boat.

He came toward her in the darkness. "Dey all gone back in de house?" he whispered.

"Yes," she breathed. "I think so."

"Ah knowed yo' was in bad times," he said. "Come 'long heah."

Together they groped their way to where the trees drooped their branches low over the river bank.

"Dey was two boats, a skiff an' a big pirogue at de landin'," he said. "Ah took de skiff. Heah it is—hid."

"You waited all this time!"

"Ah tol' yo' Ah'd wait." That was all; his simple explanation.

He helped her into the skiff that was pushed out from under the overhanging branches, and he took the oars.

At first he let the boat drift down the near side of the river, whispering that he did not want the sound of the oarlocks to be heard. After a mile or more he rowed out into the full current and then drifted again. She sat in the stern of the little boat, and he merely rested on his oars and watched for dangerous places, like snags or floating logs.

Mile after mile they floated thus. Now and then she saw a light on one shore or the other: a home beside the river. She thought once that she recognized the Glover place, but she could not be sure in the darkness.

At last, after hours had passed with the river carrying them along at the rapid pace of its current, he began to row for the Ohio shore. He was not an expert oarsman; he made so little progress in the swirling stream that the light craft was being swept down the river faster than it could make headway across.

A wide eddy caught them and threw them first out into the current, then sucked them back toward the shore. As the boat came close under the bank, helped by frantic rowing on the part of Jeff, Prudence grasped at a low-hanging tree limb and clung to it, though the force of the eddy nearly dragged her from the seat on the rear thwart before she could check the skiff so that it lay stern first by the steep bank. Without a word Jeff quickly came aft to help her and between them they brought the side of the boat to the shore, where they held it.

He was panting from his exertions. Presently he said, "Kin yo' climb dat bank, Miss Prudence? Ah'll hol' de boat."

"I think I can," she said.

"Go ahaid. We cain't stay heah."

Resolutely, she put a foot over the side, found a solid place, then stepped out from the skiff, clinging to the steep bluff. As she looked above her it seemed that she must somehow climb straight upward—how high she could not tell in the darkness. But with the instinct of a wild thing pursued she did not hesitate.

The bank was indeed steep, and at this place it was twenty or more feet high. But she found a foothold here, a vine to grasp there, and after a hard scramble she was on top.

"All right?" came Jeff's cautious voice below.

"Yes," she panted. "Come on. It's not hard if you angle like I did."

She heard him commit himself to the bank. The boat was pushed out into the stream to swirl about in that eddy until at last it was swept away downriver. Heavy breathing below indicated the Negro's upward progress. Something heavy tumbled downward with a great splash in the water.

"Jeff?" she called out anxiously.

"Hit's all right, Miss. Jes' a big rock roll into de river."

A moment later he was beside her.

"Look lak, whenever yo' an' me' is togethah, Miss Prudence, we gotta climb somewheah."

"I thought you'd fallen," she said.

"Put mah foot on a big rock, it come right out'n de bank. Neah threw me."

"At least we're across," she said. "They won't follow us, will they?"

"Dunno. Cap'n Lassiter, he don't know his own slave rowed yo'. We must of floated twenty mile befo' we reached heah."

"Would he come over after you?"

"Iffen he knew, he shore would," said Jeff. "But he ain't likely to fin' out—very soon, nohow. Dat boat, she'll float down de river fo' mebbe anothah twenty mile befo' anybody sees her. Even den dey wouldn't know who was in her—she might of got loose from de landin' somehow an' floated away."

"Let's get away from this bank," she said nervously.

Through the woods that lined the river they made their way
in the darkness until they found themselves in an open field, a
meadow of some kind. Cattle lying in the shadows chewing their
cuds heaved themselves to their feet and blew through their
noses and then, as they lumbered away, turned back from time
to time to gaze at these night invaders of their pasture.

Ahead loomed a solid darkness.

"Haystack," said Jeff.

It was old hay, too old to be of much use; and it was left
there for what good the cattle could get out of it. The animals
had eaten deeply into its sides, and their dung fouled its immediate vicinity. Nevertheless, Jeff picked his way to it, drew out arm-
fuls of the musty stuff, and strewed the hay on clean grass at
some distance, to serve as bedding.

"Mebbe things is goin' to turn fo' de good," he said. "Ah
shore was skeered somep'n bad was goin' to happen when de
witch woman hung dat charm on yo'. When yo' went into de
house, Ah took de skiff from the landin' all right, an' hid it wheah
Ah said. But yo' didn't come back. Ah waited fo' hours. All dat
time Ah kep' hopin' dat de bad spell of de conjure woman had
been broke by de ashes, silver an' water."

"I don't think that old woman meant any harm to me,"
said Prudence.

"All Ah kin say, Miss, is Ah purty nigh give up hope when
Ah seen dat man, Bad 'Lias, yo' calls him—de one dat shot at
us on de clift—ride into de clearin' an' stable his hoss. When
he went up to de house, Ah thought shore it was bad fo' yo'.
But Ah still waited, hopin' Ah could he'p yo' somehow."

"Things did look bad," she said.

"Jes' befo' dark," went on Jeff, "Ah heered men comin' down
de road. Fust thing, Ah seed Cap'n Lassiter. Ah almos' died,
becuz Ah made shore dey was afteh me——"

"They were trailing Bad 'Lias."

"Ah 'spect so," he assented. "Ah seen dey was afteh somebody else when dey begun surroundin' de house. Some of 'em

commenced shootin', an' dey all went into de house, an' yo'
still didn't come——"

"They captured Bad 'Lias and hung him," she said. "Did
you see them do it?"

"Hit was purty dark by that time. Ah seen a commotion
from wheah Ah was, but Ah couldn't see much. Ah hear some
cryin' noise by wimmins. Ah shore hoped it wasn't yo', Miss Prudence——"

"They whipped two women in the house."

"What fo'?"

"I don't know. Having stolen property, I think. Anyway, it
was awful—treating women that way, even if they were bad."

She did not tell him the manner in which Mag and Florabelle
were whipped because she could not bring herself to describe it.
She felt that it was a debasement of her sex, a dishonoring of
womankind.

"While they were doing it," she finished, "I slipped out of
the house and got away."

"Praise de Lawd!" said Jeff. "Mebbe Ah done laid dat bad
spell afteh all."

6.

Before dawn Prudence rose from her mat of hay and tried to
brush the dried stems from her dress and out of her hair. She
knew she must look terribly unkempt, but there was little she
could do about it. For the second time she had left everything
behind her in her flight. She managed, eventually, to pull her
tangled locks into some kind of order, and she tied them at her
nape with a piece of string.

Jeff, who had slept some distance away from her, stood
politely with his eyes averted while she made these preparations.

"What now?" she asked him.

"Ah foun' somep'n," he said. It was a half crock of brown
pottery, broken in two and thrown away, but it still could be

used as a container of sorts. "Ah washed it good in dat li'l pond,"
he said, indicating a small sheet of water left by some recent rain.

Through the misty half-light he looked toward the cows,
some of which already had started to graze away from them.

"Ah got a way with cows," he told her. "Done a lot of milkin'
in mah time. Iffen any of 'em is gentle—now look at dat ol'
brindle. She got a bag all swole up with milk. Likely she wants
to be milked."

He went toward the cow, walking slowly. "So, boss," he said
smoothly. "So-o-o, bossy."

The cow looked at him suspiciously, but stood still. Very
cautiously he approached her. She moved away slightly, but he
placed a hand on her hip.

"So, bossy," he crooned softly.

She seemed to understand what he wanted. Squatting beside
her and milking with one hand while he held the half crock in
the other, he was not long filling his broken receptacle.

He brought it to Prudence. "Milk's good," he said. "Heah,
yo' drink it. Ah kin git mo' from dat ol' brindle. Me an' her's
good friends now."

Prudence took the half crock. It contained perhaps a quart
of warm milk. She raised it to her lips and drank, her stomach
receiving it gratefully. But when she had taken about half of it,
she returned the container to Jeff.

"That's all I want," she said. "You drink the rest."

He looked at her and took the half crock. The cows were
ambling away evidently toward some barn, hidden in the woods
by the river, where they were accustomed to being milked. A
distant rooster crowed, answered by another.

"All right," he said, draining the receptacle. "We got to be
movin'," he added, wiping his mouth with his sleeve.

"We're in Ohio," she said. "Ohio's a free state."

"Yeah, but Ah ain't a free man yet."

"Why not?"

"Folks sees a strange black man in dis kentry; dey repo'ts
him as a slave. Sheriff come git Jeff. Sheriff keep Jeff in jail.

Sheriff git reward when he turn Jeff ovah to man who owns him. Only one way kin Ah git real freedom."

"How is that?"

"West of heah, on de river, is a town call Ripley. Ah been tol' by colored folks what Ah mus' do. Lay out by day an' travel to dat town by night. Dey's a big house on top of a hill. Yo' climb fifty stone steps to git up to it. In dat house is rooms fo' slaves to hide in. On top of dat house is a beacon light so's runaways kin fin' it. Freedom people lives in dat house. When a slave comes to dem dey take him by nighttimes to othah places fartheh no'th, an' den still fartheh an' fartheh no'th, ontil at las' dey comes to a place called Canada, wheah white masters cain't git slaves back, no matter how dey goes to law about it."

Later Prudence was to learn that at least part of this was true. Ripley, Ohio, was the southernmost "station" of what later came to be called the "Underground Railroad," which transported fugitives from slave states to Canada. There were exaggerations and embroideries in Jeff's account, but the important thing was that he knew of a place to go.

She hoped all the best for him. She remembered his faithfulness and how he braved not only real dangers, but superstitious fears that were just as real and perhaps more terrifying to him, and stoutly stood by her. But now at last they must part, for her way was toward the east, and he would have to go west, each to his destination.

"We'll have to say goodbye here, Jeff," she said.

"Miss Prudence, it tear mah heart to say goodbye to yo'."

"I can never thank you for all you've done for me."

"Ah serve yo' as good as Ah knowed how," he said humbly.

"But you didn't have to serve me. You did it of your own accord. That is *friendship*, not service. We're friends. Do you understand that, Jeff?"

"Yes, Miss. Hit's mighty sweet to know a white lady like yo' calls me 'friend.' De Lawd have his arm around yo' an' guide an' protect yo', Miss Prudence."

"God bless you, Jeff, and good luck. I'll never forget you."

They did not even shake hands, but the feeling of mutual regard was warm within them. She turned and began walking up the low hill to the top of the meadow. When she reached the top and looked back, she saw him still standing where she left him, looking after her. She waved her hand and he waved back. She never saw him again.

IV

The Paths of the Mighty

Chapter 18

1.

She had parted from Jeff and once more she was all by herself; and she felt more desolate, if possible, than before. Behind her was everything she knew. And she was beginning to realize that her sudden emotional flight from the Binns' house and Troy Lassiter had not been well thought out, or logical, or wise.

The whipping of those wretched women, Mag and Florabelle, had shocked her, particularly the shameful obscenity of the way it was done. And the lynching of Bad 'Lias, however much he deserved it, sickened her. She could not drive out of her mind Troy Lassiter's cold face as he watched these punishments; and she felt that she could never think of him again without a shudder.

And yet thoughts of him kept coming back to her: that look of surprised joy in his face when he first saw her, and the comfort of his arms about her when she ran to him. In the tangled state of her emotions, she could not now say exactly why she did run away. She only knew she had done so and crossed the river

315

with Jeff; now she had cut herself off from everything her previous life had known.

After she waved goodbye to Jeff, Prudence began walking—the draught of milk having given her strength—and she saw that the Ohio side of the river seemed more open than the Kentucky side. The great forest of hardwood trees that once covered most of Ohio now existed chiefly in hollows and on broken higher ground, where it had not yet been cut down.

Broad fields had been cleared and rail fences and houses were visible. The process of clearing, however, still was being continued, as the girl could tell by a faint scent of wood smoke prickling her nostrils—that ever-present odor of the frontier. Men continuously burned the trees they had felled in order to make room for tillage.

Not very long after the sun came up she saw a man, with a team of horses a field away, plowing; she felt a kind of pleasure in the way the moist furrows glistened in the early sun as he turned the earth. Young corn was up in some fields and it seemed to her that she had never seen greener meadows, or soil so rich, or new crops starting with such promise. As for the distant plowman, he paid no attention to a girl in a blue gingham dress walking slowly along, so far away.

Late that morning she sat down to rest beside a small brook and drank the pure water. The gentle murmur of the streamlet seemed to bring peace to her heart; she became conscious of other sounds in the still air. In the distance a cow lowed for her calf, nearby a robin was caroling with an oriole and a catbird and, so far away that it seemed to be from another world, came the sound of a bell, mellow and slumberous, perhaps calling worshipers to some church.

She wondered if this was a Sunday. She had lost track of the days, but the thought of church was soothing; all these homely sounds lulled her, making her almost forget that she was a fugitive, as if there were none to hunt or frighten her.

Presently she rose from the brook side and walked on. She was on a road now and although it seemed to run north rather

than east, she stayed on it from sheer unwillingness to tackle
a trail again through a tangled forest. Perhaps a little farther
along this road she might find another that pointed toward
Washington, for she still clung stubbornly and almost blindly
in her mind to the hope of doing something to help her father.
So now she stepped along almost confidently, her little feet in
their old moccasins winking beneath the blue hem of her skirt.

Yet at the first test, her new feeling of freedom and confidence faded. She heard a wagon coming up from a creek-crossing
in a draw some distance behind her, though not yet in sight. Her
wild fear of being seen again took possession of her, and she hid
in a thicket of sumacs beside the road.

The wagon came near and passed on by. Its driver, a stolid,
bearded man in blue jeans and a wide straw hat, did not see her.

But some distance behind the wagon walked someone more
observant—a boy with an old single-barrel shotgun. His quick
eye caught the slight quiver she made in the sumacs, and he
moved forward, gun ready, to investigate.

"Don't shoot," a weak voice implored him. "It's only me."

"Who's 'me'?" he asked. "Come out of there."

From the sumacs crept a very disheveled girl in a blue dress.

"Huh!" he said. And then, boylike, his questions came tumbling out all together. "What you doin' in there? Who you
hidin' from? What's your name?"

He was about a year younger than she, long-legged and long-
armed, with a frank, open countenance and inquisitive blue eyes.
His nose was as freckled as the back of a trout, and he did not
look particularly menacing.

She stood before him, her eyes on the ground because of
her shame at her unkempt appearance. To his questions she told
the old lies: that her name was Alice Hankins and that she was
trying to reach an aunt.

"Where at?" asked the boy.

"Near Columbus," she said, remembering her previous deception.

"An' walkin'?" he said doubtfully. "That's a pretty long walk."

"Yes, I know," she said humbly. If this boy only knew how far she had come and what she had been through! But she did not enlighten him.

He stared at her with sixteen-year-old male superiority. "You look pretty beat up. Better come along with us. Dad's waitin'."

The man with the wagon had halted his team and was looking back at them.

She did not want to go, for she had come to the place where she distrusted any stranger. But she could see no way out of it, so she accompanied him. As she walked beside him the boy was full of information, which he expounded to her.

"Lucky you spoke up when you did. I was lookin' for rabbits an' I might of cut loose with my shotgun right into them sumacs. My name's Sam Brigham. That's my father, Levi Brigham, in the wagon. We been takin' a couple of hogs down to Farrell's. We raise hogs an' corn an' purebred Holstein cattle. Our bull, Alladeb, is the meanest animal in the hull county, but he gets good calves. One of our cows won the blue ribbon for milkers at the fair. Most of the land you kin see around here, both sides of the road, is ourn. We got two hired men to help with the farmin' an' the milkin', but we lost our hired girl. Hulda was her name. She sure could make good gingerbread. You know how to cook?"

"Not—very much," said Prudence.

"Well, you could l'arn. Ma needs help in the kitchen. My sister Helen ain't much good. Too flighty. Here's the wagon."

Prudence found herself under the scrutiny of Sam's father, a thick-set man with a seal-brown beard and penetrating gray eyes.

"Dad," said the boy, "this here's Alice Hankins. She's on her way to an aunt in Columbus—walkin'."

"Walkin'?" asked the man in a deep, deliberate voice. "Where from?"

"I've been staying in Kentucky," said Prudence diffidently.

"H'mm. No baggage of any kind?"

"No, sir."

The farmer studied her thoughtfully. "Well, come on, get in the wagon."

She mounted up to the seat beside him and Sam clambered up and stood behind them. The wagon had the strong, rancid smell of the hogs it had been conveying.

Brigham started his team. Presently he said, "Runnin' away, ain't you?"

In spite of herself she flushed. "Why do you say that?"

"I ain't easy to fool," said the farmer. "Gal comes along without no extry clothes, or nothin' else. It's a cinch that she run away on a moment's impulse, so she didn't have time to take nothin' along with her. But I judge you ain't much of a criminal. Runnin' from your folks—your old man took a gad to you, mebbe?"

"No."

He tried again. "An uncle? An ornery old skinflint uncle?"

"That's pretty close," she said, to head off further questions.

"An' yet you're goin' to another relative." Brigham evidently prided himself on being able to read character and tell the business of a stranger. By this time he was sure he had worked out the girl's past, and he began thinking about her future.

"This aunt in Columbus," he said, "she related to your uncle by blood, or did she marry into the family?"

Prudence had to speak. "Married in," she said lamely.

He nodded. "Think she'll treat you better than that uncle?"

"I hope so," she said.

"How old are you?"

"Seventeen."

"You ain't exactly what I'd call a strappin' sort of a gal. But mebbe you're willin' to work?"

"I can work," she said.

"There's our house up ahead—we'll be there right soon. Mebbe we could give you a place as a hired girl. That is, if you're willin' to take sens'ble wages. We had one. Hulda Jenson. Swede. She got acquainted with a man named Joris Brown who owns a farm two mile north of here. Too well acquainted, seems like. Anyway, she's goin' to have a baby. I went over an' talked to Joris about it. I own a mortgage on his farm. So he finally concluded to marry her. If you're quick an' willin', I'd give you five dollars a month an' board an' room."

When she did not reply, he said, "Well, think it over. Here we are an' dinner ought to be about ready."

2.

He drove into a wide farmyard. The white house, with morning glories rioting up its porch posts and flanked by hollyhocks and rambler roses along the fence, was somewhat dwarfed by the huge red barn behind it. The day was warm and the windows and doors in the house were hospitably open. The noise of animals—cattle, horses, chickens, and the inevitable dog barking—made a pleasant homely sound in the air.

A man in overalls came across from the barn.

"Take the team, will you, John," said Brigham. He helped Prudence out of the wagon and she walked between him and his tall son to the house.

From the door, a slim, bright girl stared at them, then flew away to inform someone inside. Mrs. Brigham, thus summoned, was there to greet them when they entered. She was a neat, brisk little woman, and after one quick glance at the visitor, she said, "Helen, show Alice Hankins where she can tidy up."

Delighted with this commission, Helen, the young daughter, took the guest upstairs to her own room, and showed her a washstand with a large china washbowl and a china pitcher filled with water. While Prudence washed, Helen watched her, then handed her a clean soft towel.

"If I only had a comb," sighed Prudence.

"Here's one!" Helen bounced across the room and brought it back.

Prudence combed her hair, braided it in two thick glossy

braids, and wound them coronet-wise about her head. Meantime Helen helped her with a few convenient hairpins and a flow of conversation.

"How old are you? Seventeen? Sam's sixteen an' I'm twelve. They was seven of us children born, but only me an' Sam has growed up. My sister Josephine would of been fourteen if she hadn't died of black inflammation of the bowels—that's what the doctor called it. She was only nine then an' I was seven. If you listen to Ma talk, you'd think Josie was a little angel, just ready to fly off to heaven. But if you want to know the truth, she really was mean. When the others wasn't around, she'd make faces at me, an' pull my braids, an' hide my doll, an' tease me all the time. Does buggy ridin' make you have babies?"

"Why, I don't think so."

"Well, Hulda—that was our hired girl—used to go buggy ridin' with Joris Brown. An' she's sure goin' to have a baby. Joris married her. I been doin' the dishes an' helpin' with the house, an' all such, ever since. I'm sure tired of it. Are you goin' to be our new hired girl?"

"I don't expect to, Helen."

"I wish you would. I like you. An' I hate dishwashin' an' housecleanin'."

By the girl's looking glass, Prudence decided she had improved her appearance enough so that she could go downstairs with Helen. The noonday dinner was ready, and the two hired men came in and were introduced to Prudence. They went by the name of John and Len, strong tanned young men with callused hands, and they sat with the family at the table. Levi Brigham prefaced the meal with a lengthy prayer. The dinner was typical of the time and country, running heavily to starches and fried meat in gravy, and Prudence ate thankfully until her hunger was well appeased.

Afterward she insisted on doing the dishes. Mrs. Brigham watched her with approval, and finally asked her if she would not work for them, thus becoming the fourth member of the family to show interest in her as a hired girl.

"I believe I can get Mr. Brigham"—she always thus formally spoke of her husband—"to raise what he offered you to six dollars a month," she said. "We don't work our girls hard; you'd have a nice room of your own and everything you can reasonably want."

She seemed kindhearted and obviously anxious to get help.

"You ought to stay with us for awhile anyway," she went on. "You don't have any money, do you? A few dollars might get you a ride to Columbus. You can hire a seat in the stage that comes to Harney's Corners, five miles above here. Mr. Brigham or Sam would drive you to Harney's. If you stayed here a little longer you might earn enough for a few clothes, too, so you can spruce up for your aunt. Not that you aren't right pretty as you are, my dear, but a new dress wouldn't make you any the less so."

Later that afternoon Levi Brigham took Prudence into the sitting room and told her to sit down.

"How do you like us here?" he asked, after he seated himself.

"Just fine," she answered.

"Have you thought over what I said to you?"

"Yes, sir."

"An' what did you conclude?"

"Mr. Brigham, I don't want to seem ungrateful, but I feel that I have to go on——"

"You got a special date with your aunt?"

"Well—no . . ."

"I said I'd give you five dollars a month. Mrs. Brigham says she'd be willin' to make it six. Tell you what I'll do. If you'll stay with us through the growin' season an' wheat harvest, that'll be about two months, I'll make it *seven* dollars."

He sat back to see how this magnificent offer would affect her. In truth, Prudence was tempted. The house was clean and comfortable; she already liked the family, and the prospect of encountering further hardships and dangers just now was not pleasant. What she might have answered she never quite knew, for at the moment Mrs. Brigham called.

"Mr. Brigham! There's a rig coming up the lane!"

Brigham rose and went to see who the newcomers were; and Prudence followed, her decision not yet made.

3.

It was an old Dearborn wagon drawn by two bay horses. Each side of the wagon had three upright standards supporting a canvas hood, the side and end curtains of which were rolled up, but capable of being let down in bad weather. Two men rode in the front seat, and there were various articles in the back covered with a tarpaulin. Both men were clad in black, and both wore tall black hats.

Prudence found her view blocked by Sam and Helen, who crowded in front of her eagerly. So she stepped back and did not get a good view of the newcomers until the wagon pulled up to the house and one of them got out. He came over to where Brigham stood before the steps: a big man with black curly whiskers over his chin and the bottoms of his jaws, but clean-shaved on his upper lip and cheeks. His features were heavy and severe; and when he lifted his hat, he revealed a head bald on top except for a sort of black topknot curling down his fore-head. To Prudence it appeared that the whiskers on the lower part of his face were to compensate for the hair that was missing on the upper part.

"Good afternoon, Brother," he said in a hoarse bawling voice to Brigham. "I take the priv'lege of interducin' myself—Uriah Rutledge, the *Reverend* Uriah Rutledge, Brother, travelin' on the Lord's work."

He had an important way of speaking and seemed to think highly of himself, as many preachers did in that day when the clergy held an almost unprecedentedly high place in frontier society.

"Howdy, Reverend," said the farmer politely. "My name's Brigham—Levi Brigham. Where you headin'?"

"I—that is to say, myself an' my colleague yonder in the

wagon are travelin' to Lancaster whar thar's to be a mighty camp meetin', a gatherin' of godly people an' mebbe some not so godly, with powerful preachers of the Word to combat the forces of the Devil. It'll be a sockdolager of a meetin', Brother. We've drove up from Portsmouth, an' we reckon there's still two days of travel to Lancaster. Ahem—it's our custom, Brother Brigham, to seek out the good people on our way, an' offer them spiritual nourishment."

It was quite evident that the "Reverend" expected bodily nourishment in return for this spiritual fare.

"Supper will be in about an hour, Reverend," said Brigham. "You an' your friend will be needin' a bed for the night. We'd be proud to have you stay over with us. Ask the other gentleman to come in. The hired men will take care of your rig an' they'll stable an' feed your horses."

The whiskered divine swelled impressively. "'The Lord will pervide', as the Scriptur' says an', also, 'Even as ye have did this for the least of these, ye have did it for me.' I ain't sayin' but what a bait of food an' a night's lodgin' will be gratefully received, an' the Almighty will bless you."

Mrs. Brigham hurried to the kitchen taking Prudence with her.

"That Reverend looks like a chicken man," she said. "I suppose maybe we ought to cook up three chickens to give them some lunch tomorrow. Alice, if you want to help, peel some of those potatoes, and Helen, run down to the barn and tell one of the men to kill three spring roosters for us. Let's see now—I got that layer cake I made yesterday, an' I'll bake a berry pie, an' some sody biscuits. Preachers is particular about what they eat, bein' used to the best of everything. I'll serve the last of my prime apple jelly and the yellow tomato preserves. I wonder, will the Reverends want coffee or tea? We'll have to find out. Ah, you're back already, Helen? The chickens are coming? Now you go upstairs to the linen press and bring down that damask tablecloth we got last Christmas from my sister. I've been lookin' for a chance to use it. We'll put on the real silver and those shiny painted dishes from Philadelphia. I only wish folks would give a person some notice when they're comin'—but we'll just have to do the best we can."

Like a brisk little feminine field marshal she set things going in the seemingly disordered but really efficient way of all good kitchens. They heard Brigham bring the two preachers into the sitting room and they knew that weighty talk went on in there. But they were too busy to hear any of that conversation. Prudence peeled potatoes and later mashed them when they were boiled. She hulled strawberries, watched the kettles, and made herself useful to such good effect that the mistress of the house was more than pleased with her. Mrs. Brigham and she carefully placed the tablecloth—its owner's pride—on the long table, and Helen set the places.

The cooking was on an iron range, the first, Mrs. Brigham boasted, that had come into this part of Ohio. It burned firewood. It was interesting to see the rapidity with which the repast came to culinary perfection in sort of well-timed accord, so that the various dishes were placed almost all at once, and piping hot, on the table. Supper was announced and Brigham conducted his reverend guests into the dining room.

As the second preacher entered, Prudence, standing by the kitchen door, felt her breath give a hitch. He was sleek, young, handsome, clean-shaved—and terrifying to her. She recognized him: Reverend Clark Catlett, whom she had met at the country chapel with the Glovers. He had, she remembered, held her hand quite a long time—and he knew her as Prudence, whereas to the Brighams she was Alice Hankins. Disclosure and embarrassment seemed inevitable.

But there could be no retreat. Introductions were being made and in her turn she was brought forward to meet the two divines. She found herself face to face with Reverend Catlett who took her hand in that clinging grasp of his.

"This is—Alice Hankins?" he said, smiling with a dancing

little light in his eyes. From the slight hesitation before pronouncing the name and the way he looked at her, she was sure that he knew her; and she waited for him to ask why she had changed her name or otherwise expose her identity.

"Alice left her home in Kentucky because her uncle treated her mean," explained Brigham with all good intentions.

"Ah, yes." Reverend Catlett smiled again. "As a matter of fact, Alice and I have met before—haven't we, Alice? It was at a church meeting when she was living at—her home in Kentucky."

He kept her hand, his eyes never leaving the girl's face. She did not reply.

"She's living with you now?" he asked Brigham.

"We're tryin' to persuade her, but she wants to go to her aunt in Columbus," said the farmer.

"I see," said Catlett, his smile never changing. But he released her hand, for the diners began to gather about the table.

There were nine at the Brigham table that evening—Levi and Mrs. Brigham, Sam and Helen, the two preachers, the two hired men, and Prudence. Before they were seated the Reverend Mr. Rutledge took charge of proceedings and while they stood behind their chairs he edified them with a particularly lengthy and sonorous prayer. It was filled with Bible quotations and a considerable discussion of "them that's seekin' after Mammon" and "them that's too blind to see the path to redemption, an' is slidin' down the skids to everlastin' hell an' damnation"; together with a good many more references to "Thy most just wrath" than to "Thy plenteous mercy." It was a copious prayer and circuitous, and Mrs. Brigham feared that her supper would get cold before it was ended.

With his final sonorous "Amen" they were at last seated, and thereafter the divine addressed himself with exemplary attention to eating. Reverend Catlett ate more sparingly and with much better manners. Prudence nervously felt that he was continuously glancing down the table at her in a manner which she thought was amused and at the same time oddly speculative.

When he had stoked his body to what seemed the limit of its capacity, Reverend Rutledge allowed himself at last, while still picking at the viands, to sit back and discuss at leisure higher spiritual matters.

A question from Brigham started him: "What persuasion do you belong to, Reverend?"

"Ahem." The bewhiskered preacher took another mouthful of fried chicken, just to prove that he could hold more, and when he had chewed and swallowed it, went on, "Persuasion, Brother Brigham? You ask my persuasion? Brother, I know an' labor with all denominations—blue-light Presbyterians, forty-gallon Baptists, sprinkle-wrinkle Methodists, Campbellites, any an' all of 'em. I am of the Church at Large, Brother. I've received baptism by aspersion, affusion, an' immersion, so that I'm accept'ble to all faiths. I am an evangelist, Brother. A stout wrastler in any arena with the powers of Appolyon. I give my talents an' my sarvices to all who desire 'em an' to some that don't desire 'em, praise the Lord! Whar thar's a pertracted meetin', or a revival meetin', or a camp meetin'—thar you'll find me. An' the ministers welcome me, Brother. For I don't preach no mealy-mouth religion—no, I preach a religion that's a *religion*, Brother, not spoon vittles or sugar tits for babies—but strong meat for men! When the power's on me, you kin smell fire an' brimstone, Brother! An' when I exhort 'em, the sinners come a-sobbin' an' a-shoutin'—by the scores an' hundreds they come—to have their sins washed away!"

He paused and thunder sat imminent on his brow as he glanced around the table.

"An' now that we're on the subjeck," he said, "shall we not have a sarvice of worship after this excellent supper? Your sittin' room, Brother Brigham? Your wife an' two children—an' these two gentlemen are your hired hands? An' this young lady"—he favored Prudence with a contortion of the face meant to be a smile—"she's your guest? A small congregation, but the Lord

says to preach the gospel in the highways an' byways. It will
suffice."

So willy-nilly that night they all sat in the parlor for the
"exhortations." First they were led in a hymn by Reverend Catlett who "lined out" the words for them; he had a rather penetrating tenor voice. Mrs. Brigham accompanied them on a wheezy
organ. The hymn was familiar, and though Reverend Rutledge's
growling bass was far off key, and John, one of the hired men,
kept singing nasally a couple of beats behind the rest, Prudence's
voice was sweet and fresh and, on the whole, the hymn was
sung with fair enthusiasm.

Then came Reverend Rutledge's turn. He was, as he said,
an Old Testament man, and he preached from the eighteenth
verse of the fifteenth chapter of First Samuel: "An' the Lord sent
thee on a journey, an' said, 'Go an' utterly destroy the sinners
the Amalekites, an' fight ag'inst them until they be consumed.'"

In the "discourse" that followed it appeared that the "sinners an' Amalekites" included practically the entire population of
Ohio—especially those within the sound of his voice—and his
denunciations were thunderous. But he was weary from his traveling and he did not feel that the occasion was such that he should
put forth his fullest powers, so at the end of an hour he prayed,
kneeling on his bony knees and causing all the others to kneel,
also. And when he finished he rose and spoke to them almost
genially, as if he felt he had now broken the ground, even though
he had not made any immediate conversions.

Reverend Catlett, who had taken a secondary part in these
proceedings except for the hymn, also went from one to another,
shaking hands and murmuring pious blessings. When he came
to Prudence he said, "So you wish to go to Columbus? A way
may be found for you, Alice—Alice Hankins, isn't it?" He gave
her hand a squeeze and smiled his curious smile, and passed on.
Prudence, sure that he knew her real name, felt that somehow
she was in his power.

But what was his power and why was she in it? That night

in bed she lay long awake, her thoughts confused and uneasy; she wished she had the wisdom to see her way clearly.

4.

Next morning she was up early to help with breakfast. Levi Brigham came in with a bucket of milk from the dairy barn and set it on the table.

"Well, Alice," he said, "we like you an' you're a real help to Mrs. Brigham an' we wish you'd stay. But I know how you must feel about that aunt, from your own sayin'. What do you think of Reverend Rutledge?"

The question surprised Prudence.

"Well—I think he must be a very good man—" She hardly knew how to go on.

"I guess he is," said the farmer, "but he's shore tedious. We had to do our milkin' an' night chores by lantern after he got through with them exhortations. My men didn't like it. Reverend Catlett's different. How do you like him?"

"He seems——"

"Ah, here's Reverend Catlett now," said Brigham.

The younger preacher had come into the kitchen and Prudence was glad she had been interrupted, for she might have said something less than tactful about his smooth ways, which contrasted with the coarseness of Reverend Rutledge, but seemed to her to lack the rugged sincerity of the latter.

To the minister's good morning, the farmer said, "I was just goin' to tell the girl about our talk, an' your kind agreement."

Catlett made a deprecating gesture. "Nothing, really. A slight accommodation for Miss Hankins. Indeed, a pleasure."

Brigham turned to Prudence. "The Reverends are goin' on right after breakfast. Knowin' how set you are on reachin' your aunt, I took the liberty of mentionin' it to Reverend Catlett an' I asked if him an' Reverend Rutledge could find a place for you

in their rig. He said yes, right off. So you'll get started toward
your aunt's this mornin' an' you'll feel safe with them to take
keer of you."

She was taken completely unprepared. Going to Columbus
—where, after all, she knew nobody, certainly not an aunt—had
not even entered her plans.

"The Reverends are only goin' as far as Lancaster," Brigham
went on. "But a road north from Lancaster in just a few miles
hits the great National Road, which'll take you west to Columbus—or all the way east to Baltimore an' Washington, if you
had the notion, which of course you hain't. Now, Alice, me an'
Mrs. Brigham has talked things over an' you've been such a good
help around an' so willin' that we want to make you a little
present."

From his pocket he drew forth a coin purse made of leather,
with drawstrings securely tied. He opened it and, with mouth-
pursing care, took out a coin.

"A hull dollar," he said, offering it to her. "With that you
kin get a ride from Lancaster to Columbus. Take it, girl, an'
welcome."

How could she refuse? To do so would mean that she must
confess her deception; and it shamed her to think of the explanations she must make. Furthermore what he said about the
National Road came to her like an inspiration. It went west to
Columbus—but also all the way east to Baltimore and *Washington,* "if she had the notion."

Reverend Catlett was looking at her with his smile. He
knew her identity, yet he had not mentioned it. Did this argue
for friendliness? Suddenly she remembered the handbill offering a reward for her. If Catlett knew of that handbill, his silence
and his offer to conduct her to Lancaster must be a real kindness.

She felt confused and helpless. So she said the only thing she
could think of saying. "Thank you for the dollar; it's much too
generous of you two. And I'll be glad, if the ministers are so
accommodating, to ride to Lancaster with them."

Immediately after breakfast she found herself sitting as

small as she could in the seat of the old Dearborn wagon, a preacher on either side of her. Tied in a handkerchief, which she tucked into the bosom of her dress, was the silver dollar the farmer had given her. She waved an almost tearful goodbye to the Brighams.

Conversation, as the wagon rolled northward, was between the two divines; it was a desultory sort of discussion from which she gathered that Rutledge and Catlett had met at a revival in Portsmouth, and the two men knew little of each other prior to that. Catlett's use of language was better than Rutledge's, which was full of backwoods solecisms.

They paid hardly any attention to her, although she noticed that Reverend Catlett was a little more careful to sit well over on his own side of the seat to keep from crowding her. She was grateful for this in a small way, since the Reverend Rutledge, who was driving with unconscious boorishness, rode hunched over, his elbows out, his knees widespread, his huge feet encroaching on her space.

She felt no apprehension in riding with the two preachers, for her opinion of the clergy was high and she did not even think that there might be any unpleasantness toward her in such company. Nor was there any, at least of the kind she might most have feared if she were alone in the company of two strange men. They were scrupulously polite in their treatment of her. But toward noon she suddenly found herself under inquisition. It was after a period of silence, during which time Reverend Rutledge seemed to be brooding over something, that he suddenly spoke to her.

"Alice, have you received grace?"

"Why—yes—I think so," she said, somewhat taken back.

"You *think* so? Young woman, if you ever received grace you'd *know* so!" He frowned indignantly at her.

She remained silent.

"Surely you have some church affiliation?" he next asked.

She hardly knew how to answer him. It would be a mistake, she was sure, to tell him that she had spent her growing years in

a Catholic convent, for the very name Catholic was anathema to
such as he. Otherwise she had almost no church contacts. Then
she remembered that Glover had said their church was Free
Methodist.

"I—I suppose Methodist—" she began.

"What's this here 'thinkin'' an' 'supposin''?" he interrupted
harshly. "You should know these things above everythin' else—
above your very life! Know this: only through grace kin your
vile body be made incorruptible!"

Prudence had never thought of her body as particularly vile,
and the remark was unpleasant to her. But Reverend Rutledge
rolled an eye over toward Reverend Catlett.

"'Pears like we must labor with this gal, Brother," he said.

"Amen," said Reverend Catlett.

But then, almost as if he purposely wished to change the
course of the conversation, he added, "Brother Rutledge, the good
people with whom we stayed last night have prepared a hamper
of food for us. That appears to be an inviting nooning spot under
the trees by the stream."

"Now that you call attention to it, it does," said Rutledge,
guiding his team in that direction.

To Prudence's relief the "laboring" did not at that time continue, for they dismounted from the wagon, unhitched the horses,
watered them and gave them the hay that Brigham had provided,
and took the wicker hamper of food to a shady place under the
trees.

During the "nooning," while the gentlemen of the cloth
helped themselves liberally to cold fried chicken, bread and jam
sandwiches, and generous wedges of cake from the hamper, the
girl sat a little to one side by herself and ate sparingly.

Meantime the divines conversed with each other on some
questions of doctrine, which she did not bother to follow. She
observed, however, that the younger man appeared to be deferential toward the other. When he raised some point with which the
elder disagreed and proceeded, with evident relish, to demolish,
Catlett took no offense, but bowed, as it were, to superior wisdom
and authority.

And yet somehow she did not believe that Catlett really considered Rutledge his superior in either category or that he agreed with all the other's postulates, at least entirely. Then why should he be deferential and accede so easily?

It was clear that Rutledge was entirely, even fanatically, sincere about his theological doctrines, much of which sounded to her like pious gibberish. It almost followed, therefore, that Catlett, if he acceded without really agreeing, was not sincere. If so, what was his object? The more she considered this the less she liked the younger man, in spite of his politeness to her.

After lunch the journey continued; the divines apparently forgetting that Prudence was to be "labored" with, talked across her to each other instead. The Lancaster camp meeting was their topic; and the Lancaster camp meeting, it appeared, was an event of exceptional importance. Rutledge spoke unctuously of "fields white for the harvest," and there was a discussion of some of the other preachers who would be present at this mammoth meeting.

Here the girl learned something new. A Reverend Tait was mentioned. He, said Rutledge with some contempt, was an "eight o'clock." Others of the clergy named he dismissed with a shrug or a word until the name of a Reverend Cartwright came up.

"Now, thar's a power preacher!" said Rutledge. "An eleven o'clock of the first order!"

"You're widely known as a mighty eleven o'clock yourself, Brother Rutledge," said Catlett, flatteringly.

Rutledge smiled with some smugness. "Oh, I kin reach 'em," he said. "I kin raise the hair on their hands. I reckon I kin tot up my full record of sinners brought to repentance, along with any other man of my knowledge."

Out of this Prudence gained the impression that there were grades of preachers. Those who did not have the greatest power as "clinchers" and were therefore used only in the forepart of the evening meetings to "get up steam" for the real "power" preachers, were known to the trade as "eight o'clocks." But the real fulminators of pulpit oratory, those who painted the most affrighting pictures of the terrors of hell, those who could bellow the loudest and use the most picturesque language, were known as "eleven o'clocks" because they came on later at night, when the congregation was worked up and "ripe for the sickle" and "ready to be sheaved."

She learned another interesting custom of wayfaring evangelists. All homes were open to them as a matter of course, but as evening approached, Reverend Rutledge and Reverend Catlett grew discriminating in this fat land. They scanned the houses they passed, looking for the most prosperous in appearance, on the logical theory that the table set in such a house would be superior to that in a humbler home.

The house they finally selected that night belonged to a farmer named Edwards, and there they were rewarded according to their expectations by the fatted calf that welcomed them. The "fatted calf" in this case assumed various forms, such as baked ham, fried chicken, beefsteak, and spareribs, all put on the table at once in a display of hospitality quite ostentatious. And with these viands were breads, potatoes, gravies, preserves, and pastries in almost endless variety.

As a matter of course, after supper that evening, Reverend Rutledge "labored in the vineyard," with some assistance from Reverend Catlett, as they exhorted their hosts. Prudence, who was given a room by herself, slept exhausted that night.

Next day they reached Lancaster.

Chapter 19

1.

Mighty was the grove at night when the great camp meeting was in full roaring session. The huge old trees, ordinarily a massing of blackness above, were now ablaze with lights; they seemed almost afire. At each corner of the open area where the congregations gathered each night had been built a wide pedestal of clay and turf, on which flames of pitch pine leaped upward, appearing to scorch the rough knotted branches above and lighting their lofty intricate tangle in garish brilliance. Hundreds of lanterns, shedding light like huge fireflies, hung from the limbs themselves, adding to the great corner illuminations.

In the center was the "tabernacle," a considerable platform roofed with branches, but open on all four sides. It was for the use of the preachers only. Before the tabernacle, on the pulpit side, rows of felled trees drawn to position by ox teams provided rough seats for the lay public; and though these crude benches were many, so great was the assemblage that far more stood or sat upon the ground than found room on the logs when the services were in progress.

Surrounding the central area, but close at hand, was a community of hundreds of tents or brush shelters, with wagons near them and horses or mules feeding, for people had come from far distances to participate in the emotional excitement of the great camp meeting. Sleeping quarters were at a premium. Almost every house in nearby Lancaster had its "pilgrims," with as many as a dozen snoring in every available room, sleeping on floors and in chairs, as well as in the overcrowded beds. In such congestions women sometimes were jammed among the men; this sleeping in close proximity gave rise on occasion to a suspicion of possible sin, since sex is sex and when people are highly keyed with excitement, inhibitions may waver.

Prudence had been assigned to a brush shelter with a tobacco-chewing family named Hubbard—husband, wife, and two grown daughters—all chewing and spitting indiscriminately. She did not like her quarters and she hoped for an early departure. The two preachers elected to sleep in the Dearborn wagon.

When she and the two divines arrived from the south, the camp meeting was already in its second day; the girl had asked Reverend Rutledge to find her a ride, at least as far north as the National Road, for which she was prepared to pay out her precious dollar. But already he was being waited upon by a committee which knew of his reputation and wished to schedule his appearance for that night at just the proper climactic hour to obtain from it the greatest effect. He was therefore so charged with his own importance that he hardly heard her plea.

During the daylight hours the people in the tents and shelters around the meeting ground gossiped, traded horses, bought or sold articles, took occasional nips from friendly jugs, discussed crops and weather. Young men courted young women and in general, the temporary community behaved like any other of the frontier.

But when darkness fell that night and the beacon fires and lanterns were ablaze, all interest turned to the services about to start. At that hour Reverend Catlett searched Prudence out and suggested to her that she attend early and remain to the conclusion.

"There'll be nobody here," he said, "except the scoffers who always hang around meetings of this kind—evil men with evil minds. A young girl alone in this hut might find them annoying or even dangerous. At the services I can keep an eye on you."

For some reason she felt rebellious at the thought of his "keeping an eye" on her. "I can take care of myself," she said.

He gave her a look of extreme annoyance. "*Prudence Buckstone*," he said, and he emphasized her real name, "I've known of your true identity all along. I also know something of your background and history. Thus far it's been my secret. Why, do you think?"

She stared at him in terror. "I don't know," she almost faltered.

"Why else than that I wanted to help you? My dear, I even have a plan worked out to get you safely to Columbus. Now pray conduct yourself so that I'll feel justified in going to all this trouble."

At that she went with him, his hand on her arm, wondering more than ever at him, but now at last believing that she had found in him a friend.

With full night darkness fallen she could not fail to be struck by the illumination in the grove. The great interest, however, was in the people who now swarmed in the crowded area. As many as could be seated already occupied the massed tree-trunk benches. The others stood or moved restlessly about the outskirts of the multitude.

Several preachers sat within the tabernacle, and one of them was in the pulpit, a cadaverous man in a rusty black suit, evidently one of the "eight o'clocks," for he spoke in a jerky and disconnected fashion, at times hesitating for words, at other times tumbling them out so rapidly that they could hardly be understood. Yet excitement was growing in the congregation, so that even at this mediocre preaching cries went up from the listeners: "Amen!" "Hallelujah!" "Praise the Lord!" "Yeah, Lord!"

Prudence stood with Catlett wondering why he did not take part in the service. He only said, "I'm not scheduled until later."

The "eight-o'clock" preacher retired while a hymn was sung and the singing and shouting grew in volume. The crowd in its mounting tension seemed to twist and turn in gyrations of emotion as the great pulpit orator of the evening came forward: a true "eleven-hour power"—none other than the Reverend Uriah Rutledge.

2.

He came, grim faced, to the pulpit and towered over the people, like a black-clad giant of wrath who had them at his mercy. Thrilled, half-nervous tiers of white faces turned up toward him, the leaping fires of the illuminations throwing strange shadows and brightnesses upon him.

He threw his long arms upward, and he stood in that position until a hush almost like that of death fell over the assemblage.

Then his voice, hoarse and roaring and carrying to the farthest of his listeners, lifted:

"I take my text this evenin' from the Book of Revelation, chapter the fourteenth, the ninth, tenth, an' eleventh verses. Hear what the Angel, appearin' unto St. John, saith:

" 'If any man worship the beast an' his image, an' receive his mark in his forehead, or in his hand, the same shall drink of the wine of the wrath of God, which is poured out without mixture into the cup of his indignation; an' he shall be tormented with fire an' brimstone in the presence of the holy angels, an' in the presence of the Lamb: an' the smoke of their torment ascendeth up for ever an' ever: an' they have no rest day nor night, who worship the beast an' his image.' "

This he read in a tone of doom, and at its conclusion he closed the Bible and paused in dramatic silence, his harsh visage glaring out over them. Tense silence still prevailed; the people seemed to be gripped by some strange paralysis.

Now he resumed in a different voice that began in a reasonable argumentative tone, but rapidly grew into a furious denunciation.

"Now, brethren an' sisters, what's this here beast you worship? Oh, you sinful men an' women! Now I'll tell you about that beast. He's the vilest an' blasphemousest critter you ever seen. He's got seven horns an' he's got seven tails. An' them seven horns represents seven black sins, an' them seven spiked an' p'isoned tails represents seven punishments that the Lord God Almighty, in his awful wrath, deals out to them that's guilty of them seven sins."

He paused again, and the effect was masterly.

"An' what are the seven sins? Wall, thar's cursin' an' swearin' an' a-takin' of the Lord's name in vain. An' I've heerd enough of that right here in this very vicinity to burn every one of us to a crisp. Yes, a black, frizzled up, stinkin', agonizin' crisp!"

From the congregation rose shouts and cries. "Yeah, Lord!" "Forgive us, Lord!"

"An' the second sin is stealin'," shouted Rutledge. "An' lemme lay it on your souls, this don't only mean stealin' your neighbor's hog, or his silver money, or anythin' else he owns, but it means stealin' away his inclination to live a righteous life an' worship Almighty God! An' I'm talkin' now about them that gits up card games to lure their neighbor, an' them that bets on shootin' matches, an' them that tempts with the jug of red-eye, an' them—an' now I'm speakin' of the females—that bats their eyes, an' wiggles their rumps, an' causes men to lose sight of the straight path of virtue an' holiness!"

More wails and outcries from the crowd below the pulpit, which the preacher allowed to rise for a few minutes before he silenced them once more by raising his gaunt black arms.

"An' what's the third sin?" he went on, gathering force. "It's lyin'! Oh, what a generation of liars has sprang up hereabouts! An' then comes the fourth sin, which is murder! An' even if you hang a murderer, I solemnly say to you, his soul has still got to fry! An' the fifth sin is violatin' the Sabbath Day by all friv'lous an' sinful amusements an' practices, sech as tippin' the bottle, an' lollygaggin' with the women, an' horseswappin', an' chicken fightin', an' gamblin', an' stayin' away from church!"

By this time there was an almost continuous undertone of moaning, crying and wailing from the congregation, but Uriah simply raised his powerful voice above it, until he was fairly bawling his words.

"The sixth sin is covetousness! An' this don't mean jest covetin' somebody's farm. It goes a lot deeper! How many of you old he-sinners has coveted your neighbor's wife, or his daughter, or his hired gal, or any of the rest of his women folks? Ha! I see shifty eyes down thar, lookin' 'round to see if anybody has caught 'em doin' it! An' I ain't forgettin' you women, neither, for you covet purty nigh anythin' wearin' a pair of pants, an' you well know it!"

He paused portentously.

"An' this brings me to the seventh an' worsest sin of all, which comes right out of covetin', an' that's adultery an' fornication! You know better! All of you know better! But I'd hate to bet that half or more of you people here present hain't at some time or another wallowed in this terrible sin. An' remember, it's a double sin! Wharever thar's a man sinnin' this horrible sin, thar's a woman sinnin' it with him! Oh, you miserable sinners! As the Good Book says, 'Ye are altogether filthy an' thar is no health in ye!'"

For a moment he paused, while the cries and wails of his hearers went up to the vault of the night sky. But Uriah Rutledge did not wait long. He was only gathering his thunders and lightnings.

"Now!" he suddenly roared, and the congregation was stilled. "What about them punishments? Does your conscience prick you after you've sinned? Have you ever been caught in one of them sins, an' went to jail, or paid a fine, or took a lickin' for it? Lemme tell you, that ain't nothin' to what'll happen to you in the hereafter! Fire an' brimstone—so says the Scriptur'! An' you know that when brimstone gits to burnin', it makes a heat that eats through iron, an' water or nothin' else will put it out."

He looked at them, as if almost hideously triumphant over what he was to tell them.

"But fire an' brimstone ain't all! The Devil's got a lot more instruments to go along with fire an' brimstone. He's got red-hot tongs, an' he's got pitchforks with sizzlin' tines. An' thar's his whip of blazin' hot wires, with fiery hooks on the ends to tear the flesh away from your pore quiverin' bones. An' he has re-volvin' spits so's he kin tie you on with wires an' turn you over an' over them everlastin' seven-times-seven heated fires. While you slowly burns an' the fat drips out of your pore old skin, it falls on the blaze an' makes it raise up higher yet. An' all the time the Devil an' his fiends is howlin' so your voice an' your pitiful cries for mercy cain't be heered; an' even if they do hear you, it only makes 'em laugh because your sufferin'—your mortal sufferin'—is the biggest delight they know!"

A new diapason of wails for mercy, beseechings, moanings, and howlings rose from the congregation. But the long black arms went up again, and the noise subsided as Uriah Rutledge began anew, in a low, menacing voice, growing louder as his excitement grew.

"I see him now, a pore soul goin' to meet his Maker. He's been full of life, an' sperits, an' sinful meanness, an' never reck-onin' on the Day of Judgment when he leaves this earth. But now he's a-leavin' it. His eyes turn up in their sockets, his breast heaves tryin' to git air, his cheeks has fallen in, he's turnin' blue —he's turnin' blue! I hear the death rattle! Oh, this is a sad sight! He gives a gasp, his body shudders. Then it goes quiet. He's gone! Yes, he's gone, friends. Gone to his reward. His body will be buried an' the worms'll eat it. But his sperit goes—to eternal, bee-youtiful happiness? Oh, no! No, my friends! It goes to the everlastin' perdition his life has earned for it!"

The drama of his recital had silenced his listeners. They sat, leaning toward him, hanging on his words almost breathlessly.

The preacher paused and bent forward, as if looking down into a pit yawning beneath the very edge of the platform itself; and the dancing flare from the illuminations seemed to light his face in such a way that it bore a peculiarly sinister look. Suddenly his voice changed to a shrillness that indicated horror.

"What's this I see now?" he cried. "Oh, merciful heaven, our friend's in hell! Oh, the pore feller! He's in the grip of the fiends of hell! He tries to git away! They laugh like the devils they are, an' they grip him with their sharp claws. If he had the strength of ten men, or a hundred men, he couldn't git away from them now. He screeches with pain! What's this? A red-hot poker is shoved into one eye. Jest one, mind you—for after it's burnt out they want him still to see with the other the horrible things that's goin' to happen to him. Oh, I see now that he's only one of many pore sufferin' wretches! Oh, them red-hot pinchers, a-grippin' off their meat! Oh, that molten lead they drip on the pore critters' heads! Oh, the burnin' flesh, an' the nerves quiverin' with torture, an' the pitiful cries of despair an' extremity! I cain't bear it! I jest cain't look no longer! If that pore man—if any of them pore men an' women—had only come to the gospel! If they only had partook of the sincere milk of the Word!"

Sweat stood out on his forehead. From the crowded benches the wildest chorus yet heard arose to the heavens, begging the Most High for mercy.

Suddenly the preacher's voice changed again, this time to prayerful invitation, to beseeching, to urgency.

"Come—all ye that are weary an' heavy-laden! Come forward an' confess your sins! Sin is bitter in your bellies! Reject the Enemy, reject the beast with the seven horns an' the seven spiked tails, reject the Devil an' all his works! Let your sperit bear witness to the manifold mercies of God who'll receive you ag'in into his lovin' arms, an' the weight of sin an' guilt will slide off'n your shoulders, an' you'll be as a child reborn!"

Now the voice of the man in the pulpit was joined by the chanting of the other preachers who came down from the taber-

nacle and began moving through the crowd. "Come! Come up!"
they kept saying, pleading to this one or that to go forward.

"Come to the seat of the mourners!" exhorted Rutledge.
"Thar's room for all, no matter if your soul's as black as a raven's
wing, thar's room for you! The meanest an' orneriest won't be
turned away, if they beg forgiveness! Oh, my friends, humble
yourselves an' come forward! If you cain't pray for yourselves,
let me pray for you—me an' my colleagues of the ministry, an'
all the good Christian people in this great outdoor temple of
God!"

3.

Someone lifted a hymn; it was caught up by two thousand voices
and repeated over and over until it began to form a rhythmic
overtone to the mass hysteria the preacher had evoked in the
crowd. The horrifying picture of hell, which he had portrayed
with no little histrionic ability, had aroused the people to a state
of emotional frenzy. Perhaps this was partly self-induced, for
many of them had come to the camp meeting to enjoy just such
hysteria, which lifted them for the time being out of the hum-
drum of their existences.

The wildest, strangest actions were yet to be seen. Deafen-
ing yells, screams, and shouts punctuated the continual ebb
and surge of the hymn. Women went ghastly pale. Young girls
burst into tears. Some persons fell to the ground frothing and
moaning in delirium. Others rolled over and over, men and
women indiscriminately together, twisting in convulsive motions,
limbs thrown about in such abandon that feminine undergarments and even limbs were exposed in a manner foreign to the
canons of modesty.

Sometimes these writhing, shouting men and women grasped,
embraced and even kissed each other in their orgy of emotion.
Others remained erect but trembled, as if in the worst stage of

the ague. Still others stood on the log benches and tried to raise their voices above the tumult to "testify."

Penitents swayed forward toward the tabernacle platform, as if they were drunk; they even crawled in that direction on hands and knees. As always in such demonstrations, women were in the majority among those who pressed forward, and many of them were young, hardly out of childhood. The more charming of these frequently received assistance from the preachers who mingled with the crowd to exhort sinners to go forward and were caught up in the mob's emotional hysteria. It was no uncommon thing to see a weeping, babbling girl proceeding toward the repentance benches, with a black-clad reverend arm close about her, and a solicitous reverend head bent over her, whispering to her consolation perhaps.

Not all by any means went forward. In the outskirts of the crowd stood the "scoffers," men who laughed and hooted at the proceedings. And there were men who sat aloof, dark faced, as if in disapproval of a wife, or other member of the family, who was "making a spectacle" of herself. But these were hardly noticed in the riotous movement and noise.

Not far from Prudence knelt a young girl, weeping piteously and keeping up a constant series of broken outcries: "Oh, dear Jesus—oh, my dear dead mother—I have backslided—I have backslided again an' over again—oh, Bobby Marshall, who caused me to backslide when I was only fifteen—oh, Bobby Marshall—oh, take me home to heaven with you, Mother—oh, Bobby Marshall——"

A young man, perhaps the Bobby Marshall whose name she called, came up behind her, leaned over and whispered in her ear. She looked up at him, as if startled, then she lowered her head and permitted him to take her hand. A moment later she rose from her knees, and with her head still lowered, allowed him to lead her out of the crowd.

Here and there other couples seemed to follow their example, grasping hands and furtively withdrawing from the scene, stealing off into the shadows of the grove far from the lights.

Almost always they were young, almost always they were wild eyed, frequently the girl was weeping, yet going along willingly enough.

Still the hymn, evidently a favorite, was repeated over and over, its burden a background for the wild furore of the people. Watching it, Prudence felt the contagion of mounting community excitement stirring in her own blood. She seemed to understand perfectly the wild paroxysms of nerves that caused some to collapse, some to have the "jerks," some to break into sobs of hysterical laughter—"holy laughter" it was called.

The wild excitement, the whole tumultuous scene, beat against her heart as the pulse beat against her temples. She resisted an actual impulse to throw herself like the others into the orgy of rhythm, emotion, and ecstatic hypnosis.

4.

A hand grasped her arm, and she drew a deep breath as the spell broke.

"You've seen enough of this," a voice said. "Come with me."

It was Reverend Clark Catlett.

His grip was firm on her arm and his manner commanding. Almost grateful for being taken from this whirlpool of passions, she obeyed him and allowed him to lead her away.

They passed out of the fire-lit arena of excitement, and into the darkness of the grove.

"Where are you taking me?" she asked.

"Don't ask questions. Just go where I tell you," he replied.

She felt herself propelled, not toward the tents and brush shelters where a few people moved in spite of the overpowering attraction of the camp meeting, but away from them, among the black tree trunks. The roar of the crowd diminished as they increased their distance from it.

Her eye was caught by a spray of white beneath a bush, and it took her two thoughts to realize that what she saw was the

undergarments of a young woman, all lifted and disarrayed. And
—yes—another figure seemed to crouch above, dominating the
prostrate girl. Catlett hurried her on, his grip on her arm not
relaxing.

Now, as she went forward breathlessly, she sensed other
movements in the gloom of the grove. Couples slipped silently
along, clinging to each other, seeking some hiding place. Once
a glimmer of moonlight through a break in the trees above revealed momentarily a smoothly rounded white thigh, uplifted and
distinct against a darker body; and she realized that two were
there, wreathed together in the desperate embrace of passion.

She was new to this phase—recognized, however, by others—
of the hysteria of camp meetings, the result of minds bewildered
and confused, of restraints giving way, of emotions overwrought,
of men and women, youths and girls, doing as their natures
directed them, seeking to assuage with the bodies of their partners the terrible, pent-up excitement within them.

She was shocked; and a new fear came to her. Where was
Catlett taking her? She had come to believe that he was so
immersed in his ministry that he had no thoughts of her,
except as a soul to be saved. But now the woman in her sensed
danger. This was a preacher, but he was also a man. Did he
desire of her what those others were doing in the dark grove?

She held back and tried to look at his face. It was too
dark to see his expression, but she asked, "What are you going
to do?"

Fearfully, she expected that he would suggest some retreat
in these woods, and she wondered how she would resist him.
But he pushed her relentlessly forward.

"Don't try my patience, Prudence," he said.

Her name, uttered so by him, seemed to take the resistance
out of her. As if lacking volition, she went forward, his fingers
still closed on her arm.

He did not halt or hesitate. Instead he hurried her on
through the last of the trees.

Ahead was an open road. On it she saw a vehicle, and a

moment later she recognized it as Rutledge's old Dearborn wagon and team.

"Get in," he said.

"Why?" she asked. "Where are you going to go?"

As once before, he seemed to lose patience. "I'm only doing you a service! You are Prudence Buckstone, a runaway bound girl. There's a reward for you. I choose to help you. North of here, not more than fifteen miles, is the National Road. It leads to Columbus—and Columbus is where you wish to go, isn't it?"

It was all so simple! This good man was going out of his way in her behalf. Without further argument she climbed into the wagon and sat on the seat while he untied the horses and took his place beside her. The horses went into motion, and they were on their way up the dark road.

He did not speak, nor did she. But again she began to be afraid—afraid of being alone with this man who was really a stranger, afraid of his silence, afraid of what she could hardly form in her own mind.

She tried to remind herself that he was a preacher, a man of God, but somehow her mind received the thought without conviction.

Two miles, perhaps three, they progressed on the narrow country road between towering dark trees. Then, all at once, Catlett pulled the horses to a stop. Beside the road at this place she could make out, even by night, a deep, forest-choked ravine, and at its bottom she heard the gurgling sound of a small river. The man dismounted, tied the horses to a sapling and came back beside the girl.

"We get out here," he said.

Now a real wave of panic swept over her. She moistened her lips. "What for? Please, I'd rather not," she said.

"We're only going to take a little walk," he told her. But he drew her out of the wagon almost by force, his fingers pressing so painfully into her arm that she knew they would leave bruise marks.

On the ground, she looked up at him with wide, frightened eyes. "I don't want to do . . . whatever you want to do . . ."

He seemed amused. "What do you think I want?"

Conviction seized her. "I *know* what you want! And I won't!" She tore herself loose from his grasp. "You call yourself a minister of the gospel! I despise you!"

He laughed a short, mirthless laugh. "Is that your quibble? That I wear a preacher's coat? If it will relieve your mind, I'm no more a preacher than you are."

"But—you're the Reverend Clark Catlett," she almost gasped. "You're a friend and colleague of Reverend Rutledge——"

Again he seized her arm.

"I don't care who you are!" she cried frantically. "I won't! I won't let you——"

The cold laugh again. "What do you think you can do about it, if I want to?" And then, "Was there ever a woman who didn't plume herself that every man who sees her can think of nothing else but bedding with her?"

She stared. "Then—you don't . . . ?"

"Do you think I traced you to that Brigham place and then brought you up here for something as unimportant to me— as that?"

"You traced me?"

"Why, yes. I was at the house on the Ohio River the morning after Elias Blevins was lynched and Mag and Florabelle were whipped. The women weren't greatly damaged, except in whatever pride they may have possessed, though it's true that they still sat down somewhat gingerly. And they were making haste to go down the river in their pirogue to escape further visitations by the posse. But they stayed long enough to help me bury Blevins, and they told me about you, and how you listened to them talking, and that you said you were going to some relative in Columbus. On a hunch I followed—and so found you."

She caught her breath. "You're one of them! *You're an outlaw!*"

"At least I'm not a preacher—although I can preach a

damned fine sermon on occasion when I want to fool the godly. Nor is my real name Catlett. Wearing a parson's black and traveling with a sanctimonious foghorn like Rutledge is as excellent a disguise as a man might want."

She knew in that moment that he was cold and deadly like a snake.

"Now, girl, answer truthfully my questions." He drew a short pistol from his pocket and she heard the hammer click as he cocked the weapon. "I'm not going to threaten you," he went on, "except to say that your life hangs on your replies."

She waited in blank terror.

"What do you know about the Blevins brothers?" he asked.

"Nothing—except that they killed Dr. Lassiter——"

"And Elias killed his own brother?"

"Y-yes——"

"What other crimes?"

"I—I don't know. There was talk about some robbing——"

"Did you learn anything about other persons—say certain gentlemen in Turkeytoe—or elsewhere?"

"No—oh, no——"

"Peebles and Rockcastle?"

She was too completely terrified to withhold anything from him. "Well—yes—they were mentioned—as friends of Bad 'Lias— I mean Mr. Blevins——"

"Mother Colby?" he suggested.

"Yes—she was mentioned, too, but I don't know anything about her."

"Did you hear the name Murrell?"

"No—yes, once——"

"Who is he?"

"I don't know. An outlaw I suppose——"

"The greatest of them all." He paused impressively. "It can do no particular harm now to tell you that I am Murrell. John A. Murrell. I am Grand Master of the Mystic Clan, a band of bandits which will stop at nothing, and the strength of which nobody suspects. That is my true name and standing."

Now that he had revealed himself to the terrified girl, that swollen vanity, which later was to prove his downfall, seemed to expand.

"But they *will* hear! One of these days the name of Murrell will be writ in letters of blood across the whole South! I have thousands of Negroes ready to revolt at my command. Cities will be devastated and burned, blood will flow in rivers, and I and my men will come out of that holocaust the richest robbers in the history of the world!"

The boasts sounded fantastic, unbelievable. But the girl remembered the words of Bad 'Lias: "*The boss bandit of the hull damn Clan . . . kin call up two hundred or more of the toughest outlaws. . . . Smooth as silk an' sharp as a razor, an' . . . mean as the Devil red hot from home. . . .*"

This was Murrell, who stalked and killed his enemies, and who Bad 'Lias wanted to "set" on Troy Lassiter! She was tongue-tied with fear. But he peered at her through the darkness.

"Now, as to you," he said, "you know a great deal too much. And, of course, you know about me."

"I'll never say anything—" she pleaded.

"You'll have no chance to, my sweet. We are going to walk down into this hollow." He motioned with his pistol. "Just you and I. Go ahead of me."

White faced, knowing now what her fate was to be, the bitter intoxication of despair took possession of her. In the clutch of that hopeless desolation, she began to make her way down through the trees and brush of the ravine in self-hypnotized resignation, such as that a condemned criminal feels when he walks to the gallows and finds the rope fitted about his neck.

All at once a few fleeting words spoken by old Corbie came back to her: "*They was so unhuman that they'd . . . dig out his guts, fill him with rocks, an' sink him in the river. . . .*"

The journey downward took on new horror. She knew its purpose now. Catlett—or rather, Murrell—would kill her. Then, like a hyena, he would go through the dreadful process of disemboweling her, and conceal her corpse by filling the bloody cavity with stones or mud and sinking it in the river.

Her body—her own intimate perfect little body—to be desecrated, mangled, and mutilated so by this fiend . . . she gave one sob and that was all.

Forlorn and bereft as she was, she must go on down in the darkness with her murderer at her heels. A cruel last touch was that she was forced to push her own way through the bushes to go to her fate.

And presently a bough impeded her, a tough green shoot as thick as her wrist extended out horizontally from its parent tree. She had to exert her full strength to bend it, and even then its heavy and stubborn springiness threatened to throw her backward.

One quick glance behind her. Dim in the darkness but close behind, the man was following with his pistol.

Prudence stooped under the bent shoot and released it.

Viciously, almost like a steel spring, it sprang back. She heard it strike Murrell full in the face.

The whole thing was unpremeditated, almost accidental, prompted by her instinct to live, to do something, anything, to hamper or hurt him.

She did better than she knew. The outlaw staggered backward, clutching at his eyes. At the same time she ran stooping along the side of the hill, and then began as rapidly as she could to climb back to its top.

Below her the man was cursing horribly and obscenely. A lurid flash momentarily lighted the bushes, accompanied by the report of the pistol. Temporarily blinded by the blow of the branch across his eyes, Murrell had fired in the direction he thought she would be, hoping to bring her down.

But with bursting lungs she was clambering up toward the road in a frantic effort born of terror. She was above him, but now she could hear him groping and thrashing his way after her.

She was at the top. Before her was the Dearborn wagon, the

horses standing with their heads up and ears cocked back, startled
by the pistol shot below them.

"Oh, you darlings!" gasped the girl.

Gathering her skirts about her she ran to untie them. She
almost leaped into the wagon seat; then she snatched the whip
from its socket and lashed the horses. The astonished brutes
leaped forward. She continued to lash them until they broke
into a mad gallop.

Somewhere far behind she heard Murrell's pistol again. He
evidently had cleared his eyes, reached the top, reloaded, and
fired after her. But a short-barreled pistol is not designed for far
shooting. The bullet went wild.

That shot only sent the horses into a harder gallop, the wagon
careering and bounding behind them. And in the wagon seat,
holding the reins, weeping and sick now from reaction but urging
the horses on, rode the girl.

Chapter 20

1.

She knew the horses were failing, and after a long time she let them ease up.

One of them limped and both were heaving so that their flanks shook. How far behind she had left Murrell she did not know, but it must be several miles. That, however, did not mean safety. As soon as he could find a horse—and he would appropriate the nearest one regardless of ownership—he would follow her.

She crossed a bridge and she remembered that this road ran northerly, so that in a comparatively few miles it encountered the great National Road. It was still deep night and as she tried to look about her the moon enabled her to see that she was in a valley with wooded hills on both sides.

The horse on the left was limping more grievously, so much so that the wagon was slowed to a mere crawl. She felt sorry for the poor beast, and she knew he could not go much farther.

After a time she halted the team, got out of the wagon and

went to the horses' heads. They had galloped for miles, and they were still blowing and starting after the whipping she had given them. But she managed to lead them and the wagon off the road.

Knowing little about harness, she nevertheless succeeded in unhitching them. Then she unfastened their checkreins so that they could graze until someone found them.

These things done, she started walking. In the silence and darkness she felt that if her pursuer came on horseback she could hear him coming up behind and hide from him, so long as it remained night. By daylight it would be different; so she hurried as fast as she could along the lonely road toward the north.

Twice, three times, she stopped to catch her breath and listen intently. She heard nothing and she gradually ceased trembling.

The sky began to brighten. And then, just at dawn, she saw before her the great National Road. She knew it at once because it was macadamized, a wonderful thing in her day. It stretched white before her, made up of layers of crushed stone cemented together by stone dust and water.

For part of its length the highway followed the old Zane's Trace, and it was built by the Government, the first great federal construction project in the nation's history. Winding eastward across Ohio, around hills, copses and hedges, the National Road by day was often heavy with traffic. But on this early morning, Prudence at first saw no vehicles.

At the point where she reached the highway, the road from the west formed a bend around the base of a hill which was covered by a dense grove of oak trees. So busy was her mind with her fears and speculations that when a black coach drawn by four horses at a gallop, with a Negro coachman sawing at the reins, came whirling around the bend, masked by trees, she hardly saw it until it was almost upon her.

At a sudden thought she ran out into the middle of the road waving her arms. Straight toward her thundered the galloping horses, not slowing their speed, the coachman appearing to have no control over them. She continued to wave helplessly.

On galloped the horses, manes flying and muzzles flecked with foam.

At the last moment she flung herself out of the way barely in time to keep from being run down.

Prostrate on the ground she heard the coach roar past. And then she was dimly aware that it had stopped down the road, as soon as the horses could be brought to a halt, and that some-one was hastening back to her.

She managed to sit up, and she looked ruefully down at her dress. This last mishap had been too much for the poor little blue gingham. A great tear went across the skirt, and it was stained with grass and dirt. Mechanically she was trying to brush away the worst of the smudges when she heard a bellow above her.

"Are you injured?"

She looked up, startled. He was a huge, hell-roaring sort of a man in a double-breasted frock coat and a high black silk neck stock. Across his ample bosom swung a heavy gold watch chain, with an equally heavy gold ornament upon it. At the moment he held in his hand his bell-crowned beaver hat.

But it was not his size or these details of his apparel that made her shrink from him. It was his imposing presence. Never before had she seen such a person.

A great fighting hooked nose, a spade of a chin, a mouth extremely wide and without one softening curve, a tangle of iron-gray hair above a massive forehead, side whiskers that flared out like the mane of a lion, and arrogant blue-gray eyes almost threatening under their bushy brows—these were her first impressions of him. These and his bellowing voice.

"I asked you a question, young woman!" he boomed. "Are you hurt?"

His manner frightened her.

"I—I—don't know——"

"Well, get up and see!"

A huge hairy hand took her arm and assisted her to her feet. "How's that?" he demanded. "Are you all right?"

"Yes, sir. I think so," she said.

He shot her a suspicious glance from under his rather awesome eyebrows. "Sure? Don't for a minute think you can lay charges for damages against me! My horses bolted back there at a confounded rolling machine by the side of this road. You were on a public highway. The horses didn't touch you!"

She stepped back, trying to hold together the rent in her skirt. "I have no intention of making any charges," she said.

Something in the way she said it made him shoot forward his head as if to look at her more closely.

"Indeed?" he said. "Pray where are you headed for?"

His question was so almost brutal in its emphasis that it further increased her confusion. "N-nowhere—" she stammered.

"Nowhere? Well, if you're going nowhere you may as well ride there with me!"

She felt that she did not wish to ride with this man. "No—I thank you, sir," she said.

"Nonsense! Why were you trying to wave us down? Come to the coach!" This was said with blustering positiveness. At the same time he seized her by an elbow.

So overpowering was his personality that she found herself going with him in spite of her protests. The Negro coachman stood at the heads of the horses, and the coach itself, she saw, was a private vehicle, quite fine.

When he handed her into it, she found that its interior was notable for padded red leather seats; an open portmanteau was on the floor along with a wild disorder of scattered papers, books, pamphlets, and newspapers, all strewn about in confusion on the floor and on the seats. She crept to a small vacant space in a corner of the front seat, and huddled there, still trying to hide the torn place in her dress.

She heard the man with the eyebrows admonishing the coachman for carelessness in a voice that could be heard a mile, she thought. Then he followed her into the coach, closed the door, disposed of his coattails in the practiced manner of a man used to making public appearances, and sat down. In a moment the coach was on its way again, but at a more decorous speed.

At first he was silent, once or twice glancing across at her with a grim look.

"What were you doing, may I ask, walking all by yourself along the highway this early in the morning?" he said gruffly at last.

"I had nowhere else to walk," she said.

"For pleasure?"

"No."

He sat back and bent his impressive eyebrows in a frown, meanwhile twirling with one hand the large round ornament like a seal, which hung from his watch chain.

"What's your name?" he asked suddenly, exactly like a prosecuting attorney examining a recalcitrant witness.

"Prudence Buckstone, sir."

"Buckstone," he said ruminatively. "A North Carolina name. I myself am a native of North Carolina, though not now a resident of that state. You're from North Carolina?"

"Yes. But more recently from Tennessee."

"Tennessee—ha! I've lived in Tennessee and have memories of it—and Tennessee has memories of me, I'll warrant! If you're from Tennessee, what are you doing *here?*"

She did not know him and she found she did not like his examination and she did not feel like confiding in him.

"It's a long story," she said and gazed away from him out of the coach window.

"Come, young woman!" he said testily. "You must not be impertinent to me!" And when she did not answer he went on, " 'Long story'—I should think so! A cultivated girl, judging by her speech, all the way from her presumable home, walking by herself on a public highway at the crack of dawn! I insist that you explain yourself! At once!"

She was worn out; she was hungry; and she was angry. Moreover, her nerves were frayed from her experiences. Suddenly she burst into tears.

"I *won't* tell you," she blubbered. "And I want you to—to stop this coach—and l-let me out this instant! You're the rudest man I ever saw. I—I've met river men—and peddlers—and

Negro slaves—and b-bandits—and horrid people—who were politer than you are——"

She let go entirely and sobbed convulsively, holding both hands to her face.

The man cleared his throat a couple of times. His face wore a look of some concern.

"My dear young lady—" he began. "Miss—er—Miss Buckstone—I really did not intend to be—ahem—rude——"

Even in her tears she could tell by his voice that he obviously was not accustomed to apologize to anyone, and that this apology required from him an effort that was almost ludicrous.

"Here—Miss Buckstone—" he said. He was offering her a voluminous white handkerchief. After a few moments she controlled herself enough to take it and mop her eyes.

From a silver traveling flask he poured some sort of liquid in a cup.

"Soda water," he said, "with a touch of brandy. I find it efficacious——"

"I don't want it!"

"I beg you. Only taste it."

She was thirsty. After a moment she accepted the cup and tasted it. The pleasant effervescence somehow appealed to her, and she drank it.

"That's better now, isn't it?" he asked. "Clears the head and quiets the humors of the body. I've seen Daniel Webster drink near a quart of that after an all-night bout in the Indian Queen Hotel——"

The name caught her. "Daniel Webster?" she asked. "The great orator?"

"Well," he said, puffing out his lips as if begrudging his words, "I'll not deny that he has a certain facility with phrases. And a good voice, yes, I admit the voice. But his speeches lack true profundity—to my mind—to rank as great oratory. And a Whig—a rank Whig——"

"Do you know Daniel Webster?" she asked with awe, for the fame of his eloquence was abroad in the land.

"Do I know Dan Webster?" he snorted. "Ask rather if he knows *me!* Webster, Clay, Adams, Calhoun—I know the lot of that pettifogging crew. Why, when John Calhoun brought forth the secession heresy and Andrew Jackson said that if a drop of blood was shed he'd hang the leaders to the nearest tree, Calhoun expressed to me the doubt that Old Hickory would go to measures so extreme. I said to him, 'When Andy Jackson starts talking about hanging, men start looking for ropes.' The secession talk died right there. Extreme measures? Andrew Jackson makes 'em look like everyday realities when he undertakes them——"

"Do you know President Jackson, too?"

He stopped and considered her. "Young lady, I declare, I've clean forgot my manners. I haven't even introduced myself." He seemed to swell with importance. "You've heard—I'm sure you cannot fail to have heard—of Thomas Hart Benton. Young lady, you are sitting in his presence at this moment. I have the honor to present myself—Thomas Hart Benton, member of the Senate of the United States."

She gazed at him almost incredulously. "A Senator? Senator Benton? I've heard my father speak of you."

"I have no doubt of it." He gave her a tolerant smile. "My name, of course, is a household word from one end of this nation to the other. Yes, and across the seas, too. If it's not spoken by my friends—and my admirers are legion—then by my enemies, of whom I have not a few. Never have I stood back from any challenge, and when I disagree on any question of political ethics or national policy or a matter of honor, I have always felt it my duty to indicate my disagreement. It has been said that Tom Benton has a corrosive tongue when he senses any taint of double-dealing or treason. I will not deny that in a moment of righteous anger I may express myself pointedly. In some quarters this has not made me popular, but I scorn mere popularity when the truth must be spoken, however it may perchance ruffle the feathers of those to whom it is addressed."

Prudence said nothing, but he needed no comment from her to rush on.

"I am now on my way from Missouri, the state which I have the honor to represent in the Senate, and where I have been 'mending fences,' as I believe the political saying goes. Though why it should be necessary for me to do so I can hardly say, since it would seem that every honest and patriotic citizen ought to know that for integrity, forecast, breadth of view, wisdom in public affairs, and courage, there can be no equal to Thomas Hart Benton."

He paused, as if to allow this extraordinary statement fully to sink in. Then he continued in the same vein.

"But now there's need for a statesman—a *statesman*, I say, among all the time-serving politicians—to uphold the President in these critical days. Therefore Benton hastens back to his post in Washington, where events of the first importance confront this nation."

All this was uttered with an oratorical flourish, as if he were addressing a large audience instead of one timid girl.

But Prudence had forgotten everything else in a new thought. "Senator Benton, you asked me to explain how I came to be here—" she suggested when he came to a pause.

"Why, yes, yes. So I did." He spoke as if suddenly recalled from a subject on which he loved to speak—himself—to matters of less interest. "What's this you were saying, about peddlers and bandits, and so on?"

Greatly daring she said, "I'm trying to get to Washington."

"Washington? Upon my word! For what reason?"

"I hope—to speak to the President—it's about my father."

He stared. "The President is a very busy man."

"I'd detain him only a few minutes—I want to beg him to get my father out of prison." Her voice trembled with the anxiety of her plea. "If it would help, I have a dollar—" She drew from the bosom of her dress the handkerchief with the coin tied in it; then she unwrapped the coin and tendered it to him. "My father, Colonel Buckstone," she finished, "is an old friend of President Jackson."

"Colonel Buckstone?" said Benton reflectively. "I do not at the moment place him. What's he in prison for?"

"For a debt he incurred through no fault of his own."

"Ha! A friend of Andrew Jackson's in prison for debt? This may be interesting. No, put away your coin, child. And now, if you please, begin at the start and tell me your story from beginning to end. I assure you that you will have in me a most profoundly interested audience."

He had assumed an enormously massive genial manner now, which was almost as overpowering as his violent moods. She felt somehow that she had won his friendship and could confide in him.

2.

She need not have feared that she would bore him, for the Senator listened, as if rapt, while she recounted to him her experiences with the candor and sometimes the naïveté of youth, trying to make her story as brief as possible. Now and then, indeed, he interrupted her with shrewd probing questions.

At the end he looked at her, marvelling.

"Upon my word," he said, "this is a tale almost beyond belief."

He tugged at his side-whiskers, ruminating with knitted brow.

"A girl, young, small and delicate, making her way through such dangers and hardships—and yet surviving! You say you were pursued with murderous intentions all the way by outlaws—because they feared that you'd reveal your knowledge of them?"

She nodded.

"Well, at least you're safe now! I should like to see the bandit that would attempt to halt Thomas Hart Benton! Beneath this seat is a shotgun loaded with buck." He lifted the portmanteau and from it took two pistols. "Beauties, aren't they?" he said. "Made by Bond, in London. They're dueling pistols,

really, and they've already done service on the field of honor.
But they'd also be handy if some venturesome lout took a fancy
to investigate us. I've killed my man before now, and will again
if need be."

He replaced the pistols in the portmanteau and sat back.

"As for your information concerning the outlaws, my dear,
you've found a worthy repository for it. You have imparted it to
Thomas Hart Benton, and something will come of this, or I
do not know Thomas Hart Benton."

His geniality suddenly vanished and he turned on her
so harshly that she shrank back. "What a vile nest of vipers
you seem to have in that town of Turkeytoe!"

"Yes, sir," she agreed, half afraid of him again.

"Assuredly this will be looked into." Again he seemed to
be dwelling on her words. "What a miracle this child has wrought
with all her timidity and innocence! Brought about the downfall and deaths of two bloody-handed desperadoes—Blevins, you
say their name was? And overcame, by a ruse as clever as
any I ever heard, a third criminal—he called himself Murrell?
This Murrell may account the day when he met you the worst
of his life. And on this incredible flight you healed a rancorous
mountain feud, unmasked an outlaw rendezvous, and even helped
a fugitive slave make his escape, although—ahem!—I cannot properly endorse that."

She understood that as a Senator from a slave-holding state
he would rather wink at her association with Jeff in his flight
than approve it.

"However," he went on, "it was a necessity for you. I
concede that. And it was also an expression of commendable
loyalty on the slave's part, since he offered you his aid. Between
ourselves, Miss Prudence, I consider slavery a moribund in-
stitution, one that impoverishes the South, and must eventually
be extinguished. Well, we'll say no more of that."

He sat back, considering. "By heaven, the passage of Prudence
Buckstone across this country has had results as miraculous as
the visitation of some empyreal spirit!"

She did not in the least know what an "empyreal spirit" was, but she sensed in him friendship.

"My father—" she began.

"Ah, yes! Your father. My dear, not the least fortunate in all the series of events that have befallen you is the fact that you have encountered Thomas Hart Benton. There are those, as I've indicated, who may dislike Tom Benton. But nobody underestimates Tom Benton. When Tom Benton espouses a cause, that cause moves!"

He gave her a look from under his impressive brows.

"Your father, Colonel Buckstone—odd that I don't remember him—is imprisoned under the most unjust and archaic law of our legal system. At this very moment, one out of five persons held in jails in the eastern states is there for debt, and I suppose numbers approaching that elsewhere. It's an outrageous triumph of avarice over personal liberty and human spite over human rights!"

He stroked his massive chin, still ruminating.

"Twice Andrew Jackson has recommended to Congress the abrogation of this inhumane law. When we reach Washington, my dear young lady, we shall see what we shall see—and you yourself may even for a moment stand forth on the pedestal of history!"

3.

The black coach whirled on its way with frequent relays of horses. They breakfasted at Jacksontown, and at Zanesville Benton insisted on buying Prudence a pair of suitable shoes and a new dress to replace the one he said he had been the cause of ruining. She demurred, but it was hard to refuse Benton anything, and accordingly she found herself garbed in a very pretty frock of embroidered cambric. But he would not allow her to throw away the old dress. Instead, he bundled it up and took it along, saying he might find a use for it.

The great National Road was an ever-changing spectacle, and for every mile of the way, Prudence was enchanted by the sights. They met or passed other coaches—but none ever passed them —and the Senator would bow to the occupants. Gaudily painted freight wagons plied back and forth along the highway, six or eight oxen drawing each at a snail's pace, and their swearing, sweating drivers, every man of them expert with his long whip, swaggering along on foot in huge boots, wearing woolen hunting shirts with large capes lined with red, picturesque to the last degree.

Occasionally they would be held up by a drove of cattle, sheep, or even hogs, following the great common highway shepherded by their herdsmen. And then Benton would fume and swear—always apologizing to his passenger for inflammatory words that slipped out. But they could only wait until the mooing, or bleating, or grunting beasts made way for them.

When they came to a tollgate—one of which was situated every twenty miles—Benton merely showed his granite face at the window of the coach, whereupon the toll collectors fell back and passed him through with a wave, for he was known all up and down the National Road, and as a senator, he had free-passage privileges. At night they stopped at the better inns, and dined together, and Prudence had a room by herself usually, although sometimes she shared a room with other women; this she did not in the least mind.

Between whiles, on their journey, Benton entertained her with stories of the capital and his opinions of notable men. Andrew Jackson, he told her, was the greatest man of his age, perhaps of all time. Daniel Webster and Henry Clay he considered self-serving politicians, with motives subject to deep suspicions. They were, he added darkly, Whigs, both of them. He himself was a Democrat.

"I'll not deny, however, that Clay is a gentleman," he added. And he described to her the duel between Clay and John Randolph of Roanoke, which he had witnessed.

"Randolph," he said, "was the prince of denouncers and

despised Clay. Once in the Senate he characterized him thus, 'So brilliant, yet so corrupt, which, like a rotten mackerel by moonlight, shines yet stinks.' Of course Clay called him out. They exchanged shots. No blood was spilled but a hole was punctured in Randolph's coattail. They met to shake hands. 'You owe me a new coat, Mr. Clay,' says Randolph. And, 'I thank God the debt is no greater, Mr. Randolph,' says Clay. That's the way a high-toned duel should be conducted."

At another time he told her the story of Peggy Eaton, a vain and wilful woman, who wrecked a Cabinet by her ambitions and schemings.

"A designing woman is a perilous creature," he said. "But after all Peggy Eaton gained no advantage of it because her husband, John Henry Eaton, was a member of that Cabinet— Secretary of War, he was—and had to resign, too."

She smiled at this and old Benton smiled back at her. He was more charmed with her each day, and she grew fond of him in spite of his enormous, overweening egotism.

There were times when the Senator busied himself with his papers, and she sat opposite him, thinking . . . of her father and how she might now actually hope to see the President and ask for his help. And Miss Sally, wondering what she was doing and what she would think if she knew that Prudence was riding to Washington with a real Senator. Sometimes she even found her thoughts dwelling on a tall young man—and this in spite of herself, for she had resolved to put Troy Lassiter out of her mind forever. And at times she merely napped in the swaying coach, for she felt the inexpressible bliss of safety—safety even from that human ferret, Murrell—in the protection of vast old Thomas Hart Benton.

Chapter 21

1.

June neared its close, and as the summer drew on the skies were for many days cloudless, ablaze with sunlight, the breezes scarcely stirring. On the village of Turkeytoe the heat settled down like a steaming blanket. Movement, never very brisk in the hamlet, slowed almost to torpor. In the forest about, the leaves of the trees did not stir, the very birds were silent in the stifling warmth. Doors of stores and houses stood open to permit the entry of even the slightest breath of air; it was as if the world was in supplication for a moment of coolness.

In all of Turkeytoe perhaps the most unbearably heated place was the cell in the county jail that was occupied by Bion B. Buckstone. For the sake of sheer survival he had removed all of his upper garments and sat in trousers and shoes alone. The single barred window of the cell was small and high, and no freshness came through it. Buckstone sometimes felt almost faint in the heat, sitting in perspiring misery, feeling the sweat globules crawling like flies down his naked back.

On this day Buckstone's thoughts were as unhappy as was his body. He had at last accepted the belief that his daughter was dead, and his first grief had passed. There remained in his heart only a settled sorrow, and with it a futile wish that he might discover some way to exact retribution from those who were involved in her unhappiness and misery.

Troy Lassiter had not been seen for days. Buckstone had not been made a confidant of the young man's plans, and he supposed that he was taking it as easy as possible, perhaps with a fan and a cold drink, on the wide porch of Beechwood. He did not blame Lassiter for his inactivity, if that was the case. The heat made any sort of movement almost unbearable.

And yet Buckstone wished above all things that the murderers of Prudence—and Dr. Lassiter—might be tracked down. He would have been on their trail himself were he not immured in this hell hole of a jail. It struck him that he had made less than an effort to do anything constructive in this hideous period. The only person he saw, aside from the sheriff, was Miss Sally, who came to speak to him daily. Lately there had been a growing warmth between them, and Buckstone reflected that if he ever got out of prison and on his feet financially, Miss Sally might consent to a suggestion he had in mind for the first time since his first wife died—the possibility of marriage. She always turned a cheerful face up to him, and he had of late found that he looked forward with impatience to seeing that face each day. And their conversation had been more and more on a personal footing. He even believed that Miss Sally . . . but thinking along this line was not only futile but ridiculous, conditions being what they were.

Prudence was gone, his bright, beautiful daughter, and Buckstone thought with bitter hatred of those who were to blame, if not directly then indirectly, for her agonies and death. Of these Drew Peebles was one, and so was the lawyer, Ezekiel Rockcastle. Of Judge Tobias Redding he thought with some resentment; but he dismissed the judge as senile and almost childish, and obviously dominated in his actions by the others.

Toward Sheriff Taney, Buckstone felt little resentment. The fellow was a lout who no more than followed orders, and he had treated the prisoner with kindness, almost friendship.

But as to Peebles and Rockcastle, their very heartlessness condemned them. He ran over again in his mind their perfidies and injustices. With anger he remembered the trick they had attempted to play on him—bringing him those papers to sign with a promise that he would be freed to seek for his daughter, when they must have already known that Prudence was dead. That they should thus seek to obtain his signature to the release of his claims was the final clincher, in his mind, that linked Peebles and Rockcastle with Blevins—for how else would the first two know of Prudence's death if the latter did not inform them of it?

He was, of course, in error in this conclusion. If Peebles and Rockcastle really knew anything about Prudence, it could only have been that she had escaped from Blevins and possessed damning evidence against him. But Buckstone had no way of knowing that at the time. He only knew the bitterness of his heart at his daughter's death, the humiliations he himself had undergone, and his present suffering in the superheated oven in which he was imprisoned.

More than once the idea of attempting to escape had entered his mind. He had considered perhaps inducing Miss Sally to bring him some tool, like a small lever, or even a small hacksaw, if she could obtain one, and smuggle it up to him, perhaps in a quilt. She had given him a quilt once before, and nobody made any inquiries concerning it.

But two things prevented him from making such a suggestion to her. One was his innate consideration for her. He would not run the risk of having Miss Sally involved in what, perhaps, might be serious trouble because of him. Also he distrusted himself, even if such a tool were available, to effect an escape with it. He was past his youth, and he had never been handy with tools. Probably he would make a botch of things and be punished for his clumsy efforts.

Once or twice the wild thought had come to him of snatch-

ing from Taney the rifle he carried, when the sheriff escorted him
to his daily emptying of his slops. But the picture of himself
making so bold a move and then leaping for freedom was considerably dimmed by the probability that Taney would not surrender the rifle easily, if at all; and that even if he fled in broad
daylight, he must soon be overtaken, for he was not as fleet
of foot as he once had been and his mature plumpness made
him short of breath.

So he could only sit in frustration, despising himself as a
hopeless duffer, unable to do anything in his own behalf or in
behalf of anyone else. For the first time his age sat heavily
upon him.

In this fevered state of mind he asked himself again, as
he had asked himself often before, *why* should Peebles and Rockcastle be willing to take upon themselves the legal risks and
financial expenses connected with an effort to obtain the title
to his lands from those Philadelphia heirs.

He tried to remember the name of the man whose heirs
claimed the land. Waterman, that was it! Yes, Horace Waterman,
of Philadelphia.

He began to wonder if Horace Waterman's heirs really
were greatly interested in the land, or if his own imprisonment
and the events following might have been solely for the purpose of inducing him to sign away his rights, after which he would
be freed—and find himself defrauded.

Was there some reason beyond the value of the acres
themselves to stimulate the cupidity of Peebles and Rockcastle?
He had looked upon the tract but once, and he remembered
that the upper part of it was roughly cut up and heavily forested.

What could make land of especial importance and value?
A thought leaped into his mind. Quite recently—within the past
four years, if memory served—there had been gold excitement
in northern Georgia. The distance from those gold fields to
his own former holdings, he estimated, was not more than two
hundred and fifty miles. Might there perhaps be gold on his
property also?

Why, if it came to that, gold had been mined in his own

native state of North Carolina, and that was just across the Great Smoky Mountains from eastern Tennessee! Buckstone's imagination, always ready to soar, began to picture rich possibilities . . . he remembered a twelve-year-old boy in North Carolina, named Conrad Reed, who at the turn of the century picked up a gold nugget as big as a flatiron and worth eight thousand dollars! Why might not Bion B. Buckstone do something as auriferously spectacular?

But at once the bleak realities interrupted this roseate line of thought. Even if there was some reason why the land was of more than ordinary value, how could he hope to profit by it? Rockcastle was a lawyer too astute, Peebles a calculator too cunning, to have overlooked any precautions. And Buckstone was himself immured in this stinking, stifling cell, with no prospect of getting out.

2.

As so often after one of his periods of fleeting optimism, his mind relapsed into a period of gloom, in which he thought of little except his own unparalleled misfortunes. Buckstone had known a varied career, and he had resorted at times to some odd shifts to maintain his existence. But never had he violated the law, at least in any important particular. Nor had the law ever bothered itself about him. That it did so now, and for a reason which had nothing to do with any dishonesty on his part, embittered him.

Imprisonment for debt! It was unjust, barbaric, even inexpedient, for it defeated its own end of obtaining payment of the debt for which it was invoked. It was a law which long ago should have been expunged from the statutes. He wondered how many other men were groaning under its shabby injustice.

His misfortunes were accented almost unbearably by his present discomfort. The prison cell seemed even more intolerably hot as the afternoon wore on; he swept the sweat off his brow and cheeks and scattered the drops from his fingers on the floor. Obviously the builders of this jail had overlooked the advantages of ventilation.

He glanced about his cell. The walls were of stone, well laid, and reinforced on the inside with cement. The floor was of the same material, and equally impervious to the entry of air. His head almost reeled with the heat.

His eye wandered upward to the ceiling. It, at least, was of planking. Perhaps if one of those planks could be loosened, it might provide some sort of an air hole.

At least it was something to do. He rose and climbed rather laboriously and awkwardly from the lower bunk, on which he slept, to the upper bunk. It had never interested him to investigate this upper bunk, and now he found it barren of anything that might have diverted him. Still, it would do to stand upon.

Rising, he found that not only could he reach the ceiling, but it cramped him somewhat to stand erect under it. He lifted his hands and pushed upward against the boards directly over the bunk. To his surprise, one of them seemed to give a little under the pressure just where it joined another plank at one end.

He pushed harder, then exerted his full strength. There was a creaking sound of distressed wood; the plank bent, then rose, pushed loose from its fastenings. He found that he was able to get his arm through the aperture. Now he saw that it might be possible to raise the plank next to it, too.

Since warm air has a tendency to rise, he found it even hotter here close up under the ceiling than on the floor below. But it was not the heat that caused his heart to start beating rapidly. A new excitement and a new idea had come to him. They would have prompted him to experiment further, but discretion forbade it just at present. He suddenly realized that this was broad daylight. He might be caught at this interesting experiment. To pursue it further he must wait until darkness.

It was not difficult to replace the plank where it had been.

The wood seemed half rotted, perhaps from some old leak in
the roof; and when he descended to the floor and glanced up,
there was nothing in the appearance of the ceiling that might
have prompted any special investigation.

He sat as before on the lower bunk, stripped to the waist
and sweating, and the interminable day drew to its close. When
the sheriff brought Buckstone his evening meal, he seemed disposed to linger.

"They's a whisper goin' 'round that they caught Bad 'Lias,"
he said.

"Indeed?" said Buckstone. At the moment even his hatred
of the ruffian did not compare with his newer interest.

"Regulators," said Taney. "If they's anythin' to the report,
he got his neck stretched."

"A fate well merited, if true," said Buckstone sententiously.

"Didn't care much for Bad 'Lias, did you?"

"Should I? He murdered my daughter."

"Now, that ain't been proved——"

"It's the truth. I know it."

Buckstone's manner was so sharp that the sheriff wandered
away, his feelings somewhat offended.

3.

Night fell, the moon climbed the sky, but still the heat of the
jail cell did not measurably decrease. Gradually, the noises of
the town died down, then ceased.

At last, about midnight, Buckstone rose stealthily from his
bunk, his shirt on now. Once more he climbed to the upper bunk.
He tried the loose plank. It gave easily and when he had removed it and laid it away on the rafters he had an eight-inch
wide opening in the ceiling.

How to force the board next to it gave him pause. It was
fastened more securely than the other. He looked about the cell,
which was partly illumined by the moon shining through the
barred window. There was not one single implement available.

But an idea occurred to him. Descending to the floor he drew from its corner the noisome bucket allowed him for excretory purposes. It was of wooden staves, iron-bound, and it had an iron bail bent to fit. For a few minutes he studied it. Then he laboriously climbed up again into the upper bunk and with his fingers worked loose one of the hand-wrought nails that was fastened to the rafter of the board he removed.

He returned to the floor, and using the nail to chip away the wood of the slop bucket, as well as for a pry, he managed to unhook the iron bail. This took time, and he resented any loss of time. But eventually he released the bail, bent it as nearly straight as he could by pressing it with his foot against the stone floor, and so at last had a tool, awkward but fairly strong. With this he went back to his work on the ceiling.

It was easier than he had thought. By using the iron bail as a lever he was able, within a few minutes, to loosen and remove the second plank.

He was now breathing heavily as well as perspiring, not only from the heat concentrated in the upper part of the cell but also from apprehension. Time after time, when he created a small sound with his raising of the plank, he paused and listened breathlessly to see if it had attracted the attention of anyone. A night-barking dog at the upper end of the town was the only sound he heard.

Now he had an opening sixteen inches wide and perhaps ten feet long; he was in a fever of impatience to get up through it. But sixteen inches is a narrow space for a thin man to pass through, even if he turned sidewise to do it; and Buckstone had long since lost the slenderness of youth. So he resolutely set about removing the third plank.

This was more difficult than the first two. But a desperate resolve had seized upon him. With perspiration soaking his shirt and dripping from him, he used the iron bail and his own strength until at last he gained a little purchase. Then with a mighty effort he pried the end of the plank loose. As it came up the rending sound of the nails pulled from the rafter gave him new alarm, for it sounded so loud to him that he thought assuredly it must be heard at some distance from the jail.

For some minutes he squatted on the upper bunk, his ears straining. The dog up the street was still at its monotonous barking. But there was no other sound to give him concern.

Again he rose and in a few minutes had wrested the third board from its place. When he put his head through the aperture thus created, he found he could also get his arms and shoulders into it.

At that he began to draw himself up through the ceiling.

Buckstone was far past the athletic age, and the strain on his arms in drawing up his heavy body was severe. His breath came sobbingly and sweat smarted and blinded his eyes, but by kicking and struggling he got as far as the rotundity of his belly would allow—through the opening and into the intensely dark space between the ceiling and the roof.

But at his waistline he stuck. For years he had possessed a comfortable portliness, but it had never discommoded him until now. Rather, he had always felt that it added somewhat to the dignity of his presence. Now he cursed it; he would gladly have exchanged that feature of his physique with any lank, ill-fed fellow he knew.

Halfway up and halfway down he rested. He was gasping for breath and the space between the ceiling and the roof seemed even more superheated than the cell below. His ears pounded with the beat of the blood from his throbbing heart. But there was no returning now. Indeed, he thought with dismay of being caught in this most undignified situation should he fail to extricate himself. Buckstone prized his dignity and to be laughed at by others wounded him in his dearest vanities.

After a time he somehow caught his breath, and at last with one more supreme effort he drew himself upward. There was a ripping sound. His trousers had suffered some sort of irreparable damage. He was released however, so that he was able at last to pull himself wholly into the low space above the ceiling and below the roof.

Crouched there in the darkness, he felt with an exploring hand. There was a hiatus in the posterior part of his trousers. He realized that a large area of cloth had been ripped from that strategic portion of his nether garment, evidently by some nail on which it caught. Furthermore, the waistband had parted in two, so that as he gained his footing he was forced to make shift to hold up his pantaloons with one hand to keep them from falling to the floor. To a man as conscious of clothes as Buckstone, it was a humiliating situation.

But at least he was out of his cell, though by no means out of the jail. He began to step from rafter to rafter, feeling his way with his feet, to explore the roof from inside. It was of hand-riven shakes and he quickly decided it might not be too serious an obstacle. One of the shakes presently gave way at his pushing, and working from that he soon made a hole—without creating too great a racket—which was sufficiently large to permit him to climb onto the sloping surface of the roof outside.

There he paused again to regain his breath. The night air seemed wonderfully cool and refreshing after the superheated attic. As he rested, he made use of a shingle nail from one of the shakes to sketchily join together his trousers at the waistband. Even this, however, regrettably left his posterior somewhat exposed.

He now considered the best way to get down from his elevated situation on the roof. The front of the jail, he was aware, was high due to the slope of the ground—so much so that the one window of his cell was considerably above the heads of any who spoke to him from below, and the door was reached by three stone steps.

The rear of the jail, therefore, must be lower, because of that same ground slope. It was, however, nearer to the courthouse, which meant nearer to the sleeping quarters of Sheriff Taney.

Nevertheless, he must essay it because the drop from that side was several feet less than that from the front. Cautiously he climbed over the comb of the roof and worked his way down to the edge of the eaves at the rear. He tried to look over. It was very dark down there and seemed a long, long way for— well, for a man who was no longer a boy.

But it had to be ventured. Feet first he slid over the eaves and dropped off into the blackness.

He was surprised that the jar was no greater. As a matter of fact, he landed on his feet, and by catching to the wall, did not even fall prostrate.

For a few moments he stood, as if rooted there, undergoing many stages of doubt and alarm. But the sound of his landing evidently had not disturbed the somewhat less than alert Dode Taney who was snoring peacefully beside his wife in the sheriff's quarters. The distant dog still barked, but Buckstone was sure the animal was interested in someone or something other than himself.

Within a few minutes he was stealing across the jail yard for the trees beyond. He almost skipped for joy as he did so. Had he been younger, in spite of the indignity of having his pants gaping open behind, he might have tried the exploit of jumping up and cracking his heels together. He had escaped from jail!

In his past life he had done considerable reading, and in his reading he had run across some notable deliveries from jail. There was Casanova's celebrated escape out of the leads in Venice. He thought also of the feat of John Sheppard, the notorious English highwayman, in clambering like a lizard to freedom, through a chimney in Newgate prison. Perhaps his own escape was not an exploit to rank with those of more famous prison breakers. But to Bion B. Buckstone, past forty and portly, it was quite sufficient for the present time.

4.

When, late next afternoon, Troy Lassiter rode into Turkeytoe he was eyed with a lively new interest as he guided his horse down the street. The chestnut Thoroughbred appeared somewhat "gaunted" as the saying was, as if it had been hard ridden.

Standing before his harness shop Henry Tidmiller remarked to the farmer, Reedy Halcutt, who stood beside him, "That's Cap'n Lassiter. Been gone longer'n expected."

"Yep," said the other. "His business must've took him more time than he thought for."

"Wonder," said Henry, "if the 'business' done any talkin'."

"You'll never find out from *him*," Halcutt replied, indicating Lassiter with his thumb, "ontil he's ready to say."

In this manner, all up and down the street, men were speaking in low voices, almost in whispers, of some mysterious "business" in which, it was generally believed, Troy Lassiter had been engaged. What is of equal interest is that almost everyone seemed to believe that the "business" referred to a certain bad man, more notable for ugliness than any other quality, who would not again be seen in Turkeytoe.

Strange how, in a country with almost no means of rapid transportation, the rumor had raced across Kentucky to this place. Nobody appeared to know from whence came the word, but all at once it seemed to be a matter of general muted discussion everywhere.

The same report indicated that Bad 'Lias had been accused, even convicted by the posse, not only of the murder of Dr. Lassiter, but of his own brother as well. On this last, opinions varied. Some Tennesseeans, strong in their own family loyalties in a land where blood relationships were always held in high regard, felt that it was unreasonable to believe that a man would kill his own blood kin. Others, however, while agreeing that a man who would do such a thing was "lower than a snake's belly," pointed out that Little 'Lige had not been seen for quite some time and that Bad 'Lias was "as full of meanness as his hide would hold."

To none of these did Lassiter pay any attention as he rode alone down the street. Those who watched him speculated in low voices about what might be the end result of his "business."

There was a rumor that Bad 'Lias belonged to some sort of a criminal clan and there was some speculation that there might be a reprisal against Lassiter. But most were of the opinion that the one-eyed outlaw's death would throw a chill into all of his kind. Already, it was pointed out, one or two of the shiftless saloon crowd that usually consorted with Blevins had quietly departed from town while others were making a conspicuous show of virtue.

Meantime, Troy Lassiter looked to neither right nor left until he reached Jared Hume's store, where he dismounted and tied his horse to a hitching post. When he entered he was greeted by the potbellied little postmaster with respect that lacked little of being effusive.

Several persons in the store fell back as Lassiter walked to the counter and an undercurrent of whispered comments swirled behind him. Jared Hume hurried to his pigeonholes.

"I got some mail for you, Cap'n," he said, handing over a small bundle of letters and newspapers.

As Lassiter accepted the bundle, Hume said, "That thar letter with the Washin'ton frank on it looks interestin'——"

By this everyone in the store was made aware that Lassiter had received some sort of mysterious communication from Washington, and such a communication to a man like Lassiter might have important potentialities.

When Lassiter made no enlightening comment, the little postmaster said eagerly, "I suppose you heard about Buckstone?"

Lassiter, who was about to turn away, stopped. "No. What about him?"

"Why, he broke jail."

Surprise rarely showed in Lassiter's keen face, but it did so now. "When?" he asked.

"Last night. They ain't caught him neither—yet. But they's a hundred dollar reward out for him."

"How did he manage it?"

"That's the derndest thing about it. He went right up through the roof." Hume was delighted to be furnishing such information. "Kind of embarrassin' to Dode Taney, the sheriff, too. He didn't reckon that a man like Buckstone would have the guts or the getup to try such a thing. Likely, too, Dode will have to pay for the repairs of the jail out'n his own pocket."

Lassiter's momentary look of surprise was gone. "Thank you, Mr. Hume," he said and started toward the door of the store.

One man, more foolish than the others, ventured a grinning remark. "I hear things is goin' to be different now."

Lassiter did not smile. "In what respect?" he asked.

The foolish fellow found himself lacking words, because one did not openly press a man like this with questions concerning matters so secret and perhaps so personal.

With his mail Lassiter left the store and began placing the letters in his saddlebags, except for the one from Washington which he opened, scanned briefly, then placed it in an inside pocket of his coat.

A voice came from behind him. "Ah—Captain Lassiter at long last."

He turned and beheld the dry, gray figure of Ezekiel Rockcastle.

"I wasn't aware, sir, that you'd been missing me," he said.

"Only that I've heard you've been out of the state."

Lassiter nodded.

The lawyer went through his routine of taking snuff, blowing his nose, and dusting off his shirt ruffles.

"Learn anything of especial interest?" he asked.

"Some," said Lassiter shortly.

Rockcastle's face did not change. "I'll not conceal from you that we've had some report of—certain happenings up North. I suppose you understand that it's the duty imposed on me by my office to take cognizance of such matters? Be so good as to come to my office and give any pertinent details of what was said and done."

"I haven't the time now, sir."

"I think," insisted the lawyer, "that you might find it to your interests to take the time—since I'm given to understand that the happenings of which we speak were—shall we say— extra-legal? Perhaps for your own protection and good name it might pay you——"

"Mr. Rockcastle," said Lassiter, "the 'happenings' to which you evidently refer took place in another state. Since when has it become the province of a county prosecutor in Tennessee to make inquiry into a matter which assuredly concerns only Kentucky?"

"I only desired to provide myself with general information," said the lawyer, never changing expression.

"I would oblige, but at the moment I must be on my way."

"By which I suspect you mean to the jail?" A dry grin went over Rockcastle's face. "Is it possible that you haven't heard of Buckstone's jailbreak?"

Lassiter did not return the smile. "On the contrary, I have. And my business is not at the jail."

Rockcastle seemed baffled, but he could not resist a spiteful cut. "Your friend Buckstone is certain to be captured. Searching parties are at this present time working the area where his daughter was last reported. To the east and north of here. When he is taken he'll find new and graver charges confronting him. It's likely to go hard with him."

"Very interesting, Mr. Rockcastle."

But Lassiter's voice seemed the reverse of interested as he swung on his horse and rode on down the street.

For a moment Rockcastle gazed after him. Then he turned and hurried up the street toward the tavern. He could see Drew Peebles, who at the sight of Lassiter riding into town had suspended his decimation of the fly population and now stood on his veranda, the fly flicker still in his hand. As soon as the lawyer reached the tavern, the two of them went within and the door of Peebles' inner office closed on them.

5.

Lassiter was still trying to digest the news of Buckstone's escape and attempting to assess its possible effects as he rode down Turkeytoe's single street. At first thought it seemed that it might complicate matters as regarded certain plans he had in mind. Yet he could not blame the man for breaking out of that filthy jail, and if something disastrous did not occur to him when he was recaptured, it might even have its advantages.

At the end of the street, instead of immediately turning southward on the stage road toward his home, he dismounted at the door of a small log house that stood last in the row toward the river. A moment later Miss Sally opened the door at his knock.

"Captain Lassiter!" she cried, and drew him in.

And before he had a chance to speak, she asked, "Have you seen him?"

"If you mean Buckstone, no. I've only just learned that he escaped from prison. I'd hoped that you might give me some light——"

"They've been here. They came and questioned me. I hadn't seen him. I haven't seen him yet. Oh, Captain, why wouldn't he come to me?" She seemed hurt.

Lassiter regarded her gravely. "I grow to have increasing respect for him. He would not allow you to be involved."

She turned that over in her mind, and her face cleared. "Yes. Yes, now that you make it plain to me, that's exactly the way he would do."

Then she asked another question. "I've heard the rumor—everybody's heard it—of what happened up North. Can you tell me—if it's true?"

"That Elias Blevins was executed? Yes, it's true."

"Did he—that man—say anything about Prudence—her death?"

"Miss Sally, whatever else Blevins did, he did not murder Miss Prudence. In fact she's alive at this moment—or I believe she is. She certainly was a few days ago."

"How can you know that?"

"I saw her and spoke to her."

"Then where——?"

"I'd give my right arm to know," he almost groaned. "She simply disappeared."

"But she's safe?"

"I can only hope she is." Lassiter's face for the first time showed weariness and discouragement. "I came to you, Miss Sally, because I wondered if you had some inkling of what Buckstone intended to do."

"I can only guess that he went in search of Prudence."

"But he believes that Prudence is dead."

"That's true—poor man! He's so bewildered that he hardly knows which way to turn." There was a poignancy in her voice that caused Lassiter to look at her with sudden understanding.

"Dear lady," he said, "at least he's at liberty—for the present. And Prudence is alive. We must keep up our courage."

She nodded, mutely.

Lassiter made his adieus, mounted his horse and rode away.

She stood in her doorway and he lifted his hat to her, but she could read nothing in his face.

Chapter 22

1.

Riding south toward his home from Miss Sally's, Troy became conscious that the day was darkening. Toward the east a summer storm was brewing, making itself evident with distant rumblings of thunder and an occasional flicker of lightning. Rain would be welcome, he thought, because it would take the edge off this unbearable heat the country was then suffering.

But the growing darkness was not due to the clouds in the east so much as to the fact that the day was nearing its close. Long shadows lay across the road and the edge of the sun, obscured by evening haze, was cutting the tops of the trees off toward the west. It was six miles from Turkeytoe to Beechwood, and he quickened his jaded horse to a slow trot, intending to be home for supper and a good rest before the storm came, if it was coming.

He wondered what had caused Bion Buckstone to attempt—and what is more, to succeed in—something so difficult and dangerous as breaking out of prison. There must have been, he decided, some sudden urgent situation that drove the prisoner to the desperate expedient; but he could not imagine what it was, nor had Miss Sally been able to help him.

In any case this provided an added complication in a tangled skein already sufficiently complicated. Buckstone probably had gotten himself into even more serious trouble than before; and Lassiter felt that his own self-appointed task of helping the man had been made more difficult by this strange turn.

And Prudence ... the way his mind went so quickly from Buckstone to Buckstone's daughter betrayed the way in which she had almost constantly occupied his thoughts since he saw her so briefly, and lost her as suddenly as he found her.

In this preoccupation he hardly remembered the details of his long hunt for Elias Blevins, except that he followed a telltale trail of horse thefts. Sheriff John Boyd at Vanceburg, a rugged and somewhat efficient officer, provided the last link in the chain leading to Blevins.

"Now I think about it, thar's a place upriver that needs lookin' into," he said. "Could be a thieves' roost."

And with that he gathered a posse. By a sort of inevitability they found Blevins at the Binns house. The fight followed, and Bad 'Lias and the two Binns women were captured.

And, also, there he discovered Prudence—alive, and for the moment at least, unharmed.

His heart had turned over in him at the way she looked, bedraggled and thin. He remembered how she came into his arms, crying his name and nestling, as if glad to be there; and he remembered the leap of joy within him and a wave of emotion with a resolve to protect her and make her happy.

After that the posse hung Blevins. He needed hanging. He had been acquitted in the murder of Dr. Lassiter, but he died for the killing of his own brother. Prudence said she saw him do it, and that was enough for the posse.

Then followed the whipping of the two women. Troy Lassiter did not hold with whipping women. It seemed a brutality toward the sex one naturally treated with chivalry. But these two women, Mag and Florabelle, were assuredly bad, he had to admit, and the Kentucky posse claimed jurisdiction and took the matter out of his hands.

So he stood back and set his teeth to abide the curious and somewhat repellent way of the whipping. After all, the women were not severely hurt, suffering little more than red and tingling bottoms. And when they were released and allowed to rearrange their garments, they sobbingly promised to leave Kentucky at once.

It was then that Prudence's disappearance was discovered. Why and where she had gone he could not imagine. It did not enter his mind that his own face, with its harsh expression as he stood in judgment, together with the girl's horror at her share in bringing about the punishments, had sent her into flight—from him, and perhaps from something in herself as well.

He blamed himself for not having escorted her to some place where she would not have had to witness the horrifying spectacle of a lynching and a whipping close at hand. She fled from the sight and sound, and he had been too occupied with his own share in it to think of what she might be doing—until he found she was gone.

He could understand her shrinking, or thought he could, but where did she go? For days thereafter Troy Lassiter led a search that combed the valley for miles. The men of the valley helped him, particularly Alex Glover with whom Prudence had stayed and who seemed fond of her. Glover said that the girl had spoken of going to an aunt in Columbus; and an old woman named Colfax told of hearing the girl say she was walking to kinfolks in the Big Sandy country.

Lassiter was fairly sure she had no relatives on the Big Sandy, yet he rode to the mouth of that river when the lumber rafts came down. There was no word or trace of Prudence. He was equally certain that she had no aunt in Columbus, and he could hardly believe that she could have crossed the wide and treacherous Ohio River. But he ferried over and made an extensive search on the northern side. Again he encountered nothing but disappointment.

He did not, of course, know that his own escaped slave had taken her over the stream, or that Jeff allowed the skiff to drift nearly twenty miles down the river before crossing. Nor did he know that if he had been asking for *Alice Hankins*—a name he had never heard—instead of a Prudence Buckstone, he might have had some news. Since he found no trace of the girl, he at last returned to the Kentucky side of the river.

Fruitless days. And nights. At the end of them he could think of nothing further that he could do. He did not want to give up the search even then; but he had important business— business connected with the letter bearing the Washington frank —and at length he felt he could no longer delay.

There was a sinister spirit of outlawry abroad in the land and he was to be one of the instruments chosen to check it. Over Elias Blevins, over scores like him, brooded a mysterious dark influence concerning whom Lassiter had only a name—John A. Murrell—and a very sketchy description. One reason why Prudence was so important—not only to Lassiter, but to all the law-abiding people of the South—was that she might have additional information concerning a criminal conspiracy such as the world had never seen before.

So at last, reluctantly, still wondering, still mystified, still half resentful at the girl's apparently thoughtless behavior, while at the same time being fearfully alarmed about her, he turned his horse southward to Tennessee. And he found as he did so that if he had felt resentment toward her, he could not maintain it. And he could not, in fact, take his mind off of Prudence.

Was he in love with her? He was ready to admit—though only to himself—that he was. Yet when he found her so unexpectedly and amid such clashing events, he had hardly acted the part of a lover. Instead he lost her by his own neglect, as completely and mysteriously as if she had taken wings and flown

away. And in this there was an aching feeling of deprivation and
self-blame.

2.

On the ride down from the Ohio River one mystery continued to
bedevil him. Bad 'Lias was hung for the slaying of his brother
Little 'Lige. Prudence testified that she saw the act. But was
there any other proof? If Little 'Lige was dead then his body
must be somewhere, concealed or buried.

It was for this reason that he returned by the same route
he had taken north, and halted at the primitive little settlement
known as Cherry's Station. In a last effort to bargain for his life,
Elias Blevins had said something about a "sinkhole."

When Lassiter reached Cherry's Station and talked to old
Laban Cherry, the patriarch said, "Onliest sinkhole I know of
is a leetle one acrost the valley."

"Has anyone been there recently?"

"No."

But it was enough for Lassiter. "I want three or four men
to go to that sinkhole with me, and I'll pay them well," he said.

Thereafter, with more men than he had asked for, he reached
after some difficulty, the sinkhole referred to. It was typical of
the limestone country: a place where the waters below had un-
dermined the surface and caused it to sink thus creating a considerable hollow. This one was small and deep, and it was choked
with underbrush and growth. But even before they reached it,
the nauseating odor of death made itself evident to them.

"Hit's so thick with bresh them fellers cain't git to whatever
it is down thar," said one of the men. He indicated a half-dozen
rusty black buzzards in the trees about, sitting humped over
like disgusted old undertakers. Others of the obscene birds floated,
teetering on their widespread wings in the sky above.

"Wall, we kin help that a leetle," said another. He carried

an ax, and with it he began to hew the small trees and bushes at the verge of the sinkhole.

"Whew, it stinks thar," he said after a minute, handing the ax to one of his mates. "You take it fer awhile."

In a few minutes there was a sufficient clearing of obstruction on one side of the hole so that it seemed possible to see down into it. But the shaft was too narrow and dark. Nobody volunteered to go down and investigate, but the first speaker, who had pointed out the buzzards, said, "That's a pitch-pine stump yonder. Somebody cut some fat pine slivers."

The idea was excellent. By the time a fire was kindled several "slivers" half the length of a man's arm and two or so inches thick were ready. It was interesting to see how quickly the resinous pine took the flame from the fire. Whirling one of them about his head to get it fully aflame, the man with the ax tossed it down into the sinkhole. But though all crowded to see, nothing could be made out.

"Light a bunch of them at once," directed Lassiter.

This time an armful of blazing sticks went in together, and together created a considerable flare in the bottom of the hole.

"Thar he is—it's a man all right!" said one of the mountaineers.

Lassiter went close to peer downward. That it was a human corpse bloated by decay was evident. Even as he looked, a flare from the faggots gave him a momentary, clear glimpse of the upturned face. He turned away, ill at the stomach. It was Little 'Lige Blevins, beyond any doubt.

"It's him," he said. "Elijah Blevins. He was murdered by his own brother."

They stood gaping at him. "Whut you want done with him?"

"I wouldn't ask any man to get him out of there," said Lassiter. "Let him stay where he is. Roll some rocks and dirt on top of him."

He took from his pocket a ten-dollar gold piece. "Here— divide it among you."

Then he mounted his horse. Looking over in the direction of the cave, he estimated that Bad 'Lias must have dragged and carried the corpse of the brother he had slain at least a mile to dump him into the sinkhole. A new loathing for the man who could do such a thing came over him. He rode away to find the trail for Turkeytoe.

Behind him the citizens of Cherry's Station stared at the sinkhole. As they did so the pine knots and slabs that had been thrown in for illumination seemed to gather fire together. Dead brush and weeds hanging down the sides of the sinkhole caught the flames and in a moment a puff of fire and smoke like a small volcano roared upward.

When it had burned itself out the sinkhole no longer was choked by the matted growth. One of the men said, "Them critters will take care of him." He indicated the carrion birds in the trees.

The whole group turned and headed for the settlement; thus it was that the last company Little 'Lige Blevins had on this earth was the fighting, scuffling flock of buzzards that soon found him.

3.

And now Troy Lassiter was on the road south from Turkeytoe toward Beechwood, his home. The summer storm was coming nearer and the sun had set, throwing the world into gloom. Three men, all armed, came riding toward him. They nodded at him and he recognized them as men from Turkeytoe, probably a patrol out looking for the escaped prisoner.

In the gathering gloom up ahead he saw the lights of Beechwood—and even made out the white house, the barns, the paddocks with the horses grazing in them, dim in the half-light. It was a sight that always had the power to gladden him, but today he took no pleasure in it. The problems before him and the frustrations were too severe.

All at once he heard a voice: "Captain Lassiter—Troy!"

It appeared to come from a clump of willows in the ditch by the roadside. He pulled his horse to a halt. Then, without glancing at the willows, he took from his breast pocket one of the long cheroots he frequently smoked, placed it in his mouth and scratched one of the new friction matches just coming into vogue. Before he applied it to the cheroot he said, "You spoke my name?"

"Yes," came an urgent whisper. "It is I—Bion Buckstone."

"What are you doing here?" Lassiter was conscious that the patrol was still in sight behind him, and he did not turn his head as he puffed on the cheroot.

"I was trying to reach your house. I need help. They hunt me like a spring buck."

Lassiter had the cheroot glowing at the end. "Wait until full dark," he said in a guarded voice. "Then come to the house. The side door will be open. Walk directly in."

If the patrol had been watching him it would only have thought that he had halted to light a smoke, and he spurred his horse forward.

A Negro boy ran out in the carriage way and took the bridle of his mount. He spoke to the lad but did not respond to the wide smile on the young face. He dismounted, took the steps to the portico, and entered.

A tall, smooth Negro in a white mess jacket came forward hurriedly to greet him. He was Lassiter's butler and body servant.

"Duke," said Lassiter, "open the side door and put out the light on that side. We're going to have a visitor."

"Yes, suh," said Duke, who seemed impervious to surprise.

"What have we got for dinner?"

"We-all wasn't expectin' yo', suh, but—" Duke's face lit up. "Oh, yes. Mistah Melton went a-gunnin' this aftehnoon. They's some of dem li'l reed birds in de kitchen." He meant the birds usually called ortolan, in reality bobolinks, which were considered a delicacy.

"Good. What's in the smokehouse?"

"Got a prime smoked ham in an' already cut into, suh."

"Tell the cook to fix dinner for two—reed birds on country fried ham, with that gravy she makes over it. And whatever else for a tasty meal. Tell her our guest will be here soon."

Duke departed on his errand.

Lassiter waited. Presently he heard a sound at the side door, and a moment later Buckstone sidled in.

But what a pitiful sight he was compared with the resplendent Bion B. Buckstone of yore! His garments were filthy and in rags; his face was unshaved and his hair was uncut. His shirt was now tied like an apron by its sleeves about his waist, save that it hung behind and not before, to cover his exposure where his trousers had been ruined.

Lassiter was startled. "Mr. Buckstone, sir!" he exclaimed.

"Troy—I'm here. You heard of my escape from prison?"

"Yes. It was the first thing I heard when I arrived in Turkeytoe. I've been gone more than a fortnight."

"You've been gone? Then I might have missed you——"

"It was merest coincidence that I passed when you called to me. I'm just now home for the first time."

"Thank a merciful God that you are here! Troy, if ever a man was in direst need of a friend, it is I."

Duke, the body servant, had re-entered to report that the dinner was in due process of being prepared.

"Go upstairs," Lassiter told him, "and prepare a tub of water for this gentleman, Mr. Buckstone. Give him razor and soap with which to shave. And lay out for him a complete outfit of clothing, including body linen from my brother's clothes cabinet." He turned to Buckstone. "You and my brother were of like proportions, I think I noticed."

"Yes——"

"Then I suggest that before we discuss matters further you go with Duke and freshen yourself."

"Indeed, I thank you."

Buckstone followed the Negro up the stairs.

When he was gone, Lassiter sat down, lit another cheroot and thought. What was he to do? It was apparent that Buckstone expected him to aid him, probably in making a final escape. He considered possible expedients. In a buggy, traveling by night, the route might be followed to Knoxville with a fair chance of evading inquiry by patrols. But what then when he reached the Fort and the city of Knoxville, where inevitably word of Buckstone's escape would have been received? He felt impatient that the older man should have chosen this particular time to make his prison break. The more important consideration in Lassiter's mind was the renewal of his search for Prudence, and it would have been more convenient not to have Prudence's father on his hands when he undertook it. Yet he felt a certain obligation to Buckstone, because of Prudence, and he sat cudgeling his mind until at last the man himself descended.

The bath, the new clothes which fit him not badly, and the shave seemed to have made a new individual out of Buckstone. He came to Lassiter with his hand extended and with a smile made more pleasant by the absence of the disfiguring beard.

"My boy," he said, with a trace of his old flair, "you have rejuvenated me. My escape created quite a sensation in Turkeytoe, I'll wager." He seemed complacent about his exploit. "What are people saying?"

"I talked to only two or three. There seemed to be rather admiring approval among some. Miss Sally was concerned——"

"Miss Sally—ahem—yes—" said Buckstone. He reflected that she *would* be concerned. Miss Sally ... but this was no time for conjecture. "I am ready, now," he finished.

"Ready for what?"

"I am ready to return to Turkeytoe to surrender."

"What on earth for?" Lassiter was astounded.

"I broke out of that jail—no mean feat, I assure you—for a good reason. I return, because it is honorable to do so. But I had a horror of being dragged back in the wretched state you have just seen me. Now I can go back as a gentleman. Will you accompany me?"

"You can't!" Lassiter remembered the threatening face of Ezekiel Rockcastle. "It might mean the whipping post for you!"

Buckstone's expression changed at that. Still with him was

the recollection of poor Homer Phipps howling and straining at the bonds that held him while the rawhide cut his back to bloody ribbons.

"What would you advise?" he asked.

At the moment Duke entered to announce that dinner was served.

"How long since you ate?" asked Lassiter.

"In forty-eight hours nothing has passed my lips but a little green corn I gnawed off a cob in a field where I was hiding."

"I hope I can offer you something better than that. Please come with me to the dining room."

The meal was a triumph of the culinary art of Aunt Polly, Lassiter's prize colored cook. The birds were delicately flavored and so tender that even the small bones might be eaten with the wonderful sauce over them; the fried smoked ham that formed a carpet under them was of the tenderest and most fragrant; the yams, beaten biscuits with honey, and the rest of the truly exceptional feast were superb. Buckstone ate like a starving man, and Lassiter, eating with more moderation, did him the courtesy of not interrupting him with talk while he ate. Yet all the time he was wondering at the strange reversal of plans. He had been wondering how he could get Buckstone out of the country without discovery; and here Buckstone was announcing his intention of returning to the very incarceration under which he had suffered before his escape.

At the end of the meal Buckstone smiled a kind of contented apology at his host. "I fear that I've behaved rather like a glutton."

"Not at all, sir. You've behaved like a man needing and deserving food."

"It was a feast that might have made Lucullus envious."

"Let's go into the library for brandy and cigars."

4.

When they were seated in the library and Duke had poured their glasses while Lassiter offered the cigars, the younger man said,

"Now tell me, sir. You said you had good reason for breaking jail. If you were searching for Miss Prudence——"

"We both know my daughter is dead."

"But she's not dead, sir!"

Buckstone looked stunned. "What are you saying?"

"To the best of my knowledge, she's alive—and I hope, well and safe," said Lassiter, his voice dropping with the last words. And he told his story, including the inexplicable disappearance of Prudence.

"I haven't the slightest notion, sir, why she went away or where." He paused, and added, "You'll be asking why I'm here without her."

"It is on my mind."

"I spent days and nights, sir, searching every foot of that country, with the help of a score of men who knew its every cranny. We found not the slightest trace of her."

"Could she have been spirited away?"

"It occurred to me. But the house was filled with posse men. A man had just been hung and two women were being punished. I cannot conceive that any criminal would have dared come near. After all those days of searching, I *had* to return."

"Your business," said Buckstone coldly, "must have been most pressing to tear you away from the search for a missing girl."

"You may believe that, sir. There was also a consideration for riding south. It was one direction we had not searched and one of the men, a wood-lot operator named Glover, said that Miss Prudence had been brought to his place from the south by a traveling peddler. I thought there might be just a chance that she had returned over the same route with the same person." Lassiter paused and seemed to gulp. "It was no private business that brought me, sir, but public duty. Why, I almost feel as if I'd deserted her. And to desert Prudence—why, sir—why, sir——"

Buckstone never forgot the timbre in his voice; and he believed he understood in that moment how things lay with Troy Lassiter.

This was approaching perilously near matters of sentiment, and matters of sentiment should not be discussed now, at least under conditions as they presently existed.

"I assure you, sir," Lassiter went on, "the search for her is by no means abandoned. Every one in that valley is alerted. Two men especially—Sheriff Boyd of Vanceburg and Glover, who knows Miss Prudence and has a personal friendship for her—are interesting themselves in the matter. And as soon as I can discharge necessary duties here—I'll be back there myself——"

They sat silent in mutual unhappiness.

It was Lassiter who changed the subject. "If you weren't searching for Prudence, sir—why did you break out of jail?"

"Because," said Buckstone, "I came to the conclusion that there was something remarkable about that piece of land of mine, which made Peebles and Rockcastle so eager to get hold of it. I wanted to look over that land."

He told Lassiter of his deductions concerning the preissued warrant as verified by Miss Sally's recollection.

"That warrant was prepared before the notice of ejectment reached me," he went on. "They must have known its contents, because on those contents the warrant was issued. Now, how could they know?"

"Only if the letter was written and dispatched with their knowledge!" exclaimed Lassiter. "Perhaps by an agent of theirs. At least at their request."

"Or even," said Buckstone, "I am thinking *perhaps written by them*. Or by George Rivers, at Rockcastle's dictation."

"Have you the letter from the Philadelphia heirs?"

"No," Buckstone groaned. "In my confusion I left it with Peebles. If I had it now I believe I could recognize Rivers' precise hand."

Lassiter was silent, thinking.

"Why should they use such trickery merely to imprison me?" Buckstone went on.

"It doesn't sound reasonable," said Lassiter.

"I feel a deep measure of chagrin," said Buckstone, "that

from the first I took it for granted that the letter was genuine, and submitted to arrest and imprisonment without questioning it. What a numbskull I've been! I should at least have tried to get someone—perhaps Miss Sally, perhaps even yourself—to try, if only by mail, to discover something about Horace Waterman, whose heirs were the claimants. But this again raises the question, why would Peebles and Rockcastle go to the lengths they did if that land was really without valid title?"

"You reached a conclusion on that score?"

"Yes, I did." Buckstone looked suddenly shamefaced. "Frankly, I thought I might perhaps find a deposit of gold or some other precious metal on it. So after I escaped I went directly to the place—it's not many miles from Turkeytoe—and I went over it thoroughly."

"Which is why the patrols didn't capture you. They never dreamed you would be on such an errand. Did you find gold?"

"Of course not. A fool's errand."

"The land, of course, has some value."

"But not sufficient value so that if it already belongs to the Philadelphia heirs, our friends in Turkeytoe would undertake the costs and risks of obtaining it."

"It does seem a mystery."

"Troy, I've been asking myself: What if the Philadelphia heirs do *not* have any title to it after all? What if Horace Waterman and his heirs don't even exist? Once they got rid of my claims they'd have a clear field to the property. The more I think about it the more convinced I am that the so-called Philadelphia claimants are entirely fictitious. And I've been played upon like the ass I've proved to be."

Lassiter's look was remote, as if he were thinking of something hardly connected with Buckstone's words. When he spoke it was to ask a question:

"You think that George Rivers actually penned that letter?"

"I'd almost swear to it."

"If so, Rivers might be the weak link in their chain," said

Lassiter, still with that speculative look. "I know George. A good enough man, but a human rabbit. With a little luck and audacity—" He broke off, then resumed. "Your escape from prison and these questions you raise, sir, might be the entering wedge into something enormously important!"

Buckstone seemed puzzled. "I don't quite follow your——"

"This brings me to the business that brought me back from the North." Lassiter drew from his pocket the letter with the Washington franking. "Read it, sir."

Buckstone took the document.

It opened with the usual "Know all men by these presents," and at the bottom was a sprawling signature known through the length and breadth of the land as that of Andrew Jackson, President of the United States. A seal was attached.

"A commission as United States Marshal!" exclaimed Buckstone.

"In response," said Lassiter, "to a letter drafted to the President and signed by three gentlemen who are conspicuous in Tennessee and of whom General Jackson thinks highly—Judge Overton, General Coffee, and Colonel Shelby. I myself added a fourth signature. The letter outlined the outlaw menace in the South, which we think is greater now perhaps than it was in the time of the Harpes, the Masons, and the river pirates in the early days of this century. And it made recommendations."

"It was because you anticipated this reply that you came back?"

"Yes," said Lassiter. "Anticipating the duties it entails made my return imperative. With the commission is a covering letter from the President himself, addressed to me. He is good enough to mention his friendship with my brother; and he kindly remembers me with a comment on my military service, which he appears to have taken the trouble to look up."

"Troy, this is wonderful!"

"When Old Hickory takes hold of a problem, he closes on it like a steel trap. His first step is to appoint men of 'highest standing'—those are his words—as special United States marshals in all the threatened states. He gives them authority to name deputies, and requires from them immediate direct reports on all matters of consequence. By the by, that means that I must, at once, forward to him a report on the occurrences up North. He may not approve of a summary lynching by a posse—but he must know of the end of the Blevins brothers."

Lassiter blew a cloud of cigar smoke ceilingward.

"He may censure me, or even revoke my commission," he went on. "No matter, what's done is done. What is important is that state lines and jurisdictions no longer will protect the criminal. In case of need, even federal troops may be requisitioned. There will be a sweep of law forces such as the South has never seen!"

Again the puff of contemplative cigar smoke.

"You wish to return to Turkeytoe, sir," he concluded. "I will go with you. And you'll return under circumstances none of your enemies will imagine."

Thunder rumbled outside. With a spatter of rain on the windows, the long-threatening summer storm broke. It was brief, like most such storms. When it showed signs of abating, Lassiter rang for Duke.

"Send for Melton to come to me," he directed.

"Ah'm sorry, suh," said the servant. "The overseer's gone."

"The hell he is! When did he go?"

"'Pears like he took a hoss an' went right aftah he found that Cunnel Buckstone was heah."

"Hum. Well, have a boy ready to ride with some notes to the Westovers, and the Perrys, and another for Knoxville, as soon as this rain lets up." He turned to Buckstone when Duke departed. "I misdoubt that Melton, who is a hangdog sort of soul, has taken word of your arrival here to Turkeytoe."

"They'll be coming for me!"

"Not tonight. This rain storm will keep the lazy villagers at home. Tomorrow Rockcastle may move; but we will move before him. Meantime, if I find Melton has indeed done such a cur's trick, I will dismiss him."

5.

The return to Turkeytoe of Bion B. Buckstone was everything that gentleman's taste for the spectacular could have desired. Instead of the fugitive, unshaved and filthy, who escaped from the county jail, the citizens of the town that early morning saw a gentleman elegantly dressed, his face smooth shaved and rubicund, his hair trimmed and neatly combed—for Lassiter's body servant was an accomplished barber.

Buckstone bestrode one of the Lassiter Thoroughbreds, and beside him, his face as stern as a profile on an ancient Roman coin, rode Troy Lassiter on a mount equally noteworthy.

There was occasion for that sternness. The young man had set himself a tricky, perhaps dangerous program to follow. He had resolved to help Buckstone clear himself, perhaps primarily because of Buckstone's daughter. But he had a score to settle for himself and for his dead brother. Everything depended on boldness, perfect timing, and luck. Particularly luck.

Half a mile behind, but not yet fully in view of the village, rode four men, serious, silent, and armed. Lassiter was not going to enter Turkeytoe without support, and these were neighbors and friends of his, summoned the night before by messenger, sworn in that morning as deputy marshals, and given their instructions. They were to give Lassiter a mile's grace, then ride into the village and join him wherever he was.

Two of them were the Westovers, father and son. Cato Westover, the senior, was an erect, austere man with long gray hair and dark pouches under his eyes. He wore a gray cape and a gray bell-crown hat; and he was known as a man who had fought two duels, a man not to be trifled with. His son, Clark Westover, was little more than a boy, but full of the importance of this occasion and ready to do his part. The two Perrys were brothers, in their thirties, who had farms side by side four miles south of Beechwood. Henderson Perry, the elder brother, was lean

and sallow faced, while the other brother, Drexel, was strongly
built, with a more sanguine complexion and reddish hair. Both
wore long sideburns and moustaches. And every one of the four
carried a rifle and two pistols.

It was such a singular circumstance that if little Prudence
Buckstone had been there to see them, she would have recognized every one of them. They were the men whom she had
seen riding with Troy Lassiter behind the bloodhounds, that day
when she thought they were pursuing her in the forest. The dogs,
in fact, belonged to the Perry brothers.

Up ahead of them, Lassiter and Buckstone turned toward
the courthouse. The people of Turkeytoe took notice, and a man
started at a run for Peebles' Tavern.

"We don't have much time," said Lassiter as he swung off
his horse before the courthouse. "Pray that George Rivers is
in his office—and alone."

Buckstone followed him up the well-remembered stairs, and
Lassiter opened the door to the small cubicle which was the
clerk's office.

George Rivers was an inoffensive, thin-faced, young-old man
with the hollow chest and stooped shoulders of one who spends
long hours over a writing desk. He looked up in surprise when
Lassiter and Buckstone entered.

"Why, gentlemen—" he began, half-rising.

"Sit down, George," said Lassiter with a smile. "This is just
a friendly call. I've been appointed special United States Marshal
for this district; and I'm making a few visits to acquaint people
with my new office and to ask for their cooperation in helping
me with my responsibilities."

"United States Marshal?" Rivers showed his astonishment.
"Why—why—you can depend on me, Captain Lassiter, for everything in my power."

"Thank you, George. What are you writing there? May I
take a look at it?"

"Of course, sir. Just a transcript for Mr. Rockcastle."

Lassiter picked up the paper. "You write a beautiful hand,
George," he said. "An unmistakable hand."

"Thank you, sir," said Rivers with quite pardonable pride. "If I do say it, there isn't a better penman this side of Knoxville."

"And beyond that, I'll wager. Your hand is so characteristic —those little curlicues, the graceful shadings of the downward lines, the immaculate evenness of the lines themselves, the margins—I'd say your style is unmistakable, even when compared with other fine writers."

"Perhaps," said Rivers, growing smug under the praise. "Yes, I know it's said that George Rivers' hand is unique in that regard."

"You often work for Mr. Rockcastle?" asked Lassiter.

"Oh, yes. A sideline. The business of the court isn't heavy enough to keep me occupied all the time. I eke out my income by doing documents for Mr. Rockcastle's private practice."

"I see," said Lassiter. He drew a folded letter from his inner pocket. Opening it, he compared it with the newly written page in his hand.

"Unmistakable." He smiled thinly. "George, your hand is like copperplate."

"I try to do my best," said Rivers with a smirk.

"But how did you happen to write this letter I hold in my hand—the notice of ejectment by the heirs of the late Horace Waterman of Philadelphia?" asked Lassiter sharply.

Rivers looked suddenly startled.

"The—Waterman heirs—?" he gasped.

"Yes. I have it here, and there can be no mistake in your writing style. Did you do it for Rockcastle?"

Rivers seemed unable to speak.

"Do you understand that you're dealing with an officer of the United States Government?"

"Y-yes, sir."

"Then tell the truth—or face the consequences! I have the authority to place you under immediate arrest!"

Rivers was a timid man at best, and he was now thoroughly frightened.

"Captain Lassiter—my family—my wife—she's subject to spells—this might carry her off——"

Seeing his fright, Lassiter's confidence grew, for he knew now that his guess, backed by Buckstone's recollection, was correct.

"If you cooperate with the government," he said, "I'll file no charge against you. Now, do you admit that you wrote this letter for Rockcastle?"

Rivers' prominent Adam's apple went up and down, and he looked wildly from Lassiter to Buckstone and back. Almost in a whisper he said, "Yes..."

"And was Drew Peebles present at the time?"

"Yes."

"Did you write this letter by your own composition, or was it dictated?"

"Dictated." Rivers had spoken of his wife's being given to spells. It almost appeared as though he might have one himself, so frightened was he.

"By whom?" demanded Lassiter.

"I didn't even know what it was about, Captain. I didn't think I was doing anything wrong——"

"Answer my question!"

"Yes, sir—it was dictated by Mr. Rockcastle, but Mr. Peebles helped him out with descriptions of the property and so on."

"George," said Lassiter, "take some dictation."

Poor Rivers, now thoroughly cowed, wrote out a short statement of his receiving the dictation, and signed it.

"Thank you," said Lassiter, taking the document. "I must officially warn you not to leave town without notifying me. You may be needed as a Government witness."

"I won't, sir," said Rivers as Lassiter and Buckstone departed.

In the hall outside the office, Buckstone looked at Lassiter in mystification. "How in the world did you get hold of that notice of ejectment?" he asked.

Lassiter laughed as he put the letter and Rivers' statement in his pocket.

"Some Frenchman, I believe Danton the revolutionary," he said, "recommended 'audacity, always audacity.' I gambled on

George Rivers' pusillanimous spirit. I wonder what the poor man would think if he knew that letter I 'compared' with his was on an entirely different subject—and in the handwriting of the President of the United States—concerning my appointment, in fact."

"I admire the superb manner with which you carried it off," said Buckstone. "That statement settles things, as far as I'm concerned—doesn't it?"

Lassiter shook his head and his smile disappeared. "There are two great scoundrels in this town and there is more to be done."

They descended the stairs and stepped out of the courthouse.

"There you see where more audacity is going to be called for," Lassiter went on. "Do as we have agreed when they speak."

Hurrying toward them were Peebles and Rockcastle, with Sheriff Taney in tow.

6.

Peebles, puffing, led the way as they drew up before the two before the courthouse, but Rockcastle was not far behind him. The lawyer was the first to speak.

"Well, Buckstone, you're back, I see."

"I return on a point of honor," replied Buckstone, "to surrender myself."

Rockcastle smiled his lizard grin. "The sheriff, I'm sure, will be delighted to conduct you back to the jail. And I suspect that Judge Redding, who has a low opinion of prison breakers, may prescribe for you a taste of 'jack gad' at the whipping post——"

"Before Mr. Buckstone surrenders himself," interrupted Lassiter, "he desires to see the notice of ejectment from the properties he claimed."

"For what reason?" demanded the lawyer.

"The letter was addressed to me; it is my property, and I have a right to it," said Buckstone.

"Nonsense!" exclaimed Rockcastle. "You're entirely familiar

with the contents of the ejectment. There's no occasion to go into the matter again——"

"The ejectment was left in Mr. Peebles' hands," said Buckstone. "Has he by any chance lost or destroyed it?"

Both Peebles and Rockcastle were silent.

"This is his right, gentlemen," said Lassiter. "If the notice of ejectment is not in existence, there is no basis for imprisoning him."

Peebles flushed angrily. "I've got it, all right! The letter that will send you back to jail!"

"Are you unwilling to display it?"

Peebles thrust his hand into an inner pocket and drew forth a leather billfold.

"What's back of all this?" Rockcastle asked sharply, looking under his shaggy brows from Buckstone to Lassiter and back.

"Never mind," said Peebles, "I've got the ejectment——"

"Shut up, Drew!" cried Rockcastle.

He was too late. Peebles drew the notice from among other papers in the billfold. Quick as a swooping hawk, Troy Lassiter took it away.

Now Rockcastle was furious. "Return that at once!" he shouted.

"Just one moment." Lassiter stepped back, drew another paper—Rivers' confession—from his pocket and compared them.

"As I thought," he said after a moment. "No, gentlemen, Mr. Buckstone will not be remanded to jail. For the very good reason that he does not owe the debt alleged against him by Mr. Peebles, or at least, presumably, he has the resources with which to pay it. There may or may not be a Horace Waterman or his heirs, but this letter is a forgery. It was written by George Rivers, at the dictation of you, Mr. Rockcastle, and you, Mr. Peebles."

"This is outrageous!" shouted Rockcastle. "Mr. Sheriff, arrest these men!"

"Don't bestir yourself," said Lassiter. "I hold authority superior to the sheriff's. Gentlemen, I have a commission as United States Marshal."

The struggle between consternation and disbelief in Rock-castle's face was almost ludicrous. "You—a United States Mar-shal?" he exclaimed. "You're bluffing! I've never heard of this appointment!"

"It came only recently. Do you wish to examine my cre-dentials?"

"No . . ." said Peebles. His color had become the hue of putty.

"In the name of the United States Government," said Lassi-ter, "I am placing both of you gentlemen under arrest."

Rockcastle pushed his fingers wildly through his hair. "On what charge do you propose to arrest us?" he demanded. "I know something of the law——"

"What about using the United States mail to defraud—as a starter?" said Lassiter. As Rockcastle glanced furtively about him he added, "I beg you gentlemen to attempt nothing rash."

The little group of four horsemen rode up to them. The men nodded at Lassiter.

"Mr. Rockcastle, these gentlemen, including Mr. Buckstone, are sworn deputies in my office," Lassiter said. "All of us are armed."

Peebles sat down heavily on the courthouse steps.

"You have no warrant!" blustered Rockcastle. "Where's your warrant?"

"I'm sure that you're aware that I can hold you for twenty-four hours, Mr. Rockcastle?"

"Without bail? That's contrary to law!"

"You will be admitted for bail," said Lassiter, "but since this is a federal offense, no local justice or even a state judge can act on it. However, I think I can promise you that within less than the twenty-four hours I have mentioned, Judge Daniel Jameyson of the federal court at Knoxville will be here, with a member of the federal District Attorney's office and various other persons, including perhaps troops. I took the precaution to send for them last night." The sheriff had retreated and was losing himself as much as possible in the gathering crowd. "There will be a federal Grand Jury to sit upon you, gentlemen," con-tinued Lassiter. "I suspect that in addition to the charge of

using the mails to defraud, you may be called to answer to
charges of plotting and causing the false arrest and imprisonment
of Mr. Buckstone; of illegally binding into service his daughter;
of unlawfully appropriating and disposing of his property and hers
—all to his great loss in trouble and property and good name,
and all for the purpose of blackmailing Mr. Buckstone into signing over to you certain lands. There will also be inquiry into
conspiracies against the peace and welfare in other respects——"

The confidence seemed to ebb even out of Rockcastle. He,
too, sat down. He licked his lips, suddenly gone dry.

"It was Peebles who wanted that land—" he said hoarsely.

"Don't lay it on me!" exclaimed Peebles. "You thought up
the scheme. And you was in for half the take——"

With the malefactors bickering with each other, the victory
seemed complete.

7.

A few minutes after this somewhat distressing scene was enacted
and after the lawyer and tavern man were locked up, under
guard, Bion B. Buckstone might have been seen riding in haste
down the street. He was headed for a small log house at its
lower end, as if he had matters of importance to communicate to
the lady who dwelt there.

Chapter 23

1.

In Washington the heat lay its oppressive weight on the nation's capital. Each morning the sun came blazing over the elms that shaded the streets, and never was there a breath of freshness to temper it. Still skies, still leaves on the trees, the city seemed to pulse with a fever in the unhealthy torrid weather.

The capital was almost lifeless. Dogs dozed in the shadows of the verandas, and by noon all houses stood silent with drawn green blinds, behind which the residents hoped to find some comfort. Grass on the lawns bleached to a yellowish brown; flowers withered in their beds in spite of water lavished on them. Not even did the nights bring any appreciable relief. In the trees outside, cicadas rasped their metallic dissonance; and inside the houses, the sheets and pillows were so hot that turning them over did not cool them. Sleep seemed almost impossible.

Day after day householders scanned the skies for relief. Occasionally big black thunderheads did roll up over Chesapeake Bay, threatening a storm that would be welcomed for the cool it might bring. But even when the sky darkened briefly, the rain did not come to the city. After hovering about on the eastern horizon, the clouds would dissipate, or sweep to the north. With resignation, the householders threw open every window of their homes, hoping to catch whatever coolness there was in the desiccated morning atmosphere so that later they could shut it in against the wrath of the heat to come.

It was July now. One breathless night Miss Prudence Buckstone lit the candles on her bureau and lay in her bed behind the closed window shutters. Small insects frittered through the openings between the wooden slats. They made crazy little swirls about the candle flames until a sudden spurt of heat sent them dropping lifeless to the floor or the bureau top.

The feather pillows seemed superheated and she threw them aside and lay flat on top of her bed, praying for coolness. At times it almost seemed to her that she was dying; the breath going into her lungs and coming out again was so dry and warm that it did her no good. It was as if she had not inhaled it. At last, she raised her body and slid from the bed. She would write a letter.

She had been intending to write a letter ever since, some days before, she had come to this house, the home of Thomas Hart Benton and his family. But inertia after her long journey held her back. And there was the change of surroundings, the experience in getting acquainted with the family, and her natural aversion to the task of writing, all of which caused her to put the letter off.

Now, however, in her thin nightgown, which clung to her damp body, she seated herself at the escritoire, to which she brought a pewter candelabra. She stared at a blank sheet of paper for a time and then taking up a goose-quill pen began to write, with much blotting and many interruptions for thought. She had considered to whom she should write. Her impulse was to send her letter to her father, but she supposed he was still in prison—having no way of knowing the events that had transpired in Turkeytoe—and if he were in jail, she was sure any mail to him would be intercepted by his odious enemies. She therefore addressed her letter to Miss Sally. In spite of the efforts of the nuns at her convent school, she had never been too sure of her spelling; but she plunged in bravely:

Dear Miss Sally:

You will be supprized to learn that I am here in Washington. When I ran away from Peebles I wanted to get here and see the President about my father. Well, I am here, but I have not yet seen the President. I had some trouble. Sometimes I was very hungry, and some bad men were going to do something to me becauze I witnessed the sad killing of Dr. Lassiter. But they got in a fight and one killed the other and I ran away. Then I finely met a pedlar named Corbie, a nice man, and he took me to the Ohio River, where I staid for a time with a family named Glover.

So much for her perilous journey to the Ohio. She did not mention her hair-raising escape, with the help of the slave, or her sickness, or the other perils, or even the names of the "bad men." Nor did she speak of the feudists and her role in healing that vendetta. The letter continued:

After I started again for Washington I fell into the hands of some evil women, and Bad Elias Blevins came and would have killed me, but I suffered no harm because Captain Lassiter and some men from downriver saved me. I was glad to see Captain Lassiter but there was some dredful things going on in the house, and I was scared and ran away again. I got across the river and rode up to Lancaster, Ohio, with two preachers, only one of the preachers was not a preacher at all. He was an outlaw named Merrill or Murrall or some such name. He would of killed me but I excaped by good luck and on the National Road I was kindly given a ride in the coach of Senator Thomas Hart Benton all the way to Washington.

Paucity of detail was a besetting sin with the girl. Nothing of the lynching of Bad 'Lias. Nothing of the wild flight down the night-shrouded river with Jeff. Nothing of the great camp meeting. Nothing of the instinctively clever stroke by which she foiled the bandit chief. Nothing of the circumstances of her meeting Senator Benton. Nothing of her journey with him to Washington. The quill pen scratched on:

> *I have been living here with the Bentons for several days. They treat me kindly. Mrs. Benton is like a mother and there is a little girl, Jessie, age 8. Senator Benton says he has something important for me to do soon, what it is I don't know. But oh, Miss Sally, I do so want to return home. I have not the money and I fear I would be put in service again by those dreadful Peebles. What am I to do? Oh, Miss Sally, give my poor father my love and tell him I think of him all the time.*
>
> *Affectionately,*
> *Prudence Buckstone*

There followed two postscripts:

> *P.S. I hope to see the President before long, and when I do I will tell him the unjust treatment of his friend, my father.*
>
> *P.S.S. If you should happen to see a certain person with initials T.L., tell him I am sorry I ran away from him. I know he meant kindness to me, and I caused him trouble. I caused trouble for myself, too. Tell him I hope he will forgive me.*
>
> *P.*

Her maidenly reticence in giving Troy Lassiter's name had

something to do with her thoughts concerning him, but she knew Miss Sally would understand.

Her eighteenth birthday was approaching, and she was no longer a child. Furthermore, her wild experiences during that climactic summer had given her maturity and wisdom such as she might not have gained in many years of peaceful, routine existence. And the thought of Troy Lassiter had power to set her heart to wishing she could see him again, and perhaps explain her wilful waywardness, and make friends with him...at the least....

Meantime, she owed a great debt of thanks to the Bentons—to the Senator himself, and to gray-haired, plump Mrs. Benton, and their ginger-haired little daughter Jessie. Mrs. Benton had managed to "borrow" from friends one or two dresses of suitable nature—perhaps a couple of seasons old, but Prudence would not have cared if they had been older than that. They were pretty and, with a little adjustment, became her well.

They had shown her some of the sights of the capital. The city, although it was hardly half built—with large open distances between the few straggling centers of government—made a mighty impression on her. She had seen the tall, white-painted structure that was called the President's House. And she saw a much larger stone building, with an unfinished dome, many windows, and a great approach of stone steps leading to a stately entrance, which resembled, with its tall marble pillars, a Greek temple. That was the Capitol, where the lawmakers held their sessions.

She even sat one day in the gallery of the Senate Chamber, where the mighty oratorical giants of the nation roared, and Mrs. Benton pointed out some of the notables there. A short, swart man, with a massive brow, cavernous eyes of great brilliance, and a wide mouth and jaw, was the famous Daniel Webster. Another man, tall and sandy haired, with bright blue eyes and a winning smile, but having an imperious manner, was the equally famous Henry Clay. There was also a lean-faced, black-eyed man, with lank black hair hanging almost to his shoulders; and she learned he was John Calhoun, who had stirred up the nullification difficulties and was the acknowledged leader of the South. Many others, whose names she forgot, were pointed out to her by Mrs. Benton; and, of course, there was Senator Benton himself, standing at his desk, and in a stentorian voice reading forth some statistics which, Prudence was told, had to do with the banking crisis.

Yet in spite of these diversions—if such they could be called —time hung heavily on her hands. The world seemed to be moving along without her.

Her letter finished, she blew out the candles and climbed back into bed, hoping for the sleep which did not come until toward morning.

Next day she gave her letter to Senator Benton, who would frank it and mail it for her. She did not know that on its way to Turkeytoe, her letter crossed another communication in the mails. Addressed to the President of the United States, the letter was from his newly appointed marshal in northeast Tennessee, and it contained a full account of many matters in which she was intimately interested.

2.

That week the oppression of the heat broke when, at last, a storm blew in from Chesapeake Bay, bringing with it blinding sheets of cold rain which danced up and down the street before the Benton home in walls of spray, and loaded the trees with wetness. They would have broken had not the gale tossed them about, so that their heavy branches managed to keep throwing off the worst of the burden of moisture. The streets of Washington, except for partially-paved Pennsylvania Avenue, were such quagmires of mud that no traffic except the most necessary moved. The Capitol building still leaked so badly that the two houses of Congress adjourned until the seats of some of their important members, which were directly under the drips from the ceilings, could dry out.

It was a storm worth looking at and sheltering oneself from, yet on that day Senator Benton, in a poncho like a Mexican Indian, called for his horse and rode forth on some business that his restless nature would not permit him to postpone. The surprise came that evening when he returned home accompanied by another man also on horseback.

Prudence was in her room upstairs, and the candles had already been lit in the house, when she heard the men enter from the porte cochère, stamping their feet while servants hurried to take their wet outer garments. The girl heard Mrs. Benton's voice in surprised welcome:

"My land, General, you here on a night like this? Take him right into the study, Senator. There's a fire going in there, even if this is July. And there's cordials in the secretary."

The storm had, indeed, brought a radical change in the temperature, so that the air was almost raw.

A few minutes later a servant knocked at Prudence's door.

"Miss Prudence, yo' presence is desiahed downstairs at once, ma'am."

She was, at the moment, in the act of changing into a new dress—or rather a dress that was new to her—which Mrs. Benton had obtained for her. It was a gold velvet with decorative lacework and embroidery, quite the finest garment she had ever possessed. To her it seemed beautiful, and indeed, when she finished putting it on, and looked into the mirror for the last few touches to her hair, she saw that her appearance would at least not disgrace her kind hosts.

At the foot of the stairs the butler was waiting for her, and he ceremoniously conducted her to the study, where Senator and Mrs. Benton were conversing with a stranger before a hickory fire in the grate.

At her entrance the gentlemen rose.

She heard the Senator say, "General, this is the girl I told you about," and, "Miss Prudence Buckstone, I'm honored to present you to the President."

She covered her immediate confusion and sense of panic with a curtsy. And then she lifted her face and looked with all her eyes. For this was Andrew Jackson, the President of all the

United States and its vast territories, the hero of the American
people, and his glory was around him like an aura.

In her naïveté the girl did not think it strange that the Chief
Executive should be here in a private home; but it might have
astonished some of the leading personages in Washington to
know it. Yet history has recorded the quaint footnote that the
old General, a widower, and lonely, occasionally slipped secretly
away from the formalities and unending demands of the White
House. He often went to the home of his old friend, Thomas Hart
Benton, where for a season he could relax undisturbed, with a
pipe and a glass, in the heart of the family of which he was fond.

Prudence saw before her a tall man, an inch over six feet
in height and looking even taller by virtue of his extremely spare
figure and soldierly erectness, and also because his snow-white
hair, thick and stubborn under the brush, was swept up and back
from his forehead like the plume on the helmet of a cuirassier.
His face was long and pale and stern, pitted by smallpox, with
the weal of an old sword-cut across one cheek. But what struck
her most forcibly were his eyes. They were blue, the most intense blue she had ever seen in human eyes, and they gleamed
pale and memorable under his cavernous brows.

She almost held her breath while the President relaxed his
sternness in a surprisingly pleasing smile. He took two long steps
forward and held out a hand in which she placed hers.

"So this is the little lady," he said, "who has gone through
such a great big adventure. Miss Prudence, will you come sit
by me?"

He led her to the high-back chair he had been occupying
beside the fire, and she sank on a hassock beside it.

"Tom," he said, "a glass of sherry, if you please. The child
looks as if she feels faint."

"Oh, no," said Prudence. But she took the glass the Senator
offered her, and after tasting the wine felt less overpowered by
the mighty presence before her.

"Mr. President—Your Excellency—" she stammered, hardly
knowing how to address him.

He smiled again. "People usually just call me General," he said.

"Then—General—I've come a long way to see you——"

"By the Eternal, I've heard something of that journey of yours. It's hard to believe!"

"It was because of my father," she told him. "Oh, General, sir, you surely haven't forgotten your old friend, Colonel Bion B. Buckstone, who helped you so much in winning the Battle of New Orleans? He's now held in prison—unjustly. And mistreated and starved, and I don't know what awful things—and I came to beg you to do something for him——"

Jackson sat silent for a moment, and his eye went over, almost humorously, to Senator Benton.

Then he said, "Of that, too, I've heard. And I think I can set at rest your concern for—ah—Colonel Buckstone."

He laid only the slightest stress on the "Colonel" and his lips twitched, as if in amusement.

"But first," he went on, "I have some things to ask of you. Senator Benton tells me that you encountered, and almost lost your life at the hands of, a man named John A. Murrell."

She nodded.

"I am—the Justice Department is—much interested in this Murrell," he said. "Please give me a description of him and tell me everything you know about him. It so happens that you are the only person who has met and talked to the man under circumstances that enable you to give such a description—and who has lived. We are in great need of any light you can throw upon him."

She was disappointed that he switched the subject from her father, but she stood too profoundly in awe of him to change the order of the conversation. Casting back in her mind, she there and then gave Andrew Jackson a physical description of Murrell, one as only a girl could give of a man, including every aspect of his features and his style of dress; she even mentioned some of the inflections of his conversation.

Jackson occasionally interrupted her with questions.

"You saw him first in company with the lawyer, Rockcastle, in Turkeytoe?" he asked once.

At another time, "He boasted of using a minister's garb for a disguise?"

Still later, "He spoke of a slave conspiracy he was fomenting, to cause a massacre of the white population?"

When she was finished he sat back and looked at her, the steel-blue of his eyes seeming to penetrate her very soul.

"That man Murrell," he said, "is the most intensely evil individual of whom I have any knowledge. According to the best records, he has been operating for years, and his murders may run into the hundreds. Yet we do not know today even where he makes his headquarters. Your description of him is the first minute description we have ever been able to obtain. If, by its help, we run him to earth, the nation will be under a great debt of gratitude to you."

She sat speechless, afraid to interrupt his line of thought. The President rose from his chair and strode back and forth across the room, an expression of profound concentration on his face.

"This information must be sent to all my officers in the South—at once," he said. After a moment, "I'd admire to see what would happen to this sleek criminal if some of my Tennessee riflemen got him in their sights."

Then he seated himself again. "But I'm not playing square with our little guest here," he said. "I know that she's more interested in her father's situation than in all the criminals in the world. So I can tell you, Miss Prudence, that I have just received a report from a man in whom I have a good deal of confidence—Captain Troy Lassiter is his name——"

"Captain—Lassiter?" she echoed, half disbelieving.

"Yes. Of Turkeytoe, Tennessee. You must know him."

She nodded.

"I only recently appointed him United States Marshal in northeastern Tennessee," said Jackson. "Already he has achieved some remarkable results. Among these, I may say, he has not only cleared the name of your father, who is free from prison, but placed under arrest the two men who victimized him—let me see—" He drew a paper from his pocket and scrutinized it. "Peebles and Rockcastle—yes, those are the names——"

An incredibility to Prudence. "He's free—my father?"

"So my informant states."

Another incredibility occurred to her. "Captain Lassiter—you know him, sir?"

"I've had the honor of knowing the family for many years, though I knew his brother, the late Dr. Lassiter, better. A regrettable thing, that foul murder. But young Lassiter appears to have avenged it. Both criminals who were involved in it have paid for it with their lives."

She heard herself say, "I saw them both die."

"You?" Jackson, who seldom showed astonishment, showed it now.

"Yes, sir. One Blevins killed the other. And then Captain Lassiter and some other men hung the one who did the killing."

"Come, child. You must tell me more about this."

Briefly she recounted her experiences, including the violent end of Bad 'Lias and the whipping of the women by the regulators.

The General nodded. "That tallies with Captain Lassiter's report."

"But wasn't it very wrong—hanging the outlaw, I mean, without a court sentence? And the whipping of the women?"

Very gravely he said, "These are rough times on the frontier. But I must exculpate Lassiter from the dealings as regards the women—which I condone no more than you do. He reports that he protested against it, but the Kentucky men took the matter into their own hands."

"But lynching Elias Blevins—surely that was against the law."

"You think it was wrong?" Jackson answered. "Tell me, what is the law?"

"It is—well, it's the *law*. You have to obey the law, or there would be no safety, no security, for anyone—" She stopped, unable more clearly to define what she was feeling.

"Just so," said the General. "But what if the law breaks down? Why do you *have* to obey the law, as you put it?"

"'I don't know."

"That's the difficulty with most people. They place a blind trust in something they don't understand. And one thing they don't understand about the law is that behind it forever lies *force*—arrest, prison, possibly hanging, for those who violate it. The reality of force behind the law is what they do not face. But I've seen what it means. I've lived where good men were fighting to establish some sort of settled life for themselves and their families. I have personally upheld the dignity of a court over which I presided with a pair of pistols leveled over the desk. No, young lady, without the good men, the brave men, to enforce the laws there are no laws; and when there are no laws the good men must do what comes next best—act directly to apply the force which upholds laws and order. This is fundamental truth. You may find it difficult to believe that the Chief Executive of this nation should uphold an extra-legal action, but this action of Captain Lassiter's I do uphold."

She sat as if stunned, but she accepted every word from this source at fullest value. And as she thought of it later, she experienced an odd feeling of relief. Troy Lassiter had been "exculpated," as President Jackson put it, of the thing which she most seriously held against him.

3.

The great rainstorm lasted over the next day, but the President rode home alone in it that night. The second day after the storm passed, Senator Benton asked Prudence to dress in the old blue gingham gown, which she had torn and soiled so badly, and accompany him. She was reluctant to wear the torn garment, but he told her that she could wear Mrs. Benton's best coat over it.

"Today is the last day of formal debate on the question of the repeal of the law by which debtors can be imprisoned for debt," he said. "You are my exhibit, and for once you must appear shabby, for the sake of the cause."

She obeyed, but her mind was in a state of confusion as she rode to the Capitol with the Senator and his wife in the Benton coach.

The Senate was just being called to order. "You will stay with Mrs. Benton in the entrance until I signal for you," he said to Prudence, and she felt constrained to obey.

The Senate Chamber of that day was modeled after a Greek theater, and had fine acoustic properties. Opposite the central entrance where Prudence stood with Mrs. Benton, there was a dais, with a huge American flag draped above it; the flag was surmounted by a sculptured eagle carrying a sheaf of arrows in its talons. Before the dais the desks of the senators were arranged in concentric semicircles, and upon each desk was a box of snuff, while beside each desk was a brass spittoon. On the dais sat the presiding officer, Vice President Richard M. Johnson, sometimes know as "Tecumseh" Johnson, from the story that he had personally slain Tecumseh, the great Indian chief, at the Battle of the Thames during the War of 1812.

Prudence saw the Vice President recognize Senator Benton and the massive figure of her friend rose at his desk. His voice filled the chamber, like the voice of a great bull bison challenging its foes on his Missouri prairies.

"Mr. President," he said, "my remarks on this last day of the debate over repeal of the debtors' prison law will be brief. In order to give them point, I ask for a special privilege from the Senate."

"What is this privilege?" asked the chair.

"I desire to introduce to this honorable body a young person who will be the most vivid possible illustration of the remarks I am about to make."

There was a stir among the senators and the privilege was easily granted. Benton turned and came down the aisle to where Prudence stood with Mrs. Benton.

"Come with me now, my dear," he said. "Leave the coat with Mrs. Benton, and do not be afraid."

But she was intensely confused as he took her by the hand,

and slowly, with all formality and courtesy, led her forward up the aisle and caused her to stand on the lower step of the Vice President's dais. Still holding her hand, he turned to the Senate.

"Gentlemen of the Senate," he said, "this is Miss Prudence Buckstone, of the State of Tennessee. You see her ragged and torn as I found her on my way to Washington. She stands here as one example, out of thousands, of the injustices done by the present law governing imprisonment for debt."

He paused, to see the effect his exhibit created, and seemed satisfied with it, for he went on:

"The law is nefarious, for it defeats its own purpose, since a man or woman imprisoned can hardly be expected to pay the debt for which he is imprisoned. But this is not the underlying basis of the law. It has become a monstrous blackmailing device. Not the debtor himself, but those who sympathize with him or who are members of his family are the true objects of the prosecutors under the debtors' law. The dower of wives, the purses of fathers, brothers, sisters, friends, are laid under contribution by heartless creditors; and scenes of cruel oppression are witnessed in every state."

He swept the chamber with his gaze, as if he looked for someone who might challenge his statements; then he went on:

"In this iniquitous law the spirit of avarice has finally gained complete triumph over personal liberty. The sacred claims of misfortune are disregarded, and to the iron grasp of poverty are added the degradation and infamy and misery of the dungeon."

Benton turned to Prudence, with a smile of reassurance that turned to sternness as he once more confronted the Senate:

"I present to you this child—this innocent girl in the first bloom of her lovely maidenhood—as an example of the operation of the law. Miss Buckstone is the daughter of a gentleman of honor, who, through circumstances over which he had no control—indeed, which were laid as a trap for him—was cast into prison for debt. She herself, gently reared and accustomed to kindness, found herself bound out to a cruel and malicious master, one of the very men who sent her father behind the bars. She escaped from that bondage and, friendless, harmless, and defenseless, made her way through incredible hardships and dangers to bring word of her father's situation and to beg for some relief in the capital of her country."

He drew a deep breath, and finished briefly, as he had promised:

"I submit to you, gentlemen of the Senate, in a land of liberty enjoying in all other respects the freest and happiest government with which the world was ever blessed, is it not a disgrace and a matter of astonishment and shame that this cruel custom, so anomalous to all our institutions, and inflicting so much misery upon society, should be allowed further to endure?"

Prudence, by her very charm and youthful innocence, had made an impression greater than the words of any orator. There was a storm of applause and cries of "The vote! The vote!"

But she, in the midst of all this excitement, did not hear the voices of the senators, and hardly realized that Benton was leading her back to the entrance, where Mrs. Benton awaited her.

She was conscious of only one thing. While standing on the step of the dais, looking toward the Senate, her eyes had wandered up to the gallery. And there she had seen her father and Miss Sally.

4.

The reunion took place in the Senate lobby, where her father and Miss Sally found her waiting with Mrs. Benton while the Senate moved for adjournment. And there the first thing she learned was that her father and Miss Sally were married. At that she flew to Miss Sally and there were tearful embraces in the manner of women, whether in joy or in sorrow.

"But what shall I call you?" Prudence asked at last. "I can't call you Mother—you're too young!"

It brought a laugh, but her new stepmother only smiled. "Just keep on calling me Miss Sally," she said.

And indeed, in the manner of the South, which extends to women it esteems the title "Miss," regardless of their marital status, she was usually referred to as Miss Sally by everyone, high and low, in all the years that followed.

The reason for their presence in Washington was explained. Miss Sally had received Prudence's letter, and with excitement had flown to Buckstone with it. It was decided that they would go to Washington at once, and "fetch her home."

"We didn't think you'd care," said Miss Sally archly, "so we let that certain 'person whose initials are T.L.'—as you put it—read the letter also. I think he would have come with us if he had been sure of the reception he would receive."

The best that Prudence could do with this was to blush, and the blush was most becoming to her.

Supper that night was at the Bentons', and afterward the Bentons, with their guests, drove in the family coach to the President's house to meet the President, as he had sent a note requesting them to do.

Andrew Jackson received them in his office, and he was in a sly mood. With a twinkle he said, "I am told, Colonel Buckstone, that you rendered invaluable services to me in winning the Battle of New Orleans."

Buckstone looked him in the eye and said soberly, "I am not a Colonel, General, as none knows better than yourself. Nor did I—or anyone else—'help' you in winning that battle. But I was with you, though as a private soldier, at that battle, and it has remained the high spot in my life. I fear, sir, that I am sometimes given to romancing, but no man can say that I ever spoke your name without expressing the unbounded admiration I feel toward you."

"H'mm," said Jackson. "You evidently do not value yourself as highly as does your daughter."

"I have never, until now, valued my daughter as highly as she deserves," said Buckstone.

Jackson gave a laugh like the bark of a fox on a frosty morning.

"Spoken like a man, sir!" he said. "But I almost hesitate to let you take Miss Prudence on the long journey back to Tennessee—at least without an armed guard. She is the most valuable witness we have today against the accursed combination of outlaws in the South."

"I believe, General," said Buckstone, "that you needn't worry on that score. At least in our part of the state, the leaders of the outlaws are under indictment for enough crimes to take a year to try and sentence them. The teeth and claws of the conspiracy have been drawn."

Next morning, Buckstone, his wife, and his daughter left on the mail coach for Knoxville and Turkeytoe. Buckstone did not dream how far afield he was in his statement that "the teeth and claws of the conspiracy have been drawn."

5.

On a certain evening a few days later Troy Lassiter spent more than ordinary care on his appearance. His servant, Duke, had trimmed his hair and freshly shaved him. He donned a suit of black broadcloth, with the crepe band still about one sleeve for his dead brother, and gleaming white linen with a black silk cravat. Lastly he drew on his best riding boots, polished until they shone again.

Duke marked these preparations with an indulgent inward smile. His master, he divined, was going a-wooing, and he wished him the best of good fortune in the enterprise.

Lassiter's mind, as he dressed, ran back over the events of the past weeks. He remembered how, the morning after he arrested Rockcastle and Peebles, Turkeytoe gaped in awe as a detachment of dragoons from Knoxville came clanking into town, escorting a coach which contained the august persons of a federal judge, a United States District Attorney, and two clerks and recorders from the court at Knoxville.

The dragoons were especially impressive. There were only

six of them, commanded by a sergeant, but they were mounted on powerful horses, with the gleaming yellow stripes of the cavalry on their blue trousers, and impressively plumed shakos. Each dragoon wore a mustachio, this being the one privilege their corps had over the rest of the army. With a pistol in his holster, a saber at his side, and a carbine slung beneath his leg, the dragoon looked grim enough to overawe the boldest.

But there really was no need for them. Turkeytoe was more than inclined to be peaceful, and some of its more turbulent citizens had left the town for places unknown. So the dragoons, as they patrolled the street, devoted their time to twirling their mustachios and ogling the girls.

The two chief malefactors, Peebles and Rockcastle, were brought before the federal judge, who set their bail at five thousand dollars apiece—an unheard of sum for a bond, but it showed the gravity with which their crimes were viewed by the court—not only their dealings with Buckstone, but their numerous other dealings in stolen slaves, horses, and valuables.

They were, however, able to post the bonds at once; and strangely enough, it was Peebles' Tavern that both gave as security. It thus became apparent that the two men were partners, not only in the tavern but in all their affairs. They even owned jointly the mortgages and liens, which were supposed to belong to Peebles alone.

Within a few mornings after their release on bond, both men disappeared, forfeiting their bonds, for they were not present when the Grand Jury sat upon their cases. Then it was discovered that they quietly had settled every mortgage they owned for what they could get, sometimes with the owners of the property, who were glad to pay only a fraction of what they owed, sometimes discounted at the bank. By this means they managed to take several thousand dollars in gold with them, loaded in saddlebags on the horses they rode.

Obviously Rockcastle and Peebles were gone for good. And while Lassiter would have preferred seeing them behind prison bars for the rest of their lives, he did not believe they would ever dare return to annoy this community.

True, Rockcastle had left a threat.

"You can tell Troy Lassiter to watch out for himself," he told a villager who quickly relayed the information. "His snooping and wire-pulling and troublemaking won't profit him. One of these days he might be waited upon by some gentlemen who'll escort him to a place where they'll give him hell before they quit him. They'll keep him *plenty busy*, until he'll wish he was dead. And maybe he'll get that wish, too."

Lassiter did not take the threat seriously, even though it was reported that a marshal in Alabama had disappeared. It was believed that he had been murdered and his body secreted. That story was after all only a rumor and had not yet been verified and he refused to take it at face value.

Just now he had what to him was something more important to think about. The Buckstones had arrived back in Turkeytoe the day before, and he was going to call on them.

He remembered again his surprise and delight when Miss Sally gave him Prudence's letter to read. Its shy reference to him had exalted him almost as much as he had been shocked when he read that she had been in the clutches of Murrell himself and had "excaped by good luck."

He had met their coach in the village and had had a brief glimpse of Prudence, who was flustered because of the travel stains in her costume and her weariness from the long and rough ride. It was unsatisfactory, but he had succeeded in gaining from her a promise that she would see him at more leisure, and presumably under more favorable circumstances this evening. It was for this call that he was preparing, for he had made the final decision that he was going to ask the girl to marry him.

6.

Shortly after sunset he mounted his best Thoroughbred hunter and rode alone for the town six miles away. Before he set out he took the precaution of loading a horse pistol and putting it into the saddle holster, though he had no expectation of needing it.

To the west the sky was still pink with the afterglow, but rapidly darkening, and the trees on either side of the road stood starkly black in the gloaming.

For a young man who usually knew what he intended to do and how he would go about it, Troy Lassiter was distressingly uncertain this evening. He knew that above everything he desired Prudence Buckstone to be mistress of Beechwood, but he was confused in mind as to how to broach the subject of marriage with her, and even as to the wisdom of broaching it immediately, as he had first set out to do. He was by no means sure how she would receive such a proposal from him; indeed, she might resent it. He had shown himself too forward with her on one occasion, and on the next, he had appeared with bloody hands, so to speak. Furthermore he began to have doubts as to the wisdom, and even the taste, of asking the girl for her promise the very first evening they were together. Maidens were notoriously shy, and she might very likely consider such a hasty proposal as presumptuous and rude. It might indeed ruin all his chances with her.

Prudence's father, he believed, would favor his suit; and the paragraph in her letter to Miss Sally gave him hope that she at least harbored no ill-feelings toward him. But the difference between a girl who harbored no ill-feelings and one who felt the kind of emotion he wished for in her was so vast that, sure of himself as he usually was, Lassiter almost turned back to Beechwood. Only his promise to see her this evening kept him riding toward Turkeytoe, and he almost decided not to risk putting everything to the touch this time.

His horse, once he headed the animal down the road, needed no further guidance, since he knew the way to Turkeytoe quite as well as anyone. So preoccupied was Troy with his conflicting thoughts that he paid very little attention either to the road or to the surroundings until he noticed that his mount had raised his head and had pricked his ears forward. Then he sat up erect and shortened his reins.

It had by this time grown quite dark, and at first he saw nothing ahead. Then it seemed to him that he noticed furtive figures in the gloom. He half drew rein, then went on, impatient at his own apprehension. Why should he fear anyone on this road?

Nevertheless, he loosened the heavy pistol in the saddle holster, and spurred the horse into a trot.

Suddenly, as he neared the spot where he had seen the moving figures, they manifested themselves on the road. There appeared to be three of them, all afoot, one on each side of the road and one directly ahead. The man ahead raised his arm with a shout, "*Halt!*"

Lassiter reined in his mount and reached for his pistol. The man in front seized the horse by the bridle bits.

"Damn you, let go of that animal!" cried Lassiter.

"Mister, you're coming with us!" said the man.

In that moment Troy Lassiter remembered the threat made by Rockcastle. He realized that all three men were armed, and that they intended, if possible, to capture him alive. Rumors of the torments the outlaws sometimes visited on their victims came to him.

Drawing his pistol from the holster, he struck his spurs into the flanks of the horse. The animal, unable to go forward because of the man clinging to his bridle, reared high.

Leaning forward, Lassiter fired straight into the face of the assailant who was holding the horse's bits. The man went down without a sound.

Glancing to his right, Lassiter made out in the darkness that the assailant on that side was leveling a shotgun at him. Full into the man's face, he dashed his heavy, three-pound pistol. The gunman staggered back, for the weapon caught him between the eyes. At the same moment the shotgun blast came in a shocking explosion as both of the heavily loaded barrels went off at once. But the aim had been spoiled, so that the only damage the buckshot did was to tear up the ground beneath the horse's belly.

By now the Thoroughbred was free, and he leaped forward. But there still remained the third assassin, he who stood on the left. He lifted the rifle he carried and fired.

Lassiter felt a heavy jolt in his back, which sent him forward on his horse's neck. But now the Thoroughbred was in full career toward the distant town, and the rider had only to cling to his back.

At first there was no pain from the bullet, a numbing sensation being felt instead. But Lassiter knew he was hard hit. Presently he felt pain and then the nausea of wound-sickness. For what seemed to be ages, he clung to his saddle. At last he felt himself slipping from the horse's back. The animal slowed to a walk, then stopped. He fell to the ground beside the road.

After a long time he heard voices, and hands were lifting him, carrying him. At first he thought the hands were those of his enemies and he was too weak to protest. But presently he was laid on a bed and he heard women's voices and inquiries. The wound in his back gave a long throb of exquisite pain and he lapsed into unconsciousness.

Troy Lassiter did not know that he had managed to stay on his horse until the very edge of Turkeytoe was reached, nor that the house into which he was carried was that of Miss Sally, occupied at this time by her and her husband until better arrangements were completed, nor that it was Miss Sally's best feather mattress through which his blood soaked that night.

The blood of his body was running out of its natural course. Life was draining from him like water. Night thickly settled.

He did not know when a girl, frantic with anxiety, arrived at the cabin—Prudence had been staying temporarily with neighbors who had an extra bed—or how she flew to him and leaned over his white, unconscious face, and later, with Miss Sally, fought the night through to stanch the flow of blood with cold wet cloths and compresses.

Turkeytoe's medical profession was not notable for its skill and knowledge, being strongly inclined to purges and bleedings. But old Dr. Horace Davis came to look at the patient. He was a goat-bearded old fellow, with bulbous staring eyes and a shambling walk; but he knew enough to see that this patient was not suited to his favorite method of treatment—bleeding.

"He's de-sanguinized," he said.

"But he'll get better?" anxiously inquired Prudence.

The physician shook his head. "Not likely. The bullet went in under the left clavicle and perforated the body. No need for probing. But when a man's lost as much blood as he has, he usually never comes back to consciousness. Just make him as easy as you can."

He took his unhurried departure.

But Prudence refused to accept the verdict. She pressed wine between the pallid lips of the head on the pillow, and chafed the cold white hands. Not for a single minute during that night did she leave Troy Lassiter's bedside. And yet it seemed that the doctor must be right, for Troy showed no signs of consciousness. A short time after midnight he gave a little moaning sigh, and she cried out in sympathy with him. Miss Sally was beside her at once, trying to find some sign of life in him. She felt Prudence's stricken eyes upon her, but she did not express her belief that Lassiter was gone forever.

7.

In blackness deeper than any night, he was conscious of himself only, in all the universe. He felt his soul leave his body. And now he was a bodiless entity, seeming to float in intense darkness, being blown hither and yon by forces over which he had no control.

Beyond him he seemed to see a very dark headland or peak, more opaque than even the Stygian darkness of the sky behind it. Below him, as he floated in space, appeared to be a vast inchoate sea—not of water but of vapor. It was so dark as to be almost invisible, except for the troubled surface which showed a turbulence that affected it from below, its unfathomable depths growing darker as they increased, until that blackness seemed almost an inky solidity. Yet he knew it for vapor, the vapor of oblivion.

Now he became conscious of music—an unearthly harmony, not weird or eerie, but almost heartbreakingly sweet—which continually increased or decreased in volume as he approached it or went away from it.

So this was death.

He felt himself impelled into an orbit of great distance, how far he could not estimate, but astronomical in space. Alone? Yes. Death is lonely, and space is infinite. There was no pain, no fear. But he felt completely helpless in the power of the forces that had possession of him. So infinitely rapid was his flight that it did not seem to take him long to swing around the orbit, far out among the stars, and come back down toward the whirlpool of black vapor.

The orbit seemed to slope, so that its nadir was close to the surface of the vaporous sea; and he felt himself swung around in it without effort or resistance on his part.

Death seemed slow, yet lightning fast.

With each revolution, he observed that the lower curve of the orbit approached ever more closely to the troubled sea of opaque vapor. And presently, as he swept downward toward it, he saw deep in the vapor a light: just a bright spot of light, like a distant star.

Thereafter, with each succeeding downward swing, as he came nearer and nearer to the surface, the light progressively brightened. And at last, as he swung very low over it, he saw that the light was an eye—a perfect eye, except that it was illuminated, as if by some inward light.

Then he remembered that the eye had always been the symbol of the human soul.

Now, as he swung breathlessly down, the illuminated eye rose, as if to meet him at the surface; and strangely, he seemed to see in it an expression of longing or wishing. He knew that it was himself that it wished for. But once more he was swung away and upward.

The next time he returned in the orbit he came very, very close to the storm-tossed surface of the black vapor. And now the eye appeared just below that surface, following his course at the lowest point—he could almost have touched it.

He perceived that this was the culmination of death. And an overwhelming desire came over him to unite himself with the being of that eye.

He knew inwardly that this was to plunge into oblivion. When he did so, he would experience the peace and rest of forgetfulness, of eternal darkness, the chafings and worries of life forever banished from him.

But now, at the last instant, when he was almost ready to surrender to inevitability, he felt within him something that seemed to rebel. For the first time his being put forth an effort against the forces that possessed him—a feeble effort, but still an effort. And he drew away from the beseeching eye.

With that, suddenly the eye receded into the black depths until it disappeared; and he was being borne upward. The orbit ceased. How long he was carried upward through the windy dark he did not know, but at last he *felt* rather than saw light.

With a great effort he opened his eyes. He heard a voice: "His eyes are open! He's conscious!"

It was Prudence. And then she said, with such power of feeling that it went to his heart of hearts, "Oh, Troy, my darling!"

And with that he felt her smooth cheek against his, her warm arms about him.

And he knew that he was going to be all right. Everything was going to be all right, now and forever. . . .

Chapter 24

1.

Another day, early in June. A year had come and gone since that June day when this chronicle opened.

As on that far day, Colonel Bion B. Buckstone again issued from the door of the tavern. Again, as before, he stopped at the top of the steps leading down from the veranda to the street. It was a brilliantly clear morning and the Colonel was in a genial mood. He was dressed, as was his wont, in the height of fashion—a high gray hat, a fine long-tailed blue cloth coat with brass buttons, a pink waistcoat, frilled shirt, white cravat, and nankeen trousers. The smile on his face would have brought a smile to the face of any onlooker. As before, he looked out over the Tennessee landscape, at the wooded hills climbing toward the mountains in the east, and at the feathery foliage of the great forest, which still surrounded the town of Turkeytoe.

All this was unchanged in a year. But in the town itself, there were changes. The very tavern from which he had just issued was changed. No longer did it bear on its front the sign:

DREW PEEBLES—ENTERTAINMENT. Instead, the sign read: UNITED STATES TAVERN—COLONEL BION B. BUCKSTONE, PROP.

The sign illustrated the upturn of fortune he had experienced. It was due to his land, because of which he had been placed in such misery and trouble by Peebles and Rockcastle. The land did not have gold on it as he had imagined, but it contained something perhaps as valuable in the end—coal. It was their discovery that this vein of coal existed that caused the rascally tavern man and his equally knavish lawyer to scheme to gain it for themselves by the methods of abuse and harassment they employed toward him.

An agent of one of the small but growing steel mills in the Clinch River area revealed this circumstance to Buckstone when he came seeking to buy the land. The iron bloomeries and steelworks in far eastern Tennessee had been operating on the expensive basis of charcoal burning; but this newly discovered coal—since known as "Jellico bituminous"—had the quality of burning slowly, with a low ash content ideal for steel-working. Buckstone was able to lease his coal deposits for sufficient money, while retaining surface rights to the land, so that when the tavern went under the hammer to satisfy the legal claims against it, after its former owners defaulted on their bail, he was able to buy it.

The defaulters were both dead. The morning after the attempted kidnapping or assassination of Troy Lassiter, the body of one of the conspirators was found beside the road where his outlaw companions left it. In spite of the gaping bullet hole in his face, he was easily identified as Ezekiel Rockcastle, once the tyrant of Turkeytoe.

One of the other assailants was certainly Drew Peebles. Lassiter could not mistake that bulky figure, even in the gloom of night, and it was into his face that he had dashed his pistol. The fate of Peebles also was known. He met his end in the Texas Neutral Ground at the hands of a group of indignant citizens who had a rope handy, after they discovered he was a receiver and a smuggler of stolen horses across the border.

The third assailant—he who fired the rifle shot that nearly put an end to Lassiter—was almost certainly Wilbert Melton, the disloyal overseer whom Lassiter had dismissed. Melton evidently fled northward into the upper Mississippi country. He went into the Indian trade, where he made the mistake of getting a band of Santee Sioux not quite drunk enough before he began cheating them. Whereupon they tomahawked him and scalped him.

And what of frowsy, spiteful Mrs. Tabitha Peebles? Deserted by her husband, she went east and inflicted herself on some relatives in Maryland. Perhaps afflicted is the better word. They received her unwillingly and treated her as she deserved, which is to say, meanly. The rest of her life she spent chopping wood, drawing water, scrubbing floors, and becoming accustomed to the same kind of slurs and insults she had once so freely indulged in with others.

Two others deserve mention here. Judge Tobias Redding resigned from the bench to avoid impeachment and was expected, sooner or later, to die of old age and brandy. Dode Taney served out his term as sheriff, but was not reelected. He had done no wilful harm; and he relapsed into congenial obscurity.

The master outlaw, John A. Murrell, was beyond harming anyone. He had been captured the previous February by an amateur detective named Virgil Stewart and was put in prison for the rest of his life. With the exposure of their conspiracy, the other outlaws scattered like rats, some going to Texas, which was then a Mexican province, others into the wild reaches of the upper Mississippi or into the West. Those who did not flee met retribution in one form or another. The South never again would face a menace akin to the Mystic Clan.

2.

Colonel Buckstone smiled benevolently upon the town which stretched toward the river. The greatest change had been in Turkeytoe itself. It had twice its former population, and new houses occupied new side streets. There was a school and an academy, two new churches, several new stores, another tavern or two, some additional saloons, and other evidence of progress.

The genial man at the top of the tavern steps was more responsible for this prosperity than any other. Not only had the first coal been discovered on his land, but he had helped locate other deposits for the interested parties, which brought new people into the district.

A considerable change had taken place in Buckstone's character and personality. And curiously this stemmed from his escape from the Turkeytoe jail. That feat, described as the day "when Buckstone went right up through the roof of the jail," had become a piece of folklore. Buckstone gained new confidence, poise, and grasp of affairs as a result.

The purchase of the tavern had at last brought him to the occupation for which he was peculiarly well fitted. He was a natural host, and he kept his tavern in the best style, as a place befitting the gentlemen and ladies who came in increasing numbers to it. As for the practicalities of hotel-running, a very efficient person now took care of them. Mrs. Buckstone, whom everyone called "Miss Sally," operated the staff and saw that it was able and efficient.

After a few moments the lady herself appeared, and one would hardly have recognized in her the humble little seamstress of the year before. She did, after all, have a certain beauty, and with a new style of hair dress which softened her face, and pretty clothes, including a charming bonnet, her fine eyes, the clearness of her features, and the brilliance of her teeth when she smiled at him invested her with good looks, which grew partly out of her happiness.

Colonel Buckstone—the title, it was understood, was honorary now, for he no longer lived in pretenses—lifted his hat in his courtly manner.

"Sally, my dear," he said, "you look fresh as a daisy this morning."

She smiled her thanks, opened a parasol, and took her husband's arm.

"The carriage should be here in a moment," he told her.

3.

He looked forward to the ride they were to take this morning, for
the end of it was Beechwood. And at Beechwood was Prudence
—now Prudence Lassiter—and her husband Troy.

It had taken Troy some weeks to make up the blood he lost
when he was shot in the ambuscade, but they were married on
Prudence's eighteenth birthday, October 12, while he still carried his left arm in a sling.

They had, it developed, been in love with each other for a
long time—ever since a certain evening when Troy suddenly
caught Prudence in his arms and kissed her. Or almost since
that time.

If she held that stolen kiss against him, she had an odd
way of showing it, for the Colonel—even his son-in-law addressed him thus now—had just learned that, in due time, he
might be expecting a grandchild.

The carriage was brought. With a flourish of his gold-
headed cane, he descended the steps with his wife to enter it.
Things had, he reflected, turned out very well in the end for the
Buckstones. If Prudence's child were a boy, he might suggest
that they call him—he ran the name over in his mind—Buckstone Lassiter. A noble name and a perpetuation of two lines.

If it were a girl, he could not think of a prettier name than
Sally.